"Tonight may I have my desires," the woman said softly as she looked up at the night sky, her naked body bathed in the gleaming moonlight.

"May I have what I want, and in return, I pledge myself to you," she repeated, looking at the ground beside her. There was a series of intersecting lines forming a rough pentagram; in the center was a knife with a six-inch gleaming silver blade.

Her hand seemed to move of its own accord toward the hilt of the knife. Looking from the moon to the blade and then back to the moon again, she asked, "What do I have to do to prove my sincerity?"

Slowly, deliberately, she clenched her hand and carefully forced the blade to her skin. Rivulets of blood ran the length of her arm and streaked her left breast and side. The pain was a dull, distant ache that pulsed with her heartbeat. The throbbing grew steadily, until the woman could no longer separate her pain from the brightness of the moon. They were one: her life's blood, her pain, and the moon.

She felt a distant joy as the Power rose within her—and she knew that she did not control it, yet. She breathed a deep sigh and whispered, "Let the ceremony begin."

MOON-DEATH

BY RICK HAUTALA

ZEBRA BOOKS

KENSINGTON PUBLISHING CORP.

ZEBRA BOOKS

are published by

KENSINGTON PUBLISHING CORP.
475 Park Avenue South
New York, N.Y. 10016

To Anthony Herbold,
   who will never read it—damn it!

Like any other book, this one was not written in a vacuum, and throughout the telling of this story, some close friends gave much needed criticism and encouragement. Most of all, my thanks and love go to Bonnie, who was patient and understanding—well, most of the time. Terry Blouin was the toughest critic, but he had to be. Steve King and Sue Austin kept me going when my pace started to slacken. Without these and other friends, this story would still be caught somewhere between my brain and the typewriter.

PART I: "HIS FELL SOUL"

> *Thy currish spirit*
> *Governed a wolf who, hanged for human slaughter,*
> *Even from the gallows did his fell soul fleet,*
> *And whilst thou layest in thy unhallowed dam,*
> *Infused itself in thee; for thy desires*
> *Are wolvish, bloody, starved, and ravenous.*

> —W. Shakespeare
> *The Merchant of Venice*
> (IV, i, 133–138.)

PROLOGUE: THURSDAY, MAY 13

"She was right! Dear God, she was right!"

A burning pain throbbed up his left arm, piercing his shoulder with a sharp stab. It made him cringe, hunching his shoulders, but he found no relief. He staggered across the kitchen floor and flung open the front door. Stepping out into the cool night air, he gripped the stair railing and looked up at the star-sprinkled night.

"Help me! Help me!!" he shouted, throwing his head back. A violent tremor through his body intensified the pain that swept now along his spine. Stiffly, he vaulted the railing and ran across the lawn toward the lake. His voice rose and fell in wavering howls of pain.

"No! No!" he whimpered, hugging himself as he ran. The pain suddenly intensified, doubling him over. He fell to the ground, locked in a fetal position. "Dear God! Please! No!"

He looked around him, at the close-pressing night. Across the shimmering moonlit lake, he saw the distant shore. The dark forest seemed to spread around him like encircling arms. It reached for him, and he twisted in agony on the ground, pulling away from the grasp of the fores

He looked frantically for the hands, the dark hands of the forest that reached out to grasp him. Looking down, he saw his own hands, held clawlike, as they twisted and dug into the loose soil.

"No! No!"

He tried to stand, but the pain wracking his body forced him to remain crouched. He raked at the ground, as if, on level ground, he was slipping, falling away. Large clots of earth tore away in his furious clawing. Dirt smeared the backs of his hands until he was almost unable to see them, pressed against the ground.

His breathing came in ragged gasps, fighting the constricting pressure he felt. His head rolled loosely on his shoulders, but when his eyes caught the gold disk of the moon, he froze, staring. He felt the embracing arms of the forest groping, reaching. Dark hands clawed at him. With one last, throat-tearing scream, he convulsed and then, lost in pain, found relief in unconsciousness.

Chapter One

Saturday, August 23

.I.

Another car sped down Main Street, a red Buick with New Jersey license plates. It was headed toward Route 43, from there to Route 16 and south. The light at the intersection of Turner Avenue and Main Street turned yellow as the Buick, taillights flickering, swung around the corner and left town.

The afternoon was hot and sticky. The sky held a dull, almost pulsating blue. Summer visitors were beginning to nail down the shutters on their camps, stuff their cars and trailers with suitcases and kids, and head back home. There would be a few of them returning in October for apples and Halloween pumpkins, and maybe a few families would open up their cottages one or two weekends for skiing, but the locals of

Cooper Falls were beginning to feel the relief they felt every late summer when their town was turned over, once again, to them.

Bob Wentworth paused in his walk to watch as a blue Chevy station wagon jolted to a standstill at the light. When he noticed the young boy sitting in the back, staring curiously at him, he looked in the other direction up Main Street until he heard the car pull away when the light changed.

Gritting his teeth, he reached into his shirt pocket for his cigarettes and shook one out. After lighting it, he watched as the smoke hung suspended in the muggy air. He stared vacantly at his lighter before putting it away, then, shaking his head, continued his walk down Main Street.

How long had it been since Amy had given him that lighter, he wondered. He kept his hand on it and toyed with it in his pocket.

He noticed that the blue Chevy had turned into Ernie's Exxon station. Ernie was busy splashing sudsy water over the windshield. Bob, not wanting to chance another inquisitive glance from the kid in the back of the station wagon, crossed the street. He took one deep drag from the cigarette and dropped it down into an open drainpipe.

The Chevy was filled now, and it rattled past Bob, down to the corner of Barker Avenue. It looked as though these people were just coming, rather than going, and it reminded Bob that he still had a little more time before school started and he began his new teaching assignment.

The left turn signal on the Chevy began to wink, and Bob watched as the driver bolted across the street. He cut right in front of an oncoming pickup truck. Both horns blasted. The Chevy cut hard to the left and, fortunately, the pickup veered into the other lane. There was a loud scraping sound as the Chevy jolted over the curb. The driver of the pickup straightened out his wheels and continued up the street without slowing. He had his hand held high above the cab of the truck, his middle finger extended.

When the driver of the pickup was beside Bob, he stopped the truck and stuck his head out the window. "D'you see that?" he shouted. His face was flushed. "The fuckin' idiot!"

"Just up from New Jersey," Bob said with a shrug. "What do you expect?"

The driver of the truck grimaced and then pulled away. The Chevy had already made its turn and gone.

Bob's walk had just about taken him the whole length of Main Street. The rest of the street, from Barker Avenue on down to the river, had only a few more stores and a couple of rundown apartment buildings. Bob turned around and started back.

Bob enjoyed these walks through the town. It helped him in a number of ways. First of all, it gave him a sense of where he now lived and worked. As a new teacher in the high school, he wanted to have some idea of what country life was like. The only thing he was sure of was that it would be a lot different than living and teaching in Worcester.

The second thing Bob liked about his walks was that it gave him plenty of time to think, to think about how he was going to live and work in this town without Amy. They had separated in June, just after they decided to move to Cooper Falls. After Bob had learned that he had the job teaching English at the high school, he had been firm in wanting to follow through. Amy had hesitated but finally agreed to come with him, to give their lives a fresh start. That resolve had lasted about a week. His walks helped him sort out his thoughts and feelings; but still, beneath it all, he felt bitter, resentful—and scared; scared because, for the first time in a long time he had to prove something to himself—alone.

Just as he was about to cross the street, another car pulled up to the curb beside him. It was Harry and Ellen Cushing. Bob went over to Harry's window and bent down to talk. Through the open window, a blast of arctic air from the air conditioner hit him in the face.

"Gonna miss you back home," Harry said, leaning his head out the window. His puffy arm flattened against the side of the car. "You've been a good neighbor."

Bob smiled weakly and nodded. "Buy a place out at the pond, then," he said. "Country living would do you some good. 'Sides, I could use a bit of company this winter."

Bob didn't miss the sorrowful look Ellen gave

him, and he felt bad that throughout the summer he had involved them so deeply in his personal problems.

Harry chuckled, the flesh under his chin jiggling. "No, we've got to head back. Can't retire just yet."

Bob glanced down at the pavement, then forced himself to look up brightly. "Well, when you do, just make sure you get a place out on the pond." He paused, then said, "By the way, you didn't happen to see Amy out at the cabin, did you?"

Harry shook his head.

"Ummm. She said she was going to be up some weekend soon to pick up the rest of her things. I thought maybe, well."

Harry looked at Bob intently. "Now one thing I want to say before we leave, Bob, and that's that you've got to stop making things so hard on yourself."

Bob shifted his feet uncomfortably.

"It's not just your fault that—well, we've talked about it and I want to make sure you don't let this get you down. You've got a good job, a nice place to live—a new start. Let your old life slip away behind you."

"Easy to say," Bob muttered. He wasn't sure whether or not Harry heard him.

"We know it's going to be hard on you, Bob," Ellen said, leaning across the seat. "But you can hang in there."

Bob smiled at her use of slang; he knew she used it on purpose, trying to communicate with someone she felt was so much younger than she.

"But you won't catch me running around up here until next June," Harry said, trying to lighten things up. "I've heard about these winters, and you can have them as far as I'm concerned."

"They can't be that much worse than winters in Massachusetts," Bob said, smiling. He shook Harry's proffered hand. It was cold and clammy from the air conditioning. "I'll set aside a bottle or two of Scotch, and I'll see you next summer."

"Sure thing," Harry said. "If you survive the winter." They all laughed as Harry rolled up his window.

"Keep in touch," Ellen yelled as the window shut.

"For sure."

The car pulled away from the curb, and Bob stood there silently waving as the Cushings drove down Main Street and slowly rounded the corner.

As he watched them drive away, Bob felt an empty pit in his stomach when he realized that he would indeed miss the Cushings. He found that they were a nice couple, once he had gotten to know them. They had listened to him when he most needed someone to listen to him. And, as far as he knew, he was going to be the only person staying out on Pemaquid Pond for the winter.

But winter is months away, he reminded himself, squaring his shoulders. He breathed deeply and crossed the street to the park. Even the shade from the maple trees that lined the sidewalk gave no relief from the heat, and Bob decided that he would head on back to the cabin and maybe take a quick swim before supper.

.II.

Monday, June 23

"She's gonna be pissed," Billy Sikes said, exhaling a lungful of smoke and snubbing his cigarette out in the overflowing ashtray. He barely took his eyes off the dark road ahead. The twists and turns along Mountain Road, from North Conway to Cooper Falls, were dangerous for any driver, even a driver who knew the road as well as Billy Sikes did. Of course, two six-packs and numerous joints didn't help.

"Stop sweating it, will you?" the young woman beside him said laconically. Her eyelids were half-closed, and she had a dull, stoned smile spread across her face. "Just tell her you had a flat tire or somethin'."

Billy snorted. "I've already had two flat tires this summer."

"You'll think of somethin'," his passenger mumbled, and then she seemed to doze off; her breathing became shallow.

The wind whistled through the opened air-vent with a shrillness that set Billy's teeth on edge. He considered putting the radio on, but he glanced at the sleeping woman and decided to let her sleep in peace.

Her name was Joyce Brewer. She had graduated from Cooper Falls High School last June, and planned to start working full time at the local I.G.A. grocery as soon as there was an opening. Billy had been seeing her for almost a year, and he hoped that his wife, Julie, didn't have any suspicions. She wasn't much of a conversationalist; she wasn't all that bright a girl; but she liked to party and she liked to screw, and that was all Billy really cared about.

Billy shook another cigarette from the pack on the dashboard, and lit it. The flash of light made Joyce stir, and he looked over at her again. The bright light of the full moon was shining through her window, and the shadows emphasized the fullness of Joyce's breasts. He could see her nipples pressing against the soft fabric of her T-shirt. Billy felt a lump form in his throat and puffed nervously on the cigarette.

Five minutes later, a reflective sign loomed out of the darkness: Cooper Falls—Two Miles. Billy reached out and gently shook Joyce's shoulder. "Hey. Come on. Wake up," he whispered. "We're 'bout there." He smiled softly and let his hand move down and grasp her breast. He gave it a squeeze, and Joyce groaned.

"Come on, babe. We're almost in town."

Joyce sat up a bit straighter and rubbed her eyes. Billy kept his hand on her breast. An even battle ensued between keeping his eyes on the road ahead and keeping them on Joyce.

"Ummm, boy," Joyce said with a sigh, "that drive went by pretty fast."

They came up to a stop sign, and Billy had to take his hand away from her so he could downshift. The road split off left and right, but before he pulled away from the stop sign, Billy put the car into neutral and shifted around so he faced Joyce. His hand went immediately to her breast again, and now that she was awake, Joyce moaned with pleasure. They kissed long, and ran their hands over each other's body.

"Good time tonight," Joyce said, still sounding drugged. "You gonna be able to get away next weekend?"

Billy grunted, "Dunno," and slid his hand up under her T-shirt. Joyce's hand started to rub his crotch with increased vigor.

They were both lost in their embrace when something bumped against the car. They jumped up and looked around, startled.

"What the hell was that?" Joyce asked, a trace of fear in her voice.

Billy was scanning the area back and forth, his head bobbing like a chicken. "Maybe a branch dropped and hit the car," he offered. His voice didn't sound like he was convinced.

"Let's get back to town," Joyce said, sitting up and pulling her shirt back down. "You gonna drive me home?"

Billy was still looking around nervously. "I was thinking you could walk from here," he said. "It's goddamn late enough as it is. What the hell am I gonna tell Julie?"

"You'll think of something honey pie," Joyce said, smoothing his cheek. This seemed to make him relax, and he turned back to her. "And you wouldn't want me to walk all the way home from here, would you?" she asked, sounding much sweeter and more innocent than she was.

"You done it plenty of times before," Billy said.

"I just don't feel like it tonight, honey pie. And besides,"—she let her hand rest on his crotch with slight pressure—"I was thinkin' you might come up for a quick cup of coffee." She squeezed harder. "I don't have any cream for mine."

Billy laughed and then leaned forward, wrapping his arms around her. They held each other tightly for a moment. Suddenly, Joyce let out a shattering scream.

"Jesus! Look out!" she screamed, pointing, wild-eyed, over his shoulder. Billy had an instant impression that her face looked almost skull-like, then he snapped his head around.

What he saw outside the car window made his stomach tighten up like a clenched fist. He tried to say something, but all that came out of his mouth was a gagged, choking sound. Staring at him, not more than a foot away and with only the car window between them, was a large dog. Its teeth were bared in an angry snarl, and its eyes seemed to glow with a ferocious hatred. Billy watched in stunned horror as the animal pressed its muzzle against the glass. Foamy saliva smeared the window.

Joyce had stopped screaming and was pressed

against the passenger door, quivering with fear. Billy looked over at her and then back at the animal. Automatically, his hand went to the horn and pressed down, giving off a loud, blaring blast. The dog—it looked like an overgrown German shepherd—started to rumble deep in its chest.

"Christ!" Billy yelled, "let's get the fuck outta here!" He jammed the car into gear and took off from the stop sign with a squeal of tires. He had turned left, taking the road toward town. He would have turned right to go to his house.

"You gonna bring me home?" Joyce asked tightly. She was still huddled in the corner of the seat.

"Right to your door," Billy answered. He drove grimly, constantly glancing in his rearview mirror. His heart was still pounding, and he had to urinate badly.

"Who the hell's dog was that?" he asked either Joyce or himself. Neither of them had an answer. "Christ, I've never seen a dog that big before!"

The road seemed to unwind slowly. They were still two or three miles from the turnoff to Millstream Road. They were following the Conway Road along the east bank of the Sawyer River and would have to cross the river into town down by the old woolen-mill bridge. In spite of the car's headlights and the full moon overhead, Billy had a numbing sense of the darkness of the surrounding woods. He tried not to admit it even to himself, but he was still scared.

21

"Was, was that thing, you know, like standing up on the car, or was it, was it really big enough, you know, tall enough to . . . ?" He let the question drift away as he looked over and connected with Joyce's wide, blank eyes.

He knew the turn was coming up on the right, so he started downshifting and snapped on his turn signal. Once they crossed the bridge into town, Billy thought, they'd be safe for sure. He remembered something, vaguely, about how demons or evil spirits couldn't cross running water; he also wondered why seeing that large German shepherd had made him think of demons.

The turn was just around the next bend in the road. Billy smiled over at Joyce, who still hadn't moved. "I guess I won't come up for that cup of coffee. Not tonight."

Joyce nodded dumbly.

There was a sign ahead: Old Mill Bridge—Millstream Road. Billy eased the car into second gear and started the turn. He gasped and Joyce screamed again when they saw, standing in the middle of the road, its back bunched up, its legs planted firmly, as if to spring, the same large dog.

"What the—" Billy said. He laid his hand on the horn and snapped his headlights from high to low to high. The animal wiggled back and forth, ready to pounce. Billy slammed on the brakes and stopped the car about twenty feet away.

"I'll be goddamned if I'm gonna—" he started to say. He pressed in the clutch, put the car into first, and jammed the accelerator to the floor. "Get out of my fuckin' way!" he shouted, moving his foot to the side and letting the clutch pop out. Tires screamed, tearing at the asphalt as the car darted forward. The headlights, on high beam, transfixed the animal, sending back a fiery green glow from the beast's eyes.

The dog had no place to go. It would either have to jump into the river or be hit by the car. Billy smiled grimly as he bore down on the animal. "You're gonna get out of my fucking way or I'm gonna—"

He never finished his sentence. Just as he was sure he was going to smash into the dog, the animal sprang up into the air. The move was perfectly timed, and if Billy was going to hit the damned thing, he would have to swerve to the left. The trouble was, it was already too late for such a move. The animal was already clear of the car with no more damage done it than wind-ruffled fur and dust in its face from the speeding auto. Astounded, Billy jerked the steering wheel, trying to correct for his error. He glanced in his rearview mirror and then back at the road. He knew immediately that it was too late, too late for anything.

Billy's foot hit the brake pedal just as the front fender of the car smashed through the wooden railing of the bridge. When the brakes grabbed, they did nothing more than start the car spinning around in a circle. One of the cross beams, the one that had the sign reading Old Mill Bridge—Built 1886, tore into the door on the passenger side and took off the right side of Joyce's head.

The car had enough speed to shoot out over the dark, swiftly flowing water and crash flat against the sheer rock face of the further shore. Billy Sikes' body snapped forward from the impact, breaking his neck and spine in three places. The car exploded into a ball of orange flame and oily black smoke, then it dropped into the black water to be extinguished and submerged.

Chapter Two

Monday, September 1

.I.

The sudden, scraping sound of brakes behind him made Bob Wentworth jump. As he spun around, his mind flashed a quick picture of an accident, but his brain also registered that these squeaky brakes sounded familiar. He wasn't surprised when he saw Amy smiling at him through the windshield of their battered blue VW beetle. She tapped the horn twice and then wiggled her index finger at him in greeting.

Good, Bob thought, at least she's in a good mood. He nodded and walked over to the passenger door. He hopped into the car and then reached for a cigarette.

"Hi."

"How you doing?" he asked, as he fished in his jacket pocket for his lighter.

"I wish you wouldn't smoke in my car," she said firmly. The smile was beginning to fade at the corners of her mouth.

"Ahhh. That's right. It's your car now." He smiled back at her and then put the cigarette back into the pack. He looked out at the sunny day and the less than busy main street of Cooper Falls.

Amy let the car idle for a moment, but had to keep stepping on the gas to keep the motor from stalling out. "I've been out to the cabin," she said finally, once it was obvious that Bob wasn't about to start the conversation. "I had to pick up a few more things." She flicked her eyes toward the back seat, which was filled with boxes. "I was hoping I'd catch you before I left."

"You got me," Bob said, wishing he had lit the cigarette anyway. He wanted to sound casual, uncaring, but was afraid that she heard his voice catch in his throat. "So, what's on your mind?"

Amy didn't answer. She dropped the car into gear, raced the motor, and then started driving up Main Street. The smile was just about gone from her face now, and there was a deep frown forming on her forehead. The gears grinded noisily as she gained speed.

Bob's hands were beginning to feel sweaty. He looked down at them, pale knuckles and thin fingers, and wiped his palms on his blue jeans. Then he folded his hands on his lap and looked over at Amy.

God, but she's damn good looking, he thought, as he studied her profile. Maybe her jaw was a bit too sharp and her nose was too small for her face, but he had always been a sucker for women with black hair and blue eyes; there was something about the combination that got him. He detected the tension in her face, and he noticed that her thin hands gripped the steering wheel tightly as she slowed for the turn that would take them out of town.

"So," Bob repeated, "what did you want to see me about?" They were heading down the road toward Route 43. "In case you don't remember, I'm not going with you." He was glad that his voice sounded firmer.

Amy's face hardened. "I know!" The muscles in her jaw clenched and unclenched. She flicked a quick glance at him. "Are you, are you sure you want it this way?" Another quick glance. "I mean, are you sure we're doing the right thing?"

"The right thing," he echoed, and then snorted and looked at her intently. "The right thing! Amy, do I have to remind you that you were the one who decided to leave? You're the one who has to decide if it's the right thing."

"But—"

"You said that you wanted to leave. I'm staying. I've got a good job starting in a couple of days, and I'm not going to blow it, not this time."

Amy looked at him, and Bob was positive he heard her say, "Not going to fuck this job up, huh? We'll see about that!" But she remained silent. Her glance said it all.

"This is my last chance to make it, and you

know it," he said earnestly.

Amy drove slowly down the road toward the highway. The VW couldn't have done any better. She sat stiffly, watching the road with a fixed stare.

"Do you think," Amy said, after a moment, "that any of the school board members, or maybe the principal or superintendent, read the Boston papers?"

Bob's folded hands began to feel slippery with sweat again. "Come on, Amy. Cut the shit."

"Well." She shrugged her shoulders and looked at him.

His fingernails were biting into his hands, and his knuckles were white. When he answered, his voice caught in his throat. "You know there wasn't anything to all that. Those charges would have never held up in court."

"If they had ever made it to court," Amy said softly, yet accusingly.

"Goddammit!" Bob pounded his hand on the dashboard. "You know damn right well why the whole thing was dropped. There was nothing to it!"

"Just ask Beth Landry, huh?" Amy asked. "She says it's true." The sarcasm in her voice stung him.

Bob sighed deeply and tried to unwind the tension that was building up in him and ready to explode. He wanted to scream at her, shake her, make her understand, shout at her until she believed him. Instead, he said mildly, "You know, Amy, maybe that was the most of our problem to begin with. Both of us know only too well just what to say, just how to hurt, exactly what button to press."

"It's pitiful," Amy whispered.

"And now," Bob went on, "now we're beginning to realize that what we were doing all along was just hurting ourselves." Bob sighed. "Amy, honestly, there was nothing. Nothing happened between me and Beth Landry."

Amy drove, silent and unsmiling. The car chugged across the bridge that spanned Pequaket Stream, and then the town was lost behind a screen of pine trees. Bob looked at Amy and then out at the trees that seemed to lean threateningly out over the road.

"Where's Jamie been staying? At your sister's?"

Amy nodded. "She's been staying there while I get the apartment ready. She starts school next week, and I—"

"Well my school starts in two days," Bob said with a snap. "And I've got a lot of work to do between now and then; so I really don't have the time to go joy-riding with you this afternoon. Will you tell me what you wanted to see me about and then drive me back into town?"

Amy suddenly pulled the steering wheel to the right. The car rumbled onto the gravel-covered shoulder, sending up a plume of dust in its wake. She yanked the emergency brake on and twisted in her seat to nail Bob with her angry look.

"I, I don't know what in the hell I ever wanted to say to you," she said. Her lower lip was trembling, and her voice cracked. "I just, I just wish things had been different, that's all."

"This is just the way you wanted it, pal," Bob said bitterly. He snapped open the door and put one foot out onto the roadside. "I've had it, and I'm just not going to try anymore. That's it."

He stepped out of the car and wanted to slam the door shut behind him. Instead, he leaned back inside and placed his hand on Amy's shoulder. "We've made our decision," he said calmly, not at all the way he was feeling inside, "and there's just no way we can go back on it."

She looked up at him and her eyes began to tear up.

She looks so helpless, so alone, he thought, over and over. He wanted to apologize, to correct everything with one word, if he could; but he knew that everything had been said. "It's too late," he said simply.

"Yeah." Amy's voice was raspy. "You're right."

"Call me from your sister's tonight, OK?"

Amy nodded her head and reached for the emergency brake. She snapped it off and then put the car into gear. It shuddered, trying to stall, but she worked the gas and kept it going.

"I'll be home after five o'clock. Call once the rates go down."

Amy started to ease the car away, but Bob walked along beside it. "Give Jamie a kiss for me. Tell her I'll talk with her soon."

"OK."

He swung the door shut firmly, and then stood

there on the side of the road and watched as the car sputtered away. He waved his hands slowly, and then the car disappeared over a small rise in the road and was gone. He stood and listened to the receding sputter of the motor, and once it had faded away, he started back toward town.

.II.

Two miles north of Cooper Falls, the Simmons farm nestled against a barrier of woods that became the White Mountain National Forest about five miles due west. The farm was small, consisting of a house, a large (mostly unused) barn, and two smaller outbuildings, one of which was caving in and slanting badly to one side. A wire fence enclosed a small pasture. The wire was badly rusted and in need of repair or replacement. The general impression it gave, was like that of many New Hampshire family homesteads, one of poverty and decay.

What was most striking, or maybe peculiar, about the house itself was its location. It sat at the end of a long, rutted dirt driveway, barely visible from the Bartlett Road, in the shadow of Bear Ridge. The ridge was a steep rise that reared its boulder-strewn head over the farm. From the top of the ridge, you looked directly down onto the roof of the house. Squatting in the shadow of the ridge, the house didn't receive any sunlight until well toward noontime, even in the summer.

Ned Simmons had learned early in his life to hate his home and the darkness that hovered over it, especially after his father died, leaving him, his mother, and his brother Frank to keep the place going. They had not done well these past ten years, and the shadow that hung over the farm seemed to hang over Ned's life as well.

.III.

The woman bent over and stared intently at the book spread open on her knees. The book was old, having been printed in the early eighteen-hundreds, and the print was small, almost too small to read with just the light of the full moon. The tiny letters seemed to float and dart about, almost as though they were trying to rearrange their order. The old paper, turning yellow with age, glowed with a pale blue iridescence.

She puffed her cheeks with frustration and pulled the hair away from her eyes. She spread the book open, and the ancient library-binding cracked. A fine powder dusted the woman's knees. Again, she wished she had memorized the pages, but the ceremony was complex and difficult to follow. Staring up at the night sky above her, she took three deep, even breaths, and then returned to her reading. She was almost ready to begin.

"Tonight may I have my desires," the woman

said softly, as she closed the old library book and laid it gently on the ground beside her. Again, she looked up at the night sky, at the disk of the moon, and spread her arms wide. Soft moonlight gleamed over her naked body as she stood silently praying to the powers she hoped to command.

"May I have what I want, and, in return, I pledge myself to you." She had been reading at the edge of a clearing in the woods. Now she strode to the center of the clearing where, before dark, she had prepared the things she needed for the ceremony.

Dug into the ground, at a depth of about an inch, were a series of intersecting lines forming a rough pentagram. At the tip of each of the five points, a willow branch had been driven into the ground. In the center of the pentagram, there was a cup containing a sticky black mixture, a stump of a candle, and a knife with a six-inch, gleaming silver blade.

The woman walked up to the implements and knelt down. Her mind drifted, taking scattered lines from the ceremony and recombining them in a new order as she let her fingers dance lightly over the ground. She considered picking up the book and reading through the ceremony once more before beginning. Her excitement and anticipation made her confuse the lines she had to say aloud to the Power.

Was it better to have it exactly right? she wondered, or better to go ahead with it, maybe missing some of the words? She didn't know, but in answer, her hand seemed to move of its own accord toward the hilt of the knife. She grasped it and held it up so the clear, blue light of the moon made the blade glimmer.

"What do I have to do to prove my sincerity?" she asked, looking from the moon to the blade and then back to the moon again. The words and actions of the ceremony were completely forgotten as she begged for the Power to touch her, make itself known.

"I give you my life blood, to seal our pact," she said, holding the hilt of the knife with one hand and the gleaming blade with the other. Slowly, deliberately, she clenched her hand holding the blade and then slowly withdrew it. The knife cut cleanly into the heal of her hand.

"I offer myself, my life, in service if I may have your assistance." She squeezed her cut hand. Rivulets of blood ran the length of her arm and streaked her left breast and side. The blood looked dark, like ink, absorbing the light of the moon but not reflecting any of it back.

The pain was a dull, distant ache that pulsed with her heartbeat. She looked up at the moon and saw the orb begin to pulsate with her heartbeat, with her pain. The throbbing grew steadily, until the woman could no longer separate her pain from the throbbing brightness of the moon. They were one: her life's blood, her pain, and the moon.

She felt a distant joy as the Power rose within her, yet a respectful humility kept her from feeling too much excitement. The Power, after all, was entering her, and she knew that in no way did she control it, yet.

She looked at the pale skin of her left arm, still held above her head. The latticework of blood lines was beginning to dry, and the pain was receding. The moonlight became once again steady. But she knew. She had felt the Power!

Bowing down until her forehead was pressing against the warm soil, she breathed a deep sigh. Sitting up again, she whispered softly, "Let the ceremony begin."

.IV.

Bob stood at the register in Miller's Pharmacy and waited patiently as Vera Miller totaled up his purchase of pens, paper, and a new typewriter-ribbon. He was feeling uncomfortable but was trying hard not to show it. He had told Amy to call him after five o'clock, and it was now past seven-thirty. Rather than going straight home after Amy had left him off, Bob had spent the rest of the afternoon walking around town, taking the opportunity to feel the place out. Once he realized what time it was, and that he still had some errands to do, he had tried to hurry along. Vera Miller was taking too long to ring up so small a sale.

"You're driving to your cabin, aren't you?" Vera asked suddenly.

"Huh? What?" Bob said. He had been idly flipping the pages of the local newspaper, the *Cooper Falls Eagle*, and her question had startled him.

"I asked if you were driving home tonight," Vera repeated. "Because if I was you, I surely wouldn't be walking home. Not after dark."

Bob shook his head quizically. "I'm sorry?"

"Well," Vera said, drawing out the word for emphasis, "you must have heard what happened out at the Cunningham's farm last week, didn't you?"

Bob nodded. Of course he had heard what had happened. A wild animal—people weren't sure if it was a wild dog or a coyote, but something had slaughtered three of the Cunningham's baby lambs. Whatever it was that had killed them hadn't done it for food, either. None of the animals had been eaten. Their throats had been torn open and they had bled to death. Apparently the animal had killed them for the pleasure of killing. The whole town had made this the number one topic of conversation since it had happened. Even a newcomer to town like Bob had been drawn into a discussion or two about what had happened and what could have done it.

"When did that happen?" he asked, aware that Vera had been taking her time because she had wanted to strike up a conversation.

"That was, ohh, I think it was on the twenty-first of August, if my mind doesn't fail me." She looked at Bob and pulled at a stray strand of gray hair.

"Well, I'm not particularly worried," Bob said confidently. "I mean, I don't think there's any particular danger in my walking home."

"You never know," Vera said spookily, obviously playing it up just a bit. "There's some kind of wild animal out there in the forest, and it sure seems like it could be dangerous."

Bob smiled and shrugged it off.

"You moved up here from Boston, didn't you?" Vera asked.

Bob tensed, and his eyes alighted on the small stack of *Boston Globes* that were in the rack beside the counter.

"Uhh, yeah, I am," Bob replied. "Well, Dorchester, really. Why do you ask?"

"Well." Again, Vera trailed out the word for emphasis. "You just don't know what's dangerous out here in the sticks. You city people, you got your muggers and robbers. Here in Cooper Falls, we got our wild animals that kill farm animals."

"Well," Bob said with a wide smile, "at least you don't have grizzly bears that break into your house and steal your color TV's."

Vera smiled and pressed the total button on her register. With a clang and a rattle of change, the drawer opened. "That'll be five dollars and fifty-seven cents," she said, still smiling.

Bob dug into his pants pocket and produced the bills and the exact amount of change. He counted it out into Vera's outstretched hand.

"I don't need a bag for this stuff," he said. He stuck the pens and typewriter ribbon into his jacket pocket, and put the pad of paper under his arm.

"Oh, you're one of those environmentalists

that wants to save paper, huh?" she asked.

"No, not really. I'd just end up throwing it away." He started for the door. Outside, pressing against the plate glass window, a large white cat regarded him for a moment, then dashed off into the night.

Vera's voice halted him at the door. "But seriously, Mr. Wentworth, I would be more careful. You never know what's going to be out there in the woods, especially after dark."

"Yeah," Bob said, swinging the door open. The brass bell on the door jangled wildly. "Good night."

"G'night," Vera said, and then she watched as Bob stepped outside and the door swung shut with a whoosh and a jangle.

.V.

"You can leave early tonight, Sue. It hasn't been all that busy tonight," Lisa Carter said. The master of understatement, she thought, as she glanced at her watch and realized that about four people had been in since suppertime. She sighed and dropped another past due notice into the outgoing mail. She looked around on her desk and saw the cards from the books taken out that day and decided she would file them in her desk catalog.

"Are you sure it's OK?" a high-pitched voice yelled from the next room.

"I'm sure," Lisa answered. "I can close up." Her well-trimmed fingernails snapped through the cards, dropping the few she had into the correct places. She took the loose strand of hair that was hanging in her face and tucked it behind her ear.

That's the last time I'm going to get a short haircut for summer, she thought bitterly, as she held the renegade strand behind her ear and learned on her elbow to continue the task. She vowed silently to wear a scarf for work tomorrow. She put the last card in place and then slid the drawer shut.

Sue Langford, the high school senior who was helping her in the library that summer, came running into the main office. She dropped an armload of books onto the desk with a bang. "Thanks a lot, Mrs. Carter. I didn't want to say anything, but there's sort of a back to school party tonight."

"That's right," Lisa said, smiling, "Wednesday's the big day."

Sue chuckled. "Yeah."

"Senior year's the best one of all, too," Lisa added. "Lot's of fun. Where's the party tonight, anyway?"

"Out at Kevin Fowler's folks' camp," Sue said.

"Ohh." Lisa's smile widened when she saw the glow that lit up Sue's face when she mentioned the name of Kevin Fowler. She felt as though she knew just what Sue was feeling. "Well, you can get along now. Go have some fun."

Sue disappeared into the coat closet for a

second, then dashed out and scooped up the books she had left on the table.

"Well, good night," Sue said. She was about to disappear out the front door when she stopped short. She stood there beside the desk silently until Lisa looked up.

"Yes, Sue? Have you forgotten something?"

Sue bit her lower lip and looked at Lisa thoughtfully. "Mrs. Carter, is there something bothering you?" she asked earnestly.

Lisa shook her head and softened her eyes. "No," she answered, but it sounded distant.

"If it's my work," Sue said seriously, "well, I know I should have gotten all the books on the cart put away, but I just, I don't know, I guess I just didn't have my mind on my work today, that's all."

"It's not your work, Sue," she said. She smiled reassuringly. "You've done a great job this summer. In fact, I'm sort of disappointed that you have to go back to school. I've gotten to depend on you a lot."

"Thanks, Mrs. Carter."

"Now you get going before you miss your party. It's the last party of the summer, after all, and you're only young once."

With that, Sue made a dash for the door. Over her shoulder, she yelled, "I'll be in tomorrow at four, and I promise I'll get that cart cleared off. Honest." And then the heavy wooden door slammed shut behind her.

"Only young once," Lisa repeated to herself as she rose slowly from her chair. She remembered, as she had a lot lately, that it had been nine years now since she had gone to her senior class back to school party. Nine years. Remembering Sue's energy made Lisa feel suddenly very old. She felt a growing frustration within herself for all of the chances she had missed and now, unlike Sue Langford, would not be able to take.

Lisa went to the closet and got her coat. Then she went over to the bank of light switches and slowly, one by one, snapped off the lights in the library. After checking the front door to make sure it was locked, Lisa left by the back door.

Once she was out in the park, she paused and looked back at the massive granite-and-brick library, crouching in its surrounding grove of maples and pine. She felt her frustration turning slowly into anger, and she knew, she was honest enough with herself to admit, that the source of her frustration was her husband, Jeff.

She sighed deeply and started walking down Main Street toward her apartment building on Railroad Avenue. She knew that when she got home Jeff wouldn't be there, that she would cook a supper for herself and then climb into bed alone. It was just after nine o'clock now, and she knew that Jeff wouldn't be home until at least midnight, probably later, and reeking of beer and smoke. She knew all this, and she was right.

.VI.

The walk back to his cabin on Pemaquid Pond should have been soothing, but all the way along

41

Old Jepson's Road, Bob felt an eerie, almost panicky sensation trying to fight its way out of his stomach. He was surrounded by everything he had used as an argument with Amy to convince her to come with him to Cooper Falls. There was the distant whistle of the whippoorwill, the constant chirring of the crickets, a cool breeze rustling through the pines—everything to put a person's mind at ease. But Bob felt edgy and afraid.

Of course, he realized that much of it was his nervousness about starting his new job as an English teacher at the high school in two days. He always got tense before a new school year, but things were especially nerve-wracking, considering how he had left Dorchester High School. That alone was enough to keep him awake long past midnight, but there was more; there was something he couldn't quite pin down.

Perhaps it was what Vera Miller had said about the wild dog that was running in the woods nearby. It would be pretty scary meeting a beast like that on a dark road, out of earshot of the nearest house. Bob considered this and almost thought he'd rather face someone who wanted his wallet. At least in that situation, he might live if he gave the mugger what he wanted. If you met a wild dog, what could you do?

The gravel on the roadside crunched underfoot. The wind stirred his hair. The stars sprinkled the sky, looking peaceful. And still he felt this vague gnawing.

He came to the end of his driveway and started up the dirt track to his cabin. The windows were dark and he hadn't left the outside light on, so he had to fumble to get the key into the door lock. Finally, after a bit of effort, he got the door open, and he was just stepping into the kitchen when the telephone rang. He snapped on the kitchen light and ran to pick up the phone.

Well, he thought, at least Amy got home OK. I hope she hasn't been trying to call all night. He picked up the phone, but before he could say hello, he heard Amy's voice say, "Where the hell have you been?"

Chapter Three

Wednesday, September 3

.I.

Beige locker doors were opening and slamming shut as noisy waves of students swept through the central corridor of Cooper Falls High School. Bob stood in front of his classroom door painfully aware of being checked out as the new one in Room 17. There were sly glances, quick once-overs, and challenging stares as he leaned his back against the wire-mesh window. He reached down and nervously flicked the tab of his fly. The overpowering aroma of fresh paint and floor wax made his nose sting, and he wished he had time to go to the teachers' room for one last cigarette before the first bell.

A well-dressed girl with curly black hair walked past him and entered the classroom. She held a bright red, three-ring binder close to her chest, almost like armour, as she pushed her way through the crowd. Once she was in the relative quiet of the room, she looked up at Bob and said, "Good morning, Mr. Wentworth."

Bob smiled and nodded a greeting. "Good morning."

Her eyes sparkled as she looked at him, then, smirking slightly, she said, "Boy, if you think it's crazy now, just wait." She took a seat in the front row.

The noise in the corridor seemed to grow louder as the time for the first class got closer. Slowly, Bob became aware of one voice that rose above the din of the corridor. The voice sounded high pitched and angry.

"Get lost, will yah, Tate!" the voice screamed, cracking.

Bob scanned the crowded hallway, trying to pinpoint the voice. After a moment, he saw a concentration of students. They were gathering around two boys. Bob started over toward them.

"I'm tellin' yah to get lost!"

"Make me," another voice taunted.

The second voice was from a tall red-headed boy, thin, but not scrawny, who was leaning toward his opponent like a tree threatening to come crashing down.

The other boy, the boy with the angry, frightened voice, was shorter, stockier. He stood with his back pressed against the row of lockers, his shoulders slightly stooped. As Bob made his way toward them, he could see the cornered boy's lower lip trembling. From beneath a tossled mass of black hair, his eyes burned with rage.

"What's the matter, little Neddie-pooh," the redhead taunted, "did your mama forget to wipe the cow shit off your shoes, or is that your lunch?"

The crowd of students snickered. The redhead pursed his lips and made gross kissing sounds. Ned cringed back further.

"That's it!" the redhead shouted, with a glee of discovery. "Neddie-boy here eats cow shit for lunch."

Everyone surrounding the boys started to laugh and hoot. A few took up the chant, "Simmons eats pasture patties! Simmons eats pasture patties!"

As the shouting grew louder, Ned's eyes darted from face to face. He scowled deeply, and his mouth pulled back in a sneer, exposing his teeth.

"Simmons eats pasture patties! Simmons eats pasture patties!"

"Maybe we ought to take you down to the shower room and clean you up, get the cow shit off you before school starts?" the redhead suggested. "How in the world could your mother send you off to school looking like that?"

The redhead made a grab for Ned's arm just as Bob broke through the line and shouted, "All right! Fun's over." He grabbed the redhead by the shoulder and turned him around. Someone in the crowd started to boo.

"What's your name?" Bob asked the redhead, who was trying to twist out of his grip.

"Alan Tate," the boy replied. Then, after a brief pause, he added, "What's yours?"

There were scattered chuckles, but Bob ignored the affront. "OK, everyone, you can get along to your homerooms now."

The crowd started to thin out reluctantly.

Bob looked over at Ned, who was still huddled against the lockers. "And your name?"

"Ned Simmons," the boy mumbled with a low growl in his voice.

"Well," Bob said, turning back to Alan, "why don't we all go down to Mr. Summers' office and straighten this out." He looked at the few students still milling around and said, "The rest of you are going to be late for class."

Just as Bob spoke, the bell rang. Its clanging shattered the tension in the hallway, and everyone drifted away, leaving Bob, Alan, and Ned.

"Let's go," Bob said harshly.

Ned straightened up, his fists in tight balls. "I'll get you, you pigfucker," he hissed.

Alan broke away from Bob's grip and, turning, reached out to tweak Ned on the cheek. "What's the matter, is the little fairy-boy getting mad?" he said teasingly.

Ned suddenly swung his fist, but, because he was off-balance, his punch merely glanced off Alan's shoulder.

"All right, cool it!" Bob yelled, but Alan had already hauled back, and his fist smashed into Ned's face. Ned spun around, a mist of blood and mucus spraying the lockers behind him.

His knees buckled, and he sank slowly to the floor, looking dazed and hurt. He covered his face with his hands. Blood seeped out between his fingers.

Alan stood over him, threatening. "If you ever touch me again, you bastard, I'll lay you in your goddamn grave!"

Bob's hand gripped Alan's shoulder. "You go to the office right now!" He gave the boy a push in the right direction and Alan started down the corridor.

Bob turned to Ned and helped him to his feet. The boy was snorting loudly, trying to keep his throat clear. The blood was still gushing from Ned's nose and falling onto the floor, leaving huge red splotches.

"It's not as bad as it looks," Bob said, supporting the boy. He reached into his back pocket for his handkerchief and offered it to the boy.

Ned remained silent, except for his loud snorting.

"I've seen a lot worse," Bob said. "Noses bleed real easy."

Ned held the handkerchief to his nose, and the cloth was quickly saturated with blood. His stance was still unsteady, but he twisted away from Bob's support.

The second bell rang, and Bob looked nervously at his watch. "Class is starting," he said. "Can you make it to the nurse's office?"

Ned nodded.

"OK," Bob said, turning toward his classroom, "After you get cleaned up, I want you to report to Mr. Summers' office too. OK?"

Ned nodded and walked away slowly. The heels of his shoes left long scuff-marks on the freshly waxed floor.

Back in class, Bob guided the students through the process of filling in the schedule cards. He was just collecting them when everyone heard the screech of tires from the parking lot. They all turned and looked out the window. A rusted Ford pickup truck ran the stop sign, swaying heavily as it turned the corner and headed down the road. A shimmering blue cloud of exhaust hung suspended in the air, and then it faded as the sound of the truck receded.

"There goes Simmons," someone said. Bob wasn't sure who had said it, because he was still staring down the road where the truck had disappeared.

Someone else in the back of the room chuckled softly.

.II.

"So there's no way you can find out if the book is still in the library?" Bob asked, his knuckles on the librarian's desk.

Lisa Carter looked up and tucked a strand of hair under the red-and-blue paisley kerchief she was wearing. I must look like a damn Russian peasant girl, she thought.

"If the card for the book is still in the catalog,

then either the book has been stolen or it's been misplaced." She made a conscious effort to sound professional in order to compensate for her Russian-peasant look. "The card indicates that it hasn't been taken out of the library for more than five years. I mean, Hadas' *Greek Anthology* isn't on any bestseller lists I know of."

Her attempt at humor worked, and Bob smiled.

"Aren't you the new teacher at the high school?" Lisa asked, hoping to keep the conversation going. She liked the looks of this man. She became aware that she had her hands in her lap and that she was playing with her wedding ring, sliding it up and down her finger. She stopped doing that and leaned her right elbow on the desk, keeping her left hand in her lap.

"Yeah, my name is Robert Wentworth."

"Pleased to meet you," Lisa said, holding out her hand for him to shake. "My name is Lisa Carter." She found herself thinking that she was glad she hadn't let him see the wedding ring on her left hand.

They were both silent for a moment, neither of them knowing what to say to keep the interchange going. Finally, Bob said, "Well, if it does turn up, would you please hold it for me?"

Lisa nodded. "Sure."

"It was the text I used in college, and I'm going to need it for a class later this semester. I'd appreciate it."

"No problem at all," Lisa said, smiling, but feeling very foolish, for some reason. She watched as Bob Wentworth left the library, then, once the door had shut behind him, she got up and went over to the window to watch as he walked down the granite steps and out into the street. The whole time she watched, she unconsciously played with her wedding ring, twirling it and sliding it up and down her finger.

.III.

Ned's nipples stiffened as he leaned over the counter and bent his head into the sink. His nose was still throbbing from the punch he had received that morning. His mother took a pitcher of cold water and poured it over his sudsy hair.

Bracing himself with a hand on either side of the sink, he held his breath and watched the creamy white stream wash from his hair and run down the sink. The drain couldn't take the water fast enough, and the suds backed up and then swirled down in a small whirlpool. The drain began to gurgle with a deep, hollow sound.

Ned's fingers began to ache, and he realized that he was gripping the side of the sink too hard. The sink had always made that gurgling sound, and ever since he could remember, that sound had frightened him; it reminded him of the sound of someone choking. He tried to fight back the panic that was rising. The sound in the sink grew louder. Suddenly, the stream of white shampoo turned pink, and then, after his mother doused his head again, a thin red line ran from his nose and down the sink. Ned started to choke as he snorted loudly in an attempt to keep his throat clear. He was bleeding again.

In a panic, he turned his head to the side, and when he did, some of the shampoo ran into his left eye. He screamed. "Towel! Towel!" he yelled. "Quick! It's in my eyes!"

He groped wildly, blindly on the counter beside him for the towel. The drain continued to gurgle above the sounds of his shouting, and his fear rose all the more. He felt the dark, gurgling hole of the sink start to pull him and, scared out of his wits, he thought he might be drawn down into it.

"Here you are," his mother said, slapping his bare shoulder and handing him a coarse cotton towel. He rubbed his face vigorously and kept his face hidden until his fear began to recede. The sound coming from the sink had grown softer too. He pulled the towel away and saw that it was stained with blood. He folded it so his mother couldn't see it.

"Lord have mercy, boy," his mother said, "don't holler so. You'd think someone was tryin' t'kill yah!" Her voice sounded hard and cold, Ned thought, like the chilled countertop pressed against his chest.

"It hurt," he said meekly, as he turned and started to ruffle his hair with the towel. He made sure to keep the bloody side hidden. "The shampoo got in my eye."

"Well it's not like you were gonna die." She

had her flabby arms folded across her chest and was leaning against the refrigerator.

Ned was silent as he finished drying his hair and then started to comb it. "Hey, Ma, do you know where Frank is?" he asked.

She shook her head no.

He slid his comb back into his back pocket and then put his shirt on, buttoning it slowly. "I was just thinking—"

"Well, don't!" his mother said harshly. "It'll always get you into trouble.

"No, I was wondering," Ned continued, trying to get past her. "I've got all my homework done, and I kinda wanted to go downtown and . . ." He wanted to keep talking, to present his argument in full before she had a chance to refuse, but he fell silent when he saw her take a threatening step toward him.

"You were thinking what?" she asked. She took another step forward.

"I thought I might go, ummm, downtown," he managed to say before shrinking back from his mother's advance.

"Going to the Royal, right?" she said shrilly. "You were thinking you'd go hang out at the Royal, weren't you?"

"No, I, uh I—" Ned felt the cold edge of the countertop press into the small of his back. He moved backward, feeling the formica rub against his bare skin.

"You were gonna go down there and drink beer, weren't you? Drink Beer! And the girls who go down there! Girls! They'd be home, if they had any decency!"

"No, honest, Ma, I—" Ned had backed into the corner and stood there, cringing under her angry outburst. Her eyes widened, and her face became flushed. Spittle flew from her mouth.

"I'll bet you they use drugs there too. Don't they. Don't they!"

"I dunno," Ned said weakly. He felt pressure in his bladder.

"They do! I know they do!" Her eyes were bulging, the yellowed whites showing all around the pupils. She moved closer, clenching her hands into fists that started to weave and dart dangerously. Ned raised his hands to ward off the expected blow.

"Is that it?" she shouted. "Have you been smoking pot?"

Ned was silent, terror-stricken.

"Well?"

"No! Of course I haven't," he stammered. "I, I—"

"Well you better not start," she said menacingly, and then, certain that she had scared him into submission, she took a few steps backward and crossed her arms over her chest again.

"It's bad enough that I've got one runabout son. I don't want you starting in drinkin' and chasin' after girls. Drink!" She snorted loudly and looked at him piercingly. "You know, drink's what killed your father."

Ned nodded his head but still didn't dare to let down his guard. He knew from past experience that her anger could flare up again, instantly.

"I've tried to stop Frank. Honest, Lord, I've

54

tried 'n' I've failed." She glared at Ned. "But I'm not gonna fail with you! No, sir! By God and all His angels, I'm not gonna fail with you!"

"Now," she said, and Ned could tell that her tension had begun to unwind, "you must have some homework to do."

Ned shrugged his shoulders. "First day of school. I got it all done in study hall."

"Well, you just go on up to your room and see if you can do just a bit extra. Or maybe you could go to bed a little bit early tonight so I won't have to drag you out of bed in the morning. You have to finish your chores before you go to school, you know."

"I know."

"Well, I don't wanna have to remind you. But one thing's for certain." She stamped her foot on the floor for emphasis. "You're not going out. Especially to the Royal!"

Ned turned to go upstairs. He was still holding the towel loosely in his hand, and he let it drag up the stairs behind him.

"G'night," his mother called from downstairs. "Sleep well."

In answer, Ned hockered from deep in his chest and sent a ball of spit sailing through the air. It hit the wall by the door with a dull plop. There was blood mixed in with saliva and, for some reason, that made Ned smile.

.IV.

The jukebox at the Royal was cranked up to

full volume, and the worn speakers blasted a fluttery rumble with each bass note. It was playing an unrecognizable Rolling Stones song.

Frenchie, the bartender, was leaning with his elbow on the bar, swirling a damp cloth in tight circles. Bob sat on one of the stools at the end of the bar. He nodded in the direction of the bartender, and Frenchie walked over to him. His damp cloth left a wet streak the length of the bar.

"Another Mic?"

Frenchie nodded, drew a beer, and then came back. Bob left a dollar bill on the bar, which Frenchie picked up. Before going to the cash register to ring in the sale, though, Frenchie leaned on the bar, waiting for Bob to say something.

Bob glanced over his shoulder at the crowded room. Just about every booth was filled, and there were three couples dancing in the center of the floor. "Is it always this busy?" Bob asked.

Frenchie smiled. "I wish," he mumbled. There was a sink close by, so he rinsed his rag and then took a few more swipes at the bartop. "Fridays and Saturdays are usually pretty good. A crowd like this on a Wednesday night is kinda unusual." When no further conversation was forthcoming, Frenchie started to move back up the length of the bar, wiping as he went.

Bob watched the crowd for a while, then turned back around and took a swallow of beer. He settled more comfortably in his seat, then shook out a cigarette from his pack and lit it. His glass was half empty and he was just stubbing out the butt in the ashtray when a firm hand gripped his shoulder. He tensed before turning, expecting to find a drunken regular who felt compelled to challenge this newcomer. He turned and was surprised to see Lisa Carter smiling at him.

"You should be home, reading Greek drama," she said brightly.

"I would be," Bob replied, returning the smile, "if the local library had a copy of the book I need."

"Isn't that just the case," Lisa said. "One of the best libraries in the state of New Hampshire, and they don't have a copy of Hadas' *Greek Anthology*." She shook her head sadly, clicking her tongue. "So I see you decided to check out the local hot spot instead."

"You mean this is it?" Bob said, and they both laughed. He rose and pulled out the stool beside him. "Care for a drink?"

Lisa stood there, considering for a moment. "I suppose one drink wouldn't hurt. What say we sit over in a booth, though."

Bob smiled and followed her over to a corner booth. Once they were seated, Lisa leaned across the table and, in a conspirator's voice, said, "You know, one thing I always thought, though, was that teachers indulged their vices out of town." She laughed softly, but there was something in her voice that made Bob think she really meant it.

"Well," he said, throwing his hands up, "I

don't really mind if people talk. What harm is there in that?"

He couldn't believe he heard himself say that, not after what had happened to him in Dorchester!

"Cooper Falls is a pretty small town, though, Mr. Wentworth," she said more seriously as her smile faded. "Really, you should, maybe, be more careful."

He looked at her and then raised his hand over his head to signal Frenchie that they wanted something to drink. "Do you mind if I smoke?" he asked, once he saw Frenchie making his way over to the table.

Lisa shrugged.

Frenchie took her order for a whisky sour and then walked away. Bob lit his cigarette and then sat back in the booth, observing Lisa.

She sat straight up in the seat, her hands folded on the table. Bob realized that this afternoon in the library, he had hardly noticed how attractive she really was, especially her green eyes, which seemed to flash and twinkle with humor.

"I would think," Bob said finally, "that the local hangout wouldn't be exactly a great place for the local librarian to hang out either."

Lisa smiled, and replied, "Well, I don't have a school board to please, especially a school board like the one we have."

David almost gagged on the smoke he was exhaling. "You'll, you'll have to tell me about them sometime," he managed to say. He fidgeted with the ashtray, spinning it around in circles.

"What can I tell you about them? They're a cross section of a typical small New Hampshire town." She paused for effect, then added, "They wear red-white-and-blue underwear."

While she was talking, Bob became aware of two voices behind him gradually rising higher and higher as their conversation turned into an argument. It was a man and a woman, and, curious, Bob twisted around in his seat to glance at them. Lisa looked also, and Bob noticed that, when she saw who it was, she tensed noticeably. The corners of her mouth tightened.

"Who are they?" Bob asked, but before she could answer, Frenchie arrived with her drink. Bob paid him, and he walked away, giving the arguing couple a brief, harsh stare.

Bob held his glass of beer up and, clinking it against Lisa's, said, "Well, here's to pleasing the school board members, especially conservative school board members."

After they each took a drink, Bob turned around in his seat again and glanced at the fighting couple. They were still going at it and getting louder.

He could only see the back of the man's head: shoulder-length, stringy black hair. He was wearing a dirty denim work shirt. When Bob looked at the girl, though, he felt an almost electric charge jolt him. She had pale blue eyes that seemed to be focusing somewhere in outer space. They flashed from beneath a shaggy mass of dark hair. Her face was thin and angular, with high cheekbones, and, at least from what he could see of her body, she looked like she had a great shape. She was an unusually attractive woman, and Bob felt an immediate interest in her.

"Who are they?" he repeated, turning back to Lisa.

Lisa ran her teeth over her lower lip and was about to reply when the girl behind Bob suddenly shouted, "I can see whoever I damn well want to see! And you aren't going to tell me not to!" Bob looked around again and saw her stand up. He had been right; she did have a terrific body.

"And it's none of your fucking business who I see!"

"Hey, come on, Julie, sit down," the man said, nervously rising and grabbing for the woman's arm. "For Christ's sake, will you just calm down?"

Lisa leaned toward Bob and whispered, "His name is Frank Simmons. Hers is—"

She was going to continue, but the argument at the other table drowned her out.

There was a loud bang as the woman slammed her hand onto the table, sending her glass of beer flying, and then shattering it on the floor. Other talk in the bar died down. Even the jukebox was silent as the argument dominated everyone's attention.

"I don't have to take this kind of shit from anybody!" the woman screamed. "You can just stuff it!" The woman reached across the table, picked up the man's glass of beer, and flung it into his face.

"Fuck off!" she shouted.

The man sat there stunned, sputtering. The woman picked up her pocketbook and started for the door. Just before she left, she turned back and looked at the man, who still hadn't moved. "You can go to hell!" she screeched, and then stormed out the door.

The barroom sat in surprised silence, which was finally broken when an old man sitting at the bar started to clap his hands. "That's tellin' him, lady. Yessir," he said drunkenly.

The silence settled on the barroom like a crystal bell-jar. Then someone dropped a coin into the jukebox, and conversation slowly resumed.

"Frank Simmons?" Bob said, turning back to Lisa. "Is he related to Ned Simmons?"

Lisa nodded. "Yeah. His older brother. Why do you ask?"

"Oh." Bob looked down at his hands. "I, umm, I have Ned in school. At least, met him there." He took a swallow of beer, emptying his glass. "It's a long story."

"Umm."

"So," Bob said, "who's his girlfriend? Or should I say who was his girl friend?"

"Her name's Julie Sikes. She lives a bit out of town, up on Martin's Lake."

"She's a pretty woman," Bob said simply. He noticed, again, that Lisa was sitting very tensed. "Hey, come on. You can't let that fight bother you. Have another drink." He raised his hand to signal Frenchie. "Tell me about yourself. I've learned about the town's school board, Frank Simmons, and Julie Sikes, but I still don't know very much about you."

Lisa lowered her eyes and studied her folded hands. Then she shook her head and said, "No. No thanks. I've got to get going."

She stood up and started to walk away, but Bob grabbed her by the arm. She was surprised by his boldness.

"Hey. What's the matter?"

"Nothing," she said tightly.

"Something."

Lisa started for the door. Bob stood up and almost bumped into Frenchie, who was finally making his way over to the booth. Bob got out his wallet and handed the bartender a five dollar bill. He glanced over at the door and saw it closing behind Lisa.

"Here," he said, pushing the bill into Frenchie's hand, "Keep the change." He rushed out after Lisa.

She was already out in the parking lot beside her car, fumbling in her purse for her keys. Bob ran up to her and caught her by the arm. He turned her around, and was surprised by the pain he saw twisting her face. Her keys clattered onto the asphalt, and he bent down to retrieve them.

"Hey," he said.

She looked at him, her mouth working to form words. Finally she said, "It's personal, OK? So don't press, OK?"

"Yeah, yeah. Sure." Bob started to back off. "Sorry."

"Oh, Christ!" she said. "It's not your fault. I'm sorry."

Bob was still unsure, but he mumbled, "Sure."

They stood there staring at each other in silence. The sodium streetlight cast an eerie orange pall on her face, washing away all other color. The night was quiet except for the distant barking of a dog.

Lisa shivered and took a step closer to Bob. She placed her hand lightly on his shoulder. "I shouldn't act like that," she said raspily, "I'm sorry." She looked at him intently, as though trying to read his thoughts. "It's just that sometimes, sometimes I like having someone I can talk to, someone I can trust."

Bob placed his finger on her lips. "You can talk to me," he said. The sincerity in his voice made Lisa smile again.

"So what got you so upset? Was it that argument in the bar?"

Lisa nodded. "Yeah. That and other things."

"What other things?"

"Well, it's Julie. I, oh, Jesus, Bob! I don't know how to say this without sounding like a damned fool. You're going to think you've moved to the original Peyton Place, or something. I don't want to unload my problems on a total stranger."

"Not total stranger," Bob said, and he pulled her closer. "You can tell me anything you want." He leaned forward, and their lips met. Lisa didn't resist the kiss, but she remained stiff. Her lips felt cold and hard. When they pulled apart,

Bob saw that her eyes were filling with tears.

"Hey, come on, Lisa. It can't be that bad," he said. He brushed her cheek with the back of his hand. Suddenly, she pulled away.

"Oh, shit!" She covered her face with her hands and leaned against her car roof. Her shoulders shook with her sobs, then she straightened up, looked at Bob, and spoke. She fought to keep her voice steady. "Look, Bob, I've got to tell you. I should have said something before now. I'm sorry I didn't but—"

"You're married, right?"

"Yeah," she said simply, staring at him with wide, gleaming eyes. She raised her hand to her mouth as though to hold back another sob and bit down on her knuckles.

"I should have said something before," she whined. "But it wasn't like I was leading you on or anything. I like you. I liked from the moment I saw you walk into the library."

"I thought you were pretty attractive too," Bob said softly.

"I, I was afraid you saw me playing with my wedding ring while you were talking to me. I guess I kind of tried to hide it."

"No, no, I didn't," Bob said, feeling foolish. He started to pull away from Lisa. "Well, I guess I should be getting on back home." He paused, then added with a chuckle, "Read a little Greek drama before tucking in."

Lisa smiled, but Bob noticed that some of the sparkle had left her eyes.

"I can give you a ride home, if you'd like,"

Lisa offered. "It's quite a long ways to walk."

"And how do you know how far I have to go?" Bob asked, with a trace of humor in his voice.

"Oh," Lisa replied with a laugh, "I know quite a bit about you. More that you think. I told you, Cooper Falls is a small town. Now come on. Hop in."

.V.

"So how long has he been having an affair with Julie Sikes?" Bob asked. He and Lisa were sitting in her car parked on Old Jepson's Road at the bottom of Bob's driveway. They had been talking for close to two hours. His question hit her like a dull hammer blow in the darkness of the car. She looked at him and smiled weakly.

"Jeff? My husband?" she asked, sounding surprised. "I, I really don't know."

"But you're sure he is seeing her?"

Lisa shrugged. "Yeah. I'm pretty sure." She tried to keep her voice calm, but just mentioning it made her feel tense.

"So why was she in the bar tonight with Frank?" Bob asked. "From the looks of things, I'd say they were kind of involved."

"You don't know Julie Sikes," Lisa said. She swallowed hard, and Bob waited for her to continue. He lit a cigarette and blew the smoke out the open window on his side.

"Julie was a sophomore in high school when I was a senior. Even before she dropped out, she had a, a reputation." Lisa paused and shook her head with amusement. "Jesus, I sound like a class-A prude, don't I?"

"No," Bob said simply.

"Well, during her sophomore year, Julie got pregnant. She had to drop out right when she found out. It's not like today, where someone can stay in school right up to delivery. So Julie dropped out just around Christmas vacation."

"Did she get married?"

"Oh, yeah. Billy Sikes admitted right away that the baby was his. He kind of took a lot of pride in that fact, maybe because it proved to his buddies that he was screwing Julie."

"Hell of a way to prove you're growing up, isn't it?" Bob exhaled and snapped the cigarette out the window. "He dropped out of school too?"

"He already had. Billy had been or should have been a senior that year. He had a job at one of the ski resorts in North Conway. They got a house out on Martin's Lake and Julie had the baby."

"How old is the kid now? He should be about, what, nine years old?"

"She. It was a baby girl. Well, that's where it starts getting kind of weird. The baby was born that June. A real healthy kid and all. She died later that summer. The old scapegoat: crib death."

"That's a drag," Bob said. He turned and

looked out the window, his thoughts suddenly on his little girl, Jamie. He remembered wishing many times, when he and Amy were having trouble, that Jamie had never been born, that their separation would have been much easier if a kid hadn't been involved. He tried now to grasp the reality of losing a baby, and his mind rejected it. He didn't tell Lisa any of his thoughts.

"But see, one thing that's always mystified me is that the baby was buried in a closed casket."

"So?"

"For crib death? A closed casket? Come on!"

"Well," Bob offered, "maybe she just couldn't stand seeing her baby like that."

"That's what I'm getting to. It seemed not to affect Julie at all. She didn't cry at the funeral. She didn't even look upset."

"That isn't a crime," Bob said. "So she didn't care for the baby?"

"OK, OK. Maybe she didn't like the kid, and maybe it's a good thing that the kid didn't have to grow up with, with Julie for a mother."

"That's really not a very nice thing to say," Bob said.

"Come on, Bob, you saw her tonight. Can you tell me she struck you as a nice person?"

"You want the truth?" he asked sharply.

Lisa nodded.

"Well, my first impression, other than the fight they were having, was that she was quite an attractive woman. You have to admit, she's a pretty good looker."

"Oh, believe me, I know. That's just the thing. See, even before Julie got married, she was sleeping around. She's attractive and she knows it. And she uses it to get whatever she wants. So, to answer your question, how do I know my husband is sleeping with Julie? I don't know, but I'm positive!"

"What about her husband, Billy?"

"That's what I'd have to call the last, or most recent chapter. Her husband Billy was killed just this past August in a car crash."

Bob grunted and stared at Lisa. "And . . ."

"And, just like when her baby died, it seemed as though she really didn't care. She just showed no reaction to it at all."

"You know, Lisa," Bob said, shifting around and placing his hand on her shoulder, "a lot of people find it hard to express their emotions, to really let people know what they're feeling."

"You can't say that about Julie, Bob. You don't know her; I do. Her husband didn't die alone. He was driving with a local girl, Joyce Brewer. When their bodies were found, there was a lot of talk about them having an affair."

"God, Lisa, you're right. I think I did move to Peyton Place." Bob laughed, but his laughter failed to lighten Lisa's mood.

"How does the expression go? He wasn't even cold in the ground, and she was messing around with Frank Simmons, and my husband, and who knows how many other men."

"So why in the hell don't you leave him?" Bob said finally. He looked at Lisa and saw the pained expression on her face. "You could, you know?"

"I know, I know. It's just, that, well . . ." She broke down and began to sob. Bob patted her shoulder and let her cry it out. They'd have time to talk about it. Of that he was certain. One thing he had decided in the two hours they had spent together was that he wanted to see Lisa Carter again, a lot.

"Hey," he said, once her tears had subsided, "it's late. Tomorrow—" He glanced at his wristwatch. "Today's another school day."

"Yeah," Lisa said. She adjusted herself behind the steering wheel and started up the motor. Bob snapped the car door open and put one foot out onto the roadside. Even in the dark he could see that the gleam had returned to her eyes. He touched her and, with a slight pressure, signaled that he wanted to hold her and kiss her.

"Don't rush anything, OK?" she said, drawing away. Her voice was low and steady, but not cold.

"Sure."

"Thanks for being such a good listener."

"Aww," Bob said, "it was nothing." Besides," he added with a laugh, "it beats reading Greek drama any day. Good night."

"Good night, Bob."

He stood on the roadside in the darkness and watched her pull away, then he started walking up to his cabin.

When Lisa got home, it was almost one o'clock. The stack of dirty dishes was still sitting in the sink where she had left them that morning.

As if Jeff would ever bother to help with the housework, she thought bitterly, as she stuck her hand into the cold, greasy water and pulled the plug. She watched the water swirl down the drain, then filled the tea kettle with fresh water and put it on the stove.

She went over to the kitchen table and sat down with a huff. The window was open, and the yellowed curtains billowed in and out on the breeze, catching now and then on the window sill's chipped paint. She rested her elbows on the plastic tablecloth and let her breath out with a long sign. She wanted to cry, but some of the emotions she was feeling counteracted that feeling.

She looked out of the window onto the street when she heard a car approaching. When the car passed by, she felt vaguely relieved. Jeff wouldn't be home for another hour or so, she figured. For the first time in her life, she wanted the time alone to think.

The tea kettle started to whistle, so she walked over and turn it off. Then she left it sitting there until the water got cold.

Chapter Four

.I.

Roy Granger, chief of police of Cooper Falls, was sitting in his office beside the open window reading the newspaper when he heard voices outside.

"You never heard about that? Somewhere in Massachusetts, I think it is in Gloucester, or Marblehead, that this woman was killed and eaten by her dogs when they got snowbound."

"Never heard that one."

They were coming closer, and Granger recognized who they were even before he saw Ted Seavey and Gene McCann walk past his window. Granger sighed heavily and folded the newspaper up and threw it on top of the clutter on his desk.

"Come on in," Granger shouted, as soon as he

71

heard the heavy clump of their boots on the steps. As the men mumbled greetings, Granger went over to the coffee pot on the table under the wall gun-rack and poured three coffees. He had done it enough mornings to know that Gene had two sugars and milk, and Ted had his black. He handed them each a cup and then sat back down in his chair beside the window.

"What's got you up and about this early, fellas?" Granger asked. He rested his cup on the window sill and leaned back in his chair until it touched the wall.

"That damn dog, that's what," Ted replied angrily. "It got into my hen house last night and tore the shit out of it." He was pacing back and forth, his face creased with concern. "I was hoping he'd stop, that he'd gone away, 'cause he ain't been seen for a while; but he's back, god-dammit!"

Granger glanced over at Gene, who was sitting silently near the door, elbows on knees, studying the toes of his boots.

"We gotta do somethin' about it, dammit!"

Gene nodded his head in agreement but didn't take his eyes away from his boots.

"You're sure it was the same animal, this wild dog?"

"Dammit! Sure I'm sure!" Ted bellowed, directing his anger at Granger. "He was howling like hell out there last night, and you should see the henhouse!"

"I'm planning on taking a drive out there."

"When? Next week sometime?" Ted said.

"Christ, Roy, the way you're dragging your ass on this, I'm beginning to think—"

"Look," Granger snapped, "I just want to be sure. Remember last week when I got hauled out to Judkin's place at three A.M. and it turned out to be nothing but a raccoon cornered in the barn by their dog? I don't want to go off half-cocked, that's all. A coon can raise a ruckus in a henhouse, but it sure as hell ain't no wild dog."

Gene finally looked up from the meditation of his boots. "It's a dog all right, and a damn big one. I saw the paw prints." He shook his head with astonishment.

"Fucking-A straight," Ted said. "Look, I lost close to ten hens last night, and the ones that lived'll probably be off laying for weeks. The henhouse looks like a goddamn tornado hit it."

Granger took a sip of coffee and rubbed his cheek thoughtfully. "Wild dog, huh?"

"Come on, Roy, you know damn right well there are wild dogs in the woods around here. Tourists come up in the summer and let their animals run loose, even though we have leash laws; then, come September, they leave and don't even try to get their animals back. What the hell are the animals gonna do? They have to survive somehow."

"Yeah," Gene said softly, " 'n, every winter we find plenty of carcasses of deer that've been run down by dogs."

"Now wait just a minute," Granger said. "Those dogs that kill deer ain't wild ones. And summer folk ain't the only people who don't observe the leash laws. Anyone's dog can spend an afternoon chasing down deer and then come home in the evening like a perfect pet."

"Well," Ted said solemnly, "this happened at night. And Cunningham's lambs got killed at night. So if we ain't got a wild dog on our hands, we got a coyote or a wolf."

Granger snickered, shifting his weight in his chair and joining his hands behind his head. "Come on, Ted. You and I both know there ain't no wolves in New Hampshire, haven't been for over a hundred years."

Ted walked over to Granger's desk and slammed his fist down. "Well I don't give a shit what it is! Me and Gene and a few other guys have decided to do something about it." He cleared his throat as though making a speech. "We're organizing to hunt. We're here to ask for permission to carry loaded guns after dark, That's when the animal hits, so that's when we're gonna hunt it."

"Now wait a minute, Ted," Granger said, slowly rising from his chair. "You know I can't suspend the hunting laws like that." He snapped his fingers under Ted's nose.

Ted exploded. "Roy, we're gonna do it whether you give us permission or not. Enough of us have lost enough livestock and are worried enough about it to take the chance of gettin' fined." Having said his piece, Seavey went over to the door and leaned against it. His eyes bore into Granger, but the blood drained slowly from his face and he relaxed. He picked up his coffee where he had left it and took a sip. It was cold.

"Well, we do have a problem here," Granger said thoughtfully. "The first thing I want you to do is give me a list of everyone who's going to be out on this hunt."

"Sure." Ted said.

"Good, that way if I decide to arrest you, I'll be able to get you all." Seavey missed the attempt at humor and glared at Granger.

"Now another thing," Granger said. "I don't want you or anyone else spreading any stories about wild dogs in our woods. We don't need the panic, and we don't need any bad publicity."

"What if it is wolves?" Gene said, almost dreamily, as though he hadn't heard the last five minutes of argument. "I think I heard something about how they were gonna bring some Canadian timber wolves into the state, you know, to give 'em a chance to expand their range. Maybe they already started and didn't tell anyone, you know, 'cause of the fuss."

"I doubt it," Granger said, "because I think we would have heard something about it."

Ted snorted. "Not if they didn't want us to, we wouldn't."

"Well I'll tell you one thing." Granger pointed his finger at Ted. "If this here animal is a wolf, you just keep in mind that wolves are protected by federal law. You guys can hunt at night, and if I don't like it, I can get the warden to slap a fine on you. But if you kill a wolf, it's a federal crime."

Gene shrugged his shoulder, dismissing the thought. "Maybe it's coyotes, them coy-dogs, they call 'em."

"Whatever it is, I just want you fellas to be careful. I have the authority to, but I won't pick any of you up for this. Just be goddamn careful. I don't want anyone getting shot; it's bad enough once hunting season starts."

Gene shook his head sadly, but there was a twinkle in his eyes. "Roy, you know it's always out-of-staters that get shot up during hunting season."

Ted went over and put his coffee cup on the table and then started out the door. "Yeah, well, we just wanted to talk it over with you. For the next couple of nights or so, we're gonna be out in the woods."

"OK," Granger said. "And keep me posted. Ted, I'll be out your way later today to check that henhouse."

"Sure. Thanks a lot," Ted said as he left. Gene scrambled to his feet and followed him out the door. Just as he left, someone else walked into the office. Granger looked up and nodded to his deputy, Rick Thurston.

"Sorry I'm late," Thurston said. "I had a little trouble with my car this morning. Guess it needs a tune-up."

"Don't sweat it, Rick," Granger said, "it's not like we have a murder case on our hands." He paused and looked out the window for a moment, then said, "But I do think we got some trouble brewing."

76

Briefly, Granger filled Rick in on what had just transpired in the office. Thurston listened attentively, nodding but saying nothing.

"So," Granger concluded, "they're gonna be out hunting for the next few nights. I don't think there'll be any trouble, but it won't hurt to be on the alert."

Thurston squared his shoulders and said, "I try to be ready all the time."

Granger chuckled. "Good, good," he muttered. "Now to get down to more serious matters. Who's going to run over to the B&B and see what Ruthie's got for donuts?" He took a quarter from his pocket and flipped it into the air.

.II.

As he got closer to the library, Bob slowed his pace and walked leisurely along the asphalt path that angled across the park. He had had a simple breakfast of toast and eggs at the B&B and was enjoying the sense of satisfaction he got walking along the Main Street of his new town. Lisa had a lot to do with it. They had been seeing each other quite a bit during the past month; they hoped they had not generated any suspicions.

There was a football game in progress at the far end of the park, and Bob stopped for a moment to watch. Apparently there was a difference of opinion. The boys were gathered in a circle, and Bob could hear their shrill, angry voices rising higher and higher. At last the disagreement was settled, and the boys split into two opposing lines again. Bob watched the snap of the ball and the resulting pile-up, then started up the granite steps.

At the top of the steps, just before entering the library, Bob turned to look again out over the peaceful Saturday morning park. The trees and the ivy that climbed up the walls of the library were just starting to turn. A squirrel skittered across the lawn, its cheeks filled with acorns.

Suddenly, a big cloud overhead passed in front of the sun, blotting out the light and plunging the park into shadow. This had an unnerving effect on Bob, and he stood there for a moment, rigid.

Why, he wondered, does that feel so ominous? He watched the darkness shift over the park. The boys playing football didn't even notice it; they kept on playing.

While he was eating breakfast in the B&B, he had heard a few men at the counter talking about the wild dog. They were sure it was still around, running in the woods. Then one of them told everyone that something, the wild dog, he thought, tore up someone's chicken coop. All of this brought back the warning Vera Miller had given him about not walking around after dark.

"You never know what's going to be out there . . ."

Somehow, the cloud passing overhead brought all of this back to Bob, and it gave him an extremely uncomfortable feeling. He opened the door to the library and rushed in, feeling almost as though he was seeking refuge from something.

"Good morning," Lisa called to him brightly. She got up from her desk and came over to him quickly. He noticed that she was looking better and better every time he saw her. She glanced around furtively, then gave him a quick kiss on the cheek.

"Good news, too," she said, smiling. "I finally found that book you were looking for, the *Greek Anthology*. It had fallen down behind the shelf." She giggled. "Shows how much I dust around this place, huh?"

Bob nodded his head and said nothing.

"Hey! What's the matter?"

Bob shrugged. "Aww. I don't know."

"You still need the book, don't you?" Lisa asked earnestly.

"Yeah, I do. Thanks for getting it," he said dully.

"Come on, Bob. What's bugging you?"

"Nothing. Really, nothing, just, well, forget it. So where's the book?"

Lisa slapped her open palm against her forehead. "Stupid me. I was cleaning, so I put it back on the shelf and then left it there." She studied him for a moment, her green eyes sparkling. "Hey, you know, if you want to talk about it, I'll listen."

He saw that her concern was genuine and tried hard to return a brave smile. "I'll go get that book," he said, heading toward the door to the stacks, "then maybe we can talk."

"Sure," Lisa said warmly. "I'll go put on a fresh pot of coffee. It'll be done by the time you get back."

Once he was alone in the stacks, Bob felt a measure of relief. He had always felt a certain peacefulness in library stacks. The ceiling-high metal shelves jammed with dusty old books offered a pleasant quiet and protection. He walked slowly down the aisle, clicking off each title as he went. He located the Hadas book, tucked it under his arm, and continued down the line without interruption.

His thoughts were muddled as he tried to sort out why he had gotten such a funny feeling as he looked out over the park. There was no way he could deny it; there had been a distinct feeling of foreboding, of danger. He realized that he was letting little things bother him. This talk about a wild dog in the woods just wasn't as serious as the guys around town were making it. He tried to force his mind into a lighter mood.

He snapped up straight suddenly. Had it been his imagination, or had he really heard faint laughter? He cocked his ear and listened intently. He heard it again; not right-out laughter, but muffled, as if behind a hand.

Bob peered along the row of books he had been following. The stacks were quiet again except for the buzzing of the fluorescent lights. Then, a third time, he heard it: a high, almost childlike laugh.

He found that he was holding his breath as he edged his way around the bookcase into the next aisle. There was no one there, and just as he had concluded that he hadn't pinpointed the direction correctly, he caught a shadow of motion in the next aisle over.

Someone else was in the stacks. That wouldn't have unnerved him, ordinarily, but that laughter: so childlike, yet so spooky sounding.

Silently, Bob tiptoed to the aisle and sneaked a look at whoever it was who had invaded the sanctuary of the stacks.

When he first saw the woman, he had to choke back a gasp of surprise. He immediately recognized the mass of tangled black hair. The woman, sensing that someone was watching her, snapped her head around and nailed Bob with a harsh stare.

It was Julie Sikes.

She was holding a large, leather-bound volume in her hands. Keeping her pale blue eyes locked on Bob, she slowly closed the book and, without looking, slid it back into place.

Bob was transfixed by her appearance. Her wild shock of black hair framed her face which, in the harsh electric light, looked pale and waxen. She was wearing a long black dress that brushed the floor, and a white shawl over her shoulders. When she turned around, Bob saw that the top of her dress was open, exposing a vast area of her chest.

"You surprised me," she said softly, airily. Her voice was nothing like the angry voice Bob remembered from that argument in the bar. She held Bob's gaze with her eyes.

"I'm, I'm sorry," Bob stammered, feeling embarrassed. "I, uhh, I didn't know there was anyone else up here."

Julie smiled slightly. "It is a public library, isn't it?" she said, with a faint laugh.

"Oh, yeah, sure." Bob tried to take his eyes away from the woman, but the piercing, blank gaze held him.

"You gave me quite a start, too," Julie said. Her smile widened, and she ran the tip of her tongue over her lips.

"I didn't mean to," Bob said. "Sorry."

Julie took a step closer to him. He felt a tight tingling in his stomach. "Uhh, what were you reading that was so funny?" he asked, aware that his voice sounded strained.

"Oh nothing, nothing," she said, shrugging her shoulders. Bob couldn't help but notice that the movement emphasized the woman's ample cleavage. "I was just looking for something to read, a novel or something."

She took a few more steps closer to Bob, and he pressed back against the bookcase to let her pass. She stopped, standing right up close to him. He caught an aroma of cloves, and he could feel her body-heat.

Looking directly into his eyes, she said, "Do you have any suggestions?" Her breath was warm on his face.

"Ahh, no. Not really," Bob said awkwardly. He tried but was unable to look away.

"Hmmm," she said, looking thoughtful and faraway. "Well, maybe later." With that, she moved past him and walked down the aisle. Bob watched her hair bounce and flutter with each step. Just before she turned the corner to leave the stacks, she turned around and nodded, almost imperceptibly. Bob nodded back silently, and then she was gone.

Once she was gone, he would have seriously wondered whether or not she had been there had he not been left with the cloying aroma of cloves.

.III.

"She must have come in when I was in the back room or something," Lisa said, blowing on her coffee before taking a tentative sip. "I didn't know she was up there."

Bob smiled slightly, shook his head, and looked down at the floor.

"Well?" Lisa said. "Did you speak with her?"

"Uhh, no." Bob shook his head and started to raise his cup to his mouth. Some coffee spilled and burned his fingers. "God! This is hot," he muttered.

"What was she looking at?" Lisa asked. She was making an effort to sound casual, conversational, but she could see that meeting Julie had put Bob on edge.

"I don't know," Bob replied. "I didn't even check. It just startled me because I thought I was up there alone, that's all. But I'll tell you one thing, Lisa. You were right. She does have some kind of a, some kind of an energy or something. I don't know. It seemed like she had some kind of power or something."

Lisa laughed and took a sip of coffee. "Now you're starting to sound like her."

"Huh?"

"You didn't check to see what she was looking at. I'll bet you next week's paycheck it was some kind of occult book. You know, witchcraft, ESP, whatever."

Bob raised his eyebrows.

"That's all she ever takes out, books like that."

"Well then she really likes to play it up, I'll tell you that much. It's like she has this kind of control over things that nobody else has. Like, like, I don't know."

"Now, maybe you understand what I was trying to tell you that night I met you at the Royal. She always has that kind of aloof detachment, even when she was at the funerals for her baby and her husband."

"She's weird, all right. I don't know what she's into, but it sure must be a strange trip."

"She really shook you up, didn't she?"

Bob nodded and drained his cup with three gulps.

"Here. Do you want a refill?"

Bob held out his cup and Lisa started to pour. His hand was shaking. Lisa reached out with her other hand to steady Bob's cup.

"God! Your hand's as cold as ice," she said with surprise.

Bob smiled tightly but said nothing. He

reached into his pocket for a cigarette and lit it, inhaling deeply. He straightened up and said, "Hey, let's forget it, huh?" He looked into Lisa's eyes and drew her closer to him.

"The library isn't going to get very busy today. It's a beautiful September day, and it's almost time for lunch. What do you say we drive out to North Conway and see if we can find a restaurant with a decent menu?"

Lisa hesitated, cast a nervous glance into the empty library, and then said, 'Well, OK. But I have to be back by one o'clock."

"Two at the latest," Bob said, grinding out his cigarette and taking Lisa by the arm.

.IV.

Through the dust and cobwebs that covered the hayloft window, Ned could see the sun slanting down behind the hills. A beam of light sliced through the grimy window, illuminating a small cloud of dust that hung suspended, glittering over Ned's head. Below, he could hear the cows shuffling in their stalls.

Ned grunted and started to push a bale of hay across the floor to the open trap door. He paused, wiped the sweat on the back of his neck, then shoved the bale up to the opening. The bale balanced on the edge, teetered, and then fell to the floor below with a dull thud. He looked down and saw that the baling wire had snapped, and the hay lay spread out like an accordion.

Ned sat back on his heels and stared vacantly at the wall. He felt a line of sweat carve its way through the grime on his neck. Slowly he raised his hand and pulled his damp hair away from his eyes, then, shaking his head as if just waking, he stood up. From below, he heard the side-door spring stretch open, then the spring twanged and pulled the door shut. Footsteps scuffed along the cement floor and then stopped.

"You up there Ned?" his mother called sharply.

He stood tensed, unable to answer.

"Well, supper's on."

"K," he answered, his voice as thin as paper.

He heard her take three quick steps and then stop.

"You got everything done?" she yelled, and when he didn't answer, "I said, did you get—"

"Yeah, yeah, just about. I'll be right down." He glanced out the window where the sky was now tinted orange with thick purple streaks in it. A spot right between his shoulders got a sudden chill, and he shivered as he shifted his gaze back to the trap-door hole. "Be right down," he whispered as he curled his upper lip into a sneer.

He waited without moving until he heard his mother leave the barn, then he lowered himself through the hole. His arms trembled, supporting his weight, but before he dropped, he glanced down at his legs. He let them hang loosely, suspended, swaying above the floor. For a moment he fantasized that he was a hanged man, and the image amused him until he glanced at the worn, shiny wood at the edge of the trap door. The fantasy took on a harsh degree of reality. He looked at his hands; they looked pale, the skin seemed thin as onionskin.

"No, no," he whispered, the words barely above a croak. The image of the gallows remained as he snapped his arms to his side and dropped.

He hit the floor with a groan, his knees giving way with a sharp, burning pain that shot down to his ankles. Moving slowly, he went over to the stall and grabbed the pitchfork he had left there. As he was forking fresh straw into Tillie's stall, she looked at him over her shoulder. Softly she mooed.

"That's easy for you to say," Ned muttered, his eyebrows creasing into a deep slash across his forehead. "You've got it pretty goddamn easy."

He reached into her stall, grabbed her water bucket, and placed it on the floor beneath the faucet. As the water sputtered, mostly into the bucket, he waited patiently, running his hands along the tines of the pitchfork.

"Are you comin' sometime tonight?" his mother called from the house.

"Just a minute."

"And have you seen Frank? He's late again!"

"Who gives a shit about Frank?" he said, not loud enough for her to hear. He reached out to turn the faucet off and, grunting, lowered the pail back into Tillie's stall. " 's probably with Julie getting his rocks off," he said, letting his voice trail away as he became conscious of a dull ache in his crotch. He reached down and scratched himself.

Before going into the house, Ned paused to survey the barn. There was still more than half a bale of hay spread across the floor; there was a big puddle of water on the floor where it had sloshed from the bucket; there was the loft trap door gaping open like a hungry mouth.

Ned coughed a ball of spit from deep within his throat and sent it sailing off into the darkness of the barn, then he turned and went into the house for supper.

.V.

Inside the doorway, as he untied a bootlace, Ned kept glancing at his mother, who was sitting at the kitchen table, her arms across her chest. Her mouth was set in a firm scowl; her eyebrows arched questioningly.

"I asked you," she said, voice iron-hard, "if you know where Frank is. He's late again."

Ned dropped a boot to the floor, unmindful of the mud and manure that smudged the tiles. "I haven't seen him since morning." He kicked the boot over into the corner and then began untying the other. He noticed that his hands were shaking as he wedged the boot off and dropped it.

"I wish you wouldn't make such a mess," his mother said, rising and moving over to the stove, where she began stirring the pot of baked beans.

Ned studied his mother's shoulders as she worked. He heard her puff as she blew her hair from her face and then began scooping beans onto a plate. Ned dropped into his seat with a groan.

"Something the matter with your eyes?" his mother asked as she placed the plate of beans before him.

"No."

"Well, they look pretty bloodshot."

Ned glanced up at the fluorescent light on the ceiling and winced. "Maybe the dust and stuff in the barn," he replied, reaching for a slice of brown bread. They were stinging a bit.

"You getting enough sleep?"

"Sure."

His mother filled a plate for herself and sat down opposite Ned at the table. He ate in silence, knowing that if the silence were to be broken, she would be the one to do so.

"Oh."

She paused for effect. Ned tensed.

"I see you didn't get the henhouse cleaned out. I went out while you were at work, and it looks like you haven't hoed it for months."

Ned stared down at his plate, swirling the beans with his fork, and replied softly, "Mr. Pomeroy had a big delivery. I had to get there early." He felt as though he were pleading.

"What's more important, Pomeroy's I.G.A. or your family's henhouse?"

Suddenly she fell silent, and they both turned to look out the window when they heard Frank's truck coming up the driveway. Ned smiled slightly when he heard a spark plug misfire. A beam of light swept over the kitchen wall. The brakes groaned; the tires skidded in the loose gravel. When he heard his brother's heavy clumping feet on the doorstep, Ned turned back to his supper, swirling his beans again.

Frank walked into the kitchen with merely a nod of his head as greeting, and sat down at the table. "Well," he said, leaning his .308 Mustang against the table, "I'm starved. Smelled them beans half-way home." He rubbed his hands together.

"Frank, will you please not bring your rifle to the table? How many times do I have to tell you?"

Frank reached across the table and placed a hand lightly on his mother's shoulder. "Now you don't have to worry; it ain't loaded," he said. "I've been out hunting all day, and I'm beat, and starved."

His mother rose and walked over to the stove where she began serving another plate of beans. "it ain't hunting season. What 'ave you been up to?"

"Ah, ah, ah," Frank said, waving his index finger in the air. "We've got permission from Granger to try 'n' track down that wild dog that's been causing so much trouble."

Ned's fingers jerked spasmodically at the mention of the dog. His fork left a trail of beans and sauce on the tablecloth as it fell to the floor with a clatter. His face flushed, Ned bent down to retrieve it.

90

"Take it easy there, little brother," Frank said with a laugh; then, turning back to his mother, "We've been out in the woods around Seavey's place all day, hopin' to get a shot at 'im. Man, you should see what that animal did to his chickens!" His mother slid a heaping plate in front of him and he interrupted his narrative just long enough to shovel in a forkful of beans. "Anyway," he said, his voice muffled, "I guess he wants us back again tonight."

"Wait a minute, you know you can't go huntin' at night," his mother said.

"I told.you, we got permission from Granger, and like it or not, he's just not going to be able to stop us. We're gonna get that animal!" Frank sopped a piece of brown bread in his bean sauce and stuffed it into his mouth. "Hey, little brother, you wanna come with us?"

Ned shook his head with a quick snap. "Naw. I've got things to do."

"You don't have to carry a gun or anything," Frank said. Ned thought he heard a mocking tone in his voice. "We could use another pair of eyes."

Ned shook his head again and tried to speak, but something caught in his throat and he had to stifle a cough. He cast a quick glance at his brother as he reached for his glass of milk. He swallowed hard and felt his tightened lower lip begin to tremble.

"I'm pretty tired; I was thinking of going to bed early tonight," he said, surprised at how low and serious his voice sounded. He wanted to mention to his brother all the work he had done that day. Frank didn't answer and continued to eat. Ned figured that because his brother couldn't think of a quick insult or joke he had let the topic drop.

After some minutes, Frank straightened up and swiped his sleeve across his face. "Good beans. You make 'em today?"

"No," his mother replied. "They're canned."

"Hmm. B&M's gettin' pretty good."

His mother looked at him, not knowing whether or not to feel insulted.

They finished their meal in silence, and then at eight o'clock Frank took his rifle and left in the pickup. While his mother was washing the dishes, Ned went up to his room to read a little before going to sleep. Saturdays were his busiest days, and he was beat.

.VI.

The stone walls of the room were cold and damp. Where water had eaten through the mortar, there were pale streaks of lime running to the floor. In the darkest corners, patches of mold grew. There were no windows, and the air was thick like honey, difficult to breathe.

A single candle burned fitfully in the center of the dirt floor, making the low-hanging ceiling-beams sway sickeningly. Small whisps of soot twisted up from the flickering flame, curled in the rising heat, and melted into the darkness.

Bubbling wax almost guttered out the flame, but it continued to burn with a faint lapping sound.

That was the only sound in the room, other than the short, gasping breaths of the woman as she bent over, tracing a pentangle in the dirt. When the star was complete, she erased the lines within the star, carefully smoothing over her footprints before stepping back to admire her work. After running her finger along the line another time to make sure the line was unbroken, she placed the candle in the top point of the star.

She remained silent, absorbed in her work, aware only of the rising anticipation she felt. Tonight. The night of the full moon. The harvest moon. As she stared at the wavering light, she reached up and pulled a strand of dark hair from her eyes. With a deep sigh, she was just beginning to unbutton her blouse when she heard a quick, almost frantic scratching sound. It came from a wooden box that lay hidden in the shadows by the door. Beside it was a small, indistinguishable heap.

"Patience, my dear," she whispered, as her trembling fingers raced down the row of buttons. She shrugged her shoulders, and the blouse fell to the floor. Quickly she stepped out of her skirt and slid off her panties and bra. She reached down, gathered her clothes, and deposited them near the box by the door. With a quick grunt she lifted the box, carried it over to the star, and placed it down in the center, just below the candle.

Striding back to the doorway, she picked up a length of bright red cord and quickly wrapped it around her waist, tying it off with a loose square-knot. Then, her eyes staring almost unbelievingly at her shaking hand, she reached for the knife she had left on the floor. As she raised it, staring at the blade, it caught the candlelight and sent a shimmering splinter spinning around the room.

She smiled faintly and whispered, "Master, help me."

She looked over her shoulder at the wooden box when the scratching sound was repeated. Slowly, solemnly she walked over to the pentangle, hesitated for a moment at the line, and then stepped within the design.

"Aquerra goity, aquerra beyty," she began in a chanting voice. "Aquerra beyty, aquerra goity." Sweat glistened on her arms, giving them an oily look. Still mumbling the chant, she dropped to her knees and held the blade over the flame until the silver was streaked with soot. She ran her thumb along the edge and smiled, then looked down at her breasts, heaving from her rapid breathing.

Her mouth and throat were dry, and when she spoke again, the words came out crackling. "Ashtarorh, Asmodeus, Princes of Amity, I conjure you to accept this sacrifice, which I offer in return for what I ask."

Quickly she snapped the hasp on the box and flipped the lid open. She held her breath, burning in her chest, as she grabbed inside the box

94

and then slowly withdrew a black rooster. Beads of sweat stood out on her forehead, and she could feel tracks of moisture run down her side from her armpits. The thin tendons in her arms stood out from the effort as she held the bird aloft. The rooster struggled to escape, but her grip was firm. The woman felt a surging wash of dizzied excitement, and she felt as though she might faint.

The light from the candle made the rooster's dark feathers gleam with a deep blue iridescence. "This I give you," she cried out, throwing back her head and reveling in the swells of excitement. The rooster's eyes, thin golden rings, stared at her, dumb, unblinking.

"Receive this gift from your servant," she yelled and she lowered the rooster to the floor where she held it pinned with one hand. The other hand, holding the soot-smeared knife, rose above her head, and then, in one swift motion, she ran the blade across the exposed neck of the bird.

A trickle of blood ran down onto the dirt floor and stained it. The bird continued to kick, trying to escape the pain that was draining its life, but the small hand remained tight. Again the blade ran across the throat, this time with more sureness, more power. The bird's head was severed. With a quick flick of the knife, the woman knocked the head away, where it lay beside the wooden box. One gold-ringed eye stared back at her.

The woman snatched the bird's body to her

chest and she let the sticky, warm river gush over her breasts. The bird's rapid heartbeat was now stilled, but she could still feel an occasional twitching. A warm ecstasy, centered in her stomach, began to wash over her. Tangled scarlet streams ran down her legs to the floor.

She dropped the now bloodless corpse to the floor. It landed on top of the severed head.

"Ashtaroth, Asmodeus," she whispered, looking down at her legs and letting her vision blur. Then, slowly and smoothly, in ever-widening circles, she began to smear the thick blood over her breasts. Her hands moved down to her stomach. Her breathing came in rapid, stinging gasps as she ran her hands still lower. "Come, and take this," she rasped, "in exchange for what I ask."

Swaying back and forth, and then, as if in slow motion, dropping to the floor, she continued to run her fingers inside herself until she lost consciousness.

.VII.

It was after five o'clock in the morning. The full moon was riding low in the west. Frank was heading home along the Bartlett Road.

He was pissed. He had wasted a whole night. He and his friends had scoured the area around Seavey's, frozen their butts off, and hadn't even turned up a pawprint of the animal they were chasing. Also, his bladder was hurting from all the beer he had been drinking.

As he drove up the driveway to the house, he saw that all the lights had been turned off. The windows reflected the morning sky like polished marble. Out back, only the porch light had been left on.

He pulled up into the driveway and then backed the truck into the backoff. He let the motor sputter and then die. For a long moment, he sat looking out over the field and listened to the morning birds. He opened the truck door and was just stepping out when his eye caught a flicker of motion.

Just a little bit too tired, he thought, dismissing it after a close look at the barn and corral revealed nothing.

He reached back into the truck for his rifle, shut the truck door, and turned toward the house. Again, from the corner of his eye, he saw motion. He turned and looked at the barn, but this time he saw something: a swift gray shape was moving along the edge of the barn toward the open field. It was vague and ill-defined, as if a patch of moonlight had detached itself and was moving through the early morning shadows.

Frank squinted, trying to see better. His hand gripped his rifle until it began to hurt. His thumb flicked the safety catch and he brought the rifle up to his shoulder.

Just then, the shape coalesced into the form of a large dog. Frank grunted his pleasure, took aim, and squeezed the trigger. The gunshot shattered the peace of the early morning, echoing from the hills.

"Damn you!" Frank hissed when he saw the shape cringe and then bolt for the field. Frank took aim and shot again, but he knew he had already missed his best shot. If he brought the animal down now, it would be more luck than skill. He squeezed off two more shots and then watched in frustration as the silent gray shape crossed the field and melted into the forest.

"Frank! What in the dickens are you doing?" his mother shouted from her bedroom window. She looked wide-eyed, half-crazy, with red hair in curlers and nighttime coat of Noxema on her face.

"I missed the damn thing, that's what!" Frank yelled, stamping his foot on the ground with frustration. "We spend the whole goddamn night out at Seavey's place, and the damn thing's right here. Shit!"

His mother disappeared from her window and ran outside. She pulled her tattered bathrobe around her against the night chill.

"I've never seen anything move that fast," Frank said, glancing off in the direction the animal had taken. "Christ, it was big. Bigger'an a German shepherd, I'd say."

"Too bad you missed," his mother said simply. "Did he get into the barn?"

"Oh, Jesus!" Frank shouted. He ran to the barn door and flung it open. The door spring stretched with a loud twang. Inside, the barn was warm with the heat of the animals. Both cows, Frances and Tillie, were stamping in their stalls. They started to bellow as soon as Frank entered the barn. He hoped to hell it had only been his gunshots that had scared them.

"Oh, Christ!" he said when he saw that Tillie had kicked one of the boards out of her stall. The splintered pieces lay scattered on the floor on top of the broken bale of hay.

Frank moved over to the cows' stalls and patted each on the head. As he bent down to stand up the pail Tillie had knocked over, he saw the legs of the calf, Ginger, sticking out through the railing. Frank could tell immediately that she was dead.

"You bastard!" he hissed.

He walked over to the workbench and felt around for the flashlight he knew was there somewhere. He found it and flicked the switch. He was surprised when the light came on.

He ran the pencil-thin beam around the barn. He saw that one of the windows at the back of the barn was broken; not just one pane, the whole window had crashed inward. "That's how you got in, you son of a bitch!" Frank whispered.

There was a bad taste in his mouth as he slowly edged his way over to Ginger's stall. The small circle of light played along the floor until it came to rest on the dead calf. What he saw there almost made Frank vomit. The calf's throat had been torn open. A wide, gaping hole spilled blood out onto the floor, where it mixed with the hay. The calf's lifeless eye threw back a dull, silvery reflection that sickened Frank. After a moment, he realized that the calf's head had been torn completely off; it lay there beside the lifeless trunk.

Frank wiped the sweat from his forehead and angrily thumbed the trigger of his rifle. "I'm gonna get you for this, you bastard," he hissed, his eyes riveted to the dead calf. "I'm gonna make you pay for this!"

He left the barn and stood out in the middle of the driveway wondering what to do. He wanted to try to track the animal but realized that he had better wait until the sun was up. He saw that the light was on in the kitchen, and he cupped his hand to his mouth and shouted.

"Hey Ma! Ma!"

After a second, his mother appeared on the back porch. "What in the blazes is it now," she yelled.

"Give Granger a call, will you. Granger and Ted Seavey. Tell 'em to get their butts over here right away. That damn dog's killed the calf."

His mother gasped and covered her mouth with her hand.

"If they get over here right away, maybe we can track it. And get Ned out of bed. Tell him to get down here. Someone's gotta bury the calf."

His mother went inside. Frank walked over to the side of the barn and carefully scanned the ground. It was still too dark to see much detail. He straightened up and walked around back to where the window had been broken in. In the soft mud undernearth the window, he could clearly see the animal's tracks. He studied them under the beam of his flashlight and noticed that they didn't look quite right; they almost looked like some other kind of animal's track.

"Yoo-hoo. Frank," his mother called from the porch. He straightened up and came around the side of the barn.

"Both Granger and Seavey said they'd be here as soon as they could."

"Good." He looked at her, then back at the barn. When he turned, he saw a dark shape moving along the side of the barn. Frank snapped the rifle to his shoulder, but before he fired, he saw that the shape was human. He lowered the rifle and snapped on the safety catch.

"Ned!" he shouted, once he recognized the person. "What the hell are you doing out here? I thought you were still in bed." He shined the flashlight into his brother's eyes as he came closer to him. Ned squinted and turned his head away.

"Christ! Do you know that I almost blew your fuckin' head off?"

Ned shook his head and stood still, about five feet from his brother. "No, no, I, I wasn't . . ."

"What the hell's the matter with you, kid?" Frank asked. He played his light over his brother and saw that his clothes were mud-stained and torn; dead leaves and twigs hung from his shoulder.

Frank stepped up next to his brother and grabbed him by the chin. He twisted his head up to the light, and Ned tried to turn away.

"Are you all right?"

"Yeah, I'm, I'm, OK."

"Jesus! It looks like you cut your head or something," he said, when he saw that Ned's hair was matted down with caked blood. "You bang your head on something?"

"I, ummm, I guess I did," Ned said, wincing as he brought his hand up to the wound. "I must have fallen or something when I was running."

"Did you see it? Did you see that wild dog?" Frank asked anxiously.

Ned cast a fleeting glance at his brother, but had to turn away because the light from the flashlight hit his eyes painfully. "Yeah, I guess I saw something, and I guess I, I went after it."

"Without a gun? Are you crazy?" Frank shouted. "That animal's a killer. You can't go chasing after it without a gun."

"I guess I wasn't thinking," Ned said. "I—It got away pretty fast." Ned looked at his brother dazedly, then, suddenly, he almost folded up and fell onto the ground. Frank grabbed him and caught him before he hit the ground.

"You look pretty beat, kid. You better go on inside."

"Yeah," Ned said hollowly, "I am pretty tired."

"You feel pretty cold," Frank said. "Are you sure you're all right?" Ned's eyes looked dark, sunken into his brow.

Ned nodded and started walking slowly toward the house.

Frank watched his brother walk away, and he noticed that he kept his legs locked stiffly so he wouldn't wobble. He took the steps carefully, one by one, and then entered the house. The sun was just rising, tinting the eastern sky a light blue.

Chapter Five

Saturday, October 18

.I.

A lot happened in a few seconds.

Ned was carrying a load of frozen-food cartons to the walk-in freezer. His grocer's apron offered little protection against the cold. His fingers were getting numb in the joints.

He twisted his body to the side and jabbed at the button for the freezer light. He missed, and the nearly off-balance load of frozen food almost tumbled. He tried again, and this time there was a soft click. A small red light went on, indicating that the lights were on in the freezer as well.

He reached out blindly until he felt the door bar, grabbed it, and pulled. The door swung open heavily, and Ned, grunting loudly, kicked it open. When he turned to enter, he heard a scuffing sound behind him.

A fist, maybe a foot, struck him in the small of the back, propelling him forward. The stack of frozen food he was carrying flew into the air and hit the freezer floor with a clatter. Automatically, he put his hands out in front of him to break his fall. As he hit the floor, the heavy metal door slammed shut, and the lights overhead winked out.

For a moment, stunned and confused, he sat on the cold floor, rubbing his wrist. He had held it too stiffly, and it hurt like hell. If it wasn't broken, he thought, it was at least sprained. Then, as he pieced together what had happened, he started to panic. He was alone in the darkness and cold, hurt. He took a deep gulp of frozen air into his lungs. It burned.

He sat silently in the darkness, trying to master his rising panic. The thick darkness began to flicker, as his eyes adjusted. Then, for a moment, he wondered if his eyes were opened at all. Maybe he had hit his head and had gone blind. He fought back the scream so it emerged as no more than a whimper. He scrambled over to the door and was relieved to see a thin line of light at the bottom of the door. At least he was not blind.

"OK," he called out, a whine in his voice. "You can open the door now."

From outside he heard a ripple of laughter and then a faint click. He knew that that click had been the door lock.

The darkness wrapped itself closer, like a deadly blanket.

Cold and death!

I'm hurt! I could die in here! he thought.

His hand reached for the door. He balled up his fist and brought it down against the unyielding metal door.

"Come on, open the door," he said weakly.

Again, his fist hit the door, harder. He didn't even notice that he was using the hand he had hurt. He beat the door viciously.

"Open the fucking door! Right now, goddammit!"

There was a faint rattling sound from outside. "Aww, jeeze. I think it's stuck," a muffled voice said.

"Come on!" he shouted, giving the door another solid hit. He stood back and rubbed his shoulders to keep warm. "Come on, I'm freezing in here," he said, softer. He bit his lower lip to keep from crying out.

I could die in here! his mind screamed.

A wild shiver wracked his body, and he leaned forward, pressing his full weight against the door. "Will you open the door? Please?" he said, trying to keep the panic from registering in his voice.

Tears ran down his face and froze. His teeth

chattered, and he kept rubbing his arms for warmth.

There was another click outside, and then a voice said, "Jeeze, it really is stuck." This time Ned recognized Alan Tate's voice.

Ned dug in with his heels and pushed hard against the door. Then, with a loud snap, the door swung open. Ned fell forward, landing on the floor in a crumpled heap. Slowly, fighting back the pain and fear, he stood up. His body was stiff and cramped. He squinted from the sudden brightness of the lights. Through his watery vision, he scanned the semicircle of people who stood there watching him.

"Real funny," he whispered angrily, "Real funny." He stood there unconsciously rubbing his hurt wrist. He knew that they could tell he had been crying, and that galled him all the more. Besides Alan, there were Louie, Jack, and Ralph.

"You all right?" Alan Tate said, stepping forward and trying to put his hand on Ned's shoulder. "Honest, the door got stuck. Just ask Louie."

Ned looked at Louie, who merely shrugged his shoulders. "I don't know," he said with his thick French accent. "I did not see what happened."

"We were trying to get you out," Ralph said, but his faint smile gave him away.

Ned's anger burned. A curse was forming on his mouth but remained unspoken because, just then, Dick Pomeroy walked into the back room.

"Hey, what the hell are you guys doing back

here?" he shouted. "There're cases of frozen food getting warm out there. Plenty of stock to put away." He halted and then looked at everyone in turn. His eyes finally rested on Ned, whose teeth were still chattering.

"What the hell's going on?" he said again.

Louie wiped his hands on his blood-stained butcher's apron and headed back into the meat-cutting room without a word. Jack and Ralph took nervous steps backward but seemed afraid to leave. Alan stood his ground.

"Had a little trouble with the freezer door," Alan said, sounding truthful and sincere.

"Well," Pomeroy said, "the girls could use a little bit of help up front, and there's a lot of stock still to be put away."

Everyone made a move to scatter, glad that they hadn't been caught in their practical joke. As Ned walked past Pomeroy, the store manager grabbed him by the arm. "Just a second, Ned."

Ned looked at the man with fear-widened eyes.

"Granger's up front of the store. Wants to talk to you," Pomeroy said.

Ned saw that Alan was listening at the door, and when he heard this, his face broke out into a wide grin.

"You aren't in any trouble, are you?" Pomeroy asked seriously.

Ned shook his head and made to leave, but Pomeroy still held him. "One more thing, Ned. I've really had quite enough of this horsing around in the back room. We're here to work, not to have fun."

"Yeah," Ned replied. "It won't happen again."

"See that it doesn't," Pomeroy said, as he headed for the bathroom. "And don't keep Granger waiting all day."

As Ned walked up the aisle to the front of the store, his mouth carefully formed the word "Bastards!"

.II.

"So, how's everything going?" Granger asked. His smile reminded Ned of Alan Tate's innocent, stupid grin. Ned glanced outside and saw that it was still raining and that it was dark. He felt a bit anxious because he knew he had a lot of work to do before closing time.

"Pretty good, I guess," Ned replied. He was unconsciously rubbing his injured wrist.

Granger cleared his throat. "Yeah, well. I've been going over what you said to me after that night your family calf was killed by that, that wild dog, or whatever. I was wondering if—"

"I told you everything I remember," Ned said curtly. "We've been all over it."

"I know. I know," Granger said, shifting his weight from one foot to the other. "But, uhh, you said you were a little confused that night, that you fell and hit your head and your memory might've been a little scrambled up. I just wanted to get everything straight."

"Sure. OK." Ned looked at Granger and then down at the puddle of rainwater that had formed at his feet from his dripping rain-slicker.

Granger rubbed his cheek and looked up at the ceiling for a moment, collecting his thoughts.

"Well, for one thing, your brother said that when he checked out back of the barn, by the broken window, that he saw some tracks there, what he figured were the animal's tracks."

Ned grunted.

"And then, once I got out to your place, oh, about six o'clock, I didn't see a damn thing underneath that window. It looked like the whole thing had been smoothed over. Not a track to be found."

Ned shrugged. "Maybe Frank was wrong," he said. "Maybe it looked like tracks with just a, just a flashlight, but wasn't really."

"But you don't know anything about those tracks?" Granger asked. His voice had an edge of accusation. "You didn't see them?"

Ned shook his head.

"Hmm. Well, Frank says that he first saw you walking out from behind the barn. I thought . . ."

"I didn't see them, those tracks, I mean."

"But you did see that dog, right?" Granger pressed.

Ned nodded.

"You say it was a German shepherd, a big German shepherd?"

"That's right," Ned replied with exasperation. "I told you all of this before."

Granger ignored Ned's last remark and pressed on. "And you didn't see or hear any other dogs, right? Nothing to indicate that there might have been a pack of 'em out there."

Again, Ned shook his head. He peered up to the end of the aisle where they were standing, expecting to see Alan Tate watching them and enjoying his discomfort. Alan wasn't there.

"Well, one thing for damn sure. You were lucky you didn't run into that animal, if you went chasing after him without a gun."

"Yeah, I guess so," Ned answered. "Like I said, I wasn't thinking too good."

"You see," Granger said, suddenly softening, his interrogation ended, "Jeff Carter was out on the old mine road that night. He failed to mention why. I don't think it was because he was out hunting with Seavey and the others. I've got a feeling he was out visiting at Martin's Lake, but that's none of our business.

"Anyway, he says he heard something thrashing through the woods, so he hunkered down behind a bush, and he says he saw a full-grown timber wolf run right by him. Not more than ten feet from him, he says."

Ned tried to look Granger in the eyes but found that he couldn't.

"Course," Granger went on, "Jeff Carter isn't the most reliable witness in the world. He was probably, hell, I know, he was drunker'an a skunk. It could have been a cocker spaniel, for all I know. But I tell you, you were damn lucky you didn't meet up with that animal, no matter what it was."

Just then the lights in the store flickered overhead, and Pomeroy's voice boomed over the P.A. system. "The I.G.A. will close in ten minutes. Please go to the registers now. We thank you for shopping at the I.G.A."

"Now I don't want you to get all worked up about this," Granger said kindly. "Seavey's got enough people worked up as it is. But I do want you to know that we might have a serious problem here. And I would recommend that you not go out into the woods at night, not without a gun."

.III.

"But you didn't see anything," Lisa said, wide-eyed. "You just heard it?"

Bob nodded as he continued to work on the cold-duck bottle cork. Suddenly, with a bang, the cork shot from the bottle, ricocheted off the ceiling, and then spun in a wide semicircle and disappeared under the refrigerator.

"Well," Bob said, smiling, "we'll just have to drink the whole thing. He poured two glasses of wine, handed one to Lisa, and then took a noisy swallow from the other.

"No," Bob said, placing the glass back down, "I didn't see anything. Correction. I didn't see the dog. I did see something."

"What?" Lisa asked, leaning forward, her face expressing fear and wonder.

"I'll get to that in a second. You remember you let me off at the end of the driveway, right? Well, I stood there for a while, watching your car drive off. I waited until I couldn't hear the car and then started up toward the cabin. I was about halfway up the path when I heard this low moaning, real hollow." Bob tried to imitate the sound heard.

"That sounds like a dog that's been hit by a car," Lisa said with a laugh.

"Well, it didn't that night, let me tell you. At first, I thought it was a dog howling far away, you know? Like I couldn't get a fix on it. I just kept walking up the path. It had me a little bit spooked, but . . . " Bob shrugged.

"Did this really happen, or are you just making it up to scare me?" Lisa asked. Bob could tell by her expression that she was getting drawn into the story.

"Honest, it happened. I was almost up to the house, right up on the rise where you can look down on the pond. The sound came again, but this time I was sure it was pretty close. I kind of panicked, but I looked around for where it might have been coming from. Suddenly"—Bob jumped and grabbed Lisa's arm. She let out a scream—"The bushes on the side of the road started rustling. I just about died! I started toward the house at a pretty good pace, and I was almost there when this animal burst out of the brush and ran right in front of me."

Lisa looked almost as scared as Bob had felt that night. "I thought you said you didn't see it?"

"Ohh, it wasn't that wild dog everyone's been talking about. It was a rabbit, I think, or maybe a white cat. I couldn't tell for sure, it was pretty dark and my nerves were on edge. The animal ran in front of me and went down toward the pond." Bob lifted his hands into the air and concluded, "And that was it. It was gone."

He walked over to the stove and opened the oven door. Peering inside, he said, "It's just about ready. Are you hungry?"

Lisa smiled and shook her head. "I don't know, after that story."

"Aw," Bob said, as he pulled the lasagna out of the oven and placed it on the counter, "it was nothing."

.IV.

The dishes were washed and put away. A fire burned low in the fireplace, evenly and warm. The stereo had clicked off almost an hour ago. Lisa was sitting cross-legged on one of the couch cushions on the floor. Bob was lying on his side, his head supported by his hand. The empty bottle of cold duck stood on the hearth, catching the flickering flames.

"I ought to be getting back home," Lisa said, glancing at her watch. "I told Jeff that the conference would be over by nine o'clock and that I'd be home by ten."

"How 'bout a cup of coffee first," Bob said,

rolling over and slowly rising. He stood up, close to Lisa, and let his fingers twine gently through her hair. She looked blankly at the fire.

"Yeah. I suppose I can be a little late," she said.

"You don't really think he's going to be home waiting for you, do you?"

Lisa sighed. Bob went into the kitchen and filled the tea kettle with water. He put in a lot of water so it would take a long time to heat. He came back over to Lisa and sat down beside her. For a long time, he watched the flames reflected in her eyes.

"And what would the fine folk of Cooper Falls think if they knew their head librarian was here, sitting in front of a romantic fire with"—he paused for effect—"another man!"

Lisa's smile was twisted. "Come on, Bob."

"Well, have you thought any more about it?" Bob asked earnestly. "It's not like you don't have any grounds for divorce, that's for sure."

"I've thought about it," Lisa answered faintly. "Probably too much."

"And?"

"And—" Before she could continue, the tea kettle whistled shrilly. Bob jumped up and ran into the kitchen.

Lisa looked at him over her shoulder and said, "Just milk in mi—"

"I know, I know," Bob said as he poured the water. He fixed both coffees and then came back into the living room. He placed the cups carefully on the hearth. While they drank their coffee, both of them avoided the topic Bob had brought up earlier. Bob wanted to talk some more about Lisa leaving her husband, but he respected her wishes not to discuss it. Lisa just couldn't deal with the idea, not yet, anyway, she told herself.

When the coffee was gone, Lisa shifted and stood up. They walked out to the entryway, and Bob got Lisa's raincoat out of the closet.

"Hey," he said, looking outside, "it stopped raining."

He helped Lisa on with her coat and, as she was buttoning the front, he held her shoulders. He pulled her close to him.

"Thanks for the meal," she said, pulling away slightly. "I didn't realize you were such a good cook."

He leaned forward to kiss her, but she raised her hand and covered her mouth. "Please, Bob. Not now. I'm confused, and that'd only confuse me more," she said, looking at him earnestly.

Bob nodded and reached to open the door for her. "Thanks for coming over," he said, "and for the conversation."

Lisa took a step outside, turned, and said, "Hey, it was nothing. It beats reading Greek drama any day."

.V.

"Hey, Julie! For chrissakes, open up!" a voice slurred, and its entreaty was punctuated by a loud bang on the door.

Crouching behind the large oak tree in her front yard, Julie watched as Jeff Carter, propped against the door jamb at a sharp angle, continued his hammering. His hulking form was illuminated and then plunged into darkness as the clouds of the passing storm raced by.

"Hey!" he shouted, and Julie heard a muffled echo from across the lake.

"It's a damn good thing I don't have any neighbors," she said, stepping forward. "They'd be calling up Granger for sure." Her left hand rose slowly and dropped the gnarled root she was holding into her coat pocket. It bulged conspicuously, but she figured Jeff was too drunk to notice anything.

"Hey, babe, ain't yah gonna let me in?" he asked, childlike.

She stepped closer, and the smell of liquor on his breath blasted into her face. She cringed back, but Jeff reached out and grabbed her arm. His fingers dug in and started to hurt her, even through her coat.

"What you been doin' out on a night like this?" he said, wobbling, and then leaning his weight onto her. He ended his question with a bubbly belch.

"Just, uh, out for a walk. After the rain, everything's so clean and fresh." She patted the bulge of the root in her pocket.

"Well, let's get inside," he said, patting a crinkling brown bag as he held it out to her. "I've got a bottle, the night's young, 'n' we got nothin' but time."

Julie broke into a short burst of laughter.

" 'Sides, I need to have my ashes hauled," Jeff said as he turned, wavering, and opened the front door. His shoulder caught on the door and almost spun him back around, but he caught his stride and barreled his way into Julie's kitchen. Dragging a chair from the table, he sat down with a grunt and slammed the brown bag onto the formica top. Julie, still standing in the doorway, was surprised the bottle inside the bag did not break. She eased the door closed behind her, shutting out the chill night air, and slowly walked over to the kitchen counter.

"Get yourself a glass and have a drink, honey," Jeff said, unscrewing the top off the Seagram's Seven and tilting his head back to swallow a mouthful.

Julie huffed, glanced at the clock on the stove, and then said softly and evenly, "Hey, you know, it's past midnight. Don't you think you ought to go home?"

Jeff stared at her with a semiconscious squint. He wiped the saliva that was running down his chin onto the cuff of his jacket and then belched. "Now com'on, babe, have a drink with me. 'S not good to drink alone."

Keeping her eyes fixed on Jeff, Julie edged close to the sink and, reaching into her pocket, withdrew the root and dropped it into the sink. She reached in again and took out a sprig of grayish-green leaves, which she dropped onto the root. Jeff obviously didn't see her do this. He sat wavering, holding the bottle out to her.

"Seriously, Jeff, I've got to get some sleep." She feigned a wide yawn and scratched her head with her dirt-encrusted fingers.

Jeff placed the bottle on the table and rose to his feet. He dropped his jacket onto the back of the chair and began to unbutton his shirt. "You'll sleep a lot better after a little of what I've got saved for you," he said as he flipped open his belt and lowered his pants to his ankles. Julie felt revolted when she saw the bulge in his yellowed skivvies. He shook his feet free of his pants and then lunged at her.

"Hot stuff, honey," he mumbled with a slur. His hand reached out and grabbed her on the elbow before she could pull away. With his other hand he reached up and grabbed her breast, massaging it roughly as he pressed his lips to her mouth. The sticky sweetness of his breath made Julie want to gag. His fumbling finger reached inside her coat and, when he found he couldn't unbutton her blouse, he gave it a quick pull and tore the material.

"You bastard," Julie screamed, and her hand shot out, slapping his face with a rifle-like report.

"Keep your goddamn hands to yourself!" she shouted, shaking herself loose and taking a step back away from Jeff.

Off-balance for a moment, Jeff fell forward and caught the edge of the counter. He stood there for a moment with his head hanging over the sink. He still didn't see or recognize what was there in the sink. Shaking his head, as though to dispel a fog, he glared over at Julie. His red-rimmed eyes were swollen and unable to focus.

"What's the matter? You on the rag or somethin'?"

Julie shook her head haughtily.

"One drink's all I ask." He wheeled around and scooped the bottle from the table with an accuracy that surprised Julie. "One drink and then we can fuck our brains out."

He leaned back and took a long slug of whisky. He almost lost his balance and fell over backwards.

"You can fuck your brains out," Julie said, pulling the torn material of her blouse around her for protection. "I don't plan on fucking my brains out."

"Christ, woman, you sound like you need a good screwin', if you ask me." Jeff tilted back for another swallow and then walked slowly toward the bedroom door. Once he was framed by the darkness of the bedroom, Jeff turned and grabbed the elastic band of his underwear. He started to roll his underwear down slowly.

"I've been savin' this for you, honey," he slurred, once he had exposed himself. Julie looked at him with disgust. "Now come on. Get your ass in here!" With that, he walked into the bedroom.

Julie waited in the kitchen, listening as Jeff fumbled about in the dark, pulling back the sheets. She heard a long, low groan as he eased his body onto the bed, and then, seconds later, the heavy sound of his snoring filled Julie's small house. She knew he'd be asleep for a few hours at least, as long as he could keep his drinks down.

After listening to his snoring for a while, Julie eased her coat off. Her torn blouse hung loosely down, and she considered putting something else on but decided against it. A light on in the bedroom might wake Jeff up. Instead she took the blouse off and threw it into the corner of the kitchen.

She walked over to the sink and gently handled the sprig of leaves and the dirt-crusted root. She ran the faucet and began washing the root.

"Hey, babe," Jeff's voice called sleepily from the bedroom. "Are you comin'?"

"No," Julie whispered, as she continued to wash the root clean, "I'm just breathing hard."

She finished washing the root, tore off a few paper towels, and carefully patted the root dry. She left the root on the counter and picked up the sprig of leaves. After rinsing them under the sprayer, she tied them into a loose bunch and hung them from a nail in the ceiling.

The blubbering sounds of Jeff's snoring filled the bedroom when Julie entered and finished undressing. Holding her breath against the sticky sweet of booze on his breath, she slipped in between the sheets beside Jeff. She decided, as she closed her eyes to sleep, that if he woke her up in the night and wanted to have her, he could.

.VI.

Just before dawn, Julie awoke with a start when she heard the loud report of a rifle. She sat up in her bed and looked out the window. Holding her breath, she listened, her eyes fixed unblinking on the pale gray sky.

Again, a shot split the morning stillness, making Julie jump. The movement woke Jeff up, and he rolled over, forcefully sliding his hand between Julie's legs.

.VII.

The echo of the first shot was still rolling back from the hills that ringed Martin's Lake. Frank Simmons rose stiffly from where he had been hiding behind a low stone wall. There was a wide smile on his face.

"You goddamn son of a bitch," he said, almost laughing, as he moved across the field toward the fallen gray bulk.

In the early morning chill, a crow cawed.

Holding his rifle, cocked and trained on the fallen form, Frank inched his way toward the motionless dog. The animal looked ghost-like in the pale, gathering light.

As he got closer to the dog, Frank could see that the animal was still alive. His ribs rose and fell rapidly as he tried to hold onto life. A widening pool of blood spread out around the dog's belly.

"That's about all for you," Frank said, raising the rifle to his shoulder and squinting down the sights.

The dog whimpered pitifully, his lungs filled with blood. He lifted his head and looked at Frank with dimming eyes.

"You've killed your last calf, you son of a bitch!" Frank said as he took sight on the dog's head. He squeezed the trigger, and the top half of the dog's head disappeared.

Chapter Six

Monday, October 20

.I.

Bob looked over at Lisa, who sat slumped in the passenger seat with her head resting against the side window. In the dim light of the dusk, he could see her bruised and swollen cheek. It looked like it was stained with grape juice. Her eyes glistened with tears.

Bob moved his hand from the gearshift to her knee, and she jumped with a snap and then relaxed.

"Do you want to talk?" he asked softly. His voice was reassuring.

Lisa ran her hand under her nose and sniffed loudly. She winced when her knuckles brushed against the bruise.

"Was it about us?" Bob asked.

"No," Lisa answered sullenly. "Well, maybe. A little, I guess."

"Did you—explain?"

She looked at him cooly. Her face was pasty, washed of color. Her eyes looked almost vacant. When she replied, her voice sounded like crinkled paper. "What's to explain? We haven't done anything that needs explaining!"

"You know what I mean." Bob sounded firm. "I think you're a fool not to dump him. Serve papers on him." He was gripping the steering wheel with one hand; his hand on her knee tightened, almost painfully. "Nobody has to put up with that kind of treatment! Christ, Lisa!"

"Bob, please," Lisa pleaded.

"I'm serious. For your own good. He's running all over town, making you look foolish, because you're pretending you don't see it. The sooner you admit it and deal with it—Well, how many more times is he going to beat you up?"

Lisa's eyes overflowed. "He wasn't always like this," she cried, her voice breaking. "He didn't used to drink and, and run around. When we were first married, I couldn't have asked for a better husband."

"Well, I know you must have seen something in him," Bob said. There was a trace of cynicism in his voice.

"It's only been in the last year or so that he's, he's changed so much. It's like he's a different person."

"So why don't you leave him?" Bob pressed.

"I love him!" Lisa said loudly, then her voice broke, "Or, I used to love him. I just don't know him anymore. It's like, like he's turned into a beast or something."

"Then you have every right to leave him," Bob said. "Especially if he's going to do something like this to you." He reached toward her face and rubbed her cheek with a delicate touch.

Lisa looked at him. Her lower lip trembled and then, suddenly, the emotion flooded out. With a groan, she pressed her face into Bob's chest and cried.

"There, there," he said soothingly. "Let it out. Let it all out." He pulled her to him and patted her shoulder.

Bob looked out at the fading brightness of the sky. They were parked at the top of Cemetery Hill, just across from one of the wrought-iron gates to the graveyard. The sun had set behind the hill, streaking the sky with yellow. Gravestones stood out black against the sky, reminding Bob of a row of broken teeth. The image gave him a sudden, nameless discomfort.

"There, there," he whispered again, but this time he noticed a tightness in his voice.

He let his gaze wander back toward the cemetery, to the heavy iron gate that was attached to two granite pillars. He then noticed that the gate was swaying back and forth slightly, almost imperceptively. His eyes darted to the trees overhead to see if there was any wind. There was none.

Fighting back the feeling of uneasiness, he stroked Lisa's hair softly. He was relieved to feel that she was no longer shaking. Her breathing was even and deep. He thought she might be asleep.

The sky was now dark. Bob looked back at the cemetery gate. It was still swinging, just barely moving. Then as his eyes adjusted to the dark, he realized that there was something on top of the left pillar. He squinted, and finally recognized the form of a large white cat, nonchalantly licking its paw. The white fur glowed, almost glimmered against the night sky. The cat paused in its cleaning and looked over at Bob with a cold, distant stare.

Bob's breath caught in his throat, and his legs twitched. Lisa stirred and sat up slowly.

"Huh? What is it?" she asked sleepily. "Too much pressure on your leg?"

"Ahh, no. No," Bob replied, then he forced a laugh. "Just getting a little twitchy. I get nervous around graveyards after dark."

"I must've fallen asleep for a second there," Lisa said, shifting herself around.

"Yeah, you did." Bob's voice cracked.

"Hey, what's the matter? There's nothing to be afraid of," Lisa said. She surprised him by leaning toward him and kissing him full on the mouth. Automatically, he put his arms around her and pulled her tight. He shifted slightly and

126

stole a quick glance at the granite pillar. The wrought-iron gate was closed, and the cat was gone.

He pulled her closer, almost in desperation as he fought back the uneasiness he felt.

Moments later, still wrapped in a tight embrace, they both heard a sound that made them sit up, startled.

A long, hollow howl drifted through the night, rising and falling like a cry.

Bob quickly rolled his window down and stuck his head outside to try to get a fix on the direction. It seemed to be coming from the cemetery.

Lisa shook his arm anxiously. "What in heaven's name?"

"I don't know. I don't know," he said, waving her to silence. He listened to the last dying strains of the howling and then pulled his head back into the car. "That sounds a hell of a lot like the sound I heard out by the pond that night."

"God, it's creepy."

The night was silent, and Bob and Lisa sat there looking around them at the surrounding darkness. Then the baying began again, rising in quivering notes. This time it seemed to be closer.

Lisa screamed when a sudden burst of wind kicked up a whirl of leaves that clattered noisily against the car. They bounced off the car's windshield and hood, sounding like scratching, like somebody trying to get into the car. Bob looked over at Lisa. Her panicked eyes held his.

"What the . . ." Bob said tightly.

"Let's get going," Lisa said urgently. Bob rolled the window shut and turned the ignition. He snapped on the headlights and pulled away from the curb.

Bob was just shifting into second when Lisa screamed, "Look!" Vaguely and just out of reach of the headlights, Bob saw a large black shadow emerge from the graveyard. A ripple of gooseflesh spread across his arms as he watched the form slink across the road and disappear into the woods on the other side.

Bob pressed the accelerator to the floor. The car jolted forward with a squeal of tires. When he got to where the black shape had disappeared, he pressed down hard on the brakes. The car skidded to a stop in the gravel on the roadside.

"What did you see?" he shouted, looking anxiously at Lisa and then out at the dark woods. "Tell me, what did you see?"

"I, I don't know," Lisa stammered. "It looked like a big dog or something."

"Yeah, or something!" Bob said. "That sure as hell didn't sound like a dog, and by Jesus, that didn't look like a dog!"

Lisa's voice shook as she tried to gain control. "It looked like a dog to me."

"Well, it wasn't!" Bob said firmly. "That animal moved just like a wolf."

Bob peered off into the darkness. "What's through those woods there?" he asked, pointing to the side of the road.

"There's a, uh, there's a gravel pit a little way in there. And an old dirt road that goes out to the falls and the old abandoned silver mine. Then just forest." Lisa bit on her lower lip. "Hey, Bob, come on. Let's get going, OK?"

For a moment longer, Bob stared into the impenetrable darkness, then he shook his head and grunted. "Yeah, OK."

He looked at her and smiled. She returned a brave smile. "I'm telling you, though," he said grimly, "that sure as hell looked like a wolf to me!"

.II.

Simmons, you are one hot fucking shit!" Reggie Vellieux said, slapping Frank on the shoulder and then taking the seat opposite him in the booth.

Reggie's face was split by a wide grin that had always reminded Frank of Howdy Doody; he had never liked him.

Frank took the last swig of beer from his glass and wiped his mouth with the back of his hand. Reggie jumped to his feet and gestured wildly. "Hey! Frenchie! A beer over here for the hero!"

Frank hooked his thumbs through his belt loops and leaned back in his seat with a loud belch. Well, he figured, might as well stick around if the beer's free.

Frenchie came over with a cold one and slid it

in front of Frank. Reggie already had a dollar bill out, which Frenchie neatly pocketed as he moved away from the table.

"So tell me all about it," Reggie said, beaming. "I've heard about it from everyone else, but I want the details from you."

"Not much to tell, really," Frank said, purposely nonchalant and looking bored to counteract Reggie's enthusiasm. There's nothing better, he thought, than a hero who maintains his cool.

"Aww, come on," Reggie said, leaning forward eagerly. "You can't tell me it wasn't a hell of a rush to nail that bastard."

Frank took a swallow of beer and shrugged his shoulders. "I spent most of the night hunkered down beside that stone wall. I knew that son-of-a-bitch would be out that way."

"How'd you know?" Reggie asked.

Frank tapped his forehead with his finger. "I knew," he said, smiling and nodding, "I knew. And when that animal went by, it was just about dawn." Frank pointed his finger at Reggie like a make-believe gun. "Bang! I nailed the sucker."

"That's it?" Reggie asked, crestfallen. Apparently he wanted a detailed account of a hand-to-hand struggle; Frank's account was too easy.

"That's it," Frank said simply. He took one last gulp of beer and left the glass, still not empty, on the table. "Look, Reg, I've gotta get going. I've, I've got some business to take care of." He winked lasciviously.

"Ohhh," Reggie said, nodding knowingly. "You're gonna go out and see Julie, huh?"

"Yeah, I think I just might," Frank said as he rose from the booth. He strode from the table, heading toward the door. As he reached into his pants pocket for the truck keys, he mumbled to himself, "That is, if she don't have company already."

.III.

"Well, I don't know if I can thank you for a pleasant night out or not," Lisa said with a tight laugh as Bob pulled up to the curb in front of her apartment building. "It did have its moments."

"Yeah." Bob looked at her and then out at the darkened apartment building. His forehead was creased with concern. "And if he starts in again . . ." he said, but then let his voice trail off when he saw the pleading look in Lisa's eyes. "OK, OK," he mumbled finally.

Lisa cast a quick glance over her shoulder at the parking lot. She sighed and looked back at Bob.

"He's not home yet?" Bob asked.

Lisa shook her head. "I wouldn't expect him to be. Whenever we have a fight, he always stays out even later than usual." Her voice began to break. "Probably just to make me feel lousy."

They dropped into silence. Bob leaned forward and scanned the three-story apartment building. The disk of the full moon had just risen over the rooftop, outlining the eaves with silvery filigree. A low, moaning wind added to the eeriness.

"About that animal we saw," Bob began. "Do you, do you think we should report it?"

Lisa shrugged.

"I thought I heard that Frank Simmons or one of the men from town killed that dog that had been getting the animals," Lisa said.

"I'd say, by the looks of what we saw, that they got the wrong animal. Or else there are two of them."

"Maybe you should give Granger a call and report it."

"Yeah," Bob said, rubbing his chin, "maybe I will." He turned and looked at her. "Hey, I almost forgot. It's the perfect time to ask you this, I know."

Lisa looked at him and cocked her eyebrows.

"A week from Friday," Bob continued, "on the thirty-first, we're having a Halloween party at school. The senior class has hired a band from Portsmouth. They decided to do it really big this year."

"You want me to chaperon?" Lisa asked guardedly.

"That comes later. First of all, we're going to have a decorating party. Would you like to come and help?"

"You think it'd be OK?" Lisa asked. Bob recognized the question behind her question.

He nodded. "Sure. We can, you know, play it cool."

"This is tomorrow night? A school night?"

"There's a teachers' conference the next day, so the students have the day off. We thought maybe a preparty party would get everyone into the spirit of things." Bob's grin widened. "What do you say?"

Lisa looked down at her folded hands and slowly twisted them. "Sure, I guess it'd be OK." She looked at him and brightened. "After all, it'd be a school function, right?"

"Right!" Bob said, emphatically. "No funny stuff."

Lisa snapped open her door and stepped outside. "OK. What time can you pick me up?"

Bob shifted in his seat. "Well, that was my last question. I have to take this old heap into the shop for repairs tomorrow. I was hoping you could pick me up."

Lisa laughed. "So that's it!" she said playfully. "You're just using me to get what you want!"

Bob shook his head with exaggerated innocence. "No-o-o-! Honest. How does six-thirty sound?"

"Well, I suppose so," Lisa said. She eased the door shut and stood there for a moment on the curb. She waved goodbye, and Bob saw her mouth the word, "Thanks," as he pulled away.

.IV.

"Ned? Are you awake?"

Ellie Simmons cupped her hands to her mouth and called sharply from the foot of the stairs. She peered up at her son's closed bedroom door and waited what she thought was a reasonable time for an answer.

"Ned! You left the light on in the barn. It shouldn't be on all night. It might start a fire. Ned? Don't you think you should go turn it off?"

She huffed and folded her arms across her chest. Still no answer came. She placed her foot on the first step, as though, somehow, the threat would be transmitted to Ned.

"Ned!"

She put weight on that foot, and the step creaked.

"It's your responsibility, not mine!" she yelled. She listened to the ticking silence of the house, then shook her head and said softly, "My God, but that boy sleeps like the dead!"

She waited a few seconds longer, then shouted, "Never mind. I'll do it this time!"

She went to the closet and got her coat before venturing out into the chilly night. All the way to and from the barn, she was muttering about how kids these days are such lazy so-and-sos.

.V.

Tuesday, October 21

"I could use a little bit of help over here," Bob shouted. He was balanced on the edge of the

134

next-to-the-top step on the ladder, straining as he reached over his head. The large orange-and-black crepe jack-o'-lantern face bobbed up and down as he felt blindly for the coat hanger hook he had wrapped around the I-beam.

The ladder was squeaking noisily, like a frightened mouse. Bob gritted his teeth.

"Don't worry, Mr. Wentworth. We'll catch you," someone yelled from the floor. Bob didn't dare to look down to see who it was who had such a charming sense of humor. He thought he could hear Lisa chuckling with the rest of the people below.

"Terrific. Just what I need." He grunted softly. "Wouldn't I look great, dancing at the Halloween party with a cast on my leg?"

"You could go as an accident victim," someone else yelled.

Bob stretched his legs and, finally, the hook caught. "There," he said with a noisy exhale. He took a quick step down until the ladder was more stable. He stood there for a moment, admiring the colorful streamers that arched away from him in all directions. A round of applause went up from the floor as Bob scurried down the rest of the way.

"Nice, isn't it?" he asked, looking at his finishing touch.

Lisa cleared her throat and stepped closer to him. "Umm, don't you think that that red spotlight is just a bit too much?" she asked, seriously. "I mean, it's supposed to be spooky, not gory."

"I think it's just per-fect!" Bob said, rubbing his hands together maliciously. He followed it with a hollow, ghoulish laugh. Then he turned and looked in the direction of the lighting booth at the far end of the gym.

"Hey, Wendy!" he shouted to one of his students who was up there controlling the lights. "Mrs. Carter doesn't like the red! Ghostly, not bloody!" Shading his eyes, he looked into the bright light. The booth looked empty.

"Wendy? Are you still up there?" he called.

"Just a second," a faint voice answered. "I'm looking for the blue gel."

Bob saw Wendy rise from behind the low barrier that surrounded the booth. "I can't find it up here. Maybe it's in the band room."

"I'll go check," one of the students said and dashed off.

Bob looked back up at Wendy. Then his eyes caught a motion at the foot of the ladder leading up to the booth. Someone else had just been up there with Wendy. Bob nudged Lisa and pointed, but she turned too slowly to see the figure disappear out the side door. In the light of the exit light, Bob thought he recognized Alan Tate.

"Aww, the things that can happen in a lighting booth," Bob said to Lisa's questioning gaze.

A few moments later, Wendy came down from the lighting booth and walked over to the group in the center of the gym floor. She moved cautiously, as though she was shy. This wasn't at all like Wendy, and Bob knew she was wondering if anyone had seen that she had had company up in the booth.

Bob noticed that Wendy looked a bit disheveled. Her hair was messed up, and the top two buttons of her blouse were open. Her skirt looked as though it was twisted around.

"I've got it!" yelled the student who had run off to the band room. He held a blue gel triumphantly over his head. When he came up to the group, he handed the gel to Wendy, who took it and then thrust it into Bob's hand.

"I've, I've got to get going," she said. Her voice sounded edgy as she backed away from the group. "My mother wanted me home by ten o'clock."

Bob looked at his watch and saw that it was just nine-thirty. "Well, thanks for the help," he said. "Have a good day off tomorrow, and I'll see you in class on Thursday."

"Yeah," Wendy said. Her skirt swished as she turned and ran over to the pile of coats on the bleachers. She grabbed her coat from the bottom of the pile and disappeared out the door.

Wendy's sudden departure seemed to infect the other students, and they slowly started filtering out of the gym. Within fifteen minutes, Lisa and Bob were the only people left to put away the unused materials.

"Well," Lisa said, bending down to pick up a crumpled paper cup. "That sure was a dud of a party."

Bob was struggling to take down the high

stepladder. "At least we got the work done," he said. "I was afraid we wouldn't even finish, the turnout was so bad."

He got the ladder down onto the floor, then he stood up and went over to the record player and clicked on the record that was on the turntable. An indistinguishable blast of guitars and drums rumbled the speakers as Bob held out his hands and bowed to Lisa gallantly. "May I have this dance, madam?"

Lisa curtsied and lightly touched her fingertips to his hand. Oblivious to the beat of the music, they began to waltz slowly across the floor. From the lighting booth overhead, a bright red spotlight illuminated them.

.VI.

Wendy struggled to get her coat buttoned as she ran across the high school parking-lot. She crossed the street and then, at an easier trot, started across the football field. For a moment, she considered going straight home, but then she decided to cut through the cemetery to take the long way home along Strout Street. She needed time to think.

The cold night air burned her lungs, and her eyes watered as she slowed to a walk. She went through the cemetery and then came out onto the street.

There were no streetlights on this stretch of

road, but the full moon overhead cast a pale glaze over the road, and she could see her way well enough.

Wendy was caught between two extreme emotions: one made her want to scream with laughter and joy; the other twisted within her until she wanted to break down and cry.

"There's a first time for everything," she whispered softly, conscious of the dampness and pain between her legs. She stopped walking and slid her hand up underneath her skirt. Her fingers came away sticky.

"Well," she said to herself in an admonishing tone, "you can't stay a virgin all your life, right?" She was trying to sound brave, but she could feel her lower lip trembling. "I'm probably the only girl in the senior class who hasn't screwed, and it's not like he forced me."

She moved down the road in the shadow of the trees, telling herself not to cry; it had to happen sometime.

She breathed in the night air and exhaled it in spasmodic jerks. She hoped the walk home would calm her down enough so she would be able to face her mother without giving away her wonderful-horrible secret. She looked to her right and saw the glow of lights from town.

Suddenly, a pair of headlights sliced the darkness. Wendy slid down the embankment and hid until the car passed by and disappeared around the bend. She scrambled back up to the road and continued walking.

She was about a hundred yards from where

Strout Street crossed Railroad Avenue when she heard a noise. It was off to her left, in the woods.

She stood perfectly still, holding her breath as she scanned the deep darkness. It was nothing, she told herself, just the wind or something.

Then she heard it again, and this time she thought it sounded like twigs breaking underfoot. She felt the tension coiling in her stomach.

No, not the wind. A branch. A branch snapping. Someone's in the woods!

"Alan?" she whispered. "Is that you?" She looked off into the dark and listened tensely. She hoped madly that she would hear a friendly voice or a laugh.

Steeling her voice, she said, "Whoever you are, it's not funny. Come on out right now!"

The black forest remained silent for an unbearably long time.

Wendy turned on her heel and took a few quick steps back, staring at the streetlight at the corner of Railroad Avenue. The pain between her legs began to throb. Suddenly, as if coming from right beside her, a loud howl filled the night. It rose with a piercing crescendo.

Wendy screamed and then broke into a run. Over the sound of her feet slapping the pavement, she heard the howling rise higher and higher. It shifted, seeming to remain right alongside her as she ran. She gulped in air as she ran, and it burned her throat.

It seemed as though the streetlight was getting no closer as she pumped her arms madly.

Then, with a suddenness that almost made her stumble, the howling stopped. The silence that followed was as thick and impenetrable as the darkness beneath the trees. Wendy slowed for a moment and chanced a look over her shoulder. The road glimmered like smoke in the moonlight. The trees were black. Then, phantomlike, a shadow detached itself from the trees and slinked out onto the road. It was the biggest damn dog Wendy had ever seen.

She broke her stride and pulled to a stop. Her eyes were transfixed by the massive black shape that was moving slowly toward her. A tremor rose up her spine and shook her shoulders wildly when she heard a low, rumbling growl that seemed to shake the road.

"No! No!" she whined. Her hands flailed wildly behind her, searching for support as she walked backward. The throbbing between her legs intensified.

In the moonlight, she caught a glimmer of green in the animal's eyes. The growl rose louder until it seemed to enfold her. Wendy sucked in a gulp of air to scream, but all that came out was a strangled cry. The black shape drew nearer.

"No! No! Momma, Momma," Wendy moaned. It was the last sound she made as the beast went for her throat.

.VII.

An hour later, Midge Stevens and Mark McKinnon were driving back from the movies in

North Conway when they found Wendy. She was lying at the side of the road with her head resting at an impossible angle. Neither would ever forget Wendy's saucerlike eyes as she stared blankly back at the headlight's glare.

.VIII.

Lisa stood leaning on the roof of her car, her chin resting in her cupped hands and one foot on the running board. "You're sure you don't want a ride home?" she asked.

Bob shook his head.

"It's not that far out of my way, you know."

"It's OK. Really," Bob said. He took the smouldering cigarette butt from his mouth and snapped it off into the darkness. "I just need some time to think, to sort things out."

"After what we saw last night?" Lisa asked, her voice edged with fear.

Bob felt an uneasiness, but he smiled and said, "I'll be all right."

Lisa sat down in the car and started the motor. "You're sure?"

"Yeah. And thanks for the help with the decorations." He moved over and shut the door for her. "I hope you had an OK time."

"Of course I did," she said. "It was terrific."

"Well," Bob said, hunching his shoulder, "it wasn't that great. You're planning on coming to the party next Friday, I hope."

"We'll see," she said. "I'll have to think what I can wear for a costume."

Bob braced himself on the car roof and leaned closer to Lisa. "You don't have to wear a costume, you know?"

"I know. But what would Halloween be without a costume?" she asked. Then she shifted into gear and drove away.

Bob started across the high-school front lawn toward Old Jepson's Road. He walked along easily, whistling softly, trying to ease his mind. He had walked about a mile when he stopped suddenly. He focused on the thought that had been lurking in his mind all day, like a hungry shark coasting just below the surface.

The cat! That white cat that was sitting on the cemetery post!

He looked back down the road toward the high school. He knew he could cut across the football field and come out on the back side of the cemetery. He also realized that he'd be foolish to go back there and look for the cat.

Why? he wondered. It's just an ordinary cat. Probably just sitting there waiting for a mouse to pounce on. He was being silly letting something like that bother him.

So if it's so silly, why was it so unsettling?

He looked back and forth, up and down the silent, dark road.

So what's the problem? he asked himself.

The problem was, that white cat had scared the shit out of him. Worse than seeing that wolflike dog.

"So why get so damned worked up?" he asked himself softly. He stuck his hands into his pockets and started down the road toward his house. He felt a vague uneasiness, a pulling at his back that made him want to turn around and go to the cemetery, but he resisted it.

Suddenly, a shiver crept along his back. He pulled his collar tighter but the feeling didn't go away. It spread out into a chilly tickling along his scalp.

He looked over his shoulder at the blackness that filled the road like ink. A breeze shifted the trees, and the moon, shining through the leaves, spotted the road with a shifting pattern.

He was reassuring himself that he hadn't seen anything moving on the road behind him, that he was letting his imagination run away, when he realized with a start that he did see something on the road behind him: a dark shadow that seemed to absorb the scattered moonlight.

"It's nothing, nothing at all," he whispered to himself.

And then the "nothing" shifted closer to him and began to growl softly.

The darkness obscured the shape, but Bob was positive that this was the same animal he and Lisa had seen the night before. They stood there, about fifty feet between them, facing each other off. Then, uttering a low rumble, the animal flattened onto its belly and started slinking toward Bob. The moonlight caught the animal just right, and Bob could see the animal's hackles raised like battle spears. The snarling grew louder as the beast inched closer.

Bob realized with a sinking feeling that it would do no good to run. The animal could bring him down in ten paces. Instead, Bob stood still until the animal was within twenty feet of him. When he saw the baleful green glow in the beast's eyes, Bob suddenly jumped forward and yelled.

"Yah! Yah!" he shouted, waving his arms wildly. "Get! Go on! Get!"

The animal stopped moving, but continued to worm its belly against the asphalt. The rising rumble in the beast's chest told Bob that his scare tactic hadn't worked.

"Jesus Christ," Bob exclaimed. "That is a god-damn wolf!"

When Bob said this, the animal let out a loud yelp that sounded almost as if it had been hurt. Bob watched as the animal crouched, preparing to jump. Bob raised his hands to this throat in a futile protective gesture.

"Christ Almighty!" Bob said softly, and again, the beast made another pained sound

Just as the growling had started again, Bob heard a screech of tires behind him. A blast of light swept across the road and illuminated the scene in front of him.

He saw the beast, caught by surprise, as it reared back on its hind legs, almost standing up.

A wolf doesn't do that! Bob's mind screamed.

And then, in the brief flash of light, the animal did something that made a strangled cry catch in Bob's throat. The animal covered its eyes with its paws to protect them from the sudden glare of light. But what made Bob cry out was that what he saw were not animal paws! They looked like human hands!

Even as the thought registered, the animal dashed off into the woods.

"Christ Almighty!" Bob mumbled, wiping the sweat from his forehead. The chilly night air made him shiver.

The car came up behind him and skidded to a stop inches from him. He was still standing there numbly in the center of the road. He spun around quickly and shielded his eyes from the light.

"Bob? Are you all right?" Lisa's voice called to him from behind the glare. "What are you doing, trying to get yourself killed?"

He walked over to the passenger's side and slid into the seat without a word.

"What's the matter?" Lisa asked. Her voice was agitated. "You look as pale as a sheet. Are you crazy or something?"

"Maybe," he muttered. "I just saw, saw something that startled me. That's all."

"What? What did you see?" Lisa asked.

"Nothing, nothing," he answered. "I just let my imagination get carried away, that's all. It was just a raccoon or something in the woods."

"Ohh?"

"Yeah." He felt the tension unwinding and took a deep breath. "Hey, what are you doing out here anyway? I thought you went home."

There was still a concerned crease across Lisa's

forehead, but she smiled and jabbed her thumb toward the back seat. "It seems as though you left your briefcase in the library this afternoon. I forgot to give it to you earlier. I didn't think you'd want to go to school tomorrow without it."

"Oh, God, yeah. Thanks," Bob said, fighting to keep his voice steady. He reached the briefcase from the back seat. "Thanks a lot."

All the way to Bob's house, his mind continued to dwell on the image he had seen, trying to absorb it; a wolf, a wolf with human hands!

Chapter Seven

Friday, October 24

.I.

Bob had slept over an hour later than usual. It was just seven-thirty when he finished shaving and came downstairs for breakfast. He looked blankly out at the falling rain as he fried his eggs.

School had been cancelled for the rest of the week. Wendy Stillman's funeral had been yesterday, and the whole town was still in shock. The weather for the funeral had been overcast, threatening rain, which did not come until after dark.

Bob sat at the breakfast bar glumly eating his eggs. The breakfast had not filled the hollowness he felt in his stomach.

He didn't hear the car drive up to his house, so he jumped when he heard heavy footsteps on the porch. Looking up, he saw his early morning visitor through the door window.

"Deputy Thurston," Bob said, rising and going to the door. "Come on in."

Thurston entered and eased the door shut behind him. He followed Bob back into the kitchen.

"Care for a cup of coffee?" Bob asked.

Thurston said, "Thanks," and took off his yellow rain slicker. He hung it on the back of the chair before sitting down. Bob got two cups from the cupboard and filled the tea kettle with water.

"I hope instant coffee's OK," he said. He looked over at the puddle forming under Thurston's chair.

"Sure."

Bob put some coffee into the cups and then leaned back against the countertop. "It's kind of a nasty day to be out so early. What can I do for you?"

The kettle started screaming, and Bob poured the hot water into the cups. He put one in front of Thurston and then sat down, pushing away his egg-stained plate.

"Well," Thurston said, fingering the coffee cup, "you could start by answering a few questions for me, if that's all right?"

"Yeah. Sure," Bob said, feeling a lump of tension in his throat.

"I didn't see you at Wendy Stillman's funeral yesterday," Thurston said solemnly. "I was wondering why." He took a tentative sip of coffee and eyed Bob over the rim of the cup.

Bob felt himself shrink under the stare. "Well, I, uhh. Wendy was one of my better students, and I just didn't think, didn't think I could handle it." He made a conscious effort to relax, but still felt tight.

" 'S that so?" Thurston said softly. He took a noisy sip from the cup.

"Do you guys have any idea who, who did it?" Bob asked.

"We have some ideas," Thurston replied, a bit too quickly, Bob thought. "Have you got any ideas?" Thurston countered.

"I, I don't know," Bob replied. He lit a cigarette and noticed that his hands shook.

Thurston stared at him with a cold, analytical glare. "What have you heard?" he asked. His voice was tightly controlled.

"Some pretty wild stories, some of them," Bob said.

"Like the story you told Granger about seeing a wolf out on Old Jep's Road that same night?"

"I saw something," Bob said. He turned his eyes away and took a drag from his cigarette.

Thurston shifted in his chair and leaned forward. "The best we can figure, the Stillman girl was killed between nine-thirty and eleven o'clock, when she was found. Now, you say you saw something on your way home, about ten-thirty."

"What I saw looked like a wolf," Bob said forcefully.

Thurston was silent as he studied Bob with an

unblinking stare. Finally, he said, "Maybe you saw a human wolf?"

Bob jumped as the image of the animal's paws—hands—came back to his mind. "Wha—what?"

"Well, she might have been bitten by a dog, savaged some by this animal that's been bothering the farmers around, but there's evidence that she had been molested, raped."

"What?"

"Doc Stetson did an autopsy." Thurston leaned closer to Bob and spoke in a secretive voice. "Now this is kind of confidential, so I don't want you adding it to those stories circulating around town, but Doc says someone put the boots to her before they killed her."

"God! Raped and then murdered?" The thought staggered Bob, and he dropped his head into his hands and stared blankly at the countertop for a moment.

"Seems as though," Thurston said. He looked at Bob and cocked an eyebrow. "I just want you to refresh my memory. When was it you saw her last? Wendy Stillman, that is."

"When we were decorating for the Halloween party. She was helping us with the—"

"Us? You mean you and Mrs. Carter?"

Bob felt his face redden. "And some students. Wendy left before everyone else did."

Bob had forgotten entirely that he had seen Alan Tate, or someone, leave the lighting booth before Wendy came down. The shock of Thurston's revelation had driven it completely from his mind.

"Did she leave with someone, or alone?" Thurston asked.

"Alone," Bob replied quickly. He got up slowly, stunned, and filled his coffee cup with cold water. He drank it in two big gulps. "We, we stayed and cleaned up after everyone else had gone home."

"We?"

"Mrs. Carter and I."

"Ohh." Thurston nodded his head. "And did you go home alone or with someone?"

Bob's anger suddenly burst. He took a menacing step toward Thurston before he got control of himself. "Look, that's my personal life. I don't have to answer anything about it. And I resent your prying into my private life."

"You don't have to answer that question," Thurston replied cooly. "Not at all. Look, someone has been killed in this town, and that makes me and Granger nervous. It makes a lot of people nervous. You're not under suspicion for anything." Thurston pointed an accusing finger at Bob. "'Cause if you were, I'd have hauled your ass down to the station by now. And you can be damn sure you'd answer my questions there! I'm just trying to find out how Wendy Stillman died, that's all!" He brought his fist down hard onto the countertop, making the cups rattle.

"You mean what killed her, don't you?" Bob asked cooly. Seeing Thurston get so agitated had a calming effect on Bob. "What killed her!"

Thurston smiled and snickered softly. "Yeah,

right. Your wolf, huh? Look, I don't want to debate that point with you right now. I think it's bullshit thinking there's a goddamn wolf in the area."

"Just check it out!" Bob said forcefully. "It's another line of investigation. Like you said, someone's died in this town, one of my best students, and that makes me nervous, because whatever got her came awful damn close to getting me too!"

"Yeah, well," Thurston said, rising. He took his coat and shook it before putting it on. "Well, I'll be in touch if I have any more questions." He tipped his head back and finished off his cup of coffee. "Thanks for the coffee."

He left, slamming the door behind him.

.II.

The rain stopped by three o'clock that afternoon, and the sun was shining through the raft of clouds as it set. It was nearly twilight as Ned walked home slowly from the I.G.A.

He was feeling better than he had in weeks. He felt whole, rested, refreshed. He walked briskly along Old Jepson's Road, swinging his arms and whistling a tuneless song. His lips were dry, and had to wet his lips continually to keep the notes from fizzling away. With jaunty skips, he avoided the leaf-choked puddles along the roadside.

Suddenly, he stopped, the tune cut short. He knelt down and stared into one of the muddy puddles. Leaves dimpled the surface of the water and the mud on the bottom was irregular, but he clearly saw his reflection in the water.

The face looking back at him was pale, washed out, almost, he thought, as though he had lost some of the substance just below the skin. His cheeks were hollow. His eyes were dark and receding beneath his scowling brow. He could see that his lips were chalky and cracked, and as he stared at himself he ran his tongue over them again.

He tried to smile at himself, letting his mouth widen slowly, but the grin looked more like a grimace.

He stretched out his hand toward the puddle, letting his hand form a tensed claw. His fingers got closer to the water, and he had a brief image of someone else's hands reaching slowly for his face. His fingers touched the water, and his reflection shattered into a dozen ripples.

With a barely audible whimper, he jerked to his feet. He started to walk away rapidly when he heard a car coming toward him down the road. The steady hum of the car's engine was muffled as it dropped into a dip in the road. Then, as it crested the hill behind him, Ned chanced a quick look over his shoulder.

He immediately recognized the black Mustang convertible. He continued walking, never breaking his stride, as the car bore down on him from behind. He held his arms stiff and clamped against his sides. The tightness in his stomach spread into his chest and crotch.

The car was rapidly closing the distance between them. Ned wished wildly that the driver of the car would not even notice him walking along the roadside; he also wished that she would stop and pick him up.

When the car was close behind him, the driver gave a quick toot on the horn, and then the car sailed past Ned, leaving him with an uncomfortable prickling at the nape of his neck. The car was a short way down the road when Ned saw the brake lights flicker and then stay on. The car pulled over to the side of the road.

Ned watched as the backup lights came on, and then the car started coming toward him in reverse. When it was right beside him, the passenger's side door opened. For a moment, Ned considered lighting out across the field, running before he had to speak with her. What would he say? he wondered wildly. How could he ever talk with her, face to face?

"Hey, d'yah want a ride, or are you into walking?" Julie Sikes called to him, leaning across the front seat to hold the door open for him.

.III.

Bob ran the zipper tab up to his chin and snuggled into the collar of his jacket to break the chill. He was sitting at the top of the hill in Pine

Haven Cemetery. The sun was low in the west behind him, but already the gravestones below him were washed with shadows. The only sound, as he sat cross-legged beside a large marble column, was the steady flapping of a flag on one of the gravestones.

He had been out walking in the woods all afternoon. He was trying to sort out his reaction to Wendy's violent death and his feelings for Lisa Carter. There was much he wanted to think about and much he wanted to forget. He hadn't been too surprised when, once the sun started to set, he had walked in the direction of the graveyard.

Bob could look down from the hill and catch a glimpse of the town to his right. He was soothed and calmed by the small spectacle it presented. All around town, lights were being turned on. As he watched, the string of streetlights that marked Main Street came on. Peace and quiet and gathering night lay upon the town like a soft blanket.

But as he looked out over the town, Bob was filled with an unnerving foreboding. He remembered that day in the park, when he had been going to see Lisa in the library, and an uneasiness came over him. What he felt now was much like what he had felt then, when he watched the thick cloud pass overhead; but now the feeling was much more intense, still as vague as that day, but much more intense.

He noticed that he was breathing rapidly and that, in spite of the cool evening air, his face was bathed in sweat.

He got up slowly and started down the hill toward the road and home. He wanted to be home before it got dark, and he would have to hurry.

.IV.

Hunching up his shoulders, Ned looked into the car and stared at Julie. "Su—sure," he said, sliding onto the seat. "Thanks for st—stopping."

The sweet smell of marijuana filled the car. Julie gingerly held the nub of a roach to her lips and inhaled noisily. "Wanna hit?" she asked, holding the roach out to Ned.

"Ahh, no. No thanks," he mumbled.

She shrugged, took another whistling drag, and then dropped it into the ashtray. "It'd do you some good," she said, lazily smiling. Ned shrugged. Julie dropped the car into gear and pulled away.

Ned sat back in the seat uneasily. He kept his hands folded in his lap, trying to hide the bulge in his pants. The setting sun glinted on the still wet road, giving it a slippery, sealskin glow. The tires hissed like tearing paper.

Ned kept stealing fleeting glances at Julie as she drove silently. His eyes kept wandering from her face to her bulging breasts. The warm tightening in his crotch made him shift uneasily. He found it almost impossible not to reach out and grab her.

What amazed him, what he couldn't believe was that, after all his dreaming and fantasizing, here he was, alone with Julie Sikes.

Again he looked at her. The thick, curly black hair framed her pale face against the flickering view out the side window. He studied the curve of her neck that led down to the swelling of her breasts.

Go ahead! his mind screamed. Reach out! Grab her! Everyone in town has had her, including your brother. Go on! Grab her. Just reach inside her coat and grab her tits! That's what she probably wants. Why else would she pick you up?

The aching in his crotch began to throb.

You can have her! Take her! Just reach over into her blouse.

"So how's everything been?" Julie asked.

It sounded innocent, but Ned thought he saw a sly glance in his direction that said a lot more.

"Ahh, pretty good, pretty good," he answered, trying to sound at ease. "Been pretty busy."

Julie smiled and looked at him. "Doing what?" she asked intensely.

"Nothing much."

They drove a while longer in silence. Ned was cursing himself for not carrying on the conversation. He was wondering how he would ever get around to putting some moves on her.

"Did you go to Wendy Stillman's funeral?" Julie asked after a moment.

Ned shook his head. "Couldn't. Had to work."

"Oh. Horrible, wasn't it?"

Ned nodded and let his eyes wander down to the floor. His gaze immediately fell on Julie's legs. He saw that they were spread apart slightly, and he wished he had the courage to run his hand up her thigh.

"So young, and to die like that. And no one even knows who or what killed her. I heard someone say that she might have been raped, too. That it might have been a person who did it."

Ned gulped for a breath of air and managed to say, "I hadn't heard."

"Were you at the school decorating that night?" Julie asked. Again she looked at him, and Ned read more than simple conversation.

"No, ummm, I was busy," he answered.

"So was I," Julie said, apparently to herself. She dropped her hand into her lap and let it rest there. "Say," Julie said, "are you planning to go to the Halloween party?"

Ned was afraid to reply, afraid to open his mouth for fear of what would come out. He rubbed his hands together, feeling the slippery sweat of his palms.

"I don't think so," he said finally. "I don't have a date."

Julie's hand in her lap moved, and her skirt moved up about three inches. Ned ran his tongue over his dry lips.

"Would you, would you like to go with me?" he stammered. He looked at her intently, trying to mask his intense feelings.

A simple, flat no would have been enough and, feeling the way he did, it would have been accepted. When Julie burst out laughing, Ned felt his face flush with blood. He balled his hands into fists and wanted to hit her, but instead, he looked out the window at the road ahead. His eyes were stinging, and he carefully formed the word "Bitch."

She has no right to laugh at me, he thought angrily. I should take her right now and teach her a lesson.

Julie's laughter died away slowly, and then they both sat in silence as she drove up the Bartlett Road. When they came to the end of Ned's driveway, Julie pulled over to the side of the road.

"It's going to be dark soon," she said, "and I've got some things to do."

"This is fine," Ned said weakly. His ears were still stinging from her abusive laughter. He opened the door and stepped out, right into a puddle. Before he got out, though, he turned and looked at her once more. "How come?" he asked. "How come you won't come with me?" The whining tone of his voice irritated him.

"Huh?" Julie asked dully.

"Why won't you come to the Halloween party with me?" His foot was still ankle-deep in the water. His sock was thoroughly soaked and his ankle was starting to feel numb.

"Come on, Ned, don't you think I'm a little too old to be going to something like that? A high school dance?"

"Not really," he answered feebly. "It's open to the public, and I know there'll be other people there who have already graduated."

"Sorry, Ned," she said softly, and he thought she almost sounded sincere. She shocked him when she reached out and rested her hand on his leg. She squeezed his thigh slightly and said, "But who knows, maybe we can get together sometime."

Walking up to his house, Ned was limping, the pain in his crotch was so intense. "Got, I'd love to get into her pants," he muttered to himself.

.V.

"Jesus H. Christ!" Bob swore as he shook angrily on the locked cemetery gate. He had heard that, because of some recent vandalism in the cemetery, all but the front gates would be kept locked. He had forgotten all about it. Now he would have to go back up over the hill and walk around.

He looked up at the pointed spikes that lined the top of the iron fence. There was no way he could get up and over them without getting hurt. He shook a cigarette from the pack and lit it before turning back up the hill.

He picked his way carefully between the gravestones. The sun had set completely, and the cemetery pathways were indistinct, the footing unsure. When he reached the crest of the hill, he paused and scanned the small grove of cedars that surrounded the marble pillar where he had been sitting. As he turned to walk down the hill to the road, he caught a glimpse of motion beside the pillar, and when he turned carefully, he saw the white cat slink into view.

Bob's breath snagged in his throat. The animal looked at him intently. It walked back and forth a few times, rubbing its sides against the monument, then it sat down at the base and glared at him.

Bob knew he had to prove that this was just an ordinary animal, that the hunting for mice was good in the graveyard, and this cat had staked out its claim. He bent down and, snapping his fingers, called to the cat.

"Come here, kitty, kitty," he said in a friendly tone.

The animal stood up and hunched its back.

Bob took a cautious step forward, still clicking his tongue. At first, the animal stood its ground, but just before Bob could have reached out and touched it, it darted away toward the cedars.

The animal moved with a quick feline grace that looked almost unnatural in the dim light. Before disappearing into the trees, the cat paused and looked back at Bob.

Bob threw his cigarette to the ground and followed after the cat. He wondered why he was doing this, why he was wasting his time chasing after the animal, but he couldn't deny the strange compulsion of the mystery he felt about it.

Bob stood for a moment on the edge of the grove, his nerves and muscles tensed. Suddenly a loud hissing-and-spitting screech shattered the quiet of the cemetery. Bob crouched and peered into the darkness under the trees.

Caution! Caution was what he needed now, he decided. He knew he should just leave the animal alone, let it be. It was probably in heat and mating in the grove. Bob knew he should just head on home, but something drew him forward. He entered the cedar grove.

He had taken no more than five steps in the enfolding darkness when that horrible feline shriek sounded again, right beside him. In a quick reflexive move, Bob dropped to his knees and spun around, raising his hands to his face. He recognized the white shape that had launched itself at him from the darkness. There was a sharp stinging on his cheek as the cat's claws raked across his face.

And then it was gone. As quickly as it had attacked, the white cat vanished into the night. Bob stook up, confused and wondering. His cheek was singing with pain. He brushed the slash with his fingers and his fingers came away sticky with blood. He turned and ran wildly from the cemetery.

.VI.

The thin tendons in her arms strained and stood out like pencils beneath her skin as Julie carried an armload of groceries toward her house. It was almost nine o'clock.

She got up to the door, fiddled with the lock until it snapped, and then bumped the door open with her butt.

She dropped the groceries on the counter with a huff. It wasn't until she turned back around that she saw the man's jacket was hanging on one of the kitchen chairs. She immediately recognized it as Frank's.

"Hello?" she called out, not too loudly as she walked over and glanced into the darkness of the living room. "Are you in here?"

She flicked on the overhead light and saw that the room was empty. She then moved to the bedroom door and cautiously peered around the door jamb. The shades were drawn, and she could hear the faint ticking of her alarm clock. Then, as her eyes adjusted to the darkness, she saw the mountainous bulk on her bed. She cocked her ear, listening carefully, and then she heard Frank's shallow breathing.

"Let sleeping dogs lie," she whispered softly as she went back over to the counter and started putting the food away.

She emptied the bags quickly and was just folding the last empty bag flat when she heard Frank mumble incoherently. Julie tensed. "Please, please don't wake up."

"Mmmmmm, no. No! No!Frank moaned. There was a loud rustling of sheets, followed by a loud thump.

Did he bump the wall or fall out of bed? Julie

wondered. The silence descended again, and Julie went over to the sink, where she stood watching the faucet drip for a long time.

On tiptoes, she crept back to the bedroom door and looked in. Frank was lying, spread-eagle, across the bed. Sheets and blankets were tangled around his legs. His breathing sounded louder, more labored. Not wanting to disturb him, Julie was about to leave when she noticed the pile of clothing at the foot of the bed. She looked at it intently, trying to distinguish the clothes from the bedspread.

"Ahhh," she whispered softly, "there it is." Glancing over her shoulder, as if afraid that she was being observed, she slid into the darkened room, went over to the bed, and snatched Frank's shirt from the floor. Cursing the floor-board that creaked under her weight, she sneaked back into the kitchen with the rumpled shirt held tightly in her hand.

Once in the light, she held the shirt out at arm's length and examined it. "Same one," she muttered, when she saw where she had cut a small piece of cloth from the shirttail.

Frank's voice suddenly shattered the silence. "No! God! No!"

Julie quickly rolled the shirt into a ball and held it behind her back. She expected to see Frank come out of the bedroom. Her heart was pounding in her ears. Then she heard Frank turn over in the bed and groan.

She exhaled slowly. Again she held the shirt up for inspection, then she went over to the kitchen table and spread it out. The blue cotton was faded and worn.

"Well," she said, thoughtfully rubbing her chin, "maybe last time I didn't have enough for it to work. Maybe I need more." She grasped the shirt by the pocket and gave it a quick tug. The pocket let go easily with a soft hiss. She folded the pocket carefully in half and then put it into one of the counter drawers. She crumpled the shirt back up and threw it back at the foot of the bed.

When the shirt hit the floor, Frank jerked up into a sitting position. "The eyes! The eyes!" he screamed in a hissing voice. "Like fire! Burning, flaming eyes!"

Fighting back the initial surprise, Julie sat down on the edge of the bed and grabbed Frank's shoulders. She shook him wildly. "You're OK, Frank. You're just dreaming!"

His arms flailed, trying to beat her away. His eyes were open wide, staring. "No! No! No!" Awwwwwwwww.

"Will you wake up?" Julie shouted. She slapped him sharply on the face. "Goddammit! Wake up!"

Frank dropped back onto the bed. His eyes flickered and then opened. They were wild and glassy. His body was slick with sweat, and his hair was plastered to his forehead.

"Hey, man," Julie said, more calmly, "you were having one hell of a dream!"

Maybe it is working, she thought excitedly.

She started to rub his shoulders, and she could

166

feel him loosening up. "Take it easy. It was just a dream."

"Yeah, yeah," Frank muttered as he rubbed his face with his hands. "Just a dream, but God, it was like no dream I ever had before."

It really could be working! Julie thought. She made an effort not to let her excitement show.

"God, you wouldn't have believed it!" Frank said with a deep rattle in his throat.

"You scared the shit out of me when you cried out."

Frank sat slumped on the bed, his mouth drawn tightly at the corners. His eyes still looked distant and glazed. Air hissed between his teeth as he inhaled. "Christ, it was terrible."

"Well it's all over now. Just relax," Julie said soothingly. "What was it? What did you dream about?" she asked.

If it's just starting to work, maybe it works just on the dream level at first.

A thickness clogged Frank's voice as he spoke. "I can't remember for sure. It was something big and dark. It was trying to surround me, to, like swallow me up." Frank shivered as the dream came back clearer in his memory. "It felt like it was trying to eat me. Then—Oh, God! Then I saw that it had eyes. Terrible, burning green eyes! And I had this sensation that, like, I was being ripped apart." His voice cut off with a sharp intake of air.

Julie sat on the edge of the bed, rubbing Frank's shoulders and speaking soft words of comfort. All the while her mind was screaming, It is! It is beginning to work!

Chapter Eight

Friday, October 31

.I.

Bob glanced at his watch as he drove rapidly down Old Jepson's Road toward the high school. It was almost seven-thirty. The Halloween party started at eight. The janitor was going to let the band in early so they could set up, but Bob wanted to be there too, just to keep an eye on things.

Up ahead on his right, he saw the school parking-lot lights glowing brightly. As he pulled into the parking lot, he could hear the band tuning up. There would be a loud blast of music that would last for a few seconds and then stop abruptly. Bob skidded to a halt near the walkway, making sure to leave his car directly under a streetlight. He noticed Lisa's car parked off to the side.

He got out of the car, made sure he locked the doors, and then raced up the walkway to the school. In one of the alcoves, he passed a knot of students who were smoking. He wondered what they were smoking, but decided not to take the time to find out yet. It was more important to make sure everything was set for the dance.

When he entered the gym, he saw that the band members had left the stage and were milling around the refreshments table with a group of girls. He also saw that the red spotlight had not been changed, that it still directed its fiery beam onto the middle of the floor. It brought back a clear memory of Wendy, and he had to fight back the pained emotions.

Lisa was standing at the far corner of the gym, silently surveying the scene. Bob almost laughed aloud when he saw that she was dressed like a medieval fairy princess. She was wearing a long gown that trailed a piece of gauze from the pointed cap.

"Fantastic," he called, as he walked toward her, smiling. "Why didn't you tell me? I would have come up with something."

One of the students standing near the stage looking at the band's equipment turned around and shouted, "Hey, Mr. Wentworth. I really like your mask!"

He laughed with embarrassment as he joined Lisa. "Well, fair maiden, are you set for a stomping good time tonight?"

Lisa raised the magic wand she held and tapped Bob lightly on the shoulder. "At midnight," she said solemnly, "you will be transformed into a pumpkin."

"Oh, great. Just what I need." He stood beside her and scanned the gym. Indicating the band, he asked, "Are they any good? From what I heard in the parking lot, they sounded pretty loud."

Lisa smiled. "They have to be loud or they aren't any good. Don't you know anything?"

Students were beginning to wander into the gym. At exactly eight o'clock, the band took the stage and lit into their first number. A few students made it onto the dance floor; others wandered over to the refreshments.

Bob watched as several paper cups were filled with punch. He realized that the punch looked very dark, and he looked over at Lisa. "Are my eyes playing tricks on me, or does that punch look like blood?"

Another cup of punch was poured, and Bob watched the thick red stream fill the cup.

Lisa nodded. "It's not your imagination. It's someone's idea of a joke, I guess. Gruesome, if you ask me."

Bob rubbed his hands together and said in a ghoulish voice, "Perhaps it is an acquired taste."

As more students arrived and began dancing, the motion of their bodies sent the crepe decorations swaying gently. The gym started to feel quite warm, so Bob grabbed Lisa's arm and led her over to the punch bowl. "Let's take our lives into our hands and try that stuff," he said.

Lisa shook her head. "You can if you want to.

I'll stick to the water fountain."

Bob picked up a cup and took a cautious sip. "Ummm. Not bad. Not bad at all," he said, smiling. "I was right, it is an acquired taste."

Lisa smirked and looked out at the dancers on the floor. "You can acquire mine," she said.

The band finished one song and, after barely enough of a pause for applause, they broke into another.

"Hey, I know this one," Bob said with surprise, when the opening notes of "Satisfaction" filled the gym.

Lisa nodded and walked onto the floor, trailing the gauze behind her. She scooped it up and held it as they danced. Bob noticed that Lisa was keeping a respectable distance from him.

As they moved about the floor, doing steps Bob didn't even think he remembered, Bob kept surveying the students in the gym. Everybody looked as though they were having fun. The only disappointment was that not many of the students were wearing costumes.

They finished their dance and, as the band worked into another number Bob didn't recognize, they walked back over to the refreshments to try some of the Halloween cupcakes and cookies. Bob bit into a pumpkin-face cookie. He took the punch ladle and began to stir the thick red punch. He felt a wave of revulsion as he poured a glass and offered it to Lisa.

She shook her head. "I reached my limit with that before I had my first one." She looked away again, and Bob finally realized that, as they had agreed, she was playing it very cool. He nodded, took the glass for himself, and stood watching the dancing students.

When they finished the song, the lead singer announced that the band would be taking a fifteen-minute break. A wave of babbling voices filled the gym.

"Well," Bob said, "I'm glad we can finally hear ourselves think." He took a sip of punch and wiped his mouth with the back of his hand. He felt a slight jolt when he saw the back of his hand was smeared bright red.

"Not a bad turn-on, huh?" a voice close behind him said.

Bob turned and almost knocked over Ned Simmons. He was the last person Bob would have expected to see at a school social function.

"No, uh, not bad at all."

Ned smirked and looked down at his feet with an unfocused stare. Bob looked at the boy and wondered if he had been drinking. His face looked deathly pale and he was wobbling, as though he needed support.

"Have you got a date tonight, Ned?" Bob asked brightly.

Ned looked up at him. His eyes looked distant and lifeless. "Uhh, no. I asked, ahh, Julie, but she was busy tonight."

"Julie Sikes?" Bob asked with surprise. He cast a quick glance over at Lisa, who had heard the exchange. Her eyes were widened with surprise too, but she shrugged and looked away.

"Yeah," Ned continued, "she couldn't make it,

but I thought I'd drop by. There's no place else to go." Ned chuckled. "I mean, I'm not into smashing pumpkins or anything."

"Yeah. This is the place to be," Bob said cheerfully. He had watched Ned carefully as he spoke, and he was becoming increasingly concerned about the boy's health. Bob kept thinking that he looked like someone who had just gotten over a serious illness.

"You did a great job on the decorations," Ned said. "Real nice."

Bob tensed. Ned's comment again reminded him of Wendy Stillman and what had happened to her. "Yeah. We worked real hard on them that night. . . ." Bob said, but he let his voice trail off.

"The night Wendy Stillman died," Ned finished, half under his breath. To Bob, he sounded like someone talking in his sleep, and his eyes were glazed over as he looked out at the crowd of students.

Suddenly, the band started again. Someone hit the light switches, and the banks of fluorescent lights on the ceiling winked off. More students had arrived during the break, and soon the floor was packed with gyrating bodies. Bob was grateful for the sudden transition because he wouldn't have to reply to Ned's last comment. He looked down at the frayed edge of his paper cup and tossed it into the wastebasket beside the table.

He grabbed a new paper cup and started filling it. "You want some?" he called over to Ned.

Ned nodded and, walking over to the table, accepted the cup from Bob. When he looked up to hand Ned the cup, Bob was stunned into a split-second of immobility. The red spotlight was directly behind Ned, and the angle was just right so a hot red glow surrounded his head like an unholy halo.

Ned took a sip and said, "Too bad there's nothing stronger."

"Sorry," Bob stammered unthinkingly. He tried to look away but couldn't. His hands shook, sloshing cold red punch onto his wrist. The red nimbus behind Ned's head seemed to pulsate with Bob's rapidly beating heart.

The music, once loud and abrasive, now seemed muted, fading and flickering in and out as though someone were playing with the controls. Bob, feeling flushed and on the verge of fainting, struggled to fight down his rising panic.

Finally, he tore his eyes away from Ned and looked out over the sea of smiling, bobbing faces. Heads bounced lazily to the distant, hazy beat of the music. The dancers' movements, like the music, seemed to be slowing down into sluggish, plodding motions.

Happy grins suddenly took on aspects of frozen grimaces, as though everyone had worn masks. Tight mouths twisted into soundless, open-mouthed shrieks. Eyes filled with the angry red light from overhead reflected a dull, dead blankness. It appeared as though everyone in the gym was merely a part of one gigantic, writhing animal.

Bob staggered back a few steps and swiped his hand across his face. His cup dropped to the floor with a dull plop. Waves of heated panic swept over him.

He blinked his eyes forcefully, but the vision did not disappear. A quick, paranoid thought flashed through his mind that someone had spiked his drink with LSD. His anxiety rose higher, and he wanted to scream to relieve the tension.

His mouth was open, and he could feel gulps of air scratch his sand-coated throat. He wanted to shout, to cry, to scream until everything returned to normal, but his voice was frozen.

Suddenly, Lisa realized what was happening and darted forward. She grabbed him by the elbows and steadied him as she led him over to the side door. The backs of his knees ached wildly, and he leaned on her for fear of falling down.

By the side door, she let him lean against the wall. He watched as Lisa's mouth formed words, but what he heard sounded like gibberish. The darkness swelled and pressed against him.

Again, Lisa's mouth moved, and this time Bob understood her. "Are you all right, Bob? What's the matter?" she asked frowning.

Bob shook his head with a sharp snap, but still the fogginess remained. He stared into Lisa's wide-open eyes, seeing his own panic reflected there. Then, with an abrupt whoosh, the music grew louder. Once again the dancers moved normally.

"Yeah, yeah," Bob said, shakily, "I think I'm

OK." He massaged the back of his neck and looking up at the ceiling. His voice sounded strange to him. "Must be the heat that's getting to me." He forced himself to inhale deeply, evenly.

"You still don't look so hot," Lisa said. "Do you want to sit down for a minute?" Her grip tightened on his arm and pulled.

Bob pulled away from her grasp. "It's so damn hot in here. I think I'll take a walk outside and have a cigarette. Want to come?"

Lisa shook her head. "I'll stay here, I think."

"I'll be right back then," Bob said quickly. He turned and barreled through the door, ignoring everyone in his path.

.II.

Once outside, Bob let the cool air wash over him like water. He shivered because he had not taken his jacket, but the cold felt good and he decided not to go back for it. He lit his cigarette and decided that once around the school should unwind him.

He walked slowly, taking long, even puffs, watching the smoke drift lazily away. He tried not to think about what had happened in the gym. He tried to convince himself that it had been the noise, the heat, the confusion, but he couldn't shake the image of Ned standing there with the red spotlight glowing eerily behind his head. The image unnerved Bob, and for some unexplained reason, he felt that the image was connected with Wendy Stillman.

He turned a corner of the building and was just moving along the back side of the school when he saw someone else come around the corner at the far end. The man was walking unsteadily (Bob could tell that even at such a distance) when he suddenly stopped, unhitched his pants, and urinated on the side of the building. Bob could see his profile clearly against the backdrop of the lighted parking lot.

The man finished his business, zipped his pants shut, and was starting toward Bob again when someone else came around the corner. It was a woman. Bob stood still and watched as he heard Lisa's voice cry out, "For crying out loud, Jeff, will you please take it easy?"

"Shut up!" the man snapped.

"It's nothing to get excited about!" Lisa shouted. Her fairy princess veil, bunched up in her hands, glowed with a blue haze.

"I tole yah to shut the fuck up," Jeff slurred. Lisa stood still as Jeff took a menacing step toward her with a raised fist. "I tole yah I'm gonna settle things my way, you goddamnbitch."

"Jeff, please!"

Bob was not sure whether or not he should intervene in this family argument, but he knew that Jeff was drunk, and he didn't want Lisa to get beaten up again. He started toward the couple and had come to within ten feet of Jeff's back before the man knew he was there and turned around.

"Just the man I'm lookin' for," Jeff slurred thickly, as he dropped into a crouch and raised both fists. "Come on! Come on, you bastard and get what's comin' to yah!" He belched loudly and wavered unsteadily.

"Wha—what the hell are you talking about?" Bob asked in surprise.

Jeff lurched forward. "You know goddamn well what I'm talkin' 'bout, mister hot-shit English-teacher! You been dippin' your wick in places you ain't supposed to."

Bob took a quick step backward. Although Jeff was so drunk that he was almost falling over, he was still bigger than Bob, and Bob didn't want to tangle with him; his fighting reflexes might not be impaired by the alcohol.

"Please, Jeff," Lisa pleaded. Bob glanced over at her, hunched in the shadow of the school building. He had a sudden, silly image that she was a princess and he was her champion.

"Really, Jeff," Bob said soothingly, as though talking to a frightened child. "Why don't you just take a minute to cool off and think about it."

"Bullshit!" Jeff bellowed, his voice almost breaking. "You've been messin' with my wife, 'n' nobody does that without answerin' to me!" He thumped his chest with his fist and took a step closer to Bob.

"Let's go inside and—" was all Bob got to say. Jeff attacked quicker than Bob thought he could, his fist landing squarely on Bob's jaw. Bob spun around from the impact and fell to his knees.

The warm, salty taste of blood filled his mouth. He held his jaw with one hand and raised the other to ward off a second blow, but when he looked up, he saw that the momentum of his punch had carried Jeff around. The drunk man stood off to the side, yelling, "Come on, you mother-fuckin' coward. Where'd you go? Where are you?"

Bob stood up slowly and spit out a mouthful of blood. He worked his tongue around in his mouth to check for loose teeth and was relieved to find none.

Lisa was still cringing in the shadows, uncertain who to go to for help.

Jeff, from his crouch, spotted Bob standing there on weak legs, rubbing his jaw. "There you are, you prick," he shouted.

This time Bob was ready, and when Jeff threw his punch, Bob sidestepped it easily. Jeff's haymaker whistled through the air, throwing him wildly off balance. He spun around in a complete circle and flopped onto his back with a loud grunt. He lay unmoving, staring up blankly at the stars. His breath rattled in his lungs.

Lisa screamed and ran forward to her husband. She knelt down and cradled his head in her lap, stroking his forehead. Jeff struggled for a moment to get up, found that he couldn't, and then dropped back into Lisa's lap with a sigh.

"I never even hit him," Bob said as he walked over and stood behind Lisa.

Jeff rolled his head from side to side. His groaning grew louder, and then a thick gurgle rolled in his throat. Without even raising his head, he vomited all over his chest. Lisa sat, unmoved.

"Honest, Lisa," Bob pleaded, "I didn't touch him. I didn't want to hurt him."

"I know. I know!" she shouted in a pained voice that Bob could barely hear above Jeff's retching. Jeff suddenly stiffened and then, mercifully, lost consciousness.

"For God's sake, Bob, will you help me with him?" Lisa cried out. Tears streaked her face. Her fairy-princess dress was stained with vomit.

She shifted from underneath Jeff's dead weight, and Jeff's head hit the ground with a dull thud. Drool smeared his chin. His eyes were still open, gazing blankly at the sky.

Bob leaned down and grabbed Jeff under the arms. With Lisa's help, they got Jeff standing up. It took both of their strengths to support the dead weight. With one of them on each side, they slowly started to drag Jeff toward the parking lot, his head flopping loosely back and forth with each step they took.

Once they got him over to the parking lot, they laid him across the hood of his car. Lisa fished in Jeff's pants pockets for the keys.

"Do you want me to drive?" Bob asked, after they had loaded Jeff into the passenger seat. "You're going to need help getting him upstairs."

Lisa pointed at the school. "One of us has to stay. And I'm sure as heck not going in there looking like this! I can get Mr. Herlihy from downstairs to help me."

"You sure?"

Lisa nodded and managed a weak smile.

"What are you going to do about your car? Do you want me to bring it over after the dance?"

Lisa nodded. "If you don't mind."

"I don't mind," Bob said.

Lisa started to get in behind the wheel of Jeff's car. Bob caught her by the shoulders and looked at her intently. "I've got to say this, Lisa," he said seriously. He tried to ignore the tear stains on her cheeks. "I don't think he's much of a person, or husband."

.III.

An hour later, after a phone call to Lisa assured him that everything was all right, Bob stood quietly at the foot of the stage. The band was on break, and he was grateful for the relative quiet in the gym. He was standing near a group of students when a dancer rushed up and said, "He's leaving now. Come on."

In an instant, four or five students ran and got their coats and slipped out the side door. Curious, Bob followed them.

He stood for a moment, hiding in the shadows of an alcove as more of the costumed partyers went by. "Everything's set," he heard someone say as they headed toward the parking lot.

Staying hidden in the shadows, Bob watched with interest as the students gathered together around several cars. Then the door to the gym crashed open, and Ned Simmons strode out into the night.

Ned hesitated for a moment when he saw the group hanging around, then he squared his shoulders and walked over to his truck.

Everyone pretended indifference as Ned got in, shut the door and turned the key. A faint chugging sound came from the motor. Then, just before the truck should have started, there was a dull thump that sounded to Bob like a firecracker going off under water. The young people laughed loudly as a billowing cloud of blue smoke rose from underneath the hood of Ned's truck.

"Trick or treat!" several of them shouted and whooped.

"Hey!" someone yelled with mock surprise, "What's the matter with Ned's truck?"

"Do you need a tune-up?" someone called out.

The crowd spread out and made a circle around Ned. Their wild hooting filled the night as he sat tensely gripping the steering wheel.

Bob started across the parking lot when he saw Alan Tate walk up and lean against the truck door so Ned couldn't get out. The cloud of smoke still hung, suspended in the air. Bob caught the sickening aroma of burning sulfur.

"You're OK, aren't you, Neddie-pooh?" Alan said in a taunting voice. "Don't worry, we'll get your crate, I mean truck, going. Won't we?"

The crowd laughed as Ned forced his way out of the cab and went to the front of the truck. He raised the hood and waved his hands to dispel the remaining smoke. Alan Tate stood nearby, his arms across his chest and his hip cocked to the side. Everyone else backed away when they saw Bob coming.

. Bob heard Ned curse softly as he peered down at his truck motor. A small pumpkin had been smashed on top of the distributor, spewing pumpkin seeds all over the inside. Taped to the inside of the radiator was the remains of a smoke bomb. Ned ripped this out and threw it at Alan's feet.

"You prick," Ned whispered shrilly, glaring at Alan.

"What?" Alan said, with mock innocence. "I didn't do anything."

"If this is wrecked, you're gonna pay for it!"

"Sure, sure," Alan said, smirking.

Ned snatched up a piece of the shattered pumpkin and threw it at Alan. It bounced off the boy's chest, then splattered on the ground. Alan looked at Ned with surprise, then rushed forward. Bob jumped in between the two boys, holding them apart at arm's length.

"Hold it! Hold it!" he shouted. "We don't want any trouble here."

"He started it," Ned said through clenched teeth.

"Well you can end it right now by just forgetting about it," Bob said calmly. The anger that raged in Ned's eyes frightened even Bob.

"The hell I will!" Ned shouted. Spittle flew from his mouth, spraying Bob's cheek.

"Can't you take a joke, Neddie-pooh?" Alan asked.

Bob turned to him angrily and said, "You can just cut that out right now!"

Alan pinched his nose and waved his hand in front of his face. "Whew! What's that stink? Did you let one, Neddie-pooh?"

Ned pressed against Bob's restraining hand, pushing toward Alan. Bob could feel the boy's chest heaving with agitation. Then, abruptly, Ned pulled back and shook away Bob's hand. "You're gonna be sorry for this, Tate," he said, in a voice so controlled and tense that it was more frightening than his shouting. "You're gonna be real sorry you even showed your ugly fucking face around here!"

"Let's just take it easy," Bob said, still afraid something more would happen.

Ned spun on his heel and slammed the hood down. He climbed up into the cab and started the truck. Alan jumped up onto the running board on the passenger side and pressed his face against the glass. He stuck out his tongue and smiled viciously.

Ned stepped on the gas, and as the truck lurched ahead, Alan jumped off and stood with his hands on his stomach, laughing.

Ned rolled down his window and stuck out his head. "You'll be sorry for this! All of you!" he shouted to the cheering crowd as he drove out of the parking lot.

Julie's hands were shaking. Her long fingernails clicked together as she swung the red cord behind her back, looped it over once, and tied it in a loose knot that hung on her left side. Except for the braided red sash, she was naked as she stood beneath the tree in her front yard and looked up at the moon.

Tonight, she thought, tonight is the most blessed and holy of nights. All Hallows Eve! The beginning of Samhain!

Shivering, she ran her hands over her body, teasing her nipples until they stood out like spikes. She kept her eyes fixed on the moon, a thin fingernail-paring that was hanging low in the sky out over the lake.

Slowly, her hands opened as though to grab something. She reached up over her head and lowered them three times.

"Feel the rising strength of our sister moon," she muttered softly. "Feel it build. Feel it grow like the unwinding power of a coiled serpent. Come! Give me power!"

Turning quickly, she walked into her house, snapped off all the lights, locked the door, and walked ceremoniously down the steps to her cellar.

She had drawn the pentangle earlier. Five small yellow candles burned, one in each point of the star. A worn leather bag and a jar had been placed in the center of the star. Carefully, so as not to smudge the lines, Julie stepped within the magic diagram.

"Come! Aid me! Give me power!" she said in a voice loud and hard with authority. She turned slowly counterclockwise as she uttered a brief prayer for protection. When this was done, she brushed the hair from her eyes and dropped to her knees in front of the leather pouch and the jar.

Eyes closed, she sat for a long time with her hands placed lightly on her thighs. Her skin glistened with sweat, even though the room was cool and damp. Her breathing sounded almost as if she were asleep, but it began to increase in tempo as she began to move her hands over her body, caressing herself. She held her heavy breasts in her hands and moaned softly as she massaged them.

Opening her eyes, she looked around at the dark corners of the cellar. Then, sighing, she reached into the leather bag, withdrawing a small rectangle of cloth, a torn pocket from a man's shirt. In the light of the candles, the piece of cloth seemed almost to glow.

Carefully, she flattened the faded cloth out on the earthen floor. Then, uncovering the jar, she poured a small amount of its contents onto the piece of cloth, her nose wrinkling from the thick stench of belladonna, ash, sweet flag, and chicken fat. The mixture poured like coagulated India ink.

She rubbed the gooey liquid into the cloth with her index finger, then sat back on her heels with satisfaction. After a moment, she reached into the leather bag again and withdrew a square of bristly gray fir, like that of a dog.

She repeated the procedure of pouring out a small amount of the black mixture and rubbing it into the piece of fur. Taking the cloth in one hand, the fur in the other, she stood up and raised them over her head.

"On the open field shines the moon, the silver goddess," she said shrilly. The noxious odor of the substance grew stronger, and she had to fight back her gag reflex.

"On the ashen stump, in the greenwood, runs the shaggy wolf into the moonlit night." Her voice grew firmer, stronger.

She held the two pieces of material overhead and slowly brought them together. Grunting, she pressed them against each other and watched as the black mixture oozed out from between them and ran down her arms. A thrill coarsed through her body.

"Under his teeth are all the beasts of the wild!" she shrilled. Her breathing grew shorter, sharper. Lines of sweat rolled from her armpits down her sides. The now joined pieces made a faint squishing sound as she rubbed them together.

She knelt down again and carefully, so as not to burn the cloth and fur, held them over the candle at the top point of the star. Just as they started to singe, she pulled them back and sat on her heels.

Moon! Moon! Silver horns! Melt the bullet and blunt the knife that none may take the life. Strike fear into the hearts of men, beast, and reptile! None may kill the gray wolf nor steal from him his warm hide!"

Her voice broke as air came into her throat like fire. She jabbed her index finger into the black mixture and, in one quick slash, drew a thick line across her forehead. The mixture seemed to burn her skin and she began to sway wildly back and forth as though intoxicated.

She raised her hands over her head and made two fists, which she shook at the ceiling. "My word is as firm as the death of the world!"

She dipped her hand into the mixture again and this time scooped up a large glop. Spreading her legs, she applied it to her vagina. Gently, she started to rock forward and backward until the tempo gradually increased. She ran her black coated finger inside herself and groaned with a deep passion.

There was a sudden rush, a roaring in her ears like a blast of wind. Dripping sweat, her body shook with a prolonged shudder. The flames of the candles in the room seemed to sputter and flicker. Julie watched, dumb with fright, unsure if the raging wind was just in her ears or really there in the closed confines of her cellar.

Her hands fluttered to her face, covering her mouth as it twisted with soundless words. Then, falling backward onto the hard floor, she passed out. Her hand was still clutching the black-stained cloth and fur.

The coffee was still warm in his belly as Lisa pulled her car into the high school parking lot. The lot was empty except for Bob's car. The school was dark and quiet. It had, surprisingly, suffered little of the usual Halloween damage.

"Thanks for all of your help," Lisa said, as she pulled up beside Bob's car and shifted into neutral. "I'm, I'm sorry if I upset you with anything I said."

"It wasn't you," Bob replied soothingly. "But I'll tell you one thing, I sure hope to hell old Jeff wakes up with a terrific hangover and the taste of parakeet shit in his mouth."

Lisa grunted.

"Well, I'll give you a call tomorrow to see how everything is. You're not afraid he'll, he'll hurt you, are you?"

Lisa shook her head. "He probably won't even remember it."

"Good for him!" Bob said. He got out and went over to his car. He waited while Lisa drove out of the parking lot, and then followed behind her, giving her a quick toot on his horn.

Lisa turned right, heading back into town. Bob turned left toward Old Jepson's Road. Then, on an impulse, instead of taking another left toward home, he turned right and headed out to the cemetery. He was thinking that a quick swing past the cemetery would, would—"What?" he asked himself out loud.

"What the hell are you doing?"

He bit down on his lower lip as he slowed for the turn. On his right he could see the grove of cedars standing out dark against the starry sky. As he drove along one side of the graveyard, he chanced an occasional glance at the rows of tombstones.

"Well," he said to himself, "what better place to be on Halloween night?" He was driving slowly along the length of the cemetery, looking for—for what? Vandals? The white cat? A dog that looks like a wolf, with human hands?

He shuddered, and then grunted with surprise when he saw something sitting, hunched up by one of the granite gates.

Too big to be the white cat! he thought as he peered ahead at the indistinct form. He drew up close to the gate and swung his car up so the light fell full upon the driveway into the graveyard.

Sitting on the ground, leaning against the granite gatepost, stripped naked and tied with more than a dozen loops of rope was Ned Simmons.

Bob sat behind the steering wheel staring openmouthed for a moment. "Good Lord," he muttered, switching off the car and getting out.

Ned, apparently unsure who had driven up, squinted into the glaring headlights with a mixture of hope and fear. Bob walked over quickly to the trussed-up boy and started working to loosen the knots.

"Who did this to you?" Bob asked.

Ned didn't reply, but Bob thought he had a pretty good idea who was to blame for this humiliation. As Bob worked to untie Ned, Ned let his head hang loosely on his chest. Bob moved the boy around and he was surprised at how loose and flaccid the boy's body seemed.

"I don't suppose you'd care to tell me who did this?" Bob asked gently. He had Ned's hands free and started to work on the ropes that bound his ankles.

"Well," he said, "if you won't tell me, I'll—"

"You don't know who did this?" Ned said suddenly, in a voice cracked and raw from screaming. "Go on, take a guess."

Once he got Ned's feet free, Bob helped the boy to his feet. He had to support him until the circulation returned to his legs.

"Where'd they leave your clothes?" Bob asked.

"Over there," Ned replied, indicating the ditch on the other side of the road. Bob started to coil up the rope.

"Well, go and get them. Get dressed, and I'll give you a ride home."

Ned's lower lip was trembling furiously as he backed away from Bob and crossed the street. A low growl rattled in his throat. Then, suddenly, he dashed down into the ditch, scooped up his clothes, and started running down the street.

"Hey!" Bob yelled, surprised at how fast Ned ran. "Come on back! I'll give you a ride!" He cupped his hands to his mouth and shouted again, but had to stand there uselessly as Ned receded into the darkness that swallowed the road past the streetlight.

Bob turned and walked sullenly back to his car. He drove home and, feeling dejected, walked into the bathroom. He hadn't noticed that, as he drove, he had picked at the scab that remained from the cat's scratch. He looked in the mirror and saw a thin trickle of blood drying on his cheek.

PART II: "THE MOONLIGHT IN HIS CAVE"

Chapter Nine

Monday, November 17

.I.

Frank Simmons was grateful for the light dusting of snow that had fallen overnight. It made it much easier to follow the trail of the wounded deer he was following. For over an hour he had been tracking the splotches of blood that diffused and turned pink in the snow.

He knew he was getting close to the animal, but he took no precautions to try to be silent. Judging by the amount of blood he had seen, the animal would have to weaken and die soon. He hoped so. It was getting dark and the last thing he wanted was a fine for hunting at night. But he had an obligation to end the wounded animal's misery.

As he scuffled down a birch-tree-covered hill, he caught a glimpse of the full moon rising off to his left. It would provide enough light to find his way home, he thought, and then he didn't feel quite so bad when the sun dipped down below the distant mountains.

Dusk gathered quickly, and the blood stains on the snow turned brick-red. Frank could tell by the tingling on the back of his neck that the wounded deer was nearby.

He stopped and listened. The forest was silent except for the hissing of the wind in the branches. The dark purple of the sky closed over the lighter bands of clouds. Adjusting his rifle in his armpit, he followed the deer's footprints. They looked like small inkwells in the snow.

Frank chuckled softly to himself. Here it was, just one week into hunting season and soon, very soon, he would be tagging his kill. What luck! Luck? No, Frank thought, shaking his head, skill. Skill! The others can set up their jack lights and salt licks, or hope to hit a deer while driving. He was the hunter, the stalker!

The trail turned abruptly to the right and ran down the slope to a small stream that wound its way through a boulder-strewn hollow. Frank could see where the deer had stopped and drunk from the still-running water. The ice on the edge of the stream was broken, and the trail continued on the other side.

Frank paused and scanned the other side. The deer might have fallen behind any of the large boulders. It couldn't go much further, he knew. The wind picked up suddenly, and the branches of the birch trees behind him clattered wildly, like rattling dice.

Was that the deer over there? That rounded gray form? Frank raised his rifle and took careful aim. He couldn't be sure in the darkness, so he waited, hoping it would move so he could finish it off with one clean shot.

He stood by the edge of the stream waiting, savoring the end of the hunt. Behind him, he heard a sound that made him jump. It was muffled, like the tearing of cloth. He flicked his eyes to the side, but kept the fallen deer directly in the sights of his rifle.

The wind, or a falling branch, he thought, but when the sound was repeated, he turned around and scanned the slope of the hill.

He saw what looked like the shadow of a cloud moving easily between the birch trees, gliding along the path Frank had made down the hill. As it got closer, the shadow took on a more distinct form.

"No. By Jesus, no!" Frank muttered, as he finally saw clearly the shape of a large dog. Without hurry and apparently without fear, the black shape drew closer.

Thin, pointed muzzle, hunched shoulders, spindly legs, an erect tail raised like a pennant—Frank recognized with mounting horror the shape of a wolf.

"Impossible," he whispered. His rifle, forgotten, hung loosely in his hand.

Thirty feet from him, the animal stopped and rose to its full height.

Frank realized with a flood of fear that he was looking at the horror of his nightmare, the dream that had so frightened him that night at Julie's house. The black shape glared at him, its green eyes flashing in the moonlight. It tilted back its head and let loose a long, mournful howl that throbbed in the still night.

Frank took a step backwards into the stream. His hands were shaking as he watched the animal lower its head and crouch close to the ground. The wolf's haunches worked back and forth as it prepared to attack. The beast's growl rose, rumbling, keeping time with the pulsing beat in Frank's ears.

The present reality and the memory of his dream merged. In blind panic, Frank raised his rifle to his shoulder and fired.

The report shattered the night. An orange flame leaped from the rifle barrel. The animal thrust its head forward and then charged.

Quickly, Frank cocked his rifle and took more careful aim. The wolf launched just as the rifle roared. The animal let out a loud yelp as Frank saw the jaws open to engulf him. The white teeth flashed in the moonlight and Frank felt the animal's fetid breath on his face. Then the jaws clamped down on his shoulder with a tearing, ripping pain.

Frank was carried back by the weight of the animal. His arms pinwheeled wildly, looking for support behind him, and his rifle flew off into the darkness.

For a frenzied moment, Frank lay in the stream. The animal withdrew and paced on the shore, studying the wounded man. With his arm hanging uselessly at his side, Frank scrambled up the shore and finally collapsed beside one of the large boulders. He leaned back, letting his head rest against the cold stone as he watched the animal pacing back and forth on the other shore.

The warm flood of blood from his torn shoulder soaked through his shirt and seeped down his side and back. In a dull, dim way, he knew that even if the animal didn't attack again, he would probably die from blood loss before he could get out of the woods.

The beast's gravelly growl rose in intensity, and the green eyes glowed and pulsated in the dark. Then with remarkable ease, the wolf leapt the stream and in two bounds shot at Frank.

The jaws reached for Frank's throat and clamped shut, severing Frank's windpipe and neck arteries with the quick slash. A fountain of blood shot up from his neck, spattering the animal's mane.

A dark, widening abyss slid open beneath Frank, and he drifted easily into a realm where, mercifully, the pain ceased to matter.

The wolf, crouching beside the dead man, was still slightly dazed from the bullet which had creased its skull. With its muzzle resting in the warm, spreading pool of blood, the animal waited until the body stopped twitching. Once silence had settled back on the forest, the wolf tore open the man's belly and began to eat.

.II.

Later that night, as the full moon sank behind a bank of clouds, a wounded deer struggled to its feet, took three wobbling steps, and then fell down dead. At least it had not died alone.

.III.

Tuesday, November 18

The sun was not yet up when Ned awoke with a start. The dream that had made him twist and groan on his bed all night slowly faded as the sky began to brighten. Slowly, reluctantly, the dream gave way to a dull ache that soon blossomed into a sharp headache. His eyes came to rest on the lightening gray square of the ceiling, and for a moment he felt better. Then the waves of pain increased with his pounding pulse.

Ned heard the scuffling of his mother's bedroom slippers at the foot of the stairs. "Ned? Frank? Get up now!" she called.

Her voice made Ned jump, and the movement caused such great pain he almost screamed aloud. Finally, with some effort, he managed to say, "Yeah, yeah. Coming."

He ran his fingers through his hair and found that on the left side of his head, the hair was matted into sticky clumps. He sat up and looked down at his pillow. The pillow case was smeared with blood.

The dream came back, clearer and more real. He leaped from bed and stood there looking at the bloody pillow, shaking.

"Ned! Frank! Right now!"

How can a dream make you bleed? Ned wondered madly. Can a dream be so real it can really have a physical effect?

Ned took three quick steps over to his bureau and stared at his reflection in the mirror. His skin was ashy pale in the morning light, and the left side of his face was crusted with blood. He felt the wound on his forehead with his fingers, gently at first; then he pulled the cut open. Blood ran down and fell onto the top of the bureau.

"Ned! Frank!"

"I'm coming," Ned answered weakly, and then for the first time realized that Frank hadn't answered.

"Frank?" his mother shouted.

Still no answer.

It didn't really happen! Ned thought. It couldn't! How could it? The pounding in his head increased as Ned stared intently at his reflection. As he focused on the small black circles of his pupils, he had a sudden sensation of being almost transparent, ghostlike.

He shook his head slowly from side to side, all the while keeping his gaze fixed on his own eyes.

How did I get this cut? he wondered, forming the words silently with his mouth. Where did I get this cut?

"Last night, last night," he whispered to himself. He wrinkled his face with concentration as he tried to recollect his thoughts and memories. As far as he could remember, he had finished his chores and homework, and then gone to bed at ten o'clock.

The dream was coming closer to the surface of his mind. Like an ant that has been buried with sand will scramble free, the dream worked its way up to reality.

Did I go out last night? Late? Once everyone was asleep? he asked himself.

He caught a fleeting image of a ball, a cold blue ball, the moon. Yes! A full moon!

Ned ran his hands over his face as though washing it. He was unmindful of the pain when he pulled the wound open further. Blood wiggled down his cheek, tickling as it touched the corner of his mouth.

The taste of blood! There was a hill, a birch-covered hill. Something lay there by a boulder, dying!

As the image of something dying came closer and clearer, the taste of blood in Ned's mouth grew stronger until he felt he was going to choke on it.

The taste of blood!

"Ahhhhhhh!" he screamed, watching intently in the mirror as his face contorted with the painful memory. His fingers clawed at his face, leaving white lines that quickly began to well up.

"No! No! No! I didn't do it! I didn't do it!" he shouted when, instead of his own face in the mirror, he saw the face of his brother Frank. He was wearing a blank, lifeless grin. He gripped the bureau top until his fingernails bit into the soft pine.

He snapped his head around when he heard a car driving up their driveway. He dashed over to the window and felt a nauseating hollowness in his groin when he saw Police Chief Granger and Deputy Thurston get out of their cruiser and walk up to the porch.

Heavy footsteps sounded on the porch. Downstairs, Ned heard his mother shuffle to the door. "Good morning, Roy, Rick. What in tarnation brings you out this way so early? Come on in. I'll put the coffee on."

"No thank you, Mrs. Simmons," Granger said firmly. His voice sounded muffled, but it carried upstairs.

Ned went back over to the mirror and stared at himself. "It was real!" he whispered in a hollow voice. "It really happened!"

When the face in the mirror started to shift again into the lifeless face of his brother, Ned cocked his arm back and drove his fist into the glass. The mirror shattered into a spreading spiderweb.

"I'm afraid we have some bad news for you, Mrs. Simmons," Granger said compassionately. Ned pictured his mother easing herself down into the safety of a chair before Granger continued. "Frank was out hunting last night. Reggie Veilleux said he was going to be out by Cushing's Stream."

"I know," Ned whispered to his shattered reflection, "I was there too."

"After dark. It seems as though he, he met with something."

"What?" Ellie Simmons shrilled. "What happened to Frank?" Her voice echoed like thin metal in the stairwell.

Granger said solemnly, "I'm sorry, Ellie. He's dead."

"No! You can't mean it! Frank's not dead!"

"He's at Doc Stetson's now. Doc'll check him over, and we'll call the county examiner later today. You probably shouldn't go down until later this afternoon."

"Dead! Dead! No, dear God, he can't be dead!" Ellie wailed, and then she broke down into tears.

"I'm awfully sorry, Ellie. We ain't quite sure what happened, but you can be damn sure we're gonna find out."

Ned's mind was filled with the image of his dead brother's face and the warm taste of blood. "I did it!" he whispered. "I did it!" And suddenly he felt like laughing.

Ned walked over to the pile of clothes he had worn yesterday and began to dress. Quickly, he slid into his blue jeans and flannel shirt. He sat down on the bed and pulled on his socks and boots. His mind was a whirring confusion.

Frank is dead and I killed him!

Frank is dead and I killed him!

His mind kept repeating this in a rising fury.

"Ned," his mother called softly from the stairs.

It was not her usual voice at all; it sounded broken and defeated. "Could you come down, please?"

"I, I heard," he answered simply, wondering what his voice sounded like to her. He waited, listening, his teeth grinding back and forth.

He went to his closet and took out his sheep-skin lined jacket. As he pulled it on, he felt a rush of well-being, vigorous and strong.

Frank is dead and I killed him! his mind repeated. The horror of that sentence was diminishing, and Ned felt a deep sense of joy.

He went into the bathroom and washed the dried blood from his face, then he went downstairs. When he came into the kitchen, his mother rose from her chair and, arms spread wide, rushed toward him.

"Oh, Ned! Ned! What are we gonna do? What are we gonna do?" Her face was bright red and looked as though it would explode.

Ned looked down at the floor and shuffled his feet. "I need some time," he snapped, dodging away from her hug. "I need some time to think."

Frank is dead and I killed him!

He threw open the door and ran out into the cold morning air. He glanced over his shoulder as he ran and saw his mother standing dazed in the doorway.

"Ned, Ned," she called faintly, holding out her arms.

He dashed past the barn, forcing himself not to hear her. Vaulting the fence, he lit out across the field.

Those dreams were real!

Frank is dead and I killed him!

The dark, ice-green of the forest seemed to open its arms and welcome him.

.III.

"You hadn't heard?" Lisa asked, trying to keep her voice down as she glanced at the other customers in the B&B.

Bob fought to control the shaking in his hands. He had a B.L.T. sandwich halfway to his mouth, and he slowly lowered it and put it on the plate. "Of course I've heard. Ned didn't show up for school today, and by the end of homeroom, the whole school was buzzing."

"It's horrible! Do you think, do you think it was the same animal you saw? The one that killed Wendy?"

"What the hell else do you think it was?" Bob snapped angrily. He looked at her tensely.

Lisa was biting her lower lip. "Well, Granger just said it was a hunting accident, and—"

Bob snorted a laugh. "Yeah, sure, a hunting accident! What's he supposed to say? Well, folks, it looks as though there's a killer animal out there in the forest. Be careful, you might be next! I'm sure that'd go over really great with the townspeople."

"Nobody's seen that animal for about a month now," Lisa said evenly. "Frank could have been shot or something."

"Lisa, I just don't think it's likely, that's all. There's something out there that, that—" His voice broke when the sudden image came to his mind of something that looked like a wolf but had human hands.

Lisa reached across the table. "Bob what's the matter?"

Bob shook his head, picked up his sandwich, and tried to take a bite; he suddenly found he had no appetite left. "Let's go outside."

He paid his bill at the counter and held the door open for Lisa as they stepped out into the chilly afternoon sunshine. Ice skimmed the puddles on the sidewalk and crunched underfoot as they made their way toward the library.

Bob walked, holding his hands behind his back. He kept his eyes fixed firmly on the sidewalk. "There's something going on here in town that, well, that I just don't understand. Ned Simmons has something to do with it, too."

"There's a wild dog or a wolf in the woods," Lisa said forcefully. "That's what's going on. It's killing people!"

"It's not just that. It's more than that." Bob stopped abruptly and grabbed Lisa by both shoulders. "I want to tell you something that happened a while ago, something that will sound absolutely crazy, insane; but when it happened, it was so clear, so real, that no matter what I've done to try to convince myself it was otherwise, I still can't come up with anything else."

His intensity gripped Lisa, and she listened

silently as he told her about what he had seen that same night Wendy Stillman had died: the wolf with human hands.

When he was through, Lisa whistled through her teeth and shook her head. "You're right," she said simply, "it does sound crazy."

"And I can't think of any other alternative. Either I saw that animal with human hands or, or I had a hallucination. I'm going crazy."

"Don't be ridiculous," Lisa said warmly. "You're not going crazy."

"Well, I didn't worry about it until the night of the Halloween dance. When I saw Ned standing with the red spotlight behind him, it triggered something."

"Like you said that night, it was the heat, the noise, the confusion."

"But right away," Bob said intensely, "right away, that image of Ned made me think about Wendy! Like, somehow, there's a connection."

Lisa shook her head, then turned and started walking slowly down the street. "You can't help it if something like Wendy's death affected you so. The red spotlight. That was what we were discussing; changing that. I think it'd be normal to connect that with Wendy. It was the last interaction you had with her."

"So how is it all connected with Ned?" Bob asked. He looked at Lisa earnestly, as though she had all the answers, and that made her feel nervous.

"You want to know what I think?" she began. "Well, I think there's no real connection. I think you're making one. Look, you told me about what they did to his truck that night, and then later, you find him tied naked to the cemetery gatepost. I think you just feel sorry for the kid. Nobody should be treated that badly. I mean, I've heard of scapegoating, but this seems to be going a bit too far."

"You should have seen him when he drove away from the school that night. God! His face was so contorted with anger." Bob shuddered with the memory.

"So, simply, I think you feel sōrry for him. Maybe because you've been there when these things happen, you feel responsible in some way."

Bob grunted. "Huh. Maybe." It rang true to him, but deep down, there seemed to be more.

"Do you want a little bit of cheap advice?"

Bob nodded.

"I think you can offer Ned Simmons friendship. He may take it; he may reject it. That's fine. But the last thing Ned needs from you or anybody is pity."

"Yeah, but—"

"Cheap advice, like I said," Lisa chirped before Bob could continue, "but it's true. And that's gonna cost you a quarter." She held out her hand and smiled smugly.

"I think that's what I like most about you. You're so damn practical." He reached into his pocket, took out a quarter, and handed it to her.

"Your next appointment is next Monday, same time," she said, assuming a pseudo-German accent.

They were standing at the bottom of the library steps. Bob wanted to get home and correct some papers. He was about to say good-bye and leave when he remembered something.

"Oh, Lisa, you said that you have a lot of books on witchcraft and occult stuff, right?"

"Uh-huh."

"Are they in now?"

"I think so. Most of them, anyway. Why do you want that stuff for? Don't tell me you're getting into that?" Lisa was standing on the third step, and she scowled down at Bob.

"On no, no. Nothing like that," he said. He fished in his mind for a lie that would sound convincing. "We're, uhh, we're going to be starting *Macbeth* in a few classes soon, and I wanted to get some background."

"The weird sisters, huh? Old 'double, double, toil and trouble! time again."

"Yeah," Bob replied weakly. "I have to get running now, but, well, I guess I can take a look now," he said, following Lisa up the steps to the library.

.IV.

"Have you finished your aisle yet, Alan?" Mr. Pomeroy shouted. He stood at the end of the pet-foods aisle and tapped his pencil against his clipboard.

"Not yet, sir," Alan said as he angrily shoved a

209

stack of Calo onto the shelf. He added, under his breath so Pomeroy wouldn't hear, "Not when I have to do mine and Neddie-boy's aisles, I'm not."

"Well, hop-to, hop-to. We'll be closing in a half-hour!" Pomeroy disappeared around the corner, and Alan continued to open boxes and stack the contents on the shelves. He felt some slight sorrow for Ned's family because of Frank's death, but he disliked Ned enough not to care too much.

Alan had all of the cartons empty, and he was just picking up the crushed boxes when the lights overhead flickered and went back on.

"Good evening, ladies and gentlemen. The I.G.A. will be closing shortly. Please come to the registers with your purchases now. Thank you for shopping the I.G.A. way."

Alan ran with the boxes to the back room, threw them into the trash, and quickly undid the knot on his apron. "God night, and good riddance," he muttered, as he hung the apron on its peg and took his jacket.

As he started down the aisle toward the door, he saw Pomeroy still working in an aisle. "Well, goodnight. Do you want me to lock the door?" Alan asked.

"No," Pomeroy said, rising to his feet, "I'll be along in a minute. Goodnight."

Alan stepped outside and glanced up at the starry sky as he zipped up his jacket. He shivered when a vagrant breeze blew into his face. He turned back and saw Pomeroy walking up and down, inspecting Alan's aisle. Alan jabbed his middle finger in the direction of the store manager and then walked over to his car.

As he walked up to his car, he noticed that it was sitting at a sharp angle. The back right side dropped down, and he realized immediately what the problem was.

"Oh, Christ!" he said angrily, walking around the back and looking at the flat tire. "I just hope the damn spare is OK." He had wanted to swing downtown and see who was hanging out. The delay meant that he would have to go straight home. He couldn't be out past ten o'clock on a school night.

He had the trunk open and was fishing out his spare tire and jack when Pomeroy came around the corner. "Alan, how many times do I—" Pomeroy stopped short when he saw what Alan was doing. "Flat tire, huh? Want some help?"

"No thanks," he replied, dropping the jack to the ground with a clatter. "I can handle it. You were gonna say?"

"Ohh," Pomeroy shifted on his feet, "you had forgotten to punch out again. I did it for you."

"Thanks," Alan said simply. He went over to the flat tire and snapped off the hubcap. Pomeroy got into his car and drove off with a short toot on his horn. Alan ran his hand over the flattened tire, trying to feel if there was a hole or something. At the bottom of the tire, his hand encountered a wet, sticky foam.

"What the—" Alan said, raising his hand to the streetlight to see what it was. The bubbly liquid stuck to his fingers with long strings. It looked like saliva.

"Christ on a mountain," Alan said under his breath. He loosened the lugnuts on the tire and then, with some effort, got the car jacked up. He picked up the spare and rolled it over to where he was working. It was then that he saw that the spare too was flat.

"Shit!" he swore, violently punching the flat spare. "Now what the fuck am I supposed to do?"

He stood there beside his jacked-up car, considering for a moment. He knew he would have to call his parents and tell them. If he was late coming home one more time, his father had said he'd take his car away from him. That was the last thing he wanted, next to a flat tire with no spare.

There was a pay phone next to the I.G.A., in front of Drapeau's Hardware and Lumber. He fished in his pocket for change as he made his way across the parking lot.

Alan entered the telephone booth and began dialing his home number. Before he could finish dialing, something slammed into the phone booth with ferocious impact. The phone booth tilted to the side and then righted itself.

Surprised and a bit disoriented, Alan looked around. His first thought was that a car had careened into him, but he didn't remember seeing the headlight.

When he turned around he saw, to his horror, a snarling dog with its face pressed against the glass. The beast had its mouth open, showing a row of long white teeth. Saliva flecked its muzzle. Its angry growl rose steadily.

"Holy shit!" Alan muttered, as he cowered away from the beast. His dialing was forgotten, and he dropped the receiver, letting it hang.

The animal pulled back and, for a moment, Alan thought it was going to leave. But then, without warning, it sprang forward, throwing itself against the glass. With its paws flashing wildly, it clawed the phone booth glass. The sound, mingled with the animal's angry growling, set Alan's teeth on edge.

The phone booth tilted, threatening to fall over as the wild animal pressed its weight against it. Alan was shocked to see that the animal actually seemed to be pushing, its hind feet braced for leverage. Waves of claustrophobia added to Alan's panic, and he crouched on the floor of the phone booth and whimpered.

His eyes rested on the loose receiver, hanging and swinging back and forth as the booth was pushed back further and further. Alan gripped the phone and started dialing.

The animal outside let out a terrifying growl and increased the fury of its attack. Suddenly, the glass of the booth burst inward. Flying shards lacerated Alan's face and hands. His fingers wavered wildly as he tried to complete his call. A paw reached in and snagged the back of his jacket.

"Help me! Help me!" he screamed, even while he was dialing. "Help! Help!" He spun the dial with the last number just as the booth rocked precariously and then started to fall. Alan turned. He was still gripping the receiver, and when he turned, the wire ripped out of the phone.

"Help me! Help me!" he screamed into the dead phone as the booth tipped over and shattered explosively on the sidewalk. A flying piece of glass ripped across Alan's neck and blood spurted out, drenching his chest.

For a moment longer, Alan struggled. His feet kicked wildly in the wreckage of the phone booth as the beast, slowly and confidently, came closer, its mouth gaping wide.

Alan's bladder released a warm flood. He stared, wide-eyed at the gaping mouth as the beast's warm breath washed over him. Consciousness slowly began to slip away, from loss of blood from his neck wound. "Help me! Help meee."

With an angry snarl, the beast tore open the boy's belly and luxuriated in the spreading pool of blood that soaked Alan Tate's body. The wolf ate until he was satisfied, then trotted off into the darkness.

.V.

Wednesday, November 19

For the first time in weeks, Thurston arrived at the office before Granger. He immediately saw the letter addressed to him lying on top of the desk. He sat down and ripped the envelope open.

In response to your requested background check on Mr. Robert A. Wentworth, late of Dorchester, Mass, I am enclosing the following newspaper articles photocopied from *The Boston Globe*. A full background report is in progress.

Sincerely,
Timothy Hatch
Agent- F. B. I. (Boston)

Thurston unfolded the two sheets of paper and read rapidly. As he read, he congratulated himself for having a sharp investigative instinct. He hadn't trusted or liked Bob Wentworth, ever since he interviewed him the morning after Wendy Stillman's murder. Now, as he read, he felt he had even more reason to mistrust Bob Wentworth.

The Boston Globe: March 6, 1973 (Dorchester)

Hearing Held on Rape Charges.
Mr. Robert A. Wentworth, a teacher at Dorchester Public High School, has been charged with rape by Miss Beth Landry, a senior at the school.

Miss Landry alleges that, on the night of January 27, following a dance at the high school, Mr. Wentworth offered her a ride home. When she refused, saying she already had a ride, she says Mr. Wentworth forced her into his car, drove her to an abandoned warehouse lot, and forcibly raped her.

At the hearing today, the charge was sternly denied by Mr. Wentworth and his lawyer.

The date for a formal inquest has been set for next Monday.

The Boston Globe: March 20 (Dorchester)
Teacher Resigns After Rape Charges Dropped.

In an out-of-court agreement today, rape charges stemming from an alleged incident last January have been dropped by the attorney for the plantiff, Miss Beth Landry. Immediately following the decision, Mr. Robert Wentworth appeared on the steps of the courthouse and announced that, due to the harassments associated with the case, he was forced to resign his teaching position. His resignation would take effect immediately, he said.

Footsteps sounding on the doorsteps outside made Thurston jump to his feet. He quickly folded the letter and articles, and stuffed them into his shirt pocket.

Granger burst into the office, his face flushed with agitation. "Come on!" he shouted, as he went to the wall gun-rack and slid the chain to release his rifle. "Something's happened down at Drapeau's."

"What? What is it?" Thurston asked, sensing the excitement.

"I'll tell you on the way," Granger said, as he checked the rifle for ammunition. "But I'll tell you one thing, we've got another one!"

.VI.

The cigarette dangled loosely from his mouth as Bob listened to the ring a ninth, a tenth time. He was just about to hang up when the line clicked and he heard Lisa's voice.

"Hello," she said, her voice still thick with sleep.

Bob snubbed his cigarette out and took a deep breath. "Hi, Lisa. It's me. I hope I didn't wake you up but, well, I only have a minute before homeroom."

"Huh? Yeah. Sure? What is it?" Lisa said, still sounding confused.

"I'm sorry I woke you up, but this is important."

There was a prolonged silence at the other end of the line while Lisa waited for Bob to continue.

"Well, you know those books I took out of the library yesterday, the ones on witchcraft." He paused and looked up at the ceiling, almost afraid to continue.

"Yeah?"

"Well, ummm, there's a section in one on, on lycanthropy."

"Huh?"

"Lycanthropy, the ability of a, uhh, a human being to change into animal form." His neck was beginning to burn with embarrassment.

"Bob, is something the matter?"

"No," he said sharply. "Look, I stayed up late last night reading this stuff. Now I know you're gonna think I've flipped my lid, but when I read that section on lycanthropy, it just made me start to think."

"What did you say it was?" Lisa asked heatedly.

"It's the ability of a person to change into an animal. According to this book, it's a belief that is so widespread, well, they think there might be something to it."

"You mean like werewolves and stuff?" Lisa asked, astonished. "Come on, Bob, this is the twentieth century."

"It has a whole section about the spells witches can use to change themselves or others into animals. That's how they go to the Sabbaths in the woods, by turning into animals. You know, how black cats are supposed to be unlucky?"

"Yeah," Lisa responded, sounding totally unamused.

"Well, that's because witches usually took the form of a cat. Now you've told me that Julie

Sikes reads a lot of this stuff. What if, what if she really believes it, and it works. Maybe she's turning someone, herself or someone else, into a wolf."

"Bob! Don't be ridiculous! That stuff is superstition. It's garbage!" Lisa sighed loudly. "You can't be serious."

"I don't know. I just don't know. But I did see an animal that had human hands. I know what I saw! Now, in this book, it says that if you meet with like a werewolf or something, if you call out the person's name, he'll assume his human shape again."

"Is that what you did?" Lisa asked, deciding to go along with Bob for a minute, just to see how far he would go.

"No. I didn't know who it was. But it also says that if you call out the name of Jesus, the transformation will also start to reverse. I don't know, I can't remember, but if I swore out loud, that would have started changing—whoever—back into human form."

"Is this some kind of joke, Bob?" Lisa asked beginning to get concerned about Bob's mental state.

"Look Lisa," he said firmly. "I know what I saw. It was a wolf with human hands!"

"The animal that's doing this, killing these people, is a wild dog. There have been enough people who have seen it to establish it was a dog, a real animal!"

"That's my point!" Bob shouted. "That's it exactly! The magic ceremony you use for the

transformation really turns you into an animal.
Forget all those *I Was a Teenage Werewolf* horror movies. That's a cheapening of what was, at least for other centuries, a really powerful symbol."

"That's it," Lisa said, "you said it: a symbol. That stuff isn't real. It can't be."

"I'd like to think so," Bob said. The bell for homeroom rang, making Bob jump. "Look, I've got to go to class. I, I don't know what to think, but, but reading this stuff just started to make me think that—"

"It's not real. It can't be," Lisa said firmly. "Look, stop by the library after school this afternoon. We can talk some more."

"Yeah, I've got to get to class. See your later."

"See you," Lisa said. She hung up the phone and listened to her heartbeat thumping in her ears. She was beginning to feel afraid, afraid for or of Bob. Maybe he did have some deep-seated problem. Maybe, after all, he was unstable. She sat there staring at her telephone and started to cry.

Chapter Ten

Wednesday, November 26

.I.

Everyone was already in the office and seated when Granger arrived at nine o'clock. He had been in Portsmouth overnight, meeting with law officials to help with the investigations of the town's recent deaths. He entered the office and nodded a silent greeting to everyone.

Standing against the wall, Rick Thurston was silently sipping at his coffee. Seated in a semicircle around the desk were Ted Seavey, Gene McCann, Ralph Hamlin, and Chuck Doyle. Others had been asked to attend but had declined, choosing instead to spend the day before Thanksgiving with their families.

"I'm glad you could make it," Granger said over his shoulder as he filled his coffee cup from the pot. He walked over to his desk and snatched his badge from the top drawer. Before pinning it on, he buffed it on his chest.

"What we're gonna discuss here today, I want held in strictest confidence." He sat down at his desk and tapped the inkblotter for emphasis. "Things are bad enough in town without lots of wild stories circulating."

"We know it's that damn wild dog, Roy. You can stop the bullshittin' and get to the point," Seavey said. "I've been talkin' with Artie down at the lumberyard and he says—"

"That always has been Artie's biggest problem," Granger snapped. "He talks too damn much!"

The other men in the room exchanged confused glances. Granger motioned for Seavey to stay cool, and then said, "Ted's right, though. It is that wild dog. We're damn lucky there's only one of 'em. Otherwise, if there was a whole pack, this town'd be wiped right out."

Granger pointed his index finger at the group. "Now just be quiet while I talk. You all know about the Tate boy. There's no use trying to disguise the fact that something, something awful damn powerful knocked over that telephone booth before it killed him. Traces around there do indicate that it was a dog, a canine. There are large paw prints, and the lab in Portsmouth determined that the smears on the glass were dog saliva. The holes in the boy's body were also made by a dog."

Granger waved his hand to silence the excited outburst. "So, what do we have? We have three

222

people, all killed in a similar manner, all of them savaged by a wild dog. We know that. I have the lab reports to prove it!"

"So what're we gonna do?" Doyle asked. He sounded frightened.

"This thing has tasted blood, human blood. And it likes it!" Seavey added.

"That's why I called you all here. To tell you what I discussed with the authorities in Portsmouth and to determine a course of action. Of course, we've got to hunt, but we can't do it like we've been doing it. We've got to have it organized."

"That's what Simmons was doing when he got it," Doyle said. "He was hunting."

"Well, the first thing we'll make sure of is that no one goes out alone, or at night."

"But night's the only time the animal's on the prowl, it seems," McCann said.

"Well, it's not the only time that animal is around!" Granger shouted. "It's not the only time we can find him. We can get dogs from the state to track. We know what we're looking for, and if we field enough men, we'll get that damned animal."

"I don't know about that, Roy," Seavey said. "I think we've got one cagey beast on our hands. It's like it almost thinks before it kills, making sure to isolate whoever it's after."

"That's why we aren't going out alone." Granger paused and took a sip of his coffee. It had already cooled off to a point where he didn't like it.

"You said that this was a dog," McCann said, "Are you sure? Did the lab tests prove it?"

"Well," Granger said, "the tests only proved that it was a canine, not necessarily a dog."

"So, like, maybe it could be a wolf or something, right?"

Granger nodded.

"See, I was reading about those coyotes they were having so much trouble with out there in Maine, around Turner and Upton. They called 'em coy-dogs. This article talked about what they called an en-vi-ron-mental niche that was left open when the wolves were killed off in the state. Something has to take the place of the wolves, so the coyotes take it."

"What this animal is doesn't concern me," Granger said heatedly. He leaned forward and pinned McCann with his eyes. "You guys can debate what it is till hell freezes over. I want some action!"

"You're the police chief, so you tell us," Doyle said.

Granger could tell that tempers might flare any minute, so he spoke calmly. "Like I said, we're going to organize and hunt. And I'm not talking about a couple of guys out drunk at night. I mean a full-scale, systematic combing of the area. If we need to, I've made arrangements to get the Forest Service and even the National Guard to help out."

"Hold on a second," Thurston said. He pushed himself off away from the wall where he had been standing quietly. "I'm not so sure that calling in the National Guard is what we need."

"You don't, huh?" Granger asked, glaring up at Thurston as he walked over and stood beside the desk.

Thurston placed his hands on his hips. "There's another possibility that no one's mentioned yet."

"And that is?" Granger said impatiently.

"That is, that it might not be an animal at all: that it might be a person who's doing this."

The room was silent for a moment, then Granger chuckled. "You don't mean to tell me that—"

"It's an angle we haven't considered, and I think we should." He faced his superior with a harsh look of challenge. "I won't deny that there's a dog running in the woods. There have been too many reports, too many sightings to deny it. But what if someone was using the situation, the confusion, for a cover?"

"Jesus, Rick, you can't be serious," Granger said aghast.

"I'm serious! Now one of the reasons I'm not for getting the National Guard and who all knows what else involved is that if I'm right, if it's someone, not something, killing these people, the confusion of a full-scale search would only help that person hide."

"We have the lab reports," Granger said. "They found canine saliva in all of the wounds."

"It could be faked," Thurston snapped. "If the person was clever enough, an unattended death could be faked to look like a dog attack."

"Rick, come on. You think there's a psycho loose in town?" Granger shook his head.

"You got any ideas who it could be?" Doyle asked. "You're talkin' like someone who knows more 'n he's sayin'."

Thurston paused and looked up at the ceiling. His hand went to his shirt pocket and started to reach inside. He stopped and patted the pocket. "No," he said softly. "No, I don't. I don't want to accuse anyone. I'm just raising a possibility we haven't touched on."

Granger knuckled his desktop. "Well, I don't see where that would change much. I don't see where it'd be any problem to have some help from a few state services in scouring the area. Hell," he waved his hand, "we could concoct some story about a kid missing to explain the activity. Let's just get some men out there and track this animal down."

"That's another thing," Thurston broke in. "We all agree that we have a problem, a serious problem here. But I think we'd also agree that the people of this town can solve their own problems without getting the state involved."

Everyone but Granger nodded, and Thurston sensed that he had them. He leaned forward and spoke earnestly. "Especially the federal government. We don't need any of this getting into the papers. Our town has a tough enough time with a slew of bad press."

"Rick, we're talking about three, three unsolved murders. People have been killed right here in town! How are you going to keep something like that quiet?"

"Chuck," Thurston said, pointing a finger at Doyle. "You have some cabins you rent to weekend skiers. Do you think you'll be able to rent them if this story gets out?"

"Well," Doyle said, scratching his chin. He huffed and recrossed his arms over his chest. "I can't see as it would help any."

Thurston jabbed his index finger forward. "And you, Ted, don't you think something like this could hurt your business at the store?"

"I don't see where it can get too much worse as it is," Seavey muttered. "But—"

"No but's about it," Thurston said. "If Cooper Falls has a problem, I think Cooper Falls can solve it without everyone from Maine to Florida knowing about it."

Granger frowned deeply and had to hold himself back from grabbing Thurston and shutting him up forcibly. Instead, sensing the feelings in the room, he folded his hands on his desk and said in an even voice, "This is a damn serious situation. I don't see where getting outside help would hurt."

"I think Rick might be right," Doyle said, shifting his weight forward in the chair. "We sure as hell don't need something like this on the cover of *Newsweek* and *Time*. Not with skiing season just startin'."

"We can't go scaring folks away," McCann said softly.

"Ted, what do you think?" Granger asked, almost desperately.

"I dunno," Ted replied. "I just think we ought to get rid of this damn animal as soon as we can."

Granger stood up and banged his fist on the desktop. "What you're saying is that you want to take the chance that someone else will be killed before we bring this animal in."

"I didn't say that," Thurston said defensively. "There's no way of knowing if the goddamn U.S. Army could get it."

"But the more men we have out hunting, the sooner we stand a chance of getting this animal. We can—"

"We got plenty of good men right here in town," Doyle said. "I think we can take care of it."

"That's right," Thurston said. "Now, with a holiday tomorrow, most everyone'll have the day off. Why don't we get together this afternoon and work out a plan?"

Seavey shifted uneasily. "Lots of folks got plans for the holiday. Bess and I were thinkin' of going out to Vermont to see Jeffrey."

"OK. OK," Thurston said. "Then let's make it Friday. Friday evening we'll meet here. Ask around. Try to get as many people with guns as you can get." Thurston stood rubbing his hands together.

"Sounds good," Seavey said, rising. McCann and Doyle followed close behind him.

Granger cleared his throat. "Just one thing before you go, fellas. I think you're making a serious mistake. As police chief of the town, I

228

have the authority to call in anyone I want to help us. If this doesn't work, if by the end of next week we haven't turned up one dead dog, I'm gonna get in touch with Major Norman at the Armory. And"—he took off his badge and dropped it on the desk—"right after that, you can find yourself a new police chief."

Thurston shook his head. "Don't worry, Roy. We'll get him."

.II.

Ned peered ahead intently as he followed the circle of light trail along the walls and floor of the abandoned silver mine. The dried-out wooden support-beams that traversed the ceiling were thick with cobwebs. Everywhere he looked he was reminded of at least a dozen movies in which the beams would sway and creak, a little shower of dirt and gravel would sprinkle down, the ceiling would moan, and then the whole thing would come crashing down, trapping the miners underneath the mountain.

He stopped short and looked back around at the pale blue patch of sky still visible at the mouth of the mine. He had to fight back the impulse to flee the mine. He swallowed hard and pushed on into the darkness, following the dot of light.

After another hundred yards, he came to where the mine branched off in two directions.

He knew that he had to take the left passage, but before continuing, he checked for the red slash of paint he had put on one of the beams.

The bundle he was carrying—a down-filled sleeping bag rolled thick with extra clothing, a heavy winter jacket, and a dozen cans of food—was beginning to hurt his arm. He wedged the flashlight under his armpit and shifted his burden until it was comfortable, then continued on his way.

His sharp breathing echoed hollowly in the empty darkness. His feet scuffed dully in the loose gravel.

After a few more twists and turns in the tunnel, his flashlight beam caught a gleam of metal and threw it back at him. He knew he had made it. After a few more times in, he thought, he would be able to do it without thinking, maybe even without a flashlight, if he had to.

His light beam danced over the old wooden crate upon which he had placed one of the kerosene lanterns he had taken from the barn. His mother would never miss it and, hell, kerosene was much cheaper than flashlight batteries. Next to the wooden crate an old mattress was spread out on the floor. Beside the mattress were two gallon wine-jugs filled with water, a pile of empty cans, and the remnants of the campfire he had had last night. He reminded himself that he would have to gather more firewood soon.

Ned sighed deeply as he snapped a match under his thumbnail and bent down to light the lantern. The warm orange glow quickly spread out to the walls and ceiling, pushing the shadows back but not dissolving them.

He dropped the bedroll down and then flopped face-first onto the mattress. The musty odor assailed his nostrils, but he let himself enjoy the brief rest. He realized that for more than a week now he had felt run-down, exhausted. He needed rest, rest and something more to help him regain his strength.

He knew now with certainty that the dreams were real. How, he had no idea, but he had been there when his brother Frank and again when Alan Tate had died. He was probably there when Wendy Stillman had died too, but that memory of the dream was too deep. But with Frank and Alan, he knew. He had felt the soft, yielding flesh grind between his teeth. He had tasted the hot blood as it gushed into his mouth. He had crunched the bones, snapping them between his jaws. It had been real!

Damn, but it had been real!

Suddenly he jumped to his feet and began pacing back and forth across the hard-packed floor. All the while he rubbed the back of his neck at the top of his spine.

He had been there, he knew. But he had been there in a different body, a body that was hunched and sleek, strong, close to the ground. In that body he had killed his brother and Alan!

The muscles in his neck twisted with tension as he paced back and forth. He worked his fingers harder to relieve the pain.

He didn't understand it, but he knew that somehow he had been transformed.

Transformed!

The word burst in his mind with fireball brilliance.

"Transformed," he whispered shrilly as he stared unblinkingly into the orange glow of the kerosene lamp. "Transformed! I became the animal! I am the wolf!"

With a sudden sharp cry, he spun around and stared down into the darkness of the mine shaft. With the lantern behind him, the light threw his enlarged shadow down the dark corridor.

That was it! he realized with astonishment. I am the shadow, the black shadow that is formed by the light of the full moon! In the light of the full moon, I am the wolf!

He knew, fully. When the moon was full, he had the power, and he could kill whomever he wanted to kill; absolutely anyone he wanted to kill would come under his shadow!

Cocking his head back, he stared into the thick blackness of the mine until it seemed to reach out and enfold him. A low, hollow laugh built in his chest and escaped from his mouth, rising higher and higher. The laughter echoed back from the depths of the mine with a hollow booming.

"I am the wolf!"

.III.

"The body's hardly cold in the ground!" Bob

shouted angrily. He and Lisa were standing together in the church parking lot. Lisa had her coat buttoned up tightly to her chin and her arms folded protectively across her chest. Her breath was a fine mist on the night air.

Bob had his hands stuck in coat pockets. When he wasn't speaking, he paced back and forth in front of her.

"Well, don't you think it's a little bit strange?" he asked, making an effort to keep his voice down. "I mean, we've been divorced about three months now and already she's rushing back to the altar. I couldn't believe it! Calling me up and inviting me to her wedding!"

He stopped pacing and looked at Lisa intently.

"I don't know," she said finally. "I guess it is a bit early to remarry."

Bob snickered and shook his head.

"Cripes, Bob, maybe you just don't realize. She might be a very insecure person who needs to be married. A lot of people feel as though they—"

"There you go with your psychoanalyzing again," Bob snapped. "She's the one who ended it for us. She left me, not the other way around!"

"Don't sound so defensive, for crying out loud," Lisa said. "You're getting too worked up about it. Think about it. This might be the best thing in the world for her. Maybe it'll work out. Maybe this time she found the right guy."

"Oh, thanks. Thanks a lot." He slapped his thighs with frustration.

"You know what I mean," Lisa said mildly. "She's doing what she wants to do, right? You should want what's best for her, too."

They both turned and looked up at the stained-glass windows when the booming notes of the organ suddenly swelled. The bright lights inside lit up the colored patterns, throwing their designs onto the snow-covered ground.

The parking lot was full now. A few stragglers hurried past them, nodding greetings as they went. Bob huffed, looked at Lisa, and resumed his pacing.

"You just have to take it easy," Lisa said smiling. "You're putting yourself under way too much pressure lately. It's not healthy." The concern in her voice was genuine. Since his phone call about a week ago, Bob hadn't mentioned the topic of witchcraft or werewolves again. But it had bothered Lisa quite a bit, and she wondered if he was still thinking along those lines. He had sounded pretty paranoid, and she hoped he wasn't losing touch.

"Stop taking yourself so seriously," she said gently. "Why don't you come to church tonight. The Thanksgiving candlelight service is one of the prettiest of the year. It might do you some good." She reached for his arm, but he pulled away.

"No. I don't feel like it tonight. Maybe some other time."

"You always say 'some other time,'" Lisa pleaded. "I've been after you to come to church with me for months."

"I told you," Bob replied, and there was hostility in his voice, "that I just don't get into it! I'm not a churchgoer!"

Lisa turned and started for the church door without a word. Bob hurried and caught up with her. He looked at her earnestly. "Look, Lisa, I'm kind of uptight. I'm sorry I snapped."

"Yeah, well," she said, shaking her head back and forth as though scolding a child, "just take it easy."

"I promise you I'll come to church on Christmas Eve. Really." He raised his hand in the air. "Promise."

"Shake on it," Lisa said, holding out her hand.

"There," Bob said as they shook.

Lisa said, "I don't want to be late." The choir was already starting the first hymn. She ran up the steps and went into the church.

.IV.

Lisa's face was flushed as she walked up the side aisle, looking for an empty seat. She found one, two rows from the front and eased her way in. Her fingers fumbled with pages of the hymnal, and she didn't join in on the opening hymn until halfway through the last verse. Her voice sounded weak and flat to her as she sang.

When the hymn was finished, Reverend Alder strode to the front of the church and faced the dimly lit painting of Jesus praying in the garden. The music swelled to a crescendo and then dropped off abruptly. As it did, Reverend Alder let his shoulders sag slightly.

He turned and, pulling his sleeves up, faced the congregation. There was a loud explosion of creaking wood as everyone resumed their seats.

"Well," Reverend Alder said, rubbing his hands together like a workman beginning a job. "I'm glad to see so many of you here."

There was another, softer creaking of the pews as people shifted around, getting comfortable. Lisa was still too upset and nervous to feel at ease. Her conversation with Bob had ruined what she had hoped would be a joyful, peaceful night.

"And I think this Thanksgiving season, that we have a lot to be thankful for." A smile stretched across the minister's face, seeming to reach from ear to ear. He held his Bible behind his back with both hands and bounced lightly on his toes. "Of course, you realize this is the end of my dry season, my bad spell. With Christmas just around the corner, I expect to do a land-office business."

There was scattered laughter through the congregation. Lisa, still uncomfortable, shifted in her seat and stared numbly at the minister.

"With Easter coming up, I expect to see plenty of faces that I haven't seen, well, for a year at least."

Again the reverend's comment was followed by laughter. A knot of tension was growing stronger in Lisa's shoulders, and she wiggled to try to relieve it.

Reverend Alder continued, "But you're probably wondering what we have to be thankful for, here in Cooper Falls. Our town has been saddened recently by three tragic, senseless deaths." He paused and looked into the silence that filled the church.

"And then there's the wider scope," he said suddenly, waving his arms wide. "What do we see in the world today? We see hunger, war, and pollution. Our newspapers are filled with stories about child abuse, wife beatings, kidnapping, and hostages. We see close-up and in-depth coverage of every plane crash and train derailment and any other human tragedy . . ."

The reverend went on, but Lisa was having a difficult time concentrating on what he was saying. Her mind was still on the man she had been talking to in the parking lot, a man she probably loved more than her husband, a man she could see was under too much pressure, putting himself under too much pressure, and who might be cracking up.

The reverend's voice rose louder as he raised his arms dramatically over his head. "Like the tribes of Israel wandering in the desert, what do we have to be thankful for? Nothing but a promise! Like the Pilgrims who fled the religious oppression of Europe and braved the dangerous crossing of the Atlantic, what do we have to be thankful for? Only our hope! Only our faith in our Lord!"

Lisa looked up at Reverend Alder, and a thought suddenly struck her.

What if Bob is right? What if there really is something supernatural happening in town?

The thought startled her, and she jumped in her seat, looking around nervously at the faces watching the minister.

If you believe in the power of God, why not believe in the power of Satan? Doesn't one need the other? Isn't Satan the dark side of God? The shadow of God?

"Our life is a tenuous arrangement," Reverend Alder said in conclusion. "And it can be terminated like that! So what do we have to be thankful for, this Thanksgiving? Just this—our lives and our trust in the Lord our God! Let us now sing Hymn Two-hundred and thirty-seven."

There was a brief organ prelude, and then the congregation burst into song. Lisa, standing hunched and angled away from the front of the church, found that she could not sing. There was a hot tightness that gripped her by the throat.

Chapter Eleven

Wednesday, December 17

.I.

Bob had his head resting in one hand as he ticked off the right and wrong answers on the test sheet he was correcting. He heard footsteps approaching his desk but did not look up until he saw a pale hand place a pink slip of paper on his desk beside the tests.

"Would you sign here, in period five?" a dry voice asked.

Bob looked up and saw Ned Simmons. The

boy's pale face showed a hint of a smile, but there was no humor in his darkened eyes.

Bob calmly placed his red pen on top of the test, sat back in his chair, and picked up the pink slip.

"Dropping out of school, huh?" he asked, scanning the slip. It had been folded and unfolded many times. It hung limply in Bob's hand.

"Yeah," Ned answered, looking away.

"You just need mine and Mr. Summers' signatures, and that's it."

Ned crossed his arms over his chest, fluttered his eyes at the ceiling, and sighed.

"Well," Bob said, picking up his red pen and tapping it on the desk, "before I sign any drop-slips, I like to have a chat with the student, see why he wants to drop out. It could be that he—"

"Would you just sign? Please?"

"Pull up a chair, Ned. I'd like to—"

"Mr. Wentworth," Ned said tightly, "I'm kinda in a hurry, so would you just sign your name?" The hostility in his voice was restrained, just barely. Ned made a move to sit down, then compromised by leaning against the desk.

Bob cleared his throat and looked at the boy. What he saw worried him. The boy's pasty complexion had almost no spark of life. He looked underweight and tired.

"You know, Ned, I've been quite concerned about you lately. You've missed more than half the school days since September."

The boy glared at him with glazed eyes. Bob felt slightly unnerved.

"You're a bright boy, Ned. I hate to see you drop out. Heck, it's your senior year. Couldn't you just hang in there until June? A diploma would get you a lot more—"

"Mr. LaFleur already gave me that rap yesterday," Ned said dully. "He earned his paycheck for the week. If you'd just sign on line five . . . ."

"I will," Bob snapped, "when we're through talking."

Ned seemed to cringe back from Bob's outburst. His eyebrows knitted together.

"Have you been feeling well lately?" Bob asked.

Ned looked at him with a frightened stare.

"You look like you could use a little food in your belly. Have you thought of seeing a doctor?"

"I feel fine," Ned said, but the weakness in his voice contradicted him. "I'll be OK in a couple of days or so."

Bob leaned forward and folded his hands on the desktop. "You haven't been having any fainting spells lately? Any dizziness or ringing in your ears? Anything that maybe should be checked out?"

"I'm doing fine," Ned said angrily.

Bob knew he shouldn't press, but he had to; his questions burned in his mind. "Have you had any times when, you know, you just lose touch? Where you wake up and you don't know what's happened? Anything? Anything that seems out of the ordinary?"

"I told you! I've been feeling fine!" Ned picked up the pink slip and held it almost under Bob's nose. "Sign. Please."

Bob stood up and walked slowly over to the window. He stared silently out onto the snow-covered school yard. "So," he said, addressing the window and watching Ned's pale reflection, "what are your plans. You've got to do something with your time. Have you got a job?"

"Pomeroy said he might be able to work me in full-time."

"Might! That's not much of a promise to throw away your education for."

In the reflection of the window, Bob could see Ned's scowl deepen. "Yeah, well, besides, my mother needs a lot more help around the farm now that Frank's dead."

"Ummm. Yeah. I'm sorry about that. It still bothers me."

Ned suddenly snapped his head up and shouted, "What business is it of yours, anyway? I don't need you messing around with my life. Just leave me alone, will you?"

"It's not that. It's not that at all," Bob said as he turned and walked back to the desk. His knees felt weak as he took the slip of paper from Ned. "Sure. Sure. I'll sign," he said with a crackle in his throat. He dashed his name on the fifth line and handed it back to Ned just as the last bell of the day rang.

"Hmmm. Three o'clock already," Bob said,

trying to sound casual as he jogged his tests together and put them into his briefcase. "Well, I guess you won't have to run your life on a bell system any more, will you?"

Ned had already turned to leave, but he stopped at the door and looked at Bob. There was something in his gaze that unnerved Bob: a deep, smoldering hatred and—and suspicion?

"Thanks," Ned said tightly. "You've earned your paycheck for the week," he added, slamming the door shut behind him.

.II.

"I had plans for tonight. Really," Julie pleaded. She pulled back as Jeff Carter's hands ran roughly over her back and shoulders. She shuddered.

"Well you'll just have to put them off, babe, 'cause I've got something else in mind." He slid one hand around to her waist and then ran it up to her breast and squeezed. She wiggled, trying to get away, but Jeff read it as her growing excitement. He pulled her roughly to him and snapped open the three top buttons of her blouse.

The smell of booze on his breath sickened her. "Well, for Christ's sake, Jeff, can't you get it up without getting drunk first?" she asked.

Jeff belched loudly.

"I mean," Julie went on, "it's almost an insult. If you think I—"

"This is no insult," he said, taking her hand and placing it on his bulging crotch. Julie squeezed, hoping to inflict some pain. Jeff took her shoulders and pushed down, making her kneel in front of him. "There you go, babe. How about giving me a little bit of head."

Julie stood up quickly and tried to get away, but Jeff grabbed her and forced her to the couch. He ripped open the remaining buttons and then began to tug her blouse down her shoulders.

"Just loosen up a bit, will yah?" he said, pinning her by the shoulders and shaking her. "Christ, come on!"

He fastened his mouth to hers in a slobbering kiss, jamming his tongue into her mouth. The sour taste of whisky made Julie gag. She pulled away, but Jeff forced her to lie down on the couch.

"Take it easy, will you?" she said angrily. "You're hurting me."

"You love it and you know it," he said. His eyes were glowing with passion. His breathing was raspy. He grabbed his drink from the coffee table and swallowed it with two large gulps. Then he turned back to her and lunged forward.

Julie wanted to spit on him as he bent down and nibbled on her neck. His hands worked furiously behind her to release her bra. She felt it loosen, and then his hands came back around front.

"Jeff, don't you think it's a little bit late to get started?" She looked over at the clock on the mantel. "It's past eleven. Won't Lisa be wondering where you are?"

All she heard was a muffled snort as he took her nipple into his mouth and began to suck. His hands moved down and started working on her belt.

"Really, Jeff, I think Lisa will—"

"Will you just shut the fuck up about Lisa?" he shouted, raising his hand in a threatening blow. "And loosen up, dammit!"

He grasped the top of her jeans, snapped them open, and pulled them down roughly, taking her panties with them. There was a quick sound of tearing fabric. With a low animal grunt, Jeff stood up and dropped his pants down around his ankles. Pulling her legs open wide, he plunged forward and into her.

Julie gritted her teeth and kept her eyes fixed on the clock as Jeff pumped up and down, groaning. He rocked her back and forth until the couch springs squeaked in rhythm. Finally, with a shudder, Jeff stiffened and gasped, then sank onto her with his full weight.

Half an hour later, after Julie had dressed and Jeff had tossed down three more whiskies, Julie got up off the couch and walked into the kitchen. It was getting really close to the time, and she was getting nervous, wondering how she could get rid of Jeff.

Jeff wandered into the kitchen behind her. "Hey, Jule," he said with a slur, "yah haven't even had a drink wi' me all night. 'S not good to drink alone." He reached up into the cupboard and took down another glass.

"You're not alone," she said, smirking as he almost dropped the glass when he tried to fill it. "I think I'll pass tonight," she said, jumping up to sit on the counter.

"Not even a tinsy-winsy?" he asked, measuring a small amount with his fingers.

Julie shook her head.

"Well, then, how 'bout a little . . ." He winked at her lasciviously.

"Oh no! I think you've exceeded your limit on two accounts tonight."

He started toward her on shaking legs but found the effort too great and sank down into the kitchen chair.

"I think you best be getting home, don't you?"

Jeff raised his half-empty glass to the light and squinted at it. "Jus' lemme finish this one first, OK?"

Julie glanced at the clock. It was eleven-thirty. "Just make it quick," she said, jumping down and going to the closet to get Jeff's coat.

Jeff polished off the glass and, snickering, started to unscrew the cap on his bottle.

"Oh no you don't," she said. "You said you'd finish that drink and go."

"One more for the road. There's jus' a little bit left. 'Sides, it's awful cold outside."

Julie came over to him and started to slide one of his arms into the coat sleeve. "No way. It's late. Time for sleepy-bye."

Jeff stood up to put his other arm into the sleeve. He stumbled and had to catch at her to keep from falling. His rough beard scratched against her face. "That's what I been tryin' to tell yah, babe. 'S beddy-bye time."

Julie kept her voice firm as she glanced at the clock. It was eleven-forty-five. She might still make it. "That's right. For me here, and for you at home."

Jeff finally got his other arm into the coat sleeve and started to button up. He turned quickly and planted a wet kiss on Julie's cheek. She wiped the saliva away and handed Jeff his gloves.

"There you go. Got your keys?"

Jeff nodded dumbly and patted his coat pocket.

"Well then," she said, moving over to the door, "I guess you're on your way." She opened the door and a frigid blast of air entered the kitchen. She took a deep breath as she looked up at the rising full moon.

"You won't lemme sleep in your cozy little bed, huh?" Jeff said, coming toward her.

Julie neatly sidestepped him and, grabbing his coat collar, propelled him out into the cold night. He tried to negotiate the steps, but he was so blind drunk, he wasn't able to stop. He pinwheeled wildly across Julie's snow-covered lawn and then collapsed onto his back. Julie shut the door with a bang and locked it.

She sat at the kitchen table, nervously drumming her fingernails on the formica top as she waited to hear his car start up. She looked up and saw the glow of his headlights out the window, then the car roared into life. The gears ground loudly once, and then she heard the car sputter down the snowy road that led back to town.

As soon as the sound of the car disappeared, she jumped to her feet, knocking over the chair. She ran to the counter and pulled open the drawer. Reaching in, she took out the red sash and the jar filled with the black syrup.

She dashed over to the cellar stairway. Pausing for a second and casting a quick glance at the clock, she snapped the kitchen light off and descended.

She wasn't too late.

.III.

Jeff clicked on the radio as he drove and jumped into the middle of a Merle Haggard song with a voice that hit one note in ten. His eyes barely focused on the snowy road, and the ass-end of his car kept trying to take the lead for a change. Snow shot up from under his back tires as Jeff pressed the accelerator down hard.

He rolled down his window and let the freezing air hit him in the face. The dark river to his right glittered in the moonlight; it had just started to freeze up above the falls. He leaned his head back and bellowed up at the ceiling.

When he got to a point where he could see the falls through a break in the trees, he slowed down and stared up at the white plume of mist. His attention wasn't on his driving, and suddenly, there was a dull thump from underneath his car. Instinctively, Jeff gripped the wheel hard as he looked out at the road. He recognized his problem immediately. Looking out of his windshield, he was staring at the side of the road. His car was sliding sideways.

"Lousy cunt," he swore as he pumped the brake with his foot. He merely assisted the skid. He watched, frozen, as his headlights swept up into the sky and his car rocketed over the snowbank and into a stand of swamp maple.

His head was thrown forward and hit the horn, giving off a loud honk. The car jolted to a stop with its front end pointing down into the snow. He could see that the light of his headlight was diffused through the snow.

"Goddamn!" Jeff said as he sat for a moment, dazed. He turned the car off and slumped in his seat. His hand dropped to the floor beside him, and he remembered something he had forgotten all night. He had another bottle of whisky in the car.

Huffing, he got on his knees and reached under the seat. Passing over tools, oily rags, and assorted empties, his hand finally alighted on the pint bottle.

"Liquid gold," he said, smacking his lips and unscrewing the cap. He tilted his head back and took a bubbling swallow. "Thank you, Lord," he said, and belched.

Fortified now, he felt able to get out of the car

and assess the situation.

He found that his car was about twenty feet from the river, and somewhere in his clouded brain, he found the ability to appreciate that. If the car had hit the ice here, he probably would have gone through and sunk. He stared at the river and listened to the distant hissing of the falls.

He walked over to the car and, cursing, kicked it viciously on the door. "Goddamn piece of shit!"

Steadying himself with a maple sapling, he took another swallow of whisky. It was working its magic. With each swallow he felt less upset. He could deal with the situation.

"Is this like when you have a boating accident?" he asked himself, staring drunkenly at the car. "Are you supposed to stay with the car or try to get back?"

He had a rough idea of where he had gone off the road. He knew that it was just about the same distance to town as it was back to Julie's house. It'd be a bitch either way, a hell of a long walk. Finally, after a moment's consideration, he came up with a better idea.

He knew that, above the falls, there was an old wooden bridge spanning the river. From there, he figured, it would be easiest and shortest to take the old mining road back to town. He could come back in the morning with a tow truck and get his car out of the pucker-brush.

He went over to the car and switched off the

lights. Before closing the door, he sat down on the seat and, fumbling, tightened his bootlaces. After one more gulp of whisky, he pulled his coat collar tight and started out.

He took exaggerated giant-steps through the snow. The going was a bit more difficult than he had expected. He hadn't considered the depth of the snow. Slowly, and with many pauses for a haul from his pint, he made his way upriver to where he knew the bridge would be.

As he got closer to the falls, the roaring grew louder, until it filled the night, drowning out all other sounds. Mostly by luck he found the bridge and started out across it.

The bridge was old. Its timbers were rotting. With each step, Jeff was surprised that he didn't fall through. The wooden railing swayed loosely in his hand.

When he was halfway over the bridge, Jeff paused to watch the water as it swept toward the falls. It moved with an inky oiliness, glittering in the full moonlight and almost taking Jeff's stomach with it as it slid through the flume. The sound was deafening. The spray rose up into the still night air.

Taking his bottle from his pocket one last time, Jeff emptied it. Then, with a heartfelt sigh, he pitched it into the water and watched it go over the falls before continuing on his way.

He came out by the old abandoned silver-mine. The road was never plowed out this far up, so the snow was deeper here, and he had a tough time making his way through it. His steps wavered, and he fell every twenty feet or so, but he slowly made it down the slope, past the deserted buildings, and onto the wider road that led back into town.

As he walked down the road, Jeff kept glancing back over his shoulder at the falls. The white spray rose into the air and glittered as it froze. Up on the cliffs, beside the falls, Jeff could see the gaping black holes of the played-out mineshafts. Something about them made him shiver, and he picked up his pace.

When he was about half a mile below the falls, he stopped short. He realized only then that he had been running, plowing his way through the snow. He leaned over with his hands on his knees, trying to catch his breath.

He turned his gaze down the road and at the trees that silently lined the road. A soft wind suddenly picked up and swayed the branches back and forth. Jeff shivered and clapped his hands to his shoulders to keep his circulation going.

Suddenly he froze, his arms poised in midair. Something was standing underneath the trees by the side of the road. Jeff squinted and, through his alcoholic gaze, finally discerned a doglike shape.

"Just a little old pooch," he said with glee. He chuckled to himself and started forward. "Jus' a little ole doggie."

He clapped his hands together and whistled shrilly. "Come'ere, fella. Come on." He took a few more steps closer and whistled again. "Come on, boy. Come'ere."

He stopped short when he saw the animal suddenly crouch low to the ground. It snarled loudly.

"Hey, come on, fella. I'm jus' bein' friendly. What's the matter wi' you?"

Jeff cocked his head and regarded the dog who crouched about thirty feet away from him. The growling rose steadily.

"Are you feelin' nasty 'cause you didn't get a piece o' ass tonight? 'S that it? You horny little bastard!"

The animal growled again and moved forward.

"Now that ain't nice, fella. Be a good dog. Come on." Jeff snapped his fingers and whistled.

He suddenly felt his stomach drop when the animal growled and rose to its full height. It moved closer toward him, and when it stepped out into the moonlight, its eyes glowed with an angry green light.

"Big fella, ain't yah?" Jeff said, starting to back away as he realized the danger.

The animal's jaws opened, exposing a row of sharp white teeth.

"I sure hope you're jus' bluffin' me," Jeff said, trying to sound calm.

The animal's hackles shot up. The growl exploded into a loud bark, and the animal sprang. Needle-sharp teeth tore into the arm Jeff raised in front of his face for protection. His coat and his arm tore open as the weight of the beast bore him back onto the ground. The air was knocked out of Jeff. The animal held onto Jeff's arm and

253

savaged it back and forth, its teeth grinding like a saw blade.

Jeff started to shout and scream as the pain spread through his body. An icy numbness gripped his brain when he heard the sharp crunching of bone.

"Get away! Get away, you bastard!" Jeff shouted as he scrambled on the ground trying to dislodge the weight that pressed him down. With his loose hand, he swung wildly and struck the animal's nose several times. With a sudden, savage pull, the animal jerked on Jeff's arm. There was a dull pop as the shoulder was dislocated. Jeff screamed.

At last the animal let go and backed off. Jeff lay on the ground for a moment, dazed, looking up at the wild beast that crouched nearby. He tried to move away but found that his body wouldn't obey the commands of his brain.

His eyesight began to dim and soon all Jeff could see was the hazy blue expanse of moonlit snow. He knew, distantly, that the dark splotches on that blue snow were pools of his life's blood. He was sinking down.

Then, like a terrible shadow, the animal loomed up over him. The green eyes flashed with fury and, with a ferocious snarl, the animal fastened its jaws to Jeff's neck and pulled violently. Jeff's neck broke with a dull pop. The animal gave his body a few quick shakes and then began to feed.

"I'm sorry I called you so late," Lisa said as she sat on the couch with her hands pressed between her knees. "He should have been home by now. I'm really worried."

Bob leaned back in his seat and took a thoughtful drag on his cigarette. He let the smoke drift lazily out his nostrils.

"I know what you're thinking," Lisa said softly.

"No," Bob said pointedly. "No, you don't know what I'm thinking."

"I do," Lisa said with an edge to her voice. "You're thinking that I'm getting exactly what I deserve for putting up with, with his running around."

"I'm not," Bob said calmly as he snubbed out the butt in the ashtray.

"But this is different. I know it is. I just have this feeling that something's happened." She giggled nervously. "I know he's been on some real good benders, but this, this is different." She shook her head hopelessly and let her shoulders slouch as she stared at the floor.

"I'm sure he's OK. Really," Bob said, leaning over to pat her gently on the shoulder. His voice was still rusty with sleep.

"He's never been later than two o'clock in the morning!"

"Maybe he just had a flat tire or something. Look." Bob stood up and began pacing the floor.

"If he came home and found me here—well, I just don't think I want to be around for that to happen." Bob rubbed his jaw as the memory of the fight behind the school came to him. He made for the door.

"Wait!" Lisa shouted in a voice that almost froze Bob. "There's something else."

Bob walked back to his chair and eased himself down.

Lisa looked at him and ran her teeth over her lower lip. "Tonight's your night, right?"

Bob was confused. "My night?"

"It's a full moon tonight, isn't it?"

Bob felt a rush of fear, but he tried to remain outwardly cool. "Don't tell me you're starting to think about full moons and werewolves?" he asked. His voice registered disdain, but he searched Lisa's face for a reaction.

"I, I don't know," Lisa said with tears welling up in her green eyes. "I just don't know. I, I—"

"Lisa," Bob said calmly, feeling the back of his neck prickling with heat, "you don't really think I still think that, do you?"

Lisa raised her eyebrows.

"That I think there's a werewolf in Cooper Falls?"

"I don't know." Her voice was hushed, as though she was afraid to hear herself speak. She ran her fingers through her hair and then slipped her hands back between her knees. "But tonight, late, around midnight, I heard a, a howling."

"Uh-huh," Bob said. He glanced out the window at the street three storeys below.

"Oh, Bob, it scared the daylights out of me!" Her face twisted with remembered pain. "It sounded just like a wolf!"

"There are a lot of dogs around town. I'm sure, if you were upset, you could make it sound like a wolf, after what I said."

"It wasn't a dog!" Lisa shouted. She punched the couch beside her with frustration. "I know it wasn't!"

"How can you be so sure?" Bob asked calmly.

"It was so, so unearthly, deep and hollow, almost like an echo or something. I almost thought it was in my head, that I might be hallucinating or something."

"Probably just your imagination," Bob said. "From the things I said on the phone that day."

"I just know it was more than just a dog," Lisa said. Tears welled up in her eyes and overflowed. "Bob, I'm really scared!"

"Lisa," Bob began. He looked at her and felt a wave of pity. He wanted to hold and comfort her, but something made him hold back. "Can I ask you a question? It's going to sound crazy, maybe, but do you have a cross or any kind of religious medal?"

"Yeah," she replied, and snorted loudly, "I have a silver cross I got way back in high school, for confirmation. Why? What are you getting at?"

Bob twisted his hands and looked at her earnestly. "I, I want you to promise me that you'll wear it. All the time!" He reached into his shirt and pulled out a chain. At its end, a small gold cross dangled, reflecting light around the room. "Now I'm not ready to get locked away. Not yet, anyway. But I don't think it would hurt to have some, some protection." He dropped the cross back into his shirt.

"Some protection! Protection from what?" Lisa asked anxiously. "Bob, do you know what you sound like?"

"Yeah, I do." He looked out the window, straining to see the dark sky. "But you mentioned the full moon. I didn't. Lisa, I have to tell you. I haven't stopped thinking along the lines that there might be something supernatural involved here. I checked back to the nights that Wendy, Frank Simmons and Alan Tate were killed. All three were either nights of the full moon or one night on either side of the full moon."

"Coincidence?" Lisa asked, hopefully.

"Who the hell knows!" Bob said, slapping his fist into his hand. "Sure it could be coincidence. I could be a border-line paranoid who has finally taken the plunge. Is that what you think?"

"No." She didn't dare to meet his eyes.

"I don't feel crazy. I don't think I'm any different. But these three deaths were on full-moon nights!"

"Or one day away," Lisa said, "If it's a, werewolf, I thought they were only on full-moon nights. Doesn't that blow a hole in your theory right there?"

"No, it doesn't," Bob said seriously. "I have been doing some reading on the topic, and the time of a werewolf's transformation, at least in some traditions, can be on nights on either side of full. According to some legends, werewolf activity occurs throughout the month of February. It's all tied in with the Roman Lupercalia and with the severe winters that probably drove hungry wolf-packs closer to towns in the old days."

"I can't believe it!" Lisa said, shaking her head. "I just can't believe that we're two adults sitting here talking like this. It's insane!"

"No it isn't, Lisa. It may be the only explanation that fits what's been happening around town. It scares me. The possibilities are frightening!"

"So who's the werewolf?" Lisa asked. Her voice had an almost mocking note of humor, but her eyes were grim.

"I think Julie Sikes is doing it. She's pretty heavily into magic and occult things." Bob faced Lisa intently. "You want it straight? I think Julie's doing it—to Ned Simmons."

Lisa gasped.

"Think about it! He's a perfect target, with all that pent-up hostility. Just as an image, it fits. I'm convinced that the image, the legends, are real, they're working!"

"I've always felt sort of funny around Julie," Lisa said seriously. "I've never liked her."

"It doesn't have to be her. It could be anyone. For all I know, if I wanted to get really paranoid, it could be you who's doing it." Bob began pacing again.

"You do sound crazy," Lisa said, her voice registering concern.

"I know I do. And if you hadn't dragged me over here at two A.M., telling me you're worried because Jeff's not home yet, and it's a full moon tonight, and that you heard something howling, I wouldn't have said all this. I would have kept it to myself and let it drive me slowly mad."

That said, Bob appeared to calm down. He came over and sat beside Lisa on the couch.

"You want a cup of coffee?" Lisa asked after a long silence.

"No." Bob yawned and stretched. "I have one day of school left before Christmas vacation, and the day after tomorrow I'm driving down to Springfield for Amy's wedding."

"You're going?" Lisa was astounded. "You didn't tell me."

"You never asked. I'm going mostly so I can see Jamie. I miss that kid. I haven't seen her since summer. So, look, if Jeff isn't home soon, give Granger a call, send someone out looking for him."

"I've got a pretty good idea where they should start looking: at Julie Sikes," Lisa said morosely.

"I'll wait if you want me to."

"No," Lisa said, getting up from the couch. "We're both getting ourselves too worked up. You were probably right. He's got a flat tire or has run out of gas. He'll come staggering on in around dawn."

"I'm sure he's OK," Bob said, hoping his lie didn't show. The coincidence of all those oc-

260

currences on nights of full moons was too much to be dismissed. His gut feeling was that something terrible had happened.

Bob stood up and got his coat on. He started for the door, but before leaving, turned to Lisa and said, "Remember your promise. Wear that silver cross all the time!"

Chapter Twelve

Friday, December 19

.I.

Bob was about an hour out of Boston, heading west on the Massachusetts Turnpike when he heard something on the radio that made his stomach clench. He stiffened in his car seat as he listened.

"Late Thursday night, the body of Mr. Jeff Carter of Cooper Falls, New Hampshire was found by neighbors who were snow-mobiling.

Earlier in the day, Mr. Carter's car had been found abandoned off a minor road. A resident had noticed tire tracks leaving the road. The accident occurred late Wednesday night."

Bob's breathing came in sharp hitches as he adjusted the dial, trying to pull the station in clearer.

"Chief of Police Roy Granger was notified immediately. Mrs. Carter, the town librarian, had reported her husband missing earlier in the day."

"Oh, Jesus," Bob said, looking in the rearview mirror at his pale face. His hands shook as he lit a cigarette.

"The victim apparently died of exposure when he tried to walk the four miles back to town following the accident. There was no evidence of foul play, sources said."

"Bullshit," Bob muttered, as he puffed angrily.

"In North Conway today, workers at the—" Bob snapped the radio off and drove silently. His mind was whirring with thoughts.

To an English teacher, the newscaster's choice of words seemed strange. Why, Bob thought, if there was no evidence of foul play, did he refer to Jeff as a victim? Was that a newscaster's habit, after years of reporting tragedies, or was there something else lurking behind the story?

Up ahead, he saw the exit sign for Old Sturbridge Village. Bob dug out his wallet and pulled out a bill. Then he put on his turn signal and began downshifting.

"Sorry I can't make it, Amy," he whispered as

he approached the toll booth. He smiled tightly as he paid the booth attendant, then did a U-turn and took a ticket and started driving east. It would be an hour to Boston, and then another two hours or so to Cooper Falls. He checked his watch. He should get there sometime in the early afternoon. He thought of calling Lisa to let her know he had heard, but he decided not to lose the time on the road.

.II.

Thurston held the phone to his ear, braced by his shoulder, and took a quick sip of coffee. He hated being put on hold, but he was glad he finally got through to agent Hatch before the weekend. He took another sip and then put the cup down as the F.B.I. agent came back on the line.

"Thanks for holding, Deputy," Hatch said. He had a clipped, efficient-sounding voice.

"That's OK," Thurston replied. "So, have you found out anything on this man, Wentworth?"

"Deputy Thurston, we have absolutely nothing on our files about this man. You got those photocopies of the newspaper articles?"

"Yes."

"Well, that incident with the rape charges checks out. From several contacts we spoke with, we determined that it was a weak case. There was no reason to pursue it further."

"You mean he was innocent?" Thurston asked sharply.

"No. I don't. I mean that the case was never brought to trial, so we don't have an official ruling. But from the rest of this guy's background, he seems to be pretty level. Married and divorced, one kid, went right into teaching after college. Pretty straight guy."

"Ahh, when did Wentworth get divorced? I had heard something, but I don't have the hard facts."

"One source we interviewed suggested that the divorce resulted from the attendant publicity and pressure of the Landry girl's charges."

"So in your statement," Thurston said, "would you say that this incident put Mr. Wentworth under a great deal of strain?"

"It could have," Hatch replied. "I have no way of evaluating that at this point. My advice to you, Deputy, would be to keep your eye on this guy if he bothers you. Officially, he's as clean as a whistle, but that's no guarantee he couldn't be involved with these murders. If your superior requests it, we could send up an agent to assist the investigation."

"I don't think so," Thurston replied, slightly flustered. "Not at the moment, anyway. You know how these hick cops are," he added snidely. "They think they can handle it themselves. I'll be in touch if we need any assistance."

"Whatever you say," Hatch said stiffly.

"If you say this guy Wentworth is clean, he's clean. But that doesn't remove my, uhh, my basic distrust of the guy. It's these quiet ones who can snap just like that! I—"

Thurston quickly jumped to his feet when he heard footsteps outside the office door. The door banged open, and in walked Granger, followed by Seavey.

"Howdy," Granger said, nodding. The sun had set, so Granger snapped on the office lights.

"Yeah, well, thank you for your call," Thurston said into the phone. "I appreciate your help with this. I'll get back to you if there's anything else you can do." He hung up quickly, snatched up his coffee cup, and walked over to the coffee pot to refill it.

"I'll take one of those if you're pouring," Granger said as he hefted off his heavy winter coat and hung it on the back of his chair. "How 'bout you, Ted?"

"Sure." Seavey walked over and took the chair beside the gun rack.

Thurston reached down two more cups and began pouring. "How'd it go today?" he asked, not looking up. "You guys have been out pretty late."

"The usual," Granger said angrily. "Nobody saw nothin', nowhere! Anything happen here?"

Thurston walked over and handed Granger his cup. "Naw."

"Who were you talking to?" Granger asked, sounding uninterested.

"No one special," Thurston answered, handing Seavey his cup. "Just an old friend."

Granger put his cup down on the desk before

going over and replacing his rifle on the wall rack. He didn't bother to run the chain through the trigger guard, although it was standard office policy. He came back to his desk and sat down with a huff. "Of course, that didn't stop half of the guys from shooting at whatever in the hell they thought they saw."

Seavey offered a half-chuckle that was lost in a noisy slurp from his coffee cup.

"Christ, I'm beat," Granger said as he stretched and yawned.

Thurston frowned. "Well it's been deader 'n a doornail around here: no calls, no complaints, and no nothing. You should stay around here and catch up on your sleep."

Granger snuffed. "Yeah, well, we pretty much covered everything from the town dump over to Lyon Hill. If there's anything out there, it—"

"We know it's out there," Seavey said quietly.

Granger nodded and said, "Yeah. The damn problem is finding it. Hell, we can't even get a decent trail. I'm still convinced we should get some help from the state."

"What more could they do?" Thurston asked sharply.

"Increase our manpower," Granger replied.

Thurston looked over at Seavey, whose expression revealed nothing of what he was thinking. "Did anyone go out on the mine road, toward the falls? It hasn't snowed since Jeff was found. There must be tracks out there."

"We were out there," Seavey said.

"Saw plenty of tracks, too. Problem is, they

were all Jeff's, ours, and snowmobile tracks. If there was a good trail, it's long gone now."

"So we just have to keep at it," Thurston said soberly.

Granger looked over his shoulder, out into the darkened street. "You haven't seen Ralph and Gene, have you?" he asked.

Thurston shook his head.

"Hmmm. They should have been in by now. I told 'em not to stay out past dark."

The distant sound of a snowmobile made all three men glance out the window. The wasplike buzzing grew louder as it came down Main Street. "Ahh, this is probably them now," Granger said, getting up and going to the window.

A single headlight swept down the street and then, just outside, the buzzing machine was cut off. Hurried footsteps sounded on the steps, and then the door flew open. Ralph Hamlin burst in.

"Roy! You gotta come quick!" His face was pasty gray, and the fear in his eyes alerted all three men in the office.

"Sure," Granger said, snatching his rifle from the wall rack. "What is it?"

"It's Chuck Doyle. It got him!"

"Is he dead?" Granger barked, pulling on his coat and gloves. Seavey was already set to go.

"Oh Jesus, yes. Yes!" Ralph covered his mouth with his mittened hands. The man looked as though he was about to vomit.

"It must've happened last night! Oh Jesus! He's, he's—" He suddenly turned and ran outside. The sound of his retching made a bad taste flood Thurston's mouth. Granger and Seavey raced outside and got into the cruiser. The blue strobes started flashing as they pulled away from the curb and sped down Main Street toward Chuck Doyle's place.

Thurston watched from the window as the cruiser disappeared. "And I get to sit around on my ass and hold down the fort," he muttered, his breath fogging the glass. After a moment, he went outside and asked Ralph if he wanted to come in and clean himself up.

While Ralph was in the bathroom washing up, Thurston sat down in Granger's chair and idly skimmed the two photocopied newspaper clippings.

.III.

Ned watched from the bordering woods as Julie came slowly up the path to her front door. He heard the steady crunching of the snow beneath her boots. In the light of the moon, just past full, her face was washed of color. Ned tensed as he listened to her work the door lock, and as the door swung open, he stepped out of his hiding place and raced toward the door.

Julie had stepped inside and was swinging the door shut when Ned shouldered his way into the doorway. Julie screamed and tried to hold the door shut, but Ned pushed her, and finally she stepped back to let him in.

"What the hell are you doing?" she said harshly. She backed her way across the kitchen floor until she stood with her back against the refrigerator.

Ned eased the door shut, stamped his feet on the floor, and then turned to face her. He smiled and said, "I was out for a little walk tonight and I just thought I'd drop by to talk, you know?" His smile widened.

Julie eyed him suspiciously as she slowly unbuttoned her coat and hung it on the back of a chair. "We've got nothing to talk about," she said firmly.

Ned opened up his coat and took a few steps forward. "Oh, I think we do. Aren't you gonna invite me in?"

Julie shook her head and said, "Please, do. Come in."

Ned nodded and walked over to the table, where he took a seat. He slid his coat off and draped it over the back of the chair. He stared at her intently, glad to see that his sudden appearance had put her off her guard. He knew he would have to keep that advantage.

"I think we have a lot to talk about," he said again, fixing her with a harsh glance. "I have some questions I think only you can answer."

Julie was still standing with her back against the refrigerator. She was scratching her hand with her fingernails, leaving long red lines on the skin. "Would, would you care for some coffee or tea?" she asked.

Ned shook his head. "Not really."

"Just as well," Julie said. "It's getting late, and it would just keep me awake."

Ned snickered.

Julie crossed her arms and regarded Ned for a moment. "You said you wanted to talk to me. What about?"

Ned smiled and shook his head. "As if you didn't know."

"I don't."

"Of course you do," Ned said with sudden intensity. "You know damn right well!" He slammed his fist on the table. "I know that you've been the one doing it, doing it to me!"

"What the hell are you talking about?" Julie asked. She tried to sound mocking, but there was an edge of tension in her voice.

"The change!" Ned said. "The transformation!"

Julie's eyes narrowed as she studied Ned. "I haven't the faintest idea what you're talking about."

"Don't be ridiculous, Julie," Ned said standing up slowly. "I know you're the one who's been making it happen."

"Are you crazy? What are you talking about?"

Ned laughed, a deep, hollow laugh. "I just want to know, why me? Why did you pick me to do it to?"

"Do what?" Julie shouted. "What are you talking about?" She tried to stare Ned down, but his eyes riveted her and she had to look away.

He took a few steps toward her. "How have you been doing it!" The intensity in his voice was like fire. "At first I thought it was, you know, just dreams, nightmares. But I realized pretty soon that it was real, that I was really taking on that other shape and, and hunting at night!"

Julie brought her hands to her mouth and shook her head. "I didn't do anything to you."

"It has to be some kind of magic, right? I thought for a while there that I was losing my mind, until I knew it was really happening."

"Nothing's happening!" Julie said, edging away from Ned as he advanced toward her.

Ned threw his head back and laughed. "Yeah, sure, nothing's happening. Just how many people have died this year, killed by that mysterious wild animal?"

"I don't know anything about them," Julie said. She had backed into a corner. Ned reached out quickly and grabbed her arm in a vicelike grip.

"First your husband, and then my brother Frank. I figured you had to have something to do with it." His grip on her arm tightened, and Julie winced from the pain. "Of course, once I knew it was real when it was happening, I used it to, to even a few scores of my own. But I know that you're the one who started it, and I want to know why. Why did you pick me?"

Julie shook her head from side to side, and tears welled in her eyes. "I didn't—" she gasped. "I didn't mean for you . . ."

Ned started to twist her arm back. "I want to know why you picked me. Maybe, just maybe you were interested in me."

"It wasn't supposed to affect you," Julie said, her voice strained. "It wasn't. I was trying, trying to, to get rid of Frank." Ned twisted her arm back further, and the pain screamed through her shoulder. "I wanted it to affect Frank. I was, I was using magic to, to get rid of him. He was getting too serious, wanting to get married, and I, I wanted to get rid of him."

"So you used me?" Ned said with a snarl.

Julie shook her head violently. "No. No! I was trying to attract evil forces to him, to destroy him. I tried to control his dark side, the beast in him, and turn it against him." Her voice broke into a braying sob. "I, I wanted him dead!"

"And you used me!"

"I didn't mean to," Julie said, pleadingly. "You have to believe me!" It wasn't supposed to turn on anyone else. His dark side was supposed to kill him, no one else. But then, then once people started being killed, I didn't know how to stop it. I thought once Frank was dead, it would all end." She lost sight of Ned in the swimming vision as her eyes overflowed.

"It didn't stop," Ned said evenly. "It hasn't!"

"You have to believe me, Ned, I didn't want those other people to die! I didn't want you to be the one who did it! I thought, I thought it was Frank, and once I realized it wasn't, it was too late."

Ned eased the pressure on Julie's arm. He smiled and said softly, "But it's not too late."

Julie shook her head, trying to regain her composure as the pain in her arm subsided. Ned stepped closer to her, pressing her back. He grabbed her by the shoulders and tried to pull her toward him. She resisted, twisting away.

Ned continued to talk in a soft, smooth voice. "I thought you had picked me because you, you wanted me." His hands slid down and pulled her closer, grinding his hips against hers.

"Get away from me!" she said angrily. "Get your goddamn hands off of me!"

Ned smiled, holding her tightly to him. "We can be lovers, you and I. And who knows what we can do, now that we know each other's secrets."

"Get the Christ away from me!" Julie screamed.

His hold on her didn't let up. He leaned his face closer, so close she felt his heated breath on her cheek. "You can come with me," he said. "I have a place where we can stay, where nobody will ever find us. Don't you realize what we can do? We have the power of life and death over everybody, everybody in this town!"

She pushed at him, trying to get away. "No! No!"

"We can be lovers," Ned said intensely. "You can be mine!"

"I don't want you!" she said heatedly. "I don't need you to be my lover!" His looming, shadowed form pressed her back against the wall. She felt as though she could barely catch her breath, but then, with a suddenness that surprised even her, she lifted up her knee and caught Ned squarely in the crotch. With a howl, he doubled up and dropped to the floor.

Julie jumped over his crumpled form and, grabbing her coat from the chair, dashed for the door without a glance back. She heard Ned groaning and scrambling to his feet as she flung the door open and raced outside. She dashed around the side of the house and disappeared into the shadows of the trees.

From a safe distance, she heard Ned hollering as he stood on her front porch. His voice lifted into the night and echoed back from the far shore of the lake.

"You will be mine!" his voice boomed in the stillness of the night. "You will be mine!"

.IV.

Monday, December 22

The funeral for Jeff Carter was held at two o'clock in the afternoon at Riverside Congregational Church. It was a closed-casket funeral.

After a short eulogy and two verses of "Nearer My God to Thee," a slow-moving procession of cars drove out to Pine Haven Cemetery.

Bob drove last in the cortege and, as he crept along through the fine falling snow, he kept asking himself why there had been a closed casket? The reporter on the radio and the newspaper article in the *Cooper Falls Eagle* had reported that Jeff had died of exposure. Bob kept glancing at his fingers, clenching and unclenching them on the steering wheel. He commanded himself to relax, but moments later he would notice that he was tense again.

A closed casket, and he died from exposure? Exposure?

And then another thought intruded: Lisa!

Throughout the service, he had kept his eyes fixed on her. She never looked up from the floor, never looked around. The ritualistic mutterings barely registered on Bob as he stared at Lisa's slouched, shaking shoulders. She looked much older, more tired and worn than he had ever seen her.

And why was she ignoring, making it almost a point, ignoring him? He thought secretly that she would have been almost glad to be rid of Jeff. Granted, it was a horrible way to die, but, but . . . He couldn't believe he let himself think such thoughts.

The lines of cars, headlights burning feebly in the snow, drove past the two cemetery gates on Railroad Avenue, turned left onto Old Jepson's Road, and finally turned into the last gateway. Bob felt a wave of uneasiness as he drove past the stone pillars. He raised his hand and thoughtfully rubbed the cheek that the white cat had scratched. Bob turned the car heater to low and opened the window to relieve the stuffiness in the car.

As they drove up toward the cedar grove, Bob felt he knew why Lisa was being distant with him. He probably shouldn't have expressed his thoughts so openly when he went to her apartment Wednesday night. Although he was increasingly convinced that there was a supernatural agent acting in Cooper Falls, she probably had concluded that he was really crazy. After time to think, and with the shock of her husband's death, Lisa must have finally rejected the idea of a werewolf, and, with it, him.

It could also be that Lisa was waiting a decent interval before furthering their relationship. Perhaps her shock and grief were not so deeply felt as they appeared? Bob hoped that might be the case, but he felt that was wishful thinking.

He also found himself wondering if Lisa was wearing her silver cross. That would have told him plenty!

The hearse pulled to a stop at the grave site. Snow had been plowed aside, and a deep pit had been dug in the frozen ground.

The deep six, Bob thought, gritting his teeth. He put the car in neutral, pulled on the brake, and got out. He stayed on the fringe of the mourners and kept moving around, trying to get a position from which he could see Lisa's face.

Reverend Alder had his hymnal open and was reading the service for the dead. Lisa, still looking down, had her gloved hands covering the bottom half of her face throughout. She was shaking, but whether it was from the bitter winds or from crying, Bob couldn't tell.

"Ashes to ashes," the reverend intoned, taking a clump of frozen soil and crumbling it in his hand. "Dust to dust. The Lord giveth and the

Lord taketh away. Blessed is the name of the Lord."

The pall bearers stepped forward and, after hefting the casket, slowly began lowering it into the ground. Reverend Alder scanned the group of mourners and then asked them to pray for the soul of Jeff Carter.

"Oh, Lord, we ask you to receive the soul of your servant Jeff Carter . . ."

As in the church service, Bob found it difficult to listen because of the thoughts that intruded. His silent prayer was that he was grateful Lisa had been released from a life with a man who must have made it pure hell for her at times.

When the prayer was over, everyone slowly filtered across the snow-covered graveyard back to their cars. Lisa stood alone for a moment at the grave site and threw a small bouquet of flowers onto the coffin. Two groundskeepers came forward and began to shovel dirt back into the pit. Stones and frozen earth rattled loudly on the coffin lid.

From a distance, Bob watched Lisa. She walked toward him through the swirling snow and, when she was beside him, looked at him with a cold, distant stare. Without a word, she strode past him. Bob raised his hand and opened his mouth to speak, but nothing came out.

What could he possibly say? he wondered frantically.

Lisa went down to her car and stood there talking to Reverend Alder. Bob walked slowly over to the grave site and looked down at the casket. It was completely covered with dirt.

"Should've waited 'til spring to plant this one," one of the workmen said. The sound of his shovel scraping up frozen dirt set Bob's teeth on edge.

The other workmen looked angrily at his partner and then at Bob. "Pity," he said, softly. "Friend of yours?"

Bob shook his head. "No. I am—was a friend of the family. I didn't know him very well."

"Hell of a way to die," the workman said, turning back to his job. Bob headed back toward his car. Reverend Adler had left, and Lisa was standing beside her car. Bob picked up his pace and walked over to her.

"It was a nice service," he said awkwardly. His lips had dried out from the cold, and they stuck to his teeth as he spoke.

Lisa kept her eyes averted but still stood there.

"Jesus, Lisa, what's the matter? Since I got back on Friday, you've been ignoring me. Will you level with me? What's the matter?"

She turned to look at him, her eyes bright with suppressed anger. "I would think," she said evenly, "that you would have a pretty damn good idea!"

Bob reached to touch her shoulder but she drew away. "I don't know what you're talking about. Look, I can't blame you for being pretty upset and all, but I—"

"Yeah. You!" Lisa snapped. "You just couldn't wait, could you?" She glared at him and then opened her car door. Sitting down, she looked back up at Bob, her teeth biting into her lower lip, making it drain white.

"Oh come on, Lisa."

"Well?" she asked grimly.

"Don't make this any harder than it already is, for yourself or for me. You can't deny that Jeff wasn't the model husband. I know he hurt you, a lot. But if you—"

"He wasn't always like that!" Lisa screamed. Her eyes glistened with tears and rage.

"That doesn't matter," Bob replied evenly. "What matters is how he treated you recently. No matter what you had before, that doesn't excuse what he put you through this last year."

"You wanted him to die, didn't you?" Lisa asked sharply.

Bob shook his head.

"Don't try to bullshit me, OK?" Lisa asked. Her voice was sharp and cutting. Bob wanted to hold her, comfort her, calm her down, but the longer he looked at her, the more he felt his anger rise.

"You want it straight? I'll give it to you straight!" Bob yelled. "The closed casket didn't fool me. Not for a minute. I know! I know it was the werewolf that killed Jeff. No, don't act surprised, you must have seen the body."

Lisa shook her head. "No, I never did."

"Jeff didn't die of exposure, Lisa. Just like Wendy Stillman didn't get raped, and Frank Simmons didn't get shot in a hunting accident, and Alan Tate wasn't hit by a car!" He smacked his open hand on the side of the car.

Lisa looked up at him, her face twisting with pain and tears streaming down her cheeks. "I, I don't know what to think!" she screamed, choking off with a sob. "I don't know what killed Jeff, but you're right: it wasn't like it was reported. I don't know! I don't know!"

"Look," Bob said softly, reaching for her.

Lisa pulled away violently. "Just leave me alone!"

"You're too upset. You should go home and get some rest. Maybe after the holidays, you can think about moving in with me."

"What?" She looked at him, wide-eyed. "Don't be ridiculous!"

"You're going to have a tough time pulling things together. I think maybe what you need is—"

"What I don't need is to be shacking up the first chance I get after my husband's funeral! What in the hell do you think people will say?"

Bob was stung by her response, but he felt a sudden, irrational anger bubbling up within him. "What I don't care about, Lisa," he said, keeping his voice even, "is all of this small-town bullshit! That's always how it is, isn't it? The small minds clicking and the big mouths flapping, all of them poking their noses into everyone's business but their own. And when they're through, they've succeeded in ruining someone's chance for a little bit of happiness." He lowered his voice and softened it. "I care about you, Lisa. I have since I met you. I don't want any bullshit gossip to ruin it."

"Oh?" Lisa said, her voice cracking. "Really?"

"Really."

Lisa heaved a long sigh and, gripping the steering wheel, leaned back in the car seat with her arms straight out. "You don't have to play any games with me, Bob. Not any more." She paused. "I know all about what happened with you and Beth Landry, and how you lost your last teaching job."

It was like she had just hit him in the chest with a sledge hammer. Bob felt the color drain from his face, and a burning lump formed in his throat. "I, I—how did you find out? Did you—?"

"Things might have gone a little smoother, Bob, if you had leveled with me from the start."

"There was nothing to hide," Bob said feebly. He knew his voice betrayed him.

"Then you should have told me from the start," she said firmly.

"I don't know what you heard, Lisa, but you should let me explain. That whole thing was a railroad job. That student, Beth Landry, was after me, trying to get me into the sack. When I didn't pick up on her advances, well, I guess she figured if she couldn't get me, she'd get me. I, I just don't see how that affects us."

"You should have been honest with me about it. You should have told me before I heard it some other way."

"What other way?" Bob asked, his anger flaring.

"That doesn't matter," Lisa answered. "What matters is that you weren't honest with me and it

282

makes me wonder what else you're holding back from me." Her eyes glistened. "You don't seem to understand, Bob, that relationships are built on trust, trust and honesty."

Bob stood up straight and scanned the now deserted cemetery. Snow drifted between the gravestones. The sky was a leaden gray. The cold air numbed his face, making him squint. He jumped when Lisa's car suddenly started up.

"Lisa," he called. "Lisa!"

She rolled up her window and put the car into gear. As she pulled away slowly, he walked along the side of the car calling her name. She ignored him and sped up, pulling away from him. Bob was left by the side of the road, listening to the receding sound of her car. Snow swirled at his feet, and for the first time in a long time, he cried.

Chapter Thirteen

Wednesday, December 24—Christmas Eve

.I.

Reverend Alder shrugged his shoulders to make sure his vestments were hanging just right. It was minutes until the Christmas Eve candlelight service began, and as he stood in his office doorway he looked long and hard at Bob, who was standing beside Lisa. Bob felt uncomfortable under the minister's searching gaze. He shifted his weight from one foot to the other, not sure what to do with his hands.

"I had hoped to see you before this," he said, with just the right combination of sternness and welcome.

Bob shrugged.

"Well," the reverend said, warming slightly, "I'm glad to see that Lisa finally has gotten you to attend service." He touched her lightly on the shoulder, gripping gently. Lisa managed a faint smile.

"And how have you been feeling?" he asked kindly.

"I've been all right," Lisa answered quietly. "It's been difficult."

"I know, I know." He gave his robe one final tug and then, excusing himself, ducked back into his office for a moment. He returned with his hymnal in hand. Through the doorway that led into the church, the hollow sound of the organ began to vibrate.

Bob moved over to the door and looked out into the church. It was completely full now. The ushers were lining up folding chairs along the side and center aisles. A young boy of about twelve, whom Bob didn't recognize, was lighting the candles on the altar.

"Well, I have to begin the service now," Reverend Alder said when the organ swelled louder. Bob recognized the hymn but could not recall the name. "Packed house. I can't keep them waiting."

The reverend made a move to squeeze past Bob and Lisa. Bob grabbed him by the elbow. "Uhh, Reverend, I, uhh—" He let his voice drop when he felt suddenly unnerved by the minister's glance.

"Yes?"

Bob released the minister's arm and slipped his hand, slick with sweat, into his pants pocket. "I'd like to have a word with you. After the service, if it's convenient."

Reverend Alder crinkled his brow. "Well, I do have an appointment to visit Elm Tree Nursing

Home. Is it important?"

"Yes, it is," Bob replied. "It'll only take a minute."

"Sure," the reverend said. "After the service, come back to my office." Then he slipped past Bob and Lisa and entered the church.

Bob stood in the doorway, watching as the minister strode out to tend his flock. He was sure that was how Reverend Alder saw it. As the thundering notes of "Hark the Herald Angels Sing" vibrated the floor, the congregation rose to its feet singing. Reverend Alder stopped in the center of the church, turned his back to the congregation, and joined in the singing.

Bob felt a tap on his shoulder. "What do you want to talk to him about?" Lisa asked, bending close to his ear to be heard above the singing. There was a strange look of concern in her eyes. When he didn't answer, she held onto both of his arms and asked, "You're not going to talk to him about, about your werewolf idea, are you?"

The astonishment in her voice chilled him. Bob pressed his lips together and nodded. "Get a little professional advice," he said, trying to lighten things up.

"I can't believe you're serious," she said. "You *really* believe you're right!" It was more of a statement than a question.

"I do," Bob said seriously. "I know what you think, but there have been too many coincidences to ignore. You don't have to believe it, but I—"

He stopped when the singing suddenly ended.

Looking quickly out at the congregation, he grabbed her arm and said, "Come on. Let's get our seats."

He swung the door open and moved out into the congregation. Their coats were spread across one of the pews in the front row. Lisa followed a few steps behind him and then stood silently beside him.

As the service proceeded, Bob was actually surprised at how much of the liturgy he still remembered. A casual glance at Lisa's open hymnal was all he needed now and then to bring back whole paragraphs of invocation and response. It all came back, just as mechanically as ever.

Throughout the service, Bob kept looking at Lisa. Their eyes would catch and hold, then let go without the slightest change of expression on Lisa's face.

When the gospel reading was completed, and everyone had sat down, there was a brief moment of silence, of expectation. And in that expectant silence there was just enough time for Bob's stomach to gurgle loudly. He chuckled and looked at Lisa, but she remained impassive.

Swirling the wide sleeves of his cassock, Reverend Alder walked up into the pulpit. He opened his Bible to where his finger marked his place and, leaning over the pulpit, stared out at the crowded church.

"Well," he began mildly, "I'm glad to see so many of you here tonight. Around Christmas time, I'm always pleasantly surprised to see how many people actually live here in Cooper Falls. Where do you hide from now until Easter?"

A nervous titter ran through the congregation.

"Our scripture lesson tonight, although not traditionally a Christmas message, is, I think, appropriate." Bob saw that the reverend gripped the edge of the pulpit with a firm bird-of-prey grasp. "It's appropriate because the story of the seven wise virgins and the seven foolish virgins is a story about being ready, ready for the beginning!

"Christmas, the first Christmas, was the start, the beginning of the beginning. I look at Christ's death on the cross on Good Friday and Easter as the end of the beginning.

"With Jesus' birth, in the dead of winter, we are given a promise of new life to come. A guarantee that, even though there is snow and ice and death, the world will bloom once again. It will grow green with new life! This!" He raised his hands over his head in a dramatic gesture. "This is the message that came to the shepherds almost two thousand years ago tonight!

"Join me in singing Hymn Seventy-three, 'It Came Upon A Midnight Clear.'"

A thundering note sounded from the organ. Then, just before the organ burst into the hymn, another note, piercing and discordant, shattered the night. The church hushed as everyone silently counted the regular timed blasts of the town fire-horn. There was a long pause. Everyone held his breath and then the pattern repeated.

"Four-five-one-one," someone to Bob's right shouted. As if on cue, there was an explosion of noise as people put their hymnals away and pulled on their coats. The church filled with a confused babble of voices.

"Where is it? Where's four-five-one-one?"

"I don't know!"

"Where's the fire? Where's four-five-one-one?"

"On Christmas Eve, no less!"

Bob looked at Lisa and read the fear and surprise in her face. She reached out and gripped the crook of his arm. "Jeff was a volunteer fireman. Four-five-one-one is out at Martin's Lake, I think." Her voice almost broke.

Everyone was on his feet, and the men were jostling past their wives and children to get to the door. For a moment Bob watched, then he scooped up his coat and quickly began to button it.

"Upper end of Drake Road!" someone shouted above the babble of noise.

"Martin's Lake area!"

"Can you get a ride home with someone, Lisa?" Bob asked. "I'm going out there. Maybe there's something I can do to help."

Before Lisa could answer, there was a loud scream of a siren outside. The flashing red light of the town's fire truck sent splinters of light through the church as it raced up Railroad Avenue. As the siren receded, Bob could hear the cars starting up in the parking lot.

"I'll come with you," Lisa said, tugging on her coat. "I might be able to help too."

"Don't you think—? Yeah, OK." Bob started to shoulder his way through the pack of people.

Once they were outside, as Bob fumbled to get his key into the door lock, Lisa leaned close to his ear and whispered, "Julie lives out on Martin's Lake."

"I know!" The lock clicked and Bob swung the door open for Lisa. As he got in behind the steering wheel, he added, "There are lots of other houses out there. Let's not think the worst until we see what's what. OK?"

"Sure."

Bob slammed the door shut and started up the car. He had to wait for a break in the line of cars leaving the church parking lot. The drive out to Martin's Lake was bumper to bumper all the way. It looked as though, wherever this Christmas Eve fire was, it was certainly going to be a spectator event.

.II.

"It's out at Martin's Lake," Ellie Simmons called up the stairway to her son's closed bedroom door.

"Really?" came a faint reply, flat and with no emotion.

"Uh-huh. Look out your window and see if you can see the glow. It's supposed to be a big one."

She listened intently and then heard one muffled clump on the floor upstairs.

"Well?" she called, placing her hand on the banister and contemplating going upstairs to have a look for herself. "Do you see anything?"

"No," Ned replied weakly.

Ellie listened to the silence for a moment and then started up the stairs. When she got to Ned's closed door, she stopped and, pressing her ear against the wood, listened for activity inside. She thought she could hear faint breathing, but she had trouble hearing anything over the pounding in her ears from the exertion of climbing the stairs.

"Ned?" she said softly, rapping lightly on the door. "Can I come in?"

There was no answer. She knocked again. Finally, she heard a deep sigh, and then Ned answered in a whisper, "Sure."

Ellie swung the door open and caught her breath in her throat as she saw her son lying on the bed. His hands were folded on his chest and he was staring vacantly at the ceiling. His face was pasty, with a pale, bluish tinge. His eyes looked like two soot smudges beneath his brows. His body barely made a bulge beneath the sheets.

"Ned, honey, are you feelin' all right?"

She walked over to his bed when he didn't answer. A grunt of surprise escaped her when she put her hand to his forehead and felt that it was ice-cold. "You're sick, boy."

"I'm all right. Just a little worn out, that's all."

"Well, I don't think so. I'm gonna give Doc Stetson a call." She made a move to go, but Ned reached out and grabbed her dress.

"No! Don't call Doc. I'll be all right. It's just a touch of flu or something."

"You sure?" She leaned over and placed her hand on his forehead. "Let me get you some water."

"No. I, I just need, need some rest," he said with a moan. His hand dropped to the floor, rapping his knuckles against the hardwood. Ellie took a quick step backward, still keeping her eyes on her son.

"I hope you're all right," she whispered, fighting to control her voice. "You're all, all I have left, now. I can't lose you too."

There was no reply from her son, but his even, shallow breathing was some reassurance. She backpedalled out of the room, easing the door shut behind her with a dull click. "Call if you want anything," she whispered through the door. "And, and Merry Christmas," she rasped, as tears coursed down her cheeks.

An hour later, after a few phone calls, she went to the foot of the stairs and called up to Ned's room, "The fire's out at Julie Sikes' place." She wasn't sure if he heard her. She went into the living room and pulled the plug to the Christmas-tree lights. Leaving only the two Christmas candles burning in the window, she went quietly off to bed.

.III.

The approach to the lake was slow. Cars were backed up almost a mile. The closer Bob and Lisa got, the more people they saw crowding the road.

292

"It'd better be a big one, or this crowd's going to be disappointed," Bob said cynically. He looked over at Lisa and smiled. Her expression remained fixed as she stared out at the long line of cars parked along the roadside.

"Shouldn't we park back there and walk?" she asked.

"There," Bob said suddenly, pointing off to the right. Above the jagged line of trees, the sky glowed a deep, flickering orange. "It looks like a big one, all right!"

Bob jockeyed his car into a small space between two other cars and turned the ignition off. Up ahead, he could see the burning timbers of the house and the three fire trucks that surrounded it. Misty sprays of water arched into the blaze but seemed to have no effect on the tongues of flame. As they sat and watched, people rushed past them, making their way toward Julie's burning house.

Bob loosened his tie and slipped it off. "Well, do you want to get closer?"

"I, I don't know," Lisa answered, her eyes darting nervously at the leaping flames.

"I think I will." Bob twisted around and reached into the back seat. "I think I have an old sweater back here. Ahh. Here it is." He wiggled his coat and sports coat off and then pulled the sweater on over his head. "No sense ruining my Sunday best." He got out and stood beside the car, leaning through the open door.

"Maybe I'll wait here a bit," Lisa said softly.

"yYu sure?"

She nodded, then shifted uncomfortably in her

seat and said, "Aww, well. I might as well come." She snapped open her door and just about had to scale the shoulder-high snowbank before she got around the car to the road. Bob leaned out over the car hood and offered her a helping hand, but she ignored it.

They pushed their way close to the fire. The deep snow had already been trampled flat, so the going was easy. They walked past small groups of people who stood facing the blaze. As they got closer, the crackling of the fire and the hissing of the water hoses grew louder until it drowned out everything else.

A sudden shower of sparks exploded into the air and a collective gasp went up from the crowd as part of the roof caved in. The flames intensified for a while, then steadied down again.

"I wonder where Julie is?" Bob said, cupping his hands to Lisa's ears so he could be heard above the noise. They were standing beside one of the fire trucks. Bob was leaning against the front fender. Lisa stood with her hands in her pockets and her shoulders pulled up tight.

"I hope she's all right," Bob said.

Lisa didn't reply.

Bob's face was beginning to prickle from the intense heat, and he was thinking about pulling back when one of the firemen bumped into him as he ran to the back of the truck and grabbed an axe. As he was heading back to the fire, he snagged Bob by the shoulder. "Hey," he said, his face glistening with sweat, "you could make yourself useful. Keep your eyes on this length of hose and make sure it doesn't coil up. That'd cut off the water. Keep an eye out for sparks, too."

"Yeah. Sure," Bob said, but the man had already rushed away.

Lisa came up close to him and said, "I think I'll get going now."

Bob nodded.

"Are you going to stay?"

Bob nodded again.

After a pause, Lisa said, "Could you use some coffee?"

"Sure."

"Why don't I see about making some up. I'm sure the other guys could use some too. I'll go back to the church and get the big coffee urn."

Bob started when suddenly the hose pulled away across the ground, leaving a deep furrow in the trampled snow.

"Coffee'd be good. Take my car." He handed her the keys and then walked over to the hose, kicking it once for good measure. It felt as though the water in it had frozen.

Julie's house was already a complete loss. Only skeletonlike studs remained standing, black lines against the raging wall of flames. The trees around the house were safe from catching fire. They had been soaked down and, anyway, were covered with thick snow.

Bob jumped when he felt a rough tap on his shoulder. Turning, he saw Granger. The fire danced wildly in the police chief's eyes.

"Wicked, huh?" the policeman said.

"Especially on Christmas Eve. Do you think it

was from the tree lights?"

"No way of telling yet."

"How about Julie?" Bob asked anxiously. "Do you know? Was she home?"

Granger shrugged. "No one's seen her. If she was home, she's still in there." He nodded toward the inferno. "I sure hope to hell she was visiting a friend or something."

Bob tried not to think about it. "Lisa's gone for coffee."

"Good," Granger said with a sigh. "It's gonna be a helluva long Christmas Eve. Christ, if it isn't one thing it's another!"

The breeze suddenly shifted around, sending a billow of smoke and steam over the crowd. Bob covered his face with his forearm and stifled a cough. The smoke made his eyes sting.

What if she's in there! his mind screamed. What if she didn't get out!

He thought about what a friend of his had once said: that burning to death is probably one of the most painful ways to die. As soon as you open your mouth to scream, or even to breathe, your throat and lungs get fried. You don't have any vocal cords left to scream! After that. . . .

He shook his head and focused as best he could on the thick canvas hose snaking along the ground.

The last standing timbers fell, pitching out onto the snow with a fiery shower of sparks. Some of the charred wood fell onto the hose, and Bob rushed forward, stamping out whatever embers he saw. This close to the fire, the heat prickled his skin, making it feel tight. Again the thought of dying by fire entered his mind. He hoped the strangled whimper that escaped his throat was lost in the noisy confusion.

.IV.

By dawn, the house was leveled, the fire was out, and everyone who had stayed the night was cold and exhausted. Most of the crowd had left after the first few hours, once the roof had fallen in and the fire was certain to be contained.

Now, only the chimney remained—a tall, jagged black tower standing out sharply against the pale blue sky. The rest of Julie's house was a blackened pit in the ground surrounded by soot-smeared snow and ice. Charred timbers lay scattered about on the snow. Steam still hissed up from the burned-out cellar where three firemen wearing hipboots were prodding the wreckage.

Bob was sitting on a blanket some distance from the destroyed house. He leaned his head back against the cold bark of the tree and looked up at the sky. His hands cupped an empty coffee mug.

Lisa stood beside him, watching the firemen as they milled about the ruin. She looked down at Bob, her face an unmoving mask.

"Would you like some more?" she asked.

"I'm going to be awake for a week after all the coffee I've had tonight. Sure. Fill 'er up." He handed his cup to Lisa and tried, for a moment, to close his eyes and rest.

"I wonder where she is?" he said, half to himself. "I mean, if my house was burning, I'd sure as hell want to stick around and—"

"How do you know she was around?" Lisa asked sharply, startling Bob, who thought he had been talking to himself.

"She might have been away, visiting relatives or friends for the holiday."

"Let's hope so," Bob said, reaching for his cup again. "Let's just hope so." With a groan, he got to his feet and started over to where the men were sifting through the rubble. Lisa remained beside the tree, and Bob was just as glad; she still wasn't acting all that friendly to him.

He walked over to Granger and mumbled a greeting.

"Well," the police chief said, straightening up, "it looks as though she wasn't home. Least, so far we haven't found a body." He took a few quick puffs from the cigarette that dangled from his mouth and then let it drop to the ground. He crushed it out with his heel.

"That's a relief," Bob said. "There's more coffee over there."

"In a bit," Granger said as he resumed prodding the frozen ashes with a shovel. He reminded Bob of a derelict dump-picker. Watching him, Bob had to hold back his laughter.

He was just turning to go back to Lisa when the toe of his boot struck something under the snow. He glanced down and was about to step over it when he saw the edge of a book sticking out of the snow.

Bob scooped the book up, glancing to see if anyone was looking at him. The book had been burned badly. The flames had sliced it almost neatly in half from top to bottom, leaving a tall, thin volume. He wiped it on his pants leg. On the top of the black leather binding, on the spine, he could barely make out the spidery letters of the gold-stamped title. He brushed the book again with his hand and read: *Witchcraft: Forms and Functions.*

Reflexively, Bob snatched the book to his chest, covering it with his forearm as he let the shock register and then subside. His heart was pounding in his ears, and his mind was racing wildly over dozens of logical steps to an illogical conclusion. His knees started to feel watery, and there was a bad taste in the back of his mouth that was growing stronger.

Sliding the book into his coat pocket, he walked over to the edge of the cellar and looked down inside. The men were still raking the ashes into piles and then poking through them. Their soot-smeared faces made them look like demons.

Granger was standing in the center of the cellar, where there had been a small, central room. There was just a low doorway in the stone wall now, probably indicating where the root cellar had been. Granger ducked into the little room. Bob started back toward Lisa.

"Hey," he called. "Check this out." His voice was low and intense as he eased the burned book out of his pocket.

"Yeah?" Lisa squinted, trying to make out the title.

"This is it," Bob said assuredly. "This is Julie's book of magic." He thumped it authoritatively.

"So." Lisa was either unimpressed or very successful at masking her reaction. "She had a lot of books like that. I told you, she was always taking out occult books from the library. What does that prove?" She folded her arms across her chest.

Bob tried to keep his voice from sounding too eager. "You don't think it might add a little weight to my theory? Look." He flipped through the pages rapidly. "It's loaded with spells and incantations and stuff."

"Bob, Julie wasn't a witch!" Lisa said firmly. "Just because she was into reading that kind of stuff, doesn't mean she, she practiced it and turned herself into a werewolf!"

"Ssshhh! Will you keep it down?" Bob looked over at the working men to see if they had heard them. He continued to speak in a whisper. "This is just one more coincidence, huh? Is that it?"

Lisa shrugged and looked down at the book. Her teeth ran across her lower lip. She took the book from Bob and flipped through the pages, each one trimmed on the edge with a jagged black line of ash that flaked off and dusted the ground. "I don't know," she said distantly, and handed the book back to Bob.

"Yeah, well, I plan to check this out later," Bob said, sliding it back into his pocket.

"Hey, Wentworth!" Granger's voice shouted from the cellar. "We're trying to move this piece of flooring. Are you here to help or to socialize?"

300

"Be right there," Bob called. He started back toward the cellar.

"I hope you don't find anything," Lisa said weakly. She smiled at Bob as he stood on the edge of the cellar about to jump down inside. It was the first smile he had seen on her face in days, and it warmed him more than the dozen or so cups of coffee he had consumed since the interrupted church service.

"I guess I'll head on home and get some sleep," Lisa said.

"Sure. You could use it, I bet."

"Hey!" one of the men shouted suddenly, making Bob look down into the cellar.

"What the fuck!"

Bob couldn't see what was going on because of an obstruction, but he heard a loud scrambling sound and then a babble of voices.

"There it goes! Over there!"

"I can't—son of a bitch!"

Bob raced along the edge of the cellar, peering down, trying to see what was going on. He heard a loud, spitting hiss that sounded like water hitting something hot, but it also brought back an instant memory of the night in the cemetery at Cedar Grove.

"I can't get it! Jesus!"

"There it goes!"

Bob stood in amazement as he saw the cat, the white cat, scramble up the side of the burned-out cellar and then, with a loud yowling, dash off into the surrounding forest.

"D'you see that?" Granger shouted up to Bob. "D'you see that fucker go?"

Bob stood in silent amazement, unable to move.

"How the hell did that bastard get in here?" one man asked, shaking his head from side to side.

"Christ!" Granger answered. "It couldn't have been here all along, could it? It would have fried!"

.V.

Bob got up from his chair, took a nervous puff from his cigarette, and began pacing back and forth across the kitchen floor. He kept rubbing the back of his neck to relieve the stiffness he had gotten from bending over while reading. The partially destroyed book he had found at Julie's house lay open on the counter. Every time his pacing brought him back to the counter, he would glance down at the book. The series of half-sentences was maddening.

He sat back down in his chair, propped his chin on his hands, and started reading again, trying to make sense of the passage. To help complete the thoughts, he started reading aloud.

Trials in medieval Germany in which se
were accused of "going out at night in
wolves), seizing and devouring the bodies
until they were satiated, whereupon they
removing the fur pelts from their waists a
three times counterclockwise (widdersh

Witches were not, of course, rest
wolves. They could assume the shape of
often to travel many miles to a coven
worshipped the Man in Black (that is, S

The fragmentary book continued like this for
page after frustrating page. Bob puffed angrily on
his cigarette as he pondered what the missing
words were. What he could understand fit quite
well into the pattern Bob had seen developing, and
that made what was left out all the more in-
furiating. Bob slammed the book shut with a loud
thump and resumed his pacing.

Was the pattern really there? he wondered, or
was he forcing it? He walked over to the Christmas
tree he had set up in the living room and ran his
fingers lightly through the tinsel. It sent glimmers
of light dancing.

Maybe Lisa's right! Maybe he was way off
track! What had she said? That paranoia is just
seeing coincidences and patterns in life and ascrib-
ing them to evil. Evil!

"Just an overactive imagination," he whispered
softly, letting his breath sway the tinsel. "Just
having too much time to think." He was trying to
convince himself to drop it all, to start thinking
along other, more fruitful lines, but he couldn't
shake the gnawing, creepy feeling he got whenever
he looked at the remains of Julie's magic book.

So why was he so convinced that it was witchcraft, magic, at work in town? The evidence he
had would never stand up in a court. He knew
that. It would be thrown out as circumstantial, in-

admissible. He snickered to himself and said softly, "Hell, Beth Landry had a better case."

Walking over to the living-room window, he bent down and looked outside. The sun was shining brightly, glaring off the snow that stretched out to the forest. The sky was a rich, deep blue. The beauty and serenity made Bob's thoughts seem absolutely ridiculous and even laughable, but he wasn't laughing.

He thought again of giving Reverend Alder a call. He had missed his appointment with him after the Christmas Eve service because of the fire. He knew he should talk to him. If anyone in Cooper Falls was going to believe his werewolf theory it would have to be the reverend. It was his job to believe in the supernatural.

A sudden, loud knock at his door made him turn around. Somehow, he wasn't surprised when he looked and saw Deputy Thurston standing on the porch. He forced a smile and opened the door.

"I'm not disturbing you, am I?" Thurston said upon entering.

Bob shook his head, forcing himself not to tell the truth. "You guys work even on Christmas Day?" Bob asked.

Thurston didn't say a word as he walked over to the counter and sat down. "Have to," he said, zipping his coat open.

Bob walked over to the stove and filled the tea kettle with water. "I didn't see you out at Julie's house last night," Bob said, glancing over his shoulder.

Thurston shrugged. "Had to stay at the office, for calls and such."

"You missed a big one."

"I know. I was out there this morning with Roy."

Bob tensed when Thurston shifted in his chair and his elbow bumped against the burned book. Thurston glanced down and placed his hand lightly on the charred cover.

"So," Bob blurted out, "you don't have any time to spend with your family, huh? Out on duty all day?"

Thurston drummed his fingers on the book cover. "I'm not married," he said.

Somehow, that didn't surprise Bob. He came over and sat at the counter opposite Thurston. He shook a cigarette from his pack and lit it. He wanted to meet the deputy's eyes, but he kept looking down at his hands.

"This book's pretty badly burned," Thurston said evenly. "You get it out at Julie's last night?"

Bob nodded and exhaled. He tensed when Thurston flicked the burned edges of the pages, and ashes sprinkled to the counter top.

"Huh," Thurston said, picking up the book and glancing at the title. "Witchcraft." He slid the book back toward Bob.

Thurston leaned back in his chair and sighed. "You know, Wentworth, I've been wanting to have a talk with you for quite some time. Ever since our little chat last fall, really."

Bob tried to maintain an even stare at Thurston. "What about?" he asked. In his ears he heard a distracting whooshing sound.

"Ever since Wendy Stillman got killed by that dog or whatever," Thurston said. "Do you recall that I mentioned that she had had sexual relations before she was killed?"

305

Bob nodded.

"And you know, it's been bothering me all this time. I mean, I've been wondering if those relations were voluntary."

Bob shifted uneasily. "You know," he stammered, "since we spoke then, I, well, I kind of remembered that there was something I forgot to tell you."

"You forgot?"

Bob told him that he had seen Wendy together with someone else, probably Alan Tate, in the lighting booth the night they had decorated for the Halloween party.

When he finished, Thurston was frowning. "That's a pretty significant detail to forget, wouldn't you say?"

Bob shrugged. "I was pretty upset about what had happened to Wendy. It just slipped my mind."

"Yeah, well, it makes me wonder. And now this Sikes girl. She's missing."

"She hasn't come back yet?" Bob asked, surprised.

Thurston shook his head. "It's kind of weird, don't you think? She seems to have vanished like smoke. I was wondering if you might be able to help me out a little."

"I don't know," Bob replied. "I was out there last night at the fire, but I—"

"You forgot what I consider something pretty important relating to Wendy Stillman's death. I'm wondering if, maybe, you're forgetting something you know about Julie Sikes, something that might help us figure out what happened to her. You know, usually if someone knows something and doesn't tell the police, it's usually because he's got something he doesn't want to talk about, something in his past."

Oh, Jesus! Bob thought.

Thurston's hand slipped into his coat pocket and produced two pages of photocopied newspaper clippings. With a smooth twist of his wrist, he placed them on the countertop in front of Bob like a winning poker hand.

Bob's eyes darted over the headlines as a burning lump began to form in his throat.

Thurston said softly, "I thought you might have some idea where this Sikes girl has gone, that's all. It seems like you knew more about the Stillman girl than you were willing to tell me."

Bob clenched his fists in his lap. For a flickering moment, he considered hauling back and punching Thurston. The smug self-assurance galled Bob, but he forced his fingers to unclasp slowly.

Too many times, he thought, too many times, I've jumped too fast, and it usually makes things look worse.

"I just thought if you saw these newspaper stories, you might, well, jog your memory a bit more. You understand?" Thurston smiled with satisfaction. "Well, you don't want me to have to come right out and say it, do you?"

"That's blackmail," Bob said through clenched teeth.

"I just want you to know that if there's something you should be telling me, and you don't—well, you never know whose desk these might end up on." Thurston rose from his chair and started toward the door, zipping up his coat.

You son of a bitch, Bob thought angrily. He now

knew who had told Lisa about his problems with Beth Landry. She must have believed that he was innocent because she had been slightly, not much, but slightly warmer to him. But Bob knew that it would be futile to argue his innocence with Thurston. The man obviously had a grudge against him. The only thing about the whole damn situation that felt good was that Bob had just as strong a dislike for the deputy.

"I'm glad you're leaving," Bob said, holding the door for Thurston. "I wouldn't want to have to ask you to leave."

Thurston smiled slightly and started toward his cruiser.

.VI.

"Doc Stetson, I'm awfully sorry to be callin' you on Christmas Day, but I have to talk with you. I'm worried sick about Ned."

"What's wrong?" the doctor asked, his concern registering in his voice. "Just relax and tell me what the problem is."

"It's Ned," Ellie Simmons blurted out, close to tears. "He ain't been well at all!" She sniffed loudly.

"Yes?" Doctor Stetson said patiently.

"He don't look well. He don't eat right. Lord, he's losin' weight and he's so pale. I swear to God, his eyes are bloodshot bright-red, like he's, like he's been taking drugs. Is that it? Could takin' drugs make him so sick?"

Stetson paused. "Well, I can't say, not without

seeing him first. Why don't you call my office Monday morning and make an appointment to bring him in?"

"He looks so poorly," Ellie said, her voice breaking. "He ain't eatin' right or nothin'. He stays awake all hours."

"Yes, Mrs. Simmons. If you'll make an appointment and then we can—"

"You can't see him sooner?" she broke in. Her throat tightened.

"Mrs. Simmons, I understand your concern, but I'm quite busy right now. The best thing for you to do is to bring him in Monday morning. I'll check him over. And stop fretting!" he commanded. "You'll just make yourself sick."

Ellie nodded her head in agreement as though the doctor was there in the room with her and could see her.

"All right?" Doctor Stetson said.

"Yes, Doctor," Ellie said softly. "Thanks, and, and Merry Christmas."

.VII.

Ned smiled down at Julie's upturned face and combed his fingers through her hair. Her face glowed with an orange dullness in the flickering light of the kerosene lamp. They were deep in the mine shaft where it was warm and silent.

"Everything will be all right," Ned whispered, close to her ear. She remained immobile, unblinking, with her eyes fixed on the ceiling of the mine. "Really, it will."

Ned shifted and lay down beside her, pulling her close. He gently pressed his lips to hers in a long kiss.

"Ohhh, you feel so cold," he said, pulling away. "Are you warm enough?"

There was no reply. Julie's gaze was still fixed on the ceiling.

Ned's fingers hovered over Julie's face and then slowly moved down to her throat. "Oh, Julie," he groaned as he began to work on the top button of her blouse. "You don't know how much I've wanted this." The button opened, and he ran his hand down to the next one.

"I'll keep you warm," he said, opening the last button and spreading her blouse open. Sliding one arm under her shoulders, he lifted her up and started to work the blouse off. All the while, he kissed her cheeks, forehead, lips, and neck. Still holding her away from the musty mattress, he unfastened the catch to her bra and pulled it off with a quick motion. He lowered her back down.

"Oh, Julie," he moaned, lowering his head and kissing her breasts. He glanced up at her motionless face.

"It won't be like this for long. You can stay here with me for a while and then, pretty soon, I'll take you to my house. You can stay there with me. I'll treat you real good."

He moved his head down, kissing her stomach as he worked to unfasten her pants. The snap came open and then the zipper slipped down.

Again, he looked up at her passive face. Then

he tugged on her pants, working them down her legs. They were tight-fitting, and he had to pull hard to get them over her hips. When he gave a sharp tug, Julie's hand slipped from beside him and flopped onto the dirt floor. Ned looked at her hand for a moment, lying there with its fingers stiffly opened. He gave the jeans a final yank, threw them onto the floor, and then took Julie's hand and laid it on her chest. It looked like it was reaching for her throat.

"There, there," he whispered, sitting back on his heels and running his hands over her body. "I just wish you had listened to me. We could have done so much! We have the power and can use it!"

He stared at her face for a long time, feeling a deep glow of contentment. Then he slowly, lovingly rolled her panties down. With the thin garment hanging loosely in his hand, Ned stood up and regarded Julie. He was transfixed by her vacant, glassy stare. Then, slowly, he undressed and lay down beside her.

"Oh, you're so cold, so cold," he whispered, pulling her to him and glorying in the feeling of their naked bodies pressed together. "You need to get warm. I can make you warm. I can give that to you now."

When he lifted her up and hugged her close, her head fell backwards and her mouth gaped open, expelling a wave of putrid gas as Ned's hug compressed her stomach. Her arms were beginning to stiffen, and he had to bend each at the elbow until they encircled his waist.

A low, rumbling groan escaped his throat as he rolled Julie onto her back, pressing his weight against her. With his knees, he spread her legs wide and entered her.

"We could have done so much together with the power!" he said between grunts as he began to pump his hips.

Tears welled in his eyes when, vaguely, he realized what he was doing, realized that Julie was dead. But he was swept up in a raging, spinning desire, and he held Julie's corpse tightly until he shuddered and spent himself.

Chapter Fourteen

.I.

Ted Seavey sat on the edge of his chair, his feet laced through the rungs. He pressed his head against the cold glass of the kitchen window, which was opened about two inches. A cold draft made the lace curtains billow in and out. Ted squinted his eyes with concentration as he listened to the clamor coming from his henhouse.

His fingers were drumming on the stock of his Winchester rifle, which lay across his lap. He cocked his head around and asked, "Hey, Edna, did you call?"

"He said he'd be right over," Edna answered from the next room. Ted shifted his gaze back to the window. Edna, a slouching, graying woman walked into the kitchen and rested her hand lightly on her husband's shoulder.

"Christ, I wish he'd get here," Ted muttered. His fingers were still dancing along the edge of the gunstock.

Edna was about to reply when a sudden, terrified squawking sound came from the henhouse and cut her off.

"Lord God Almighty! It must be tearing the place apart," Ted said, not looking around at her. He could see her faint reflection in the window. She had one hand raised, covering her mouth.

There was a loud crashing sound; boards splintered and chicken wire tore. Hens clucked wildly. Even at this distance from the house, it was almost deafening.

"I hope you told him I wasn't goin' out there alone," Ted said.

Edna drew up a chair beside him, sat down, and said, "I told him."

"Get a sweater on if you're gonna sit here by this open window," Ted snapped. "You want to catch a cold or something?"

Edna got up and went into the living room, returning soon wearing a cardigan and holding out a sweater for Ted.

"Did Roy say when he'd get here?"

"As soon as he could," Edna replied patiently, sitting back down beside her husband.

"Ummm."

There was another, even louder explosion of wood from the henhouse. The clamor continued without pause as Ted and Edna sat listening tensely.

It was after eleven o'clock before Granger pulled into Seavey's yard. Coming into the driveway, his headlights swept across the face of the barn, cutting the shadows in a wide arc as he turned around in the driveway and stopped the cruiser. Only one light, in the kitchen, was on. The pale blue glow of the full moon washed the roof and the snowy field behind the house.

Granger sat for a moment and scanned the darkness. He rolled his window down before snapping on the spotlight and running the thin, intense beam over the barnyard. The beam of light darted about the face of the barn, cutting the darkness like a heated knife.

Everything was quiet now, but Granger could see that the henhouse had been almost totally destroyed. All of the wired windows were torn out, and the door was hanging on one loose hinge. There were feathers and what looked like blood all over the ground.

For a moment, Granger thought Seavey had gone to bed. Then the back porch light snapped on and Ted stepped out into the cold. He leaned forward, hanging on the door, and waved Granger in.

Granger shut off the headlights and the spotlight, and killed the engine. He debated leaving his shotgun in the cruiser, but then picked it up before opening the door. He left the box of ammunition on the front seat.

"I didn't see much—moving, that is," Granger called out as he came up the pathway shoveled out of the drift of snow.

"You should've heard it half an hour ago," Seavey said, stepping back as the police chief entered the house. He cast an apprehensive glance at the destroyed henhouse. "It's been quiet now," he added, almost under his breath.

Granger stepped into the toasty warm kitchen and nodded a greeting at Edna.

"It sounded like there was a whole pack o'dogs out there," Edna said.

"You didn't see anything, though, huh?"

Ted and Edna both shook their heads. "If you think I was gonna go out there and take a look, well . . ." Ted said.

"Well, let's go take a look now," Granger said. "I've got a flashlight in the cruiser, and ammo."

As they left the house, Ted let Granger lead the way.

When they returned half an hour later, Edna met them at the door. The tension didn't leave her face until they were both inside and the door was closed and locked. Then she smiled weakly and walked over to the stove to heat up some coffee.

"You wouldn't believe it!" Seavey said, looking at his wife with amazement on his face. "It looks like a bomb went off in there. Dead chickens everywhere. None of 'em left alive. The coop's about good for firewood, that's all."

"You didn't see the animal?" Edna asked.

"Nope."

Ted took the bullets from the chamber of his rifle and then stood it up in the corner beside the refrigerator. Granger sat down heavily at the kitchen table, placing his shotgun and flashlight in front of him.

"Saw some pretty good tracks, though," Seavey said, shaking his head. "Some damn big ones."

Granger sighed and scratched his head. "Course, it might be deceptive. Those tracks might look bigger in the snow than they really are. Still . . ." He whistled through his teeth.

The pot on the stove began to boil, and Edna reached down two cups. Seavey was over by the window, still staring out at the moonlit snow.

"No. No coffee for me, thanks," Granger said, rising slowly to his feet. He hiked his pants up and bounced on his heels. "I don't want to be up all night. I just might take a swing out around the loop, though. See if I can see anything." He zipped his coat up and made for the door.

"You want me to come along?" Seavey asked.

"Naw." Granger swung the door open. "I doubt I'll see anything. 'Sides, it's after midnight. You get some sleep. But drop by the office tomorrow, OK?"

"Sure."

"Good enough. Goodnight Ted, Edna."

As Granger drove away from the Seavey's, he scanned both sides of the road carefully for any sign of the animal. Looking out at the still, calm night, he found it difficult to believe that somewhere out there was a killer, an animal that had killed four residents of Cooper Falls. It was out there in the forest somewhere, and Granger knew with a gut-wrenching dread that he would have to find that beast and kill it, soon.

He reached out and picked up the radio microphone. He pressed the button to talk, but then remained silent. No sense in calling in when there was nothing to report. He placed the microphone back on its clip as he turned onto Farthling's Loop Road.

He drove slowly, watching the high sides of the snowbanks, stopping now and then to scan the woods with his searchlight whenever he saw what might have been tracks. He kept thinking about the amount of damage done to Seavey's henhouse and the size of the tracks in the snow. If the tracks were any gauge, he figured the animal must weigh close to a hundred and fifty pounds. The paws had measured close to six inches across.

"One hell of a big fucking animal," Granger whispered softly.

He came to where a fire road branched off to the right, just about at the point where the Loop Road began to curve back toward Bartlett Road.

The snowbanks were flattened down where snowmobiles had crossed the road. The fire road headed east out toward Martin's Lake, about a mile away.

Granger stopped the cruiser and got out. He had his shotgun clutched in one hand, his flashlight in the other. Puffing, he climbed up onto the snowbank and took a look around.

The wind moaned deeply in the pines, sending ghostlike sprays of snow sifting down from the branches. Granger's pencil-thin flashlight beam danced in and out of the shadows, revealing nothing. His grip on his shotgun loosened slightly. The peace and stillness of the night remained unmarred. Granger sighed to relieve the tension he felt building, then turned back down toward the cruiser.

Once he was sitting behind the steering wheel again, Granger felt safer. He took a pad of paper from the console and jotted down: "Farthling's Loop. 12:35 A.M. Not a damn thing." He put the pad of paper down and picked up the radio microphone.

"Rick, this is Roy. You got your ears on? Over."

He waited, tapping the steering wheel as he listened to the static of the radio and the faint chatter of a trucker out on Route 43. Thurston did not respond.

"Rick, you there? Over."

His eyes darted from the radio to the snowbank as he waited.

Suddenly, as though it had moved into place

in the time it took him to blink his eyes, he saw it: the animal standing at the top of the snowbank. It squared its shoulders and looked down at Granger with a cold, hard green glint in its eyes.

"Holy ole Jesus Christ," Granger muttered, letting the microphone drop to the floor. It continued to sputter static.

Granger couldn't take his eyes away from the animal as it stood tall and proud, the wind puffing its pale gray fur. The animal threw its head back and let loose a long, wavering howl.

Moving slowly, Granger went to pick up his shotgun, but then he realized that he would probably have a better chance of dropping the animal if he used his service revolver. He knew damn well that the .38 was no good for a distant target, but with the beast no more than fifteen feet away from the cruiser, Granger wasn't concerned with getting any closer before firing. He drew his pistol and was just bringing it to bear on the wolf—

Christ, yes! Granger thought. I know a wolf when I see one!—when the animal disappeared behind the ridge of snow.

"Come on, you fucker," Granger said angrily. He sat counting the seconds with slow precision as he cocked the pistol's hammer back and held it close to the window. He debated swinging the spotlight around, but before he could, a streak of silver off to his right caught his attention. He twisted around to look, scanning the side of the road anxiously.

It's close! he thought. It's coming in close!

He leaned across the seat and tried to pierce the darkness, but all he could see was the ridge of snow and the forest beyond. Just then, a massive weight slammed into the driver's side of the car. The cruiser rocked on its suspension. Granger turned around and reflexively shielded his face as the window glass shattered. Granger saw the wolf no more than six inches from him, snarling loudly as it battered with flailing paws the spiderweb patterns of the broken window.

"Cock-suck-er!" Granger shouted, waving his hand at the animal. The revolver in his right hand was momentarily forgotten, until he felt its weight. Teeth flashing, the wolf was punching at the window with its snout until a small hole appeared in the center of the spiderweb. Then it reared back and pressed against the window with its full weight.

Granger swung the revolver up just as the window exploded inward. Flying fragments of glass lacerated Granger's face. The gun discharged with a hollow, thundering blast. The bullet tore through the door and ricocheted from the frozen asphalt. Granger's face stung with dozens of slices from the glass, and it took him a few deadly seconds to realize that he hadn't hit the wolf.

The animal thrust its head into the cruiser. Its foam-flecked jaws opened wide and grabbed Granger by the shoulder with a vicelike grip.

Granger yelled as searing pain flooded his body, splashing along his nerves like acid. Again the gun exploded, this time ripping off the spotlight.

The strength quickly drained from Granger. After the second shot, his revolver dropped to the floor. He felt himself being dragged jerkily toward the door as the wolf pulled viciously on his shoulder. The throaty growling of the wolf, although almost at his ear, was sounding fainter, as though at a great distance. His eyes, fixed on the glow of the headlights on the snowbank, began to lose focus. The light grew brighter and brighter in pulses, and the view grew less distinct until it began to recede, like the view through the wrong end of a telescope.

Granger became aware, dimly, of a hollow, thumping sound beneath the angry growling of the wolf. When the sound came in conjunction with stinging stabs of pain in his head, he realized that he was being pulled roughly through the broken window. His head banged repeatedly against the roof of the cruiser. His body jostled wildly in time with the savage pulls of the beast.

Just before Granger sank down into merciful unconsciousness, he heard a grating, crunching sound, and then the long, drawnout echo of someone screaming.

.IV.

The wolf dragged the flopping body of the police chief out through the window and up over the snowbank. Once out of sight from the road, the animal settled down and ate its fill.

.V.

Bob's mind clicked rapidly. Whenever Mr. Jack Summers called you into his "inner sanctum" on a Friday afternoon and asked you to make yourself comfortable, you could be damn sure he wasn't going to ask you how you liked the new carpet that had been installed in the office.

No, Bob thought, aware of the tight grip he had on the arms of the chair, that isn't what he's going to do.

Summers leaned out of the office and said something to his secretary, then eased the door shut and took his seat at the desk. Except for a manila folder in the center of the ink blotter, the desk was clear.

"Well, Mr. Wentworth. May I call you Bob?"

Bob nodded.

"Bob. We haven't really had much of a chance to talk, you and I, have we?"

Bob shook his head, feeling stupid and awkward. "Uhh, no. We haven't."

"Too bad, too bad," Summers said, leaning his elbows on his desk and steepling his fingers. He gave Bob a cold, hard look before continuing. "Well, you see, the reason I've called you in today is, well . . . ." He searched the ceiling as though he had lost his place on a cue card. "I've been hearing some vague stirrings, some rumblings, you might say, that have me quite concerned."

"Oh?" Bob managed to say, hoping to keep this a dialog.

"Yes." Summers leaned forward slightly and stared into the pyramid of his fingers. "Now it's quite difficult for me to believe that what I've heard is true. But what I've heard, and the people I heard it from, have me concerned and, well, I thought we both might benefit from a little chat. You understand."

He knows! Goddammit, he knows! Bob thought. The casual tone didn't fool him. He knew he was being manipulated, expertly manipulated. He knew he would have to keep his guard up.

"What I've been hearing, from more than one source, I might add, is that you have not been quite prepared in your classes lately; that for the last two months or so you have, shall we say, let things slide." He leaned forward even more and arched his eyebrows.

That isn't all you've heard, I'll bet, Bob thought. A sour taste filled his mouth. "I, I wouldn't say so," he said softly, irritated by the weakness in his voice.

"Really?" Summers' eyebrows went up further. "Of course, I wanted to speak with you first, to hear what you had to say about it before I said too much. But, as I said, these reports have come from a number of sources. Your last evaluation was not the best aNd—" He tapped the manila folder with his forefinger. "And your lessons plans have been skimpy at best."

Bob shifted back in his seat and loosened the grip on the chair arms. Don't let him get to you, he thought.

"I wonder," Summers went on with a more menacing tone in his voice. "I can't help but wonder exactly how much you are getting done in your classes."

"I've been having some personal problems lately," Bob said, "but they have not affected my teaching."

Take it easy. Don't let him get to you!

"You leave your personal problems outside the door as soon as you walk into that classroom, Mr. Wentworth," Summers said firmly. "I am concerned only with your performance in the classroom, nothing else."

"My performance in the classroom has been just fine," Bob said, forcing himself to remain cool. "But there have been things going on in this town that have, have me concerned. For one this, this wild dog or whatever. There have been four unexplained deaths in this town, and that bothers me."

"I don't see how that affects your teaching," Somers said dryly.

"Because one of them was a student of mine," Bob said, his anger flaring. "That bothers me! I'm not just a teacher, I'm a member of this community, and these recent deaths have me greatly concerned."

"Indeed," Summers said, shaking his head and clicking his tongue. "These deaths are horrible, but I would think that it would not affect your job."

"It's not affecting my job!" Bob said, trying hard not to shout. "I would just like to help, if I could."

"A fine sentiment, indeed, but I think you'd be best off leaving this matter to those people whose job it is to deal with it. You were hired to teach English, not to get involved in other peoples' responsibilities. This—" Again he tapped the manila folder. "This tells me that you are not doing the job you were hired to do."

Bob leaned forward and was about to reply when his eye caught an edge of a piece of paper that was sticking out of the folder. It looked like a photocopied newspaper clipping.

That bastard does know, he thought. He's toying with me.

"Where did—" he started to say, but then cut himself off. He knew immediately that Thurston must have given those clippings to Summers. He slumped back in his chair feeling defeated.

"I think a word to the wise is sufficient, don't you?" Summers said softly, his voice like oil. He rose and extended a hand to Bob. As they shook, Summers added, "My advice to you, Bob, is that you concentrate a little more on your job and let other people handle this, this problem in town."

"Sure, sure," Bob said, as he turned and headed for the door. "I'll do better in class." He left without closing the door behind him.

Bob drove with one hand draped over the steering wheel, the other resting lightly on the gearshift. Lisa's hands were clasped in her lap. She had said all of two words since he had picked her up after work.

The car was having trouble making the grade of the cemetery hill. The spark plugs misfired, and Bob had to downshift to make the rise. He looked over and saw that Lisa was biting her lower lip.

"That's all you heard?" Bob asked as they drove alongside the cemetery.

"Uh-huh."

"After Granger left Seavey's house last night, he hasn't been seen or heard from," he said. It was more a statement than a question. They came to the intersection and, instead of turning left onto Old Jepson's Road, Bob went straight, up the Bartlett Road.

"That's all I know," Lisa said distantly.

"Christ! You know what I think."

Lisa's gaze remained fixed on the road.

Bob sighed. "And what the hell is Thurston doing about it? Sitting on his hands?"

"Bob."

"Huh! He probably sees this as his chance to become police chief."

"Bob!"

"Well," he grunted. The sun had set, and purple clouds were closing in on the bright bands of light in the western sky. Cold shadows reached across the road, turning the snowbanks deep blue. Lisa shivered, so Bob turned up the heat in the car.

After a moment, Bob said, "You know, this is Thurston's big chance. Maybe he will wear the star."

Lisa flared. "Bob! I really don't think you're being fair. Just because he—"

"He blackmailed me! That's what he did. He told Summers about those charges. I know he did. I'm telling you, Lisa, he's a lot more devious than you realize, or will admit." He didn't dare look at Lisa, so he kept his gaze fixed on the shadowy road.

"He's just doing his job, Bob," Lisa said mildly. "He has to check out any angles there are."

"Hmmmmp." After a moment of silence, Bob pointed up to the sky off to the right. "Look. The moon's full tonight." A large silver disk had just risen above the horizon. A cold, pale face.

"Come on, Bob. Don't start that." There was an edge in her voice that told him she was still afraid to consider that possibility.

"Granger is missing!" Bob said emphatically. "The only thing is, I was hoping that once Julie was gone, things wouldn't happen."

"Bob, please! Drop it!"

"You don't think this is all pretty strange? Her house burns down. She's nowhere to be found. And now Granger's missing."

"Yes, I think it's strange," Lisa snapped. "But I still just can't accept your idea that it's a werewolf killing these people. I mean, come on!" Her teeth ran over her lower lip.

Bob snorted and drove in silence.

"Did you get all your homework graded?" Lisa asked after a moment.

Bob shook his head. "No, I didn't. It always seems so much easier to leave it until Sunday night. I do my best under pressure." He concluded with a tight laugh.

They drove along the twisting turns of Bartlett Road. The car had stopped backfiring and was now humming smoothly as it took the bumps in the road with a pleasant sway. Bob snapped on the headlights, and this made it look as though they were driving down a long, twisting, snow-covered tube.

"Have you had supper?" Bob asked, when a low rumble in his stomach reminded him that he hadn't eaten since breakfast. The little chat he had had with Summers had ruined his appetite, but now he felt it returning.

"Not yet," Lisa replied.

"Well, let's drive out to that restaurant, Horsefeathers. I've heard it's supposed to be pretty good. Then we could find a bar with a band and do a bit of dancing."

Lisa didn't answer.

"What d'yah say?"

"I, I really don't feel like it." Lisa kept her eyes averted. They had come to the end of Bartlett Road and stopped at the intersection of Route 43. Bob backed the car into a cleared-out space beside the road.

"Hey, Bob. I don't want to be a spoilsport. I

just don't feel like eating out, that's all," Lisa said apologetically.

"Sure. Sure. It's OK by me," Bob said. He jockeyed the car around and headed back down Bartlett Road.

"Well, we don't have to call it a night," Lisa said. "I don't want to ruin your evening."

"Ruin my weekend? Hey. It's OK. I just thought that a little something different might, might, I don't know, loosen us up a bit, that's all."

"We don't have to go right back," Lisa said. "I wouldn't mind driving around for a bit. There. There's the turnoff for the Loop Road." She brightened up as she pointed at the turn coming up on the left. "Let's take the long way around going back, at least."

Without reply, Bob snapped the steering wheel to the left and turned onto Farthling's Loop Road.

.VII.

Doc Stetson carefully folded his glasses and slipped them into his breast pocket behind a row of multi-colored pens. He shifted his eyes from the blood-stained sheet that covered his examination table to the two men who stood in his office doorway. He rapped the clipboard he was holding with his knuckle and then dropped it onto his desk. He looked back at the mounded shape of Roy Granger's body.

"Well," he said, sounding tired, "that's it. Same thing. That wild dog killed him."

Thurston and Seavey exchanged anxious glances. Thurston said, "You said that both of them found him, right?"

Doc nodded as he sat down in his chair and rubbed his face with the palms of his hands. "Yes. They were driving out on the Loop Road when they found his cruiser. They stopped and looked around and found him. Of course, I didn't ask too many questions. I wanted to get the preliminary examination done right away."

"We'll be wantin' to get statements from them, huh?" Seavey asked, looking at Thurston.

"Of course we will," Thurston snapped. Then he locked eyes with the doctor. "But Mrs. Carter said that she was with Wentworth the whole time?"

"Yes, yes," Stetson muttered. He took the clipboard and stared vacantly at the report. "It's difficult to get an exact time of death, but I can place it roughly at sometime early this morning. He's been dead at least twelve hours for sure. Once we do the full autopsy, we'll know more exactly what the time of death was."

Seavey shifted closer to Thurston and whispered in his ear, "You know, Rick, this means you're police chief, at least until a new one's appointed by the town council."

Thurston grunted. "Yeah. I guess so." He was still watching Stetson, who was writing something on the report.

"You haven't been out to the scene yet, have you?" Stetson asked.

"Just briefly. We're heading out there now, if you don't need us. Can you drop a copy of that report off at the office in the morning?"

"First thing," Stetson answered, not looking up from his writing. "And you guys be careful going out there now, for Christ's sake. That animal's probably still around."

"Don't worry. We'll be careful," Seavey said. Then both men departed, leaving Stetson alone with the body of his friend.

The doctor sat for a long time, staring blankly at the sheet-draped form. His fingers tapped steadily on the autopsy report on his clipboard. It was the worst form he had ever had to fill out. In all his thirty-odd years as physician in Cooper Falls, he had never been more shaken by a death, never.

Must be getting on in years, he thought. Seeing the mutilated body of Roy Granger, one of his closest friends, stretched out on his shiny aluminum examination table had sounded the death rattle in his own ears.

Horrible! Horrible way to die!

"I can finish tomorrow," he whispered, sliding the clipboard back onto his desk. He let out a hissing sigh and reached to snap off his desk light. Just before he did, his eyes rested on another report that was on the desk.

Feeling a vague shudder in his stomach, Stetson picked up the report and scanned it for what must have been the tenth time that day. He had gotten it from North Conway General Hospital that morning.

It was a simple blood test for a patient of his: Ned Simmons. He had been admitted overnight on Wednesday, two days ago. Upon admittance, the patient's hematocrit had been low: thirty percent. Stetson had decided to prescribe an iron supplement for the boy and take another blood test in a few weeks to see how it was working.

The following morning, though, Ned had seemed quite rested, had lost most of the pallor in his face, and was anxious to be released. What was curious was that, when the hematocrit was repeated that morning, it came out forty-five percent: high, if anything. That was more than unusual. But after a quick check, Ned was released Thursday afternoon with a clean bill of health.

There was no way Doc Stetson could account for such a dramatic change in the patient's hemoglobin count. Blood composition just could not change that fast. The only thing Stetson could think of was that the first test had been a lab error. It had happened before.

He took the report on Ned Simmons and placed it back on the desk, beside the autopsy report on Roy Granger. He clicked off his desk light, made sure the front door was locked, and left his office. It had been a long day, full of pain and confusion.

"I don't know about you," Bob said, "but I sure could use a stiff drink right about now." He swung his front door open and stepped back to let Lisa enter. Before he followed her in, he glanced back over his shoulder at the jagged line of trees that ringed his back yard. Stars winked in the cold sky. Silence swept over him like a chill wind.

When he got inside, he hung his coat in the hall closet. Lisa was already crinkling up newspaper to start a fire in the fireplace. He watched her work for a moment and then went into the kitchen for two glasses and a bottle of Cutty Sark. When he returned with two tall drinks, the flames were already licking up through the sticks Lisa had piled up.

"Where'd you learn to make a fire?" Bob asked.

"Girl Scouts," Lisa said, reaching for the offered drink. "Thanks. How'd you mix it?"

"Straight," Bob replied, taking a sip and pursing his lips. He stared at the rising flames. He felt vacant, washed, drained.

"That's a pretty deep frown you've got," Lisa said. "Try not to think about it, OK?"

"Yeah," Bob answered, unable to push away the mental image of Roy Granger dead and partially eaten. He sat down beside Lisa and started rubbing her shoulders. She sat still for a moment, then leaned forward and placed a larger

334

log on the bed of snapping kindling.

"Don't you think we should contact someone? The F.B.I. or something?" Her voice was wire tight.

"What could they do?" Bob asked.

"I don't know," Lisa said emphatically, "but something's got to be done. People are being killed!" Her voice almost broke.

"I know," Bob replied coolly. "Every month people die. It just happens to be on the night of the full moon."

"Something's got to be done," Lisa repeated.

"I know Thurston and Seavey and the other men have been trying," Bob said. "But they won't succeed. I know they won't, not until they—"

"Bob, please. I don't want to hear about any werewolves." She leaned forward and threw two more logs onto the blaze.

"I see you took my suggestion, though," Bob said smugly.

"Huh?"

"The cross. You're wearing a cross," he said, pointing to the small crucifix that dangled from her neck. Lisa reached to her throat and grabbed the cross. She twisted it around, letting the silver reflect the light from the fire.

"I, I wear my cross a lot," she said, sounding defensive.

Bob snorted and, leaning his head back, took a deep swig of whisky. He gasped and then put the drink down between his legs.

"You better take it easy with that stuff. I am

going to need a ride home a little later."

Bob started to stand up, grunting from the effort. "Not necessarily," he said with a laugh, and then went into the kitchen to refill his glass.

"So," he shouted from the kitchen, "I guess Thurston got the job as police chief, at least for a while."

"Yeah. Guess so."

"I can hardly wait," Bob said, laughing. "His first official act will probably be to organize a posse to tar and feather me. Maybe burn me at the stake. Child molester! Accused rapist!"

"Don't talk like that, not even joking," Lisa said, sounding hurt. "You're being silly."

"I sure hope so," Bob said, leaving the kitchen and turning off the lights before he sat down. "I sure as hell hope so."

"What is it between you two, anyway?" Lisa asked.

Bob held up his whisky glass and studied the flames through the amber liquid before answering. "I really can't say, for sure. I just know that, from my point of view, I've never liked the guy, not since I first saw him. There's just something about him that rubs me the wrong way."

"Must be that he feels the same," Lisa said.

Bob noticed that she hadn't taken a sip of her drink, and he gestured at it.

"I mean," Lisa said, "why in the heck would he give those newspaper articles to Summers and threaten your job? It's almost like he has an axe to grind or something."

Bob shrugged. "I don't know. I never crossed him, not that I know of, anyway. I'm not worried," he concluded, and then took another long drink.

"You should be," Lisa said worriedly. She shifted closer to him and placed her hand on his leg. She leaned forward and kissed him on the mouth. "But I believe you."

Bob smiled, trying still to force the image of Roy Granger from his mind as he held Lisa close to him.

"What was that?" Lisa asked suddenly, pulling away from him and looking around. Her eyes were wide and glistening in the fire light.

"Just the sound of my little heart going pitter-pat pitter-pat," Bob said good naturedly.

"I heard something!"

"I didn't," Bob said, trying to pull her close again.

"No! I swear I heard something!"

"Will you just calm down? God! It's just the—"

This time, Bob heard it too, a low gritty sound, like someone scraping. It came from the darkness of the kitchen. Bob sprang to his feet and stared into the darkness as the sound was repeated. "I don't think the mice in the walls have hammers and saws," he said, fighting the tension.

"I think it's at the door," Lisa whispered hoarsely. "Is it locked?"

"I can't remember," Bob said, taking a cautious step toward the kitchen.

Both of them jumped when they heard a heavy thud followed by a rapid scratching at the door. Bob edged his way into the kitchen and peered down the short hallway that led to the door. The shade was pulled but, faintly, he could see a shadow, a silhouette on the curtain.

"Christ," he whispered, his eyes trying to distinguish the shape. The only thing he was sure of was that it was not human.

He jumped with a start when Lisa put her hand on his shoulder from behind. He hadn't heard her come up close. They exchanged nervous looks and listened to the snuffing sound outside the door. Bob took another few tentative steps closer to the door.

"Do you have a gun in the house?" Lisa whispered harshly.

"No I don't, dammit!"

The sniffing and scratching sound got louder, and then the door began to rattle. Bob flattened against the wall and cautiously inched his way forward. His breath caught in his throat like a wad of phlegm. Hand shaking, he reached out for the curtain drawstring. He was afraid for a moment that he would be unable to grasp the string, his hand was shaking so badly. But he took it, held his breath, and snapped the shade.

The shade flipped up, fluttering noisily, but the sound was drowned out by Lisa's ear-piercing scream. Staring at them through the pane of glass was a huge wolf. Its eyes burned with a cold, evil green fire. It pressed its nose against the glass and snarled viciously. A circle of fog blossomed on the glass from the animal's heated breath.

Bob's stomach clenched like a fist. Sweat broke out on his forehead as he backed away from the door.

"Oh my God! Oh my God!" Lisa screamed as she grabbed at Bob.

"Get into the living room. Get the hell out of here," he yelled, not daring to take his eyes away from the animal. He was transfixed by the cold gleaming of the wolf's eyes. The widespread, foam-flecked jaws seemed to form an almost human smile, and the eyes, the eyes glared at him with what looked like more than animal cunning.

"Go on!" Bob shouted to Lisa. "Get in the other room!"

The animal lifted its front feet up and pressed them against the glass. The door rattled loosely, threatening to break under the wolf's weight. The paws flattened out under the pressure as the animal pressed harder. Then with a loud crash, the window exploded inward.

Bob jumped back, knocking into Lisa, who stood rooted to the spot. He spun around and stared at her, eyes wide with fear. The sound of the animal crashing and tearing through the door filled the small kitchen. Bob was about to push Lisa back when his eyes caught the glint of her silver cross. Without a word, he snapped the chain from her neck and turned to face the wolf.

The front half of the wolf was inside the house. Its paws scrambled wildly, trying to pull forward. With a low, guttural growl, it looked at Bob and widened its jaws.

Bob took a step closer to the wolf, holding out the crucifix, dangling from the length of silver chain. "Get! Get out of here, you bastard!" he shouted. The wolf pushed the rest of the way into the house and stood squarely on its four feet glaring at Bob.

"Go on, you bastard!" Bob shouted. The chain swung back and forth in wide arcs and—was it a trick of his eye, or was the silver cross beginning to glow with a dull blue? The wolf crouched, growling, preparing to leap.

"Go on. Get the hell out of here!" Bob pressed forward.

"Are you crazy?" Lisa shouted, her voice breaking.

"Go back to hell!" Bob shouted, taking another step closer. "I know who you are, and you're not going to get us. Now leave!"

The wolf seemed to shy back. And, yes, the cross was shining with a deep blue glow.

"I command you to go! In the name of Jesus!"

There was a short, pained yelp, and then the animal bolted forward. Bob didn't have time to react, but the dangling cross of silver hit the animal on the nose as it sprang. There was a crackling explosion of blue fire, and the wolf was thrown backwards, landing in the pile of broken glass and wood. The choking smell of burning hair filled the hallway.

"Holy God!" Lisa cried out.

Bob reached forward and again let the cross touch against the animal. Again there was a shattering explosion that sent the wolf flying through the door and onto the porch. In the brief flash of light, Bob was positive he saw that the beast now had human hands. Saying the name of Jesus must cause it to change back to human form, Bob thought.

"What does it take to kill you?" Bob shouted, his throat ragged. The wolf snarled ferociously, but it no longer sounded like an animal. There was a pained, almost human quality to the sound.

"Come on! Come on!" Bob taunted, stepping out onto the porch and reaching out to let the cross touch the animal again. The cross was glowing with a ghostly light that flickered and wavered like it was on fire. It cast shadows that wavered back and forth in wide, sickening circles.

The animal suddenly turned and ran toward the woods. Bob stood on the porch and watched as the beast made its way across the snowy field. He wasn't sure, but just before it entered the woods, it looked as though the animal was running on just its hind legs, like a person. The shadowy trees reached out and engulfed the form. Bob was left standing on the porch alone with the cold wind blowing into his face.

Lisa came up behind him and wrapped her arms around him. She buried her face into his back and sobbed. "Oh God! God! I can't believe it! I can't believe it!"

Bob shivered and looked out over the field toward the forest. From far off came a sound that rose slowly until it filled the night. It was the sound of someone, a person, screaming with pain.

Chapter Fifteen

Monday, February 2

.I.

The sky was overcast, and it was starting to snow as Bob swung his door shut and locked it. He still cringed inwardly whenever he remembered the night, three weeks ago, when the werewolf had come crashing through the door. He was convinced now—no doubt left at all—that the beast was supernatural in origin. The effect the animal's presence had on the cross, making it glow with blue light, and the reaction the mere touch of the silver cross had was too convincing. It couldn't be attributed to coincidence or paranoia any longer.

Bob walked down to his car, thick, wet snowflakes hitting him in the face and melting. He had hoped last night, when he had heard that the storm was coming, that it would snow enough through the night so school would be cancelled. It was with a curious sense of resignation that he started his car and drove down the driveway.

He had woken up late this morning and

hadn't taken time for breakfast. His stomach was churning when he pulled into the parking lot and saw that the schoolyard was empty. He was late again. Quickly, he parked the car, grabbed his briefcase from the back seat, and raced into the school just as the first warning bell rang, signalling homeroom.

He saw, at a distance as he approached his room, that there was a small envelope taped to the door. He reached for it, tore it open, and read quickly: Please stop by the office before homeroom. J.S.

"Oh, shit," Bob muttered, folding the paper in half and stuffing it into his pocket. He took off his coat and folded it over his arm before going to the office. The hunger knot in his stomach was getting tighter.

He entered the office, placed his coat and briefcase on the floor, and took a seat after giving Leona Gleason, the secretary, a quick nod of greeting. He fiddled with his tie a few times before lighting a cigarette, but after two or three puffs, he put it out. It wasn't helping his unsettled stomach any.

The late bell sounded and then, after a moment of silence while the rooms said the pledge of allegiance, Leona began to read the morning messages over the intercom. The last item she read made Bob look up, startled.

"Mr. Wentworth's first period literature class is to report to study hall with Mrs. Winslow."

Leona clicked off the intercom and looked over at Bob.

343

"What's this all about?" he asked anxiously.

Leona's mouth twisted as though she wanted to say something, but she remained silent and shrugged her shoulders. Looking down at the announcements in her hands, she finally said, weakly, "I haven't the faintest."

Bob could tell that she did have the faintest but couldn't say. The tightness in his stomach was burning now. He got up and walked over to Leona's desk.

"Is Summers on the warpath?" he asked, jabbing a thumb over his shoulder in the direction of the principal's closed door.

Leona's eyes revealed that she didn't want to say a word; a battle between loyalty and confidence creased her face. Finally, she said, "I think so, he and Barry have been talking for over half an hour."

Trouble, Bob thought, with a fainting feeling. Big trouble.

Just then, the office door swung open and Summers stood in the doorway. "Please come in," he said, with just the right touch of command in his voice to irritate Bob.

As he entered the office Barry LaFleur rose from his seat and nodded. "Morning, Bob."

Bob merely nodded. He had never liked the assistant principal, and throughout the school year they had gone head to head on quite a few issues. Bob sensed the stiff formality in both men and knew that he was in for a tough morning. He sat down beside Summers' desk without a word and folded his arms across his chest.

Summers shut the door firmly and walked over to his chair. He marked the end of any social amenities by clearing his throat as he sat down.

"Well, Bob," Summers began, "I'm sure you have some idea why I called you in this morning." His eyes sparkled with a coldness that did nothing to relieve Bob's tension.

"No, sir," Bob answered. "I'm afraid I don't." He rubbed his sticky palms together. Looking briefly at LeFleur, he had the flickering impression that the assistant principal was a clinical psychologist observing the interaction from behind the safety of a two-way mirror.

"I spoke with you a while ago and expressed my concern about several issues," Summers said. "It's been brought to my attention that these matters have not been corrected; that matters have worsened."

"My performance in class has been fine," Bob said, making an effort to sound professionally detached.

"To the contrary," Summers said, interrupting him with a wave of his forefinger. "Your work has not improved. Mr. LaFleur's last evaluation of your classroom work indicates that you have not been prepared for class."

"A brief look at your lesson plans is enough to convince me that you are not coming to class prepared," LaFleur interposed.

Bob glanced angrily over at the man, whose small, dark eyes bored into him. The stare reminded Bob of a rodent.

"In the past two weeks, Bob, you have been late for school five times. Such a record with a student would call for immediate disciplinary action," Summers said.

Bob wanted to say something, anything, even lie in his defense, but he remained silent.

"This, in conjunction with your romantic involvement with Lisa Car—"

"My what?" Bob shouted suddenly, his anger no longer contained.

Summers coughed and leaned forward in his chair. "Your not very discreet affair with Mrs. Carter seems to be impinging on your work. As a teacher in this community, you are expected to present a moral example for your students."

"My personal matters don't concern this school or you," Bob said evenly, fighting to control himself.

"Since I spoke with you last, your attitude has steadily deteriorated," Summers said. Bob glanced over at LaFleur, who was sitting back smugly in his seat.

"Mr. Wentworth," Summers said, "I called you to the office to inform you that your contract for next year is not going to be renewed. You have a choice: you may either resign or, when the contracts are discussed at the school board meeting, I will recommend that you not be hired."

Bob immediately remembered what Lisa had said to him that night last September, when he had first met her at the B&B: "Well, I don't have a school board to please. Especially a school board like the one we have. They're a cross section of a typical, small New Hampshire town. They wear red-white-and-blue underwear."

"What I do and who I see on my own time is of no concern to anyone," Bob said tightly.

"Your performance in class is," LaFleur said.

"If you have some legitimate complaints about my work, I'd like to see them in writing and I'd like the opportunity to respond to them," Bob said, glaring at LaFleur. The small man sat looking at him, unblinking.

Summers shook his head with mock sympathy. "I'm afraid, Bob, that the decision has already been made. I would like a letter of resignation from you before you leave school today. If not, your name will be—"

"Like hell!" Bob stood up and pounded his fist on the desk. "You can't pull this shit on me. You have to have legal, legitimate grounds not to renew a contract. The teachers' union will be behind me on this."

Summers shifted in his chair, leaning back and holding his folded hands in front of his face. "In the privacy of this office, strictly off the record, I'd say that you could take this to the union, to the court, if you have to, and you would probably win a contract renewal. But . . ." Summers tapped his forefinger on the desk and, for the first time, Bob noticed the photocopied newspaper clipping in the desk tray. "There are some things in your past which, if known, would hurt your credibility."

Bob stood there beside the desk, open-mouthed.

"I can assure you that even with a court order

to renew your contract, you wouldn't last long in this school system. My advice to you, Bob, is to make it easy all the way around. Don't make waves. Just write out a brief letter of resignation and—"

"That's blackmail!" Bob shouted.

"Do you want your students to know that in your last job you were accused of raping one of your students?"

Bob swallowed hard, feeling a throbbing pressure in his head. "You can take your god-damn contract and stuff it!" he said, firmly, evenly. "As far as I'm concerned, last Friday was my last day on the job."

He strode to the door and flung it open. Without a word, he picked up his coat and brief-case and left the school by the front door.

"Go ahead," he muttered as he walked out to his car. "Try to sue me for breach of contract. I'd love to bring that one to court."

He drove away from the school. His stomach was on fire. He considered going straight home and starting to pack, but then decided to go downtown and see Lisa first.

.II.

Ellie Simmons was pushing a grocery cart down the ice-covered sidewalk, heading toward Pomeroy's I.G.A. The loose front wheels of the cart rattled and jittered. Lisa was walking up the sidewalk in the opposite direction, so she stopped and stepped up onto the snowbank to allow the old woman to pass.

When Ellie was beside Lisa, she stopped, looked up at her, and said, "Morning, Mrs. Carter. Surely looks like more snow, don't it?"

Lisa nodded, said, "Yeah," and stepped down onto the sidewalk behind the old woman. Ellie turned around and looked at her, making her feel extremely uncomfortable.

"And how have you been, Mrs. Simmons?" Lisa asked, aware that the interaction was going to continue.

"Gettin' along," Ellie said, shaking her head and pulling at her coat collar. "Gettin' along."

"Ummm," Lisa said, wanting to be on her way. Then, automatically, she said, "And how's Ned been feeling?"

"Better, now, thank yah. The Doc says he's on the mend. But the bill from just a few tests 'bout set us back a full week's wages."

"Times are tough," Lisa said sympathetically.

"Still 'n' all, it's good knowin' everythin's OK."

"I didn't know Ned was sick," Lisa said. "When was that?"

"Couple of weeks ago. He had to spend a night at the hospital."

"In North Conway?"

Ellie nodded. "Yeah, but he's better now. Got his strength now."

Lisa was going to wish her well and depart but just then Bob drove up and called out to her. "Hey, Lisa. I've got to talk with you."

"Just a minute," she called back. Then she

turned to Ellie and said, "Well, nice talking with you. I'm glad to hear Ned's feeling better. Have a nice day." She watched as Ellie departed, pushing her rattling cart in front of her.

"Lisa," Bob shouted impatiently.

"That wasn't very nice of you," Lisa said, walking over to the car. "You could have been a bit more civil."

"Well, I—"

"That poor woman's got it tough. You could have said something to her. She isn't feeling well, and Ned just got out of the hospital. The least you could have said was hello to her."

"Sorry," Bob said agitatedly. He paused and then said, "Well, it happened."

"Huh? What happened?"

"Summers and LeFleur. They dropped the axe this morning. I'm no longer a teacher at Cooper Falls High School."

"You're kidding!"

"For once in my life I'm glad I'm not," Bob said. He reached over and clicked open the door. "Hop in. I'll fill you in on all the gory details."

As they drove toward the library, Bob related the incident of the morning. He was just finishing when they pulled into the parking lot behind the library. They got out and walked toward the back entrance.

"Well, don't you think you could take it to court?" Lisa asked, unlocking the heavy oak door and swinging it open.

"Sure. Sure I could," Bob said, slapping his fist into his open palm. "Jesus, those bastards.

Especially that little shit, LaFleur! But Summers has photocopies of those newspaper clippings."

"You really think they'd use them?" Lisa placed her hand on Bob's elbow and looked at him, wide-eyed. "You really do?"

"I don't know." Bob shrugged. "But even if it gets out, I mean, it'd sort of ruin my credibility don't you think."

"Not if it isn't true," Lisa said, not too convincingly.

Bob looked at her with a tight grin. "Yeah. Not if it isn't true. Just like it didn't hurt me with my job in Dorchester."

"I think you ought to make a case out of it, if only to show them that they can't pull that kind of stuff."

Bob grunted.

"Summers isn't the sweetheart of the school committee. There are a few members who aren't satisfied with his work."

"Come on, Lisa. Not in a case like this."

"Well, you won't be the only one who comes out looking bad, Bob."

"Oh, gee. Thanks a lot."

"You know what I mean," Lisa said angrily. "I don't think Summers would have his guts to bring out your dirty laundry, not unless—"

Bob laughed out loud, and Lisa was surprised that he could find humor in the situation.

"No pun intended, I assume," Bob said, still chuckling.

"What?"

"The girl's name, the one who accused me. Her name was Beth Landry."

Lisa didn't even smile as she went to the closet and hung up her coat. She slipped her snow-crusted boots off, then went over to the sink and started filling the tea kettle with water.

"So," Bob said, letting his palms slap his thighs, "I've decided to leave town."

"Huh?" Lisa was stunned. She turned around. "You're what?"

"I'm leaving town," Bob repeated simply.

"You aren't serious," Lisa said.

"Oh, yes I am," Bob said, nodding his head. He looked at her intently. "I'm serious and, and I want you to come with me."

"Do you know where you're going?"

"I'm not sure. I was thinking it might be nice to spend the rest of the winter in Florida."

"Just like that?" Lisa snapped her fingers. "You want me to leave my job and everything and come with you to Florida?"

Bob nodded. "Yeah. What the hell do you expect me to do? It feels to me like Cooper Falls would just as soon spit me out. I'm not gonna let it chew me any more! They can have the damn job. And as for this, this werewolf, or whatever, I've had it!" He cut the air with the knife edge of his hand. "I'm not going to wait around until this beast gets me! This isn't my home town. I've got no responsibility."

"Well I do," Lisa said with an edge in her voice. "It's my home town and I don't think I can just, can just give up on it and leave. After what we've seen and what we know, don't you think we have to do something or tell someone or try somehow to stop it?"

Bob's resolve suddenly strengthened. He walked over to Lisa and took her arms with a firm grip. Fighting to keep his voice steady, he said, "I have had it! I'm leaving by noon tomorrow. If you want to come with me, you can. But I'll be goddamned if I'm going to spend another full day in this town! I'll give you a call tonight."

With that, he turned and left the library.

.III.

Bob was up in the attic, digging out his suitcases, when the telephone began to ring. He stuck his head down through the trapdoor and glared at the phone as it jangled again.

"Damn!" he whispered harshly, shifting his body around so he could drop down to the floor. He hurried because he figured it was Lisa calling. It seemed perfectly timed; as soon as his feet hit the floor, the phone cut off in midring.

He stared at the silent phone for a minute, then went to the kitchen for a cigarette before heading back up into the attic. The phone started ringing again, and Bob dashed over to it quickly and picked it up.

"Hello," he snapped, exhaling smoke into the receiver. He was expecting to hear Lisa's voice, so he was surprised when Amy said hello.

"Oh," Bob stammered. "Hi. How you doing?"

"I'm just fine," Amy said. She sounded happy, and Bob wondered if it was real or put on.

"And how is married life treating you?" Bob asked. "This time."

There was a long silence, and then Amy said, "Fine."

"Did you try to call just a second ago?" Bob asked.

"No," Amy replied.

"Hmmm."

"So, how have you been doing? The winter's not too tough for you, is it? You never did like snow," Amy said.

"It's, it's OK."

"And teaching's going well for you?"

Bob inhaled from his cigarette and debated whether or not he should tell Amy that he had quit—been fired. "It's going OK, I guess."

"Well," Amy said, "the last Jamie and I heard was a Christmas card with a pretty short note. We were wondering if you had forgotten about your promise."

"My promise?"

"Jesus, Bob, you know, Jamie's your daughter too. You could show a little more interest in what she's been up to. You don't remember that you said you wanted her to come out there and stay with you for February vacation?"

"Oh, shit," Bob muttered, looking down at the floor. He knew now that there was no way of getting around it. He would have to tell her what had happened.

"You've made other plans?" Amy said, her voice taking on the harsh edge he remembered.

"No, I, uhh . . ." His eyes darted around the kitchen. "I'm not sure that's a good idea right now, I—"

He looked at the door, at the window looking out onto the snowy night, and for a brief flash, he thought he saw a shadow shift through the darkness outside.

"Bob? You there?"

"Yeah, uhh, what I was saying was that, well, things have been going on here and I'm not sure I want Jamie around right now."

"Who are you shacking up with?" Amy asked snidely.

"No, no. It's nothing like that." His voice was shaking. The cigarette in his hand had burned down to the filter. "It's, well, I'm not teaching anymore."

There was a stunned silence at the other end of the line.

"I, uhhh, I had a little bit of trouble with a few of the administrators and I, uhhh, I resigned. Just today, in fact."

"Jesus, Bob!"

"It's a long story, but I'm packing. I'm going down to Miami or Orlando for the rest of the winter."

"You haven't even seen Jamie since last August, Bob," Amy said pleadingly. "Don't you think you could just stay around for that week so she could see you? I want her to know she does have a father, too."

"Yeah, well, that, that's not all. I—" he stopped himself before he told Amy about the series of deaths that had plagued the town. He didn't even want to mention a wild dog in the area, much less a werewolf. She'd think he was cracking up for sure.

"Well?"

"Well, there's been some trouble out here. No one's really sure what's going on, but it looks like there's a wild dog or something that's been attacking people."

"Really?" Amy sounded surprised, but there was an edge to her voice that suggested that she suspected Bob was making up the story just to get out of having Jamie come to visit.

Bob felt a twisting in his bowels, and he ran his fingers through his hair. "I just don't think this would be a safe place to be, that's all."

"I haven't seen anything about that in the papers," Amy said.

"Yeah, well, they're trying to keep the whole thing under wraps, you know?"

"I know there was that story about the student nurse in North Conway who was killed by a wild animal, but I hadn't—"

"What?" Bob shouted. "What are you talking about?"

"You didn't hear about it?" Amy asked. "It must have been, oh, two weeks ago or so. It was in all the papers down here. It must have been in the Sunday paper, because that's the only one I get to read. A student nurse at General Hospital was attacked and killed by a wild dog."

"Holy shit!" Bob looked out at the doorway again and his mind replayed the sound of smashing glass and wood as the beast crashed its way into the house. He shivered. "They said it was a wild dog?"

"I think so. I just skimmed the article."

"You don't remember if it said that there were

356

any eyewitnesses, do you?" Bob asked agitatedly. "Anyone else who saw the, the animal?"

"I don't recall it mentioning any," Amy said distantly. "Of course, that doesn't mean there weren't."

"Jesus," Bob said softly. He held the phone tightly against his ear. Glancing at the wall calendar, he ran his fingers across the dates. He went back two weeks, and his fingers stopped on Thursday, January 15. At the top of the dated box was a picture of a full moon.

"Could it have been on Wednesday or Thursday?" he asked excitedly.

"I told you, I can't remember. It was about two weeks ago. Why, why do you ask?"

"Oh." Bob glanced again at the kitchen door. "It was about that time that I saw a dog, a stray, sniffing around my house."

"I think you might be right, Bob," Amy said at last. "I think we can wait a while before Jamie comes out to visit."

"That's a damn good idea," Bob replied. "I have to get packing. I'll give you a call once I get down there and let you know my new address."

"Sure. Bye."

"Bye. Thanks for calling," Bob said, and then hung up.

He was still standing beside the phone, contemplating calling Lisa, when a sudden thought hit him. When he had seen Lisa earlier that day, hadn't she said that Ned Simmons had been in the hospital?

"Oh, Christ!"

He thought back, trying to remember. He had been so worked up about getting fired that he hadn't really listened to her, but as he dredged through his memory, he was sure Lisa had said Ned had been in the hospital. And the only hospital in the area was in North Conway!

He had to find out when Ned had been in North Conway, he realized with a deep urgency. Some intuitive glimmer told him that it would coincide with the night the student nurse had been killed. And if it did . . . .

"It wasn't Julie Sikes at all!" Bob said aloud. "All this time I've been thinking it was Julie Sikes, and it wasn't! All this time it's been Ned Simmons!"

He knew. The final piece had fallen into place with the click on the end of the line as Amy had hung up. He knew!

He lifted the receiver and started dialing Lisa's number. "Well," he said, listening to the phone ring, "if she's coming, she's coming now."

.IV.

Monday, February 16

Bob held the envelope in his hand, turning it over and over as he walked down the wide steps of the Miami Post Office. He kept reading the postmark each time it came around: Cooper Falls, N.H. February 14, 11:17 A.M. The return address was Lisa's.

He sat in his car and took a deep breath before sliding his finger under the envelope flap and ripping it open. Enclosed was a single sheet of blue stationery, neatly folded. As he opened the letter, a small newspaper clipping dropped onto his lap. He snatched up the clipping and glanced at the headline. It gave him a quick chill in spite of the warm Florida sun. He quickly read the letter.

Dear Bob,   Friday nite

I'm writing this in a hurry. It's almost twelve and I've got to get to bed and sleep, if I can. I know you said you wanted to write first, but I thought you'd better know about Sue. I hope you'll drop her folks a note. I know you didn't have her in any of your classes, but a note would be appreciated. I know what you're thinking! The official story from Thurston, still, is that it's a wild dog. I just don't know what to think! I can't accept your idea, but after that night at your house, I don't know what else could explain what happened.

I want to make it clear to you too that I understand why you were so upset the night before you left. I wish neither of us had gotten so angry, but none of my reasons have changed. I love you, Bob. I really do. I miss you a lot, and I wish you'd reconsider what I said. If you don't do anything, who will?

It's been a real hard winter. You wouldn't have believed the last storm we had!

Almost two feet a day for two days! School's been cancelled for three days, and we're just getting dug out now. Did they mention the storm on the news down there? It's been real bad.

One more thing. You've got me paranoid enough so I checked out when Sue was killed. It didn't come close to the night of the full moon. Sue died on Wednesday, the 11th, and the full moon wasn't till Sunday, the 15th. Doesn't that screw up your idea? I don't know. I'm so confused. All I know is that a friend of mine, someone I loved and worked with, has been killed and I'm scared! I wish to God this would stop soon!!! Please write. Let me know what's going on with you. So far, all I've got was a post-office-box number in Miami. Communicate!!!

Love, Lisa

Bob's eyes began to water as he read the article about Sue Langsford's death. Lisa was right; the official story was the same. She was also right that Sue had died four days away from the full moon. His shoulder shook with a wild shiver as trickles of sweat ran from his armpits and down his side.

.V.

"I sent him a letter a few days ago," Lisa said,

smiling as she looked at Mrs. Miller. "He should have gotten it by now." She paused, then added, "I'm sure he'll send his regards."

Mrs. Miller carefully placed Lisa's purchase into a bag and stapled it shut.

"Well," Lisa said, making a point of counting her change when Mrs. Miller handed it to her, "have a nice evening."

"I'll be closing soon," Mrs. Miller said, nodding past Lisa toward the fading evening light. "Until this wild animal's caught, I'm closing before dark."

Lisa wrinkled her eyebrows and said, "I don't blame you in the least." There was a knot of uneasiness in her stomach.

"Specially after what happened to the Doyles."

"What?" Lisa reached for the countertop for support.

Not again! she thought. Not again!

"You hadn't heard?" Mrs. Miller asked, surprised. She tapped the top copy of the newspaper on the counter. "Right here."

"Cooper Falls Couple Found Dead," the headline read; and below that, "Mystery Animal Strikes Again."

"I swear," Mrs. Miller said, shaking her head solemnly, "I swear, it's the curse of God."

"Good Lord, no," Lisa said distantly. Her head began to hurt with a distant throbbing.

They must not have had a silver cross, Lisa found herself thinking. They must not have had protection.

"Dearie, are you all right?" Mrs. Miller asked. "You look a bit peaked."

"I'm, I'm all right," Lisa said, shaking her head to clear it.

"Dear me, I didn't mean to frighten you," Mrs. Miller said with genuine concern. "I thought you knew."

"No I didn't," Lisa said. Her voice was strained.

They must not have had protection!

"Can I get you a glass of water?" Mrs. Miller said, rushing around the counter. "Here. Sit down for a minute."

"No. Really. I'm all right," Lisa said weakly. "I just got a bit dizzy for a moment."

"I'll be closing soon. Can I walk you home."

"You don't have to do that," Lisa said, feeling suddenly foolish. "My car's right outside. I'll be OK."

"You sure?"

"I'm sure."

They must not have had a silver cross!

"Good night, Mrs. Miller." Lisa started toward the door.

"You take care of yourself," Mrs. Miller called out. "And if you need anything, just let me know."

"I will."

When Lisa got back to her apartment, she dialed directory assistance and asked for a new listing for Mr. Robert Wentworth in Miami. She was surprised when the operator didn't tell her, "Sorry. There's no listing under that name," and, instead, gave her the number. Lisa wrote it down on the chalkboard beside the telephone.

For almost half an hour, she debated whether or not she should call Bob and tell him about the Doyles. Would he want to know about it, or had he had enough? she wondered. Instead of calling Bob, she went into the kitchen and made herself a cup of tea.

Just before she went to sleep, around eleven o'clock, she saw the flashing red light of the town's ambulance swing across her ceiling as the emergency crew raced up Main Street.

.VI.

Thursday, February 19

"I had just been with her last night," Lisa said hoarsely, her voice breaking with tears. "I was probably the last person to see her alive!" Her voice broke off in a choking sob.

Groping for words and finding none, Bob listened to Lisa's sobbing. Finally, he said, "There wasn't anything you could have done. How could you have known?"

"I know! I know! It's just that, that—" Again her voice broke off into crying.

"Just take it easy, will you, Lisa?" Bob said patiently. "For Christ's sake."

"It's just," Lisa sniffed loudly. "It's just that whatever killed her was, was right there outside the pharmacy. Right when I was talking to her, maybe. It could have, could have—"

"Do you think that might be why you got that fainting feeling?" Bob asked calmly. "If I'm right and it is a werewolf, maybe it was exerting some kind of psychic force that you picked up. Maybe subconsciously you were aware of its being nearby."

"I don't know. I don't know," Lisa said, whimpering. "I think it was just from the shock of hearing about the Doyles."

"Maybe it was more than that," Bob said evenly. "Maybe the werewolf—"

"How can it be a werewolf?" Lisa said sharply. "How can it be when there have been four people killed this month, and none of them has been killed when the moon is full?"

"Well—"

"There's nothing supernatural, and there's no werewolf!" Lisa shouted, so loudly that Bob had to pull the receiver away from his ear.

"Not necessarily," Bob said after a moment.

There was a long silence at Lisa's end of the line. Finally, she said softly, "What do you mean."

"I mentioned it to you before, but you probably don't remember. Also, I've been doing a bit of research on werewolves since I've been down here and, if most of the legends are correct, it's during the month of February that werewolves are most active. Most accounts say they're active for the whole month, and don't need the full moon during February."

"Come on!"

"I'm just telling you what I've read, what the legends are. Of course, most of the folklorists who try to dispel the werewolf legends say that it was during the dead of winter that the wolves in the wild would prowl closer to town. An especially harsh winter, when food was scarce, would drive them right into the towns and villages. I forget what year it was, but there's a documented case of a pack of timber wolves right in the streets of Paris in midwinter."

"But those are real wolves," Lisa said.

"I know," Bob replied, "But like a lot of myths, there might be more than a grain of truth in all of this. If there is a werewolf, if Ned or whoever is transforming, he would be able to do it for the whole month of February."

"That's ridiculous, Bob. I mean, what—"

"After what you've seen?" Bob said, angrily. "After what you've seen for yourself, you can say it's ridiculous?"

"And you won't do anything about it," Lisa said harshly. "If you're so damned convinced, why don't you do something?"

"Well," Bob said, swallowing hard, "I told you what I think. I think you should come down here."

"You know I can't," Lisa replied. "I told you why."

"And neither can I. I can't come back to Cooper Falls. I can't do anything about it! I just wish you'd get out of there before, before something happens."

"Bob!"

"Well, it's the only thing that worries me. I

could give two shits for Cooper Falls!" He was
tempted to hang up right then, to leave her with
that final, bitter thought, but he resisted the temp-
tation. "The only reason I'd come back to Cooper
Falls," he said, "would be to pick you up and get
you the hell out of there!"

"Yeah," Lisa said, sounding defeated. "You're
probably right. There's nothing you can do about
it. See you."

"I love you," Bob whispered, but he wasn't sure
if she heard him. There was a loud click at the
other end of the line, and he was left with the
wavering buzz of the dial tone.

.VII.

Friday, February 20

"Damn it all!" Thurston said, roughly placing
his 30-30 shotgun and a box of shells onto the desk.
He looked over at Ted Seavey, who was standing
by the doorway with one foot up on a chair.
Thurston's newly appointed deputy shrugged his
shoulders and said nothing.

"You'd think that after this goddamned long a
time we'd have got the bastard!" He picked up the
shotgun, snapped open the barrel, and peered
down the inside. "Something. Anything!"

"It ain't for lack of tryin'," Seavey said.

"No!" Thurston shouted. "But it ain't 'cause this
fuckin' animal is makin' itself scarce either! Christ!
Four people within a week! And anyone who ever

sees the fucker doesn't live long enough to tell anyone." He blew down the gun barrel and then snapped it shut.

"We're doin' what we can," Seavey said softly.

"But why is it us? Why is it only around here?" Thurston asked, pained. "There haven't been any reports from any other towns of any trouble with this wild dog."

"There was that nurse in North Conway a while ago," Seavey said, shrugging. "I don't know. Maybe they're keeping it quiet like we are. Who knows? Maybe the bastard is running the whole county. It seems like he's here for a while, a couple of nights or so, then he disappears. Maybe he has a whole circuit he runs."

"If the situation wasn't so damned serious, I'd laugh at that," Thurston said. He opened the box of shells and put a handful into his coat pocket. Glancing at the clock on the office wall, he said, "It's getting dark. We'd better get out to the ridge and check that line of traps. See if we got something this time."

Seavey put his foot back onto the floor with a heavy clump. "I'll tell yah, Rick, that bastard's just too damn smart to go for a trap or poisoned bait. We gotta see it and shoot the fucker if we're gonna stop him."

"Let's go."

.VIII.

Saturday, February 21

Ellie Simmons had a huge pot of baked beans

bubbling away in the stove, just like she did every Saturday night. A blast of hot air slammed against her face as she opened the oven door, satisfied herself that they were ready, then put on her thick cooking mitts and pulled the pot out onto the oven door. With a puff of breath, she blew away the strand of hair that was dangling in front of her face. She was just putting the pot of beans up on the countertop when she heard a loud bang from outside. She jumped, emitting a high, mouselike squeek.

" 'S that you Ned?" she asked hopefully, looking over at the kitchen door. Through the door she could see the darkening blue of the snow as night approached. Then a familiar form stepped into view.

"Ned," she said. "you're just in time for supper."

Instead of moving toward the door, she reached up into the cupboard for their plates. The kitchen door swung open, and Ned, with barely a grunt of greeting, walked in and sat down at the table facing his mother. He sat slouched in his chair, his chin resting on his chest.

"You feelin' OK?" Ellie asked, concern in her voice.

"Yeah. I'm OK."

" 'S gettin' dark in here. Snap on the light and fetch us some silverware." She looked at him carefully, squinting in the dim light. His pale face, creased with deep lines, almost frightened her. He was breathing shallowly, barely moving.

She scooped some beans onto a plate. "Goodness, son, you look a fright. Why don't you go wash up. I'll set the table."

She continued scooping out beans. Glancing over her shoulder, she saw that Ned had not moved. "Ned? Are you sure you feel OK?" she asked. "The doctor said that—"

"I'm OK," Ned snapped, his voice sounding with a ragged edge. He shifted his shoulders uneasily, and Ellie thought she heard a low, guttural moan.

"Ned?" she said, louder and with more alarm. She was thinking that Ned must be either drunk or stoned. In the dim light of the kitchen, he appeared to be sinking down in his chair, slipping toward the floor. His breathing was louder now, raspy and bubbly.

"Go clean yourself up now," she repeated. She looked out at the deep purple sky, the long stretch of blue snow. A sudden wave of chills made her teeth chatter. She looked back over at her son.

"Ned?"

Was it the dimness of the kitchen? she wondered. Maybe just getting old, eyesight's going.

She wasn't sure what it was, but Ned looked like he was sliding down to the floor and he looked—thicker, was the first word that came to Ellie's mind. The gathering darkness was playing tricks on her eyes, making Ned's body look like it was shifting, changing subtly.

"Ned?" she said again, softer. She wanted to go over to him, but something held her back.

Ned suddenly collapsed and dropped onto the floor, landing in a crouching position on his hands and knees. Ellie heard a low grumbling sound. She found that her mouth had suddenly gone dry, and she licked her lips to no avail. Horrified, she stared at her son, crouching on the floor in the darkened kitchen. His body seemed to shift, elongate, grow sleeker.

"What the devil?" Ellie said.

A low, steady growl began to build, pulsing in rising waves. The spoon Ellie had been using to scoop beans clattered to the floor. With that sound, Ned suddenly snapped his head up and glared at his mother. His eyes were two burning green coals. His body, Ellie now realized with mute horror, really was changing.

"Help me," Ned managed to say with a rumbling growl in his throat. "I don't want to hurt you." His voice broke off in what sounded almost like a bark.

"I must be losing my mind," Ellie said blankly.

Suddenly, Ned threw his head back, and Ellie could see that his face now looked like a dog's, a wolf's! Ned stretched his neck out and howled wildly. The kitchen was filled with wave after wave of ululating howls. Ellie stood frozen, leaning against the counter unable to move.

"God have mercy," she whispered, her throat feeling like sandpaper. The longer she stared at her transformed son, the more his body shifted, lost its human shape, and took the form of a wolf.

Ellie's hands moved blindly behind her. Her elbow knocked over the pot of beans, and there was a quick hissing sound as her fingers were scorched. The pot rolled to the edge of the counter and then crashed onto the floor, spilling beans everywhere.

Ellie glanced down at her legs. They were burn-

370

ing painfully from the splattered bean juice. When she looked back up at Ned, he no longer retained any of his human form. A large wolf stood in the dark kitchen, glaring at her, panting with its mouth open. The wolf bared its teeth with a snarling hiss.

"Oh, Oh," Ellie mumbled as her legs gave way beneath her. She slid to the floor, and ended up sitting in the steaming pile of beans. She watched with numbed, fascinated horror as the wolf—she could no longer believe that this was her son—coiled back on its haunches and then, jaws wide, leapt for her throat.

.IX.

Friday, March 19

The dinner shift was over at the Ebb 'n Flow, and the supper crowd wouldn't come for another hour or so. The pots and pans were washed and stacked to dry, so Bob had time to go to the post office and pick up his mail. He hadn't been there for over a week, so he expected something would be there. He felt a strange mixture of joy and nausea when he saw the thin letter with the Cooper Falls postmark. He leaned against the row of mailboxes as he tore the letter from Lisa open. There was no accompanying letter, just two newspaper clippings.

Cooper Falls, N.H, Tuesday, March 16

The body of Richard Pomeroy, manager of a local grocery store, was found this morning in the parking lot behind the store by one of the store's employees. This is the most recent in a series of mysterious deaths which have plagued this small New Hampshire town since last September.

Police Chief Richard Thurston states that his department, recently assisted by the National Forest Service, is following every possible avenue in an attempt to track down and destroy the animal responsible. Local dog owners are asked to keep their pets confined. Citizens are asked to stay at home or in well-lighted areas after dark.

There have been no authenticated eyewitness reports, but numerous townspeople interviewed report hearing wolflike howling in the surrounding forest. Judging by the tracks found at several locations, Thurston says that they are looking for a large canine, probably a wild German-shepherd. Rumors in the area persist that the animal is, in fact, a timber wolf.

Bob swallowed hard and noticed that the article had come from *The Boston Globe*.

"Word's getting out," he muttered, turning to the next clipping.

Eleanor T. Simmons

Cooper Falls—Mrs. Eleanor Thomas Simmons, 63, widow of Everett Simmons of Bartlett Road, was found dead last Thursday at her home. Cause of death was reportedly heart failure.

She had lived all of her life in Cooper Falls, the daughter of Henry and Margaret Thomas. She attended local schools, graduating from Cooper Falls High School in 1936. She was active in local church and community affairs until the death of her husband.

She is survived by her son, Ned Alexander Simmons. There are no other members in the immediate family.

Funeral services will be held at 2 P.M. Monday at St. Jude's. Interment will be in Pine Haven Cemetery.

Bob's fingers shook as he folded the clippings back up and stuffed them back into the envelope. All through the evening rush at the Ebb 'n' Flow, he worked slowly, sullen and uncommunicative. When, at nine o'clock, his boss asked him if he was feeling all right, he lied and said that he thought he was coming down with a flu or something. He punched out early and went to his small apartment.

.X.

"Planning on doing a little skiing this winter?"

the late night newscaster asked, arching his eyebrows sharply. "You may want to reconsider when you hear the next news story when News Center returns after these messages."

Bob swung his feet to the floor and sat leaning forward anxiously as he watched a string of commercials for aspirin, deodorant, and dog food. He reached out blindly, grabbed his cigarettes, and lit one without taking his eyes from the small screen of his black-and-white portable TV. The first puff of smoke was drifting toward the ceiling when the news announcer returned.

"If you have reservations for a ski weekend in New Hampshire, you just may want to cancel them. There has been a series of brutal deaths, all of which have been attributed to a wild dog in the area of the small town of Cooper Falls, a community on the eastern edge of White Mountain National Forest."

A blocklike profile of New Hampshire with a dog's head superimposed over it appeared on the screen behind the newscaster.

"Authorities are baffled. Sheriff Richard Thurston insists that the deaths are due to one wild dog. He and a group of local residents have been hunting the animal to no effect since the incidents began last September.

"But townsfolk have a different story. Rumors are circulating that the town is being ravaged by a timber wolf. Many people claim to have heard howling in the woods. For a full report, we switch to Michael Fleischer, in New Hampshire."

The map of New Hampshire disappeared, and

the studio closed in on the screen behind the announcer. The screen burst into a shifting snowy pattern. The cigarette wedged between Bob's shaking fingers, grew long and then dropped to the floor unnoticed. The snow on the screen continued unabated for a few seconds longer, then the camera slowly pulled back. The announcer rubbed his neck with embarrassment.

"Well, we seem to be having some technical difficulties with that report," he said, looking over his shoulder at the screen. "We'll try to have that report for you on our noon newscast tomorrow. That's it for News Center 12 tonight. The Johnny Carson Show is next."

As Doc Severenson's blaring trumpet filled Bob's apartment, Bob stared vacantly at his burned-out cigarette.

I could have warned her, he thought. Her own son, and I could have warned her!

He looked up and stared, unseeing, as Johnny strode out onto the stage and began his monologue. Bob reached out numbly and snapped the TV off.

If I don't help, who will? he wondered.

He rose quickly from his chair, dropping the cigarette stub into the ashtray. He had already decided that he would return to Cooper Falls.

Chapter Sixteen

Tuesday, April 6

.I.

Bob pulled into the parking lot of the Howard Johnson on Interstate 95 in Portsmouth at a quarter past five in the morning. The sun was edging its way up over the horizon.

During his stay in Florida, Bob had forgotten, or at least gotten used to not having, snow. He was glad to see that spring had made some headway this far north. In the restaurant parking lot, there was just a brown-stained ridge of snow left by the snowplows.

Bob got out, locked the car, and, patting the book he had in his coat pocket, leaned his head back and drew in a deep lungful of clean, crisp air. That was one thing New Hampshire had over Florida: the air was much better.

As he entered the restaurant, he looked longingly at the empty newspaper rack. He wanted something to read other than the book he was carrying. Anything, even a copy of yesterday's

Union Leader. He patted the book in his coat pocket again and took a stool at the end of the deserted counter.

"Just a coffee and a plain donut, please," he said to the waitress, who stood in front of him, tapping her pencil on her order pad. Her eyes were red-rimmed and watery, and he didn't want to take the chance of having her confuse a more complex order. Besides, his stomach was feeling a bit upset.

"That'll be all?" the waitress asked, sounding very tired.

"Yeah." Bob closed the menu and placed it back between the salt and pepper shakers. A few seconds later, the waitress set the coffee, donut, and bill in front of him.

Bob took a tentative sip as he slid the book from his pocket and placed it on the counter beside his elbow. The book had a black edge where fire had seared away about half of it. Bob opened the book and began to read, tracing each word with his forefinger and mouthing each word like a person learning to read.

were active only during phases of the fu
Greece and Turkey, they also prowled
when the
new. In more northern climates,
werewolf ac
continue throughout the month of
Februar
remnant of the ancient Roman rite celebr
Lupercalia, held on the fifteenth of Feb
the god Fannus, often associated with th
footed Pan.

"More Coffee?"

The question startled Bob, and he looked up at the waitress wide-eyed. Then he glanced down at his almost full cup.

"Uhh, no. No thanks," he mumbled, shifting his arm to cover the book. He picked up his donut and bit into it.

"Well, let me just warm that up for you," the waitress said, pouring coffee into his cup until it threatened to spill.

"Thanks," Bob said, as he watched her walk away. He wondered if she had a quota of coffee she had to use up every hour. When he saw her disappear back into the kitchen, he pulled the book back out and continued reading.

He had puzzled over this book nearly every night he had been away from Cooper Falls. By now, he was familiar with every page. He still found its incompleteness maddening in places. He could guess at the meaning of most pages, but some key passages remained unclear.

He thumbed past the chapters on the theory and rituals of werewolfery and finally stopped at the chapter titled: Destroying the Werewolf.

He read carefully, trying to piece it together.

There are, as would be expected, many ways
rid of a werewolf, both religious and quasi-
most common way, of course, is to shoot the
silver bullet; but this has not always been

A person can be cured of lycanthropy if
he
three times. In order to prevent the ret
werewolf, most folk customs *require* that
the
Otherwise there is the possibility that the
wer
pire.

It went on from here, breaking down the
various customs of different countries for
destroying the werewolf. Bob was satisfied at
this point, though. He had decided to use the
most common, the Hollywood method of
shooting the beast with a silver bullet.

The only problem he could think of, other than
getting in a position to shoot, was how he was going
to get a silver bullet.

Leaving his brim-full cup of coffee and his donut
with one bite out of it, Bob paid his bill at the
register and went out to his car. He wheeled
around the rotary, got onto Route 16, and, with
the sun rising behind and to the right, sped toward
Cooper Falls.

.II.

When he pulled into town two hours later, Bob
drove slowly down Main Street. The view absolutely astounded him. It looked like he had been
away for years and, in that time, the town had
died. Cooper Falls had never been a thriving town,
but now, at seven-thirty in the morning, it looked

as though the town was in a state of siege.

The plate glass windows of the pharmacy were starred with holes. Plywood covered the bottom of the windows. Every store window along Main Street was either boarded or soaped over, or had its blinds drawn.

Bob pulled over to the side of the road beside the library and looked up at the cold stone and bricks. It seemed like years, lifetimes ago, that he and Lisa walked up those stairs holding hands. Now there was a thin covering of dirty snow on the steps. Bob shivered as he looked up at the thin, skeletal trees, not yet budding. He lit a cigarette and drove the length of Main Street toward Lisa's apartment building.

Like the rest of the town, Lisa's building looked asleep or deserted. Bob realized with a start that he hadn't seen anybody on Main Street. There should have been someone—a milkman or a paperboy or someone!

Bob pulled up to the curb in front of Lisa's apartment and looked up. He felt his spirits rise when he saw the curtain billowing in and out with the morning breeze.

He raced up the steps two and three at a time up to the third-floor landing. His hand was shaking as he reached out and pressed the buzzer beside the door.

No answer.

He put his ear against the door and pushed the buzzer again, listening to it sound within the apartment. After a moment, he heard a faint scuffing sound. Then the door lock was being worked.

"Who is it?" Lisa called out, her voice still thick with sleep.

"Me," Bob replied simply.

The lock clicked and the door swung open, then Lisa's surprised face filled the opening. She stood there in the doorway for a moment, then she collapsed into his arms and burst out sobbing.

"Oh God! Oh God! I can't believe it. It's really you!" she sobbed, her voice muffled by his shoulder.

Bob patted her on the back, then held her away at arm's length. "Well," he said, forcing a smile, "aren't you going to ask me in?" Then he kissed her, long and deep.

They went into the apartment and sat down at the kitchen table.

"I can't believe you're here," Lisa kept repeating. "Why didn't you call or write? Oh, God. Are you here to stay or are you passing through."

Bob could tell that she was trying hard to restrain any emotion that might show in her voice, but she was doing poorly.

"I'm not sure," he said calmly, locking her with his gaze. "I'm really not sure."

"So," Lisa said, smiling weakly.

"So," Bob said, nodding his head. "I got all your letters." He watched Lisa, who sat looking from him to the table cloth to him again. "I can't believe what's happened to the town. Why didn't you say something in your letters, when you wrote?"

Lisa shrugged. "I don't know." She sighed and looked up at the ceiling, fighting tears. "It's been terrible. Lots of people are scared, lots have left town for good. It's been terrible."

"I can't say as I blame them for leaving," Bob said. He noticed that Lisa's face paled. "They've got plenty of good reasons."

Lisa was gnawing at her lower lip.

"Yes, Lisa," Bob said, reaching across the table and taking her hand. "I've come back to, to do what I have to do to stop it."

The tears streaked down Lisa's cheeks, and fear registered in her eyes. "Bob! You don't—I can't—"

He squeezed her hand tighter, reassuringly. "I know what it is. I know who it is. And I know what I have to do to stop it," he said intensely.

"Not now, Bob," Lisa said, eyes overflowing. "Let's not talk about it now. Later."

"Sure." Bob said, getting up and walking over beside her. He grasped her by the elbow and, guiding her gently, led her into the bedroom.

.III.

"I don't think we should be doing this," Lisa said as Bob stopped his car at the foot of the Simmons' snow-filled driveway. The late afternoon sun threw out a slanting ray of light that illuminated the house, making it stand out in sharp relief against the dark forest behind it. The weather-worn shingles, the crumbling masonry of the chimney, and the boarded-over windows stood out with such sharp detail that Bob felt as though he was looking at a painting.

"What?" Bob said. "We're just stopping by to—"

"To break the law, that's what," Lisa snapped as she pointed to a sign tacked to the gatepost. No Trespassing. Police Take Notice.

"The house has been boarded up for over a month now," Lisa said. "I don't think we have any right to be prying around."

Bob snuffed loudly and, feeling his resolve build, reached into the back seat for the two flashlights he had brought. He held one out to Lisa and said, "Look, you don't have to come up. If you want to wait in the car you can. I want to take a look around."

"Inside?"

"Yeah, inside. If what I read was right, there must be some evidence in the house. If Ned was doing any kind of magic, there would have to be some signs of it, some implements or something. Do you want to stay in the car?"

"Are you kidding? Stay here alone?" She bit at her lower lip. She hefted the flashlight in her hand and switched it on and off a few times. The beam made a pale circle on the glove compartment.

"Don't worry," Bob said, "they're brand new Ever-Readys." He glanced once more up at the still house and said, "Come on."

They stood at the bottom of the driveway for a moment, silently surveying the gently sloping land, the house, and the towering ridge behind the house. Then they started trudging through the snow. The going was harder than Bob had expected, and before they were halfway to the house, they were both puffing for breath.

383

"Looks spooky, doesn't it?" Lisa said. "It almost looks like a ghost ship riding waves of snow."

"You wax poetical," Bob replied, breathing rapidly.

The sun was lower in the sky, and the slanting gold lighting brought out darkening purple shadows. The ridge loomed taller, darker, more threatening.

"Bob," Lisa said suddenly, surprising him. "Don't you think we should go back. We shouldn't be out here. I mean, if there's any investigating to be done, let Thurston do it."

"Oh, sure. I'll just give him a call tomorrow and say his troubles are over, all he has to do is arrest Ned Simmons. He's a werewolf. He's the one who's been killing all these people. They'd throw the net for sure, Lisa."

"Maybe you could approach it a little more rationally," Lisa said defensively.

"How can you be rational about something that's so irrational?"

"I don't know," Lisa said, looking down at her feet. "Maybe you could say that there are hippies or someone living out here and he ought to check it out. Anything. I just think we shouldn't be out here."

"I'm going to have a look around," Bob said firmly. He turned away from Lisa and continued walking toward the dark, silent house.

One end of the porch had caved in from the weight of the snow. The floor boards creaked underfoot. Bob and Lisa stood at the door, looking nervously at each other. Wind whistled in the eaves, loosening snow that had accumulated there.

"After you," Bob said, in a deep, Boris Karloff voice. He swept his hand in a grand gesture toward the door.

Lisa was unamused. "Let's take the boards off the door first, OK?"

"Sure," Bob replied. He grabbed the No Trespassing sign that was nailed to the door and ripped it off.

"Bob!"

He shrugged and slid his gloved fingers under one of the rough planks. Grunting loudly, he gave it a quick tug. The board squeaked loudly as it began to give. Bob braced his foot on the side of the house and pulled again. The dried-out board suddenly snapped in half. Arms windmilling wildly, Bob fell backwards over the porch railing and landed flat on his back in the snowbank.

"Bob!" Lisa screamed. "Are you all—" She stopped and smiled when she saw that he was laughing.

"Jeeze, we're off to a flying start," he said, standing up and brushing himself off.

He mounted the steps and started working on the boards again, this time more carefully. The rest of the boards pulled away easily. When he was finished, Bob looked at Lisa quickly and then reached for the doorknob. He was surprised to find it unlocked. Hinges complaining, the door swung slowly inward.

"God! What a stench!" Lisa said, covering her face with her mittens.

"You just can't get good help these days," Bob

385

said, wrinkling his nose. He was smiling, but careful not to take a deep breath of the noxious air in the house. "It'll air out soon enough and, besides, we'll get used to it in a minute."

"You can get used to it," Lisa said.

Bob clicked on his flashlight and let the beam dance around in the hallway. After a moment, they both stepped inside.

"The power's off, no doubt," Bob said, flicking a useless wall switch.

"What could make this place smell so bad?" Lisa asked.

"Just being closed up so long," Bob said, walking further down the hallway. His light beam illuminated wafting cobwebs and flickering dust motes.

When nothing unusual appeared in the hallway, Lisa seemed to relax. She snapped on her flashlight and began scanning the floor and walls.

"You know, you haven't really told me what we're looking for," she said. She was breathing shallowly through her mouth, and her voice sounded weak.

Bob walked over to the living room door and leaned inside. The wall creaked from the pressure of his weight. His throat felt tight from the stale air, and he had trouble speaking. "Well, I told you that I've done a bit of reading about werewolves, lycanthropy. That book we got, the one burned at Julie's house, wasn't much good because half of it was burned."

"Oh," Lisa broke in, "I forgot to tell you. I ordered a copy from the publisher for the library. It came a few days ago."

"Oh, good," Bob replied. "Anyway, I read some other books and, well, if someone want to turn into a werewolf, he—"

"Or she, right? A woman can do it too?"

"Oh, yeah, sure. But the person has to have some magic implements. You know, potions and all that. As it turns out, most of the witches' potions were organic hallucinogenics. A lot of scholars think those old witches were just tripping their brains out. When they were flying, they were really just stoned."

"So what does this all have to do with your werewolf?" Lisa asked sharply.

"Well, for becoming a werewolf, the primary drug potion used contained belladonna. Also, the person had to have a piece of wolf fur. Usually it was a belt that they wore while doing the ceremony."

"You think we'll find one here? That Ned really is doing magic?"

"I'm not sure," Bob said. "You see, people could become werewolves either voluntarily or involuntarily. Now, if Ned was doing it on purpose, he would have to have something like that wolf pelt. The other thing I'm thinking is that Julie Sikes might have been doing it to Ned, that, for Ned, it was involuntary. In that case, what we're looking for probably burned with Julie's house. We probably won't find anything here."

"Except maybe a warrant for breaking and entering," Lisa said. She walked back to the front door and looked down at the car parked at the bottom of the driveway. The sun had set, but she could still see the wavering line of tracks they had made through the snow.

Bob snuffed and entered the living room. All of the furniture was covered with sheets. The chairs sat like hunchback ghosts in the gloom of evening. The clock on the mantelpiece had stopped at ten past ten. As Bob looked around, Lisa followed closely behind him.

"You said that Ned hasn't been seen around town for a month or so, huh?" Bob asked as he got down on his hands and knees and peered under the sofa.

"At least," Lisa said. "No one's sure when they saw him last, but it was quite a while ago."

"Does Thurston think he was killed by the wild dog and just hasn't been found yet?"

"I guess so. After Ned had been missing for a week or so, they came out here and boarded the house up."

Bob stood up and wiped his hands on his pants legs. "You could start looking around too, you know."

"Sure." Lisa walked over to the TV and pulled it away from the wall. She shined her light behind it but found nothing. She wasn't even sure she'd know it if she found anything important, but she kept looking.

For a few minutes longer they poked around in the living room. Then, as if by unspoken agreement, they both went into the kitchen and continued their search. Suddenly, Lisa screamed. She heard a wild scrambling sound behind her. She spun around and trained her flashlight beam on the walls and floor but saw nothing. "Did you hear that?" she asked nervously.

"Your scream? Yeah."

"No, I—" Again, the scratching sound came. This time she was ready for it, and she pinpointed it with her beam.

"In the walls," Bob said, "it sounds like. Probably just mice in the walls."

"Whew!" Lisa wiped her forehead and loosened her coat collar.

In the kitchen, they looked behind everything: pulling the refrigerator away from the wall, looking inside the cupboards, shifting everything around. They even knocked on the walls in hopes of locating a hidden hollow place. They finally concluded that the kitchen would yield nothing.

They were heading into the hallway when Bob suddenly slipped and fell. He landed on one knee and bumped his head against the counter. His flashlight clattered to the floor and went out as it rolled away.

"Aww, shit!" he yelled, rubbing his head with one hand and his knee with the other.

"You OK?" Lisa asked. The beam from her light hit his eyes, making them hurt.

"Yeah. Yeah. I saw that before but stepped in it anyway." He groped in the darkness for his flashlight and found it. He sighed with relief when he snapped it on and it worked.

"What? What did you see?" Lisa asked.

"That." Bob pointed his light at a dark brown stain on the wooden floor. He touched it tentatively and found that it was sticky and had begun to moulder.

"Something spilled here," he said, studying the brown ooze. "Probably from the stove."

"Look here," Lisa said, training her beam a little to Bob's right. There was another, deep rust-colored stain on the floor.

"Looks like dried blood to me," Bob said.

Lisa gasped softly, then said, "I think they reported that Ellie was found dead in the kitchen."

Bob snickered. "Well, you don't find blood like this if someone dies of heart failure."

Bob got up slowly, keeping his light on the brick-red stain. "I just thought," he said, stopping Lisa from heading down the hallway. "I didn't check in the fireplace. A classic hiding place, as long as they didn't use it."

"After you," Lisa said.

Bob went into the living room and, getting down on his hands and knees, peered up into the fireplace. The narrow flue was crusted with thick soot. It looked empty. Shifting into a better position, he held his flashlight with one hand and gingerly reached up behind the damper. He ran his hand along the edge, reaching as far down back as he could.

"Hmmmm. Nothing. Wait a minute." He grunted as he stretched up into the chimney. "I felt something." He reached, then dropped back with a sigh. "Christ," he muttered, rubbing his face with his soot-smeared hand. "That can work up a sweat. I don't know how the hell Santa Claus does it!"

He smiled and angled his body around to reach again.

He was breathing rapidly as he shoved his arm up over the damper and grabbed for what he had felt. "It's furry, all right," he grunted. "Just a little bit—Got it!" His fingers closed on the bundle of fur.

He withdrew his hand slowly so he wouldn't scrape it on the corroding damper. A shower of soot rained onto his face as he pulled his hand out triumphantly and shined his flashlight on his find.

Lisa screamed and, in a quick reflex action, Bob tossed the object away, "Key-rist!" he shouted, looking down at the partially decomposed body of a large rat. He wanted to laugh at his surprise, but the way the dead rat's eye absorbed the light like a chip of black marble made his stomach do a quick flip-flop.

"Must have gotten caught up there," he managed to say, once his pulse had slowed.

"Sure as hell isn't a pelt of wolf fur," Lisa said grimly.

"Let's check the rest of the house."

.IV.

Seavey and Thurston sat in the idling cruiser not speaking. The spotlight on the side of the car was fixed on the rear license plate of the car they had found parked at the bottom of the Simmons driveway. Thurston took a clipboard from the console and jotted down the plate number. "For later," he said, not particularly to Seavey.

"You're sure it's Wentworth's car?" Seavey asked, furrowing his eyebrows.

"Of course I'm sure," Thurston snapped. He tapped his pen on the edge of the clipboard.

"Well, don't you think we ought to go on up there and see what the hell he's up to? We've got the place posted."

"I don't know," Thurston said, rubbing his nose with his gloved finger. "I think I'd just as soon leave him alone for now."

"How long you s'pose he's been back in town?" Seavey asked.

"Good question." Thurston looked over at Seavey and then leaned forward to stare up at the house. "I had no idea he was here until tonight. All we gotta do is ask around a bit. We'll find out."

"Do you think he might have had something to do with Ned Simmons' disappearing? As far as we knew, Wentworth was supposed to be in Florida."

"I told you," Thurston said evenly, as though to a child, "that I've never trusted that guy. Something makes me think he knows more than he's telling. Once I found out about his background, that he had raped a girl, well—"

"I thought that had never been proved," Seavey said. "That it had never gone to court."

Thurston spoke as if he hadn't heard Seavey. "And if he raped a girl once, why, who's to say he would do it again, and then maybe kill."

"And you don't think we should go up there and

check it out?" He turned and looked up at the house. It stood out like a soot smear on the darkened snowfield. Seavey shivered and looked back at Thurston. "What could he be up to?"

"Look!" Thurston said suddenly, pointing up at the house. "In the window to the right."

"I don't see anything."

"It's gone now. But there was a light in one of the windows. He's in the house."

"Come on, let's go back to the office," Seavey said. "This place gives me the creeps."

Thurston dropped the cruiser into gear and slowly pulled into the road beside Bob's car. Then he started driving down Bartlett Road slowly, staring into his rearview mirror more than at the road ahead.

"I wonder what he's doing up there," Seavey said softly as they drove back toward town.

.V.

The door leading to the cellar was bolted tightly. Even by throwing his full weight against the door, Bob couldn't budge it. All he got was a sore shoulder. He grasped the door knob and rattled it furiously. "Goddamned thing!"

"We've come up empty handed, Bob. Let's go back. We're not going to find anything." Lisa's voice was almost a whine. Bob looked from the cellar door to her and back to the door.

"We may as well finish our search," he said with exasperation. "Let's see if we can find something to get this door open with."

They went back into the kitchen and looked around. In the anteroom, Bob found a rusted tire-iron. "Just right," he said, hefting the heavy metal bar. "Let's give it a go."

Back at the door, Bob shoved the end of the iron in by the lock. He gave the bar a few light shoves, then with a fierce grunt, he threw his weight into it.

"If—I—can—just—spring—it."

His face flushed, and he could hear his heart thundering in his ears.

"Just—get—it—to—"

Suddenly, the door kicked open, swung away from him, and banged against the wall. He lost his grip on the tire-iron, and it fell to the floor with a bang.

They had gotten used to the stuffy, noxious air of the house and had forgotten about it. But now, as the cellar door swung open, another, stronger wave of putrid air hit them in the face.

"Whew! Now we know where it's coming from," Bob said, staggering backwards. Both he and Lisa had their hands up over their faces. Lisa started to retch but controlled it. Heaving a little sigh, she winked at Bob over her mittened hand.

"You don't have to come," Bob said, his voice muffled. He trained his light on the stairway leading down.

"Ummmm, I think I'll wait up here, if you don't mind," Lisa said from behind her mitten. She stepped back and leaned against the wall opposite the open cellar door.

"Sure. Be just a second," Bob said as he placed his foot on the top step. The stairway creaked under his weight, and he cast one quick look at Lisa before starting down.

The awful smell got stronger as he took a few steps down. "I'll be right up," he called. He paused on the steps and fished his handkerchief from his back pocket. He tied it outlaw fashion across his face. That would keep one hand free to hold the light and the other free, if he needed it.

He walked the rest of the way down the steps, letting the thick, clammy air of the cellar embrace him. He felt as though he were walking into a dark, murky pool of water.

At the foot of the stairs, he stopped, adjusted the handkerchief on his face, and looked back up to where he could see the glow from Lisa's flashlight. It reassured him as he turned and began to scan the cellar.

"Bob?"

Lisa's voice sounded far away, and the impression he had that he was submerged under water came back stronger. He tugged at the mask, wanting to pull it aside and take a deep breath to dispel the drowning feeling. He knew, though, that the putrid odor would gag him if he did.

"Bob! Did you find anything?" Lisa shouted.

"Just a second. I'm looking." The handkerchief was damp and clung uncomfortably to his face.

Bob swung his flashlight around in a wide arc. The low wooden beams, rough-cut and rotting, were draped with cobwebs. They hung motionless in the still, stifling air. The dirt floor was damp. Mold grew in the corners and up the sides of the walls. Black earth clung to his shoes as Bob walked over to a long-unused tool-bench. The tools were corroded brick-red; like the blood on the floor upstairs, he thought.

He walked past the stairs over to the thick bulk of the chimney. For a moment, he scanned the crumbling masonry, streaked with lime and cement. He picked at a loose brick that fell to the floor with a dull plop.

"Anything?" Lisa shouted from the top of the stairs.

"No."

"Come on up, Bob."

He didn't answer as he moved around the mass of the chimney to the back of the cellar. "I guess I'll—" He stopped short.

"Bob?"

"I—"

"Bob! What is it?"

He moved his mouth to answer, but all that came out was a strangled sound.

"Bob!"

He heard her at the top of the steps. He knew that if he turned around he would see her flashlight beam reaching down into the cellar's darkness. But his eyes were held by the sight illuminated by his flashlight. He staggered back and bumped against the chimney, pressing his back against the crumbling bricks, hoping their solidness would ground him in reality.

The stairway creaked as Lisa started down. Bob

turned quickly and ran to the foot of the stairs.

"No!" he shouted, holding up his hand to block her way. "Stay up there!"

"What is it, Bob!" Lisa yelled, panic coloring her voice. She was poised in mid-step.

"Get upstairs!"

When he saw her take a quick step backwards, he aimed his light into the corner behind the chimney, thankful that he could see it from there. He raced up the steps three at a time. Once he was in the hallway, he turned Lisa around roughly and pushed her toward the door.

"Let's get the hell out of here!"

It wasn't until they were back in the car with the doors locked and the motor idling that he told her what he had seen down in the cellar. He knew that from then on, for the rest of his life, he would be haunted by what he had seen. In the corner of the cellar, the mummified body of Julie Sikes was lying face up on the dirt floor. Her head, hands, and feet were all touching a point of the pentagram that had been dug into the cellar floor. What most horrified Bob was that there had been a wide smile on her face!

Chapter Seventeen

Sunday, April 11 (Palm Sunday)

.I.

Lisa stood at the side of the church, watching as the congregation filed slowly out the door following the early morning Palm Sunday service. She was nervous and shifted continually from one foot to the other.

There was a clatter behind her as the acolyte snuffed out the altar candles. She looked around, saw him eyeing her suspiciously, and gave him a curt nod. Sighing, she sat back down in the pew.

She hadn't really intended to speak with Reverend Alder. But when she had arrived for church, he had commented that she looked pale, or worried, and asked if there was something he could do. A valiant effort not to let her emotions show failed, and he had asked her to wait for him after the service.

Snatches from the service that morning kept echoing in her mind as she waited. She crossed her legs and folded her arms across her chest. Reverend

Alder's sermon had been on guilt: just what she needed to hear. It had dampened the bright spring morning. Although the connection had never been made explicit, Lisa was sure the reverend had meant for the congregation to see the parallels between Jesus' suffering on the cross and the town's recent suffering.

Both were dying, Lisa thought with a shudder. The old spiritual the choir had sung also hit home.

Whose hands were drivin' the nails, O
Lord?
Whose hands were drivin' the nails,
Lord, O Lord?
My hands were drivin' the nails, O Lord!
And I did crucify my God!"

Tears welled in Lisa's eyes, threatening to spill. She wiped them until they began to sting. The spiritual kept changing in her mind to:

Whose fangs are destroyin' the town, O Lord?
Whose claws are destroyin' the town, Lord, O Lord?

A hand came to rest gently on her shoulder. Lisa was surprised that, feeling as keyed up as she was, she didn't scream and jump. She looked up at the smiling face of Reverend Alder.

"Can we talk here, or would you like to take a walk?" he asked softly. His bushy white eyebrows came together over the bridge of his nose.

Lisa shrugged. When she made no move to stand, the reverend sat down beside her. He put his arm on the back of the pew almost touching her shoulder. Again, Lisa was surprised that she didn't pull away. She felt reassured that there was someone she could talk to.

With watery eyes and a voice that threatened to crack at any second, she told Reverend Alder everything. She told him about her relationship with Bob; Bob's idea about what was killing the people of the town; even, although she had promised not to, about Bob's discovery of Julie Sikes' body in Ned's cellar. The whole time she spoke, the reverend sat, silently nodding his head whenever she paused.

"And that's it," she said at last. Her constricted throat was barely able to get the words out. "The whole thing is driving me crazy, and I don't know what it's doing to Bob!" She did feel a measure of relief just for having said it to someone besides Bob.

Reverend Alder sat for a minute with his hands folded in his lap. His eyes were fixed on the cross on the altar. Finally, he cleared his throat and spoke. "You know, Lisa, this past winter has been without a doubt the most difficult time of my life. That included when I was a chaplain in World War II. There, at least, the deaths had some sense of purpose. The senseless deaths this past winter leave me feeling hollow."

"I know," Lisa said, sniffing. "Sometimes it seems as though God is so cruel."

"No. No." the reverend said, gripping Lisa's shoulder. "Not God! It isn't God who's testing us. It isn't God who's killing these people. It's

Satan, the Enemy. He's the one who brought this to our town."

"You mean," Lisa said, looking up, "you mean that you think Bob might be right? That there is something supernatural, a werewolf who's doing this?"

A trace of a smile twitched at the corner of the reverend's mouth.

"Well, perhaps not quite that literally, Lisa. But, yes, in a way I think Bob might have, well . . ." He leaned back and craned his neck, rubbing his hands vigorously together. "There might be an element of truth there. Like God, Satan can work in mysterious ways, ways we mortals cannot discern."

"That night at Bob's house, when that, that animal came through the door. You wouldn't have believed it! I still don't believe what I saw, but my cross was the only thing that stopped it, my silver cross!"

Reverend Alder said nothing.

"And all that stuff about Julie Sikes doing magic. Bob found one of her magic books in the ashes of her house the night it burned. It was pretty badly damaged, but he pieced enough of it together to find some of the incantations she might have used."

"People have been known to engage in some rather bizarre practices," Reverend Alder said. "And for them, a lot of times, they seem to work."

Lisa gasped.

"I said seem to work," he repeated, looking at Lisa intently. "You and I know that there is a lot of wrong in the world. A lot of people delude themselves into thinking—"

"But it's more than that!" Lisa said sharply. "I saw! That night at Bob's house, I saw! There is something in Cooper Falls, something supernatural that's killing people!"

"You missed the point of my message this morning, didn't you?" the reverend said, patting Lisa's shoulder.

Lisa looked at him quizzically.

"It's Palm Sunday, the day Jesus rode into Jerusalem, knowing that he was going to his death. But winter and death are behind us now, Lisa. Easter is not a celebration of death, it's a celebration of life. The promise of spring. The eternal process of new life coming from the old. Our Lord said, 'He that believeth in me shall not perish, but have eternal life.' "

Lisa sat wringing her hands in her lap. They were slippery with sweat.

"But Julie Sikes' body! Ned had it there in his cellar, inside the magic pentagram. Reverend Alder!" Lisa sat forward and gripped the reverend's arms. "If what you say is all true, that means there can be eternal death too!"

.II.

Wednesday, April 14

Bob sat at the kitchen counter, feeling like Captain Queeg in *The Caine Mutiny* as he tumbled three bullets from one hand to the other. These bullets were not ordinary. Where most bullets would have been dull lead, these were, instead, brightly polished silver. Bob looked at them and rattled them like dice.

"I felt like such a damn fool, asking that guy in the gunshop to make them for me," he said, looking at Lisa. "Finally I told him that a friend of mine was a Lone Ranger fan and that these were for his birthday. That seemed to satisfy him, and he finished making them without any more are-you-crazy looks."

Bob glanced down at the partially burned book that lay spread open on the counter.

"I wish you had remembered to bring the new copy with you," he said.

"Sorry."

"Oh, well." He dropped the bullets one by one into the crack in the spine. As they landed, he half-expected to see them glow with a dull blue light like the cross had the night they had been attacked.

"I just can't believe that this is really happening," Lisa said distantly. She shook her head and bit her lower lip.

Bob snickered and picked up the bullets. He started passing them from hand to hand again.

"And you're sure this will do the trick?" Lisa asked. "That this will destroy the werewolf?"

"It's probably the most traditional way. I mean, you have to assume that there were werewolves long before gunpowder was invented, so there must be other ways. It isn't mentioned that often in the book." He tapped the charred pages. "But that night at the house here, when the werewolf came through the door, I don't think it was the cross that drove him away."

"Huh?" Lisa said, surprised. "I thought a religious symbol would always protect you." She looked worried.

"Against vampires, yes," Bob said. "But not for werewolves. They operate on a much lower, more bestial level than vampires. No. I think it was the silver in the cross that made the explosion when it touched the animal."

"But you feel that you can depend on the silver bullets?"

"There are plenty of other ways," Bob said with a tight laugh. "But if it's good enough for Hollywood, it's good enough for me."

"Some recommendation," Lisa muttered.

"It depends on which country you check, but there are other ways to reverse the spell and destroy the werewolf. I guess it all comes down to whether you want to kill it or just have it resume its human shape."

"Are there any other, safer ways?" Lisa asked.

"Well, you can rap the beast on the head with a stick, three times between the ears. That's supposed to reverse the spell. Or you can repeat the person's Christian name three times. That is supposed to reverse the change. Or you can just draw blood."

"Sounds like just about anything will do it," Lisa said.

Bob chuckled and thumbed the charred edges

of the pages. "I think I've got enough out of this to do the job."

"You're sure," Lisa said after a moment, "that you don't want to go to Thurston and tell him. After all, there is a body in the cellar up there. The police should know."

"Thurston would probably just love it if I came in and told him where to find the body. He'd have me locked up, either there or in the looney bin, and throw the damned key away."

"You don't have to be so melodramatic," Lisa said.

"Yeah, well. . ." Bob replied. He shifted uneasily in his seat when the image of Julie's smiling face rose in his mind. He shook his head to clear it away, as if the image was water in his ears.

"I mean it, Bob. You're acting as though you're the only person involved in this. Think of the other people, the ones who have died, the families. Ned! Think about what Ned must be going through!"

"Well, that all depends on whether Ned is doing it on purpose or not." He shifted again. "I know, Lisa. Really. I feel it a lot more than, maybe, I let on. It's just that I think, I'm sure that unless I do this—" He indicated the silver bullets. "Unless I do this, there's no hope." His mouth twisted into a hard grimace.

"But there is hope, Bob." Her eyes were watering. "I believe in you, and I believe you're right. It contradicts everything rational I've ever learned, but I'm convinced there's something supernatural going on."

"Well." Bob shrugged his shoulders. "At least I'll have company in my rubber room." He felt better when Lisa's mouth spread slowly into a smile.

"Then you'll talk to Thurston?"

"I didn't say that!" He clenched his fist holding the bullets and pounded it on the counter top. "No! I've got to do it this way!"

.III.

Ned had seen them as they came up to the house. He had seen them and recognized them. He had been hiding behind one of the pine trees in the back yard. After they had broken through the front door and entered, he had crept around to the edge of the porch and crouched there. He caught snatches of what they said as they went from room to room. Once the sun set, he could see the glow of their flashlights through the slats covering the windows. He had wished violently that he could have had his other shape then!

He sat now beside the small campfire in the abandoned mine, thinking about what he would have to do. His upper lip tightened into a grimace. He snapped a wrist-thick branch in half and threw it into the blaze. Tilting his head back, he waved his hands over the fire and watched the shadows wash over the dirt-and-stone ceiling. A laugh built slowly in his chest.

He knew that he could never go back to his house now. Even if they hadn't found his secret in the cellar, he was just as pleased to get rid of that house forever. It reminded him of his humanity—the weaker part, the part he rejected. He longed for his other shape.

What he also knew now was who he would have to find next, when the change came. He didn't have to go outside to know that the full moon was near. He could feel the strange, subtle pulling that began in his groin and slowly spread out to his stomach and limbs.

Soon! The time is soon! Not yet. Soon!

He stood up and made his way along the twisting tunnels to the mine-shaft mouth. He walked with long, sure strides.

Soon!

As he neared the mine opening, he felt the pulling in his groin grow stronger. The power was rising!

From the ledge, which hung some fifty feet above the abandoned-mine office-building, he could look out over the surrounding forest. The glow of light from the town shone just above the thick black line of trees. The night air was filled with the rushing sound of the falls. The winter ice had broken up, freeing the river once again. Ned looked to his left at the misty spray rising from the falls. It looked like a dense silver cloud, obscuring the further shore.

Behind him, the nearly full moon threw his shadow along the ground and out over the edge of the cliff. As he focused his gaze on his shadow, the brilliantly lit ground in front of him seemed to grow brighter, more distinct.

The other shape's eyes! he thought with barely

contained pleasure. I'm getting the night animal's vision. It will be tonight, later!

He turned around, looked up at the pale silver disk of the moon, and raised his arms as if to embrace it.

The urge, the power stirred deeply in his bowels as he opened his arms to the moon. The light grew brighter, making him squint. The moonlight seemed almost to pierce him, right through his body as if he had no substance left, or as if he were changing into another substance.

A low sound beneath the hissing of the falls made him start, turn around, and drop to his hands and knees in one swift motion. Down below, on the road by the old office, a car was pulling to a stop. He skinned his lips back across his teeth. A low rumble came from deep within his chest. With his altered night-vision, Ned could clearly see the black-and-white police cruiser.

Ned watched, coiled with tension and ready to sprint off into the mine if he was seen. He wished anxiously that the change would come faster. Then he would know how to take care of the people down below!

Thurston opened his door and got out. Ted Seavey stepped out on the passenger's side. The headlights were still on, shining onto the office building. Above the roar of the falls, Ned, with his acute animal hearing, could hear the buzz of their voices.

"Uh-uh. Not me," Seavy said, shaking his head and looking up the face of the cliff. "I ain't going up there. Not after dark. Footing would be too risky."

"We ought to check that line of traps up there." Thurston said. They both stood for a moment, looking up at the cave mouth. Ned was sure they couldn't see him.

They don't have the power! They don't have the vision!

Thurston turned, said something Ned couldn't quite make out, and then they both got back into the cruiser. Before driving away, Thurston directed the spotlight across the side of the cliff. The circle of light darted back and forth across the mine opening. Ned pressed his body close to the ground until he heard the cruiser driving away. The tension in his body slowly unwound as he got up and brushed himself off.

He looked back up at the moon, smiled, and then walked back into the mine to his campsite.

The fire had burned low, but it had made the cave warm enough for comfort. Ned quickly undressed and lay down on the musty mattress. He felt a deep ache in his joints, as though his bones and muscles were tightening, twisting, reforming. He forced himself to relax and let the change come. He fixed his eyes on the vaulted ceiling of the mine and let himself drift.

Soon. Soon.

.IV.

"You're sure you don't want to come along?" Bob asked for the third time. "It'd be kind of nice just to relax a bit, maybe have an early breakfast at a truck stop out on the highway."

"No," Lisa said. "It's too late to be running around. You should go home and get some sleep."

"You think I'd be able to sleep?" Bob asked. "Besides." He glanced at his wristwatch. "It's only eleven-thirty. We should do something different to, to take our minds off it."

Lisa paled. "You're going to start the hunt tomorrow night?"

Bob nodded.

"You could stay here. Have an early breakfast with me," Lisa said.

Bob shook his head. "No. We'd spend the whole time either dwelling on it or talking around it. I have to do something different, so I won't think about it so much." He put on his jacket and started toward the door. "I think a nice long drive will help clear my head. Tomorrow night's the full moon, you know."

"Will you stop reminding me," Lisa snapped. "Anyway, I think I'd rather get some sleep, especially if I had some company," she added demurely.

Bob chuckled and shook his head. "Don't tempt me, woman!" he said with mock anger. "I have business to tend to first!" He realized that his attempt at humor was not cutting the tension, so he added, "I'll stop by tomorrow afternoon, before I start hunting."

He put his hand on her shoulder, and she tensed. "Yeah. OK."

"See you tomorrow," he said, kissed her quickly. And then he went down the steps.

"Yeah, see you," Lisa said to the door as she

410

swung it shut. She locked it and stood there for a moment with her cheek pressed to the wood.

She forced herself to go through her usual motions of preparing for bed: brushing her hair, washing her teeth, washing her face with Noxema. She finally admitted to herself that she was kidding herself. She stood in the bathroom, staring at her pale reflection in the mirror. She shuddered and then walked over to the bathroom window and looked out on the street below.

The quiet street was bathed with bright moonlight. She couldn't see the moon from where she was, but she knew that there was a small, imperceptible rind missing from the left side of the moon's face. That thought and what it meant to her and Bob brought tears to her eyes.

The sudden knock on her door made her jump. She snatched a square of toilet paper and dabbed at her eyes as she started for the door.

"Who is it?" she called, hoping that Bob had decided to come back after all.

"Thurston, Mrs. Carter. May I come in?"

Lisa clasped one hand to her throat as she unbolted the door. "Is something the matter?" she asked anxiously, thinking something might have happened to Bob. Lisa stepped back to let Thurston and Seavey enter.

"Evening," Thurston said, tipping his hat. Seavey nodded and remained silent, standing by the open door.

"Is something the matter?" Lisa repeated. "Has something happened?" Her hands twisted together.

"No, no. Take it easy, Mrs. Carter. Nothing's wrong."

"Then isn't it a little late to be making social calls?" she asked sarcastically. She glanced at the wall clock and saw that it was after midnight.

"Well. . . ." Thurston hitched his belt importantly, glanced at Seavey, and squared his shoulders. "We've been out to your boyfriend's place."

"He's all right, isn't he?" Lisa asked. She felt a stomach-wrenching wave of fear, even though Bob had left no more than half an hour ago.

"I dunno," Thurston said slowly, cocking his eyebrows and glancing toward the bedroom door. "We've been out there looking for him, you know, just wantin' to talk to him about a few things. He wasn't there. We just thought we might find him here." He finished the last statement with a suggestively rising inflection that galled Lisa.

"He's not here," she said coldly, swinging her arm wide to indicate the empty apartment. "Obviously."

"Hmmm. Well."

"If you have a message for him, I could give it to him." She paused, then added, "Provided you don't intend to drop by later tonight."

Thurston shook his head thoughtfully. "Not really. I just wanted to—"

"To ask him what he was doin' out at the Simmons place a couple 'a nights ago, for one," Seavey piped in.

Thurston turned and glared at his deputy.

"The Simmons place," Lisa said weakly. She

412

looked down and saw that her hands were trembling. She clasped them behind her back and bounced on her toes in an attempt to conceal her agitation. "I, I have no idea."

"You don't?" Thurston looked at her sharply. "Well, we were just anxious to talk with him, saw the lights on, and figured we wouldn't be disturbing you."

"Actually," she said, feigning a yawn, "I was just getting ready for bed, so if that's all . . ."

"Sorry to bother you, ma'am," Thurston said, touching his hat.

"Good night," Lisa said. She started to close the door on the two policemen. "I'll tell Bob you were by."

"You just do that," Thurston said, looking at her harshly. He stood with one foot poised over the steps. "You just do that. Evening."

Lisa shut the door firmly and listened as the two men went down the stairs. Her throat was dry, and a trickle of sweat ran down the back of her neck. When she heard the door at the foot of the steps close, she went into the living room, switched off the lights, and sat huddled on the couch. Sleep came an hour later.

.V.

Thurston flattened himself against the wall of the house when he saw the bouncing headlights coming up the driveway to Bob's house. The motor stopped and the lights winked out. He heard the car door open and slam shut, footsteps crunch on the gravel walkway, the key jitter in the lock, and then the door open and close.

Cautiously, he peeked around the edge of the house and saw that the car was Bob's. When a light came on in the kitchen window, Thurston flattened back against the wall.

So where the hell has he been? Thurston wondered. He glanced at his watch and saw that it was a little after four in the morning.

He pressed his ear against the house and tried to distinguish the sounds he heard from inside. There was a steady banging sound, then a loud clump. Crouching low, Thurston ran away from the house, making sure to keep out of the light that spilled from the window into the back yard. He made his way over to a sheltered position behind a tree, from which he could see into the kitchen.

Bob was standing near the window, back-to, drinking a cup of coffee. The early morning chill made Thurston shiver as he thought about how good a cup of coffee would taste. He rubbed his arms to drive away the chill; there would be time enough for coffee as soon as he checked out what Bob was up to.

After several minutes of watching, Thurston started to get impatient. It looked as though Bob was staring at something, either on the table or the floor in front of him.

Won't learn anything standing out here freezing my balls off! he thought angrily. Ought to just go in and talk to him.

He glanced again at his watch. It would be light soon. He thought about making his way back to where he had left his cruiser parked, about a mile through the woods on Route 43.

Suddenly he saw Bob raise a rifle to his shoulder, bend over it, and take a quick practice aim. Bob turned around, facing out the window, and pointed the rifle again. Thurston panicked for a second, thinking Bob had seen him and was going to shoot. He cringed back into the darkness under the tree and didn't relax until, after several tense seconds, the shot didn't come.

Who's he going to hunt? Thurston wondered. If it was the wild dog, why did he think he had any better chance than the rest of them?

"I always thought he knew more than he was saying," Thurston whispered to himself with satisfaction.

What if he has another target in mind? Not the wild dog at all.

Thurston watched with held breath as Bob snapped open the barrel of the rifle and sighted down its length. He lowered the gun, studied it in his hands, then placed it on the counter. The light in the kitchen blinked off, and Thurston was left alone in the dark.

"Have to talk to him in the morning for sure," Thurston whispered. Then he turned and started making his way back through the woods to his car.

The silence of the forest seemed to intensify as Thurston trudged through the snow. It was deeper here in the cover of the woods, and he found the going tough. He was grateful that the moon was so bright, helping him find his way more easily.

He was at the top of a ridge, looking down at the thin span of woods, beyond which he knew his car was parked, when he heard a soft rustling sound behind him. There was no wind; it couldn't have been the trees. He turned and saw the black shadow bearing down on him. He didn't have time to draw his service revolver. He didn't even have time to scream.

Chapter Eighteen

Thursday, April 15

.I.

Bob was in the bathroom shaving when he heard someone coming up his driveway. He wiped the shaving cream from his face and, looking out the window, saw a battered Chevy pickup truck stop at his front door. The truck door opened and Ted Seavey stepped out. Bob's immediate impression was that he looked nervous, distraught. He kept glancing over his shoulder as he came up to the door and knocked.

Bob went to the door and opened it. His initial impression was confirmed as Seavey pushed his way into the kitchen. The deputy stared at Bob for a moment, ashen-faced.

"Good morning, Deputy," Bob said warily. "What can I do for you?"

"Last night," Seavey stammered. "Did you? Thurston was killed, out by 43." He stopped, gulping air furiously.

"What?"

"Sure as shit," Seavey said. "That fuckin' wild dog killed him. God! His face was missing!"

His own face had paled considerably, and Bob was afraid the man might faint.

"Out by 43? Nearby?"

Seavey nodded his head violently. "He dropped me off last night, 'bout one in the morning. Said he was gonna swing by here. Wanted to talk to you. We was looking for you. You didn't see him?"

Bob shook his head slowly. "No, I was out until pretty late. I didn't get home until almost dawn."

"Christ, it's terrible! We have him over at Doc Stetson's now. He, he—" Seavey tried to continue but his throat closed off.

"Here, let me get you some water." Bob walked over to the sink and filled a glass. He handed it to Seavey, who took a deep swallow. Water dripped down his chin.

"We found his cruiser out on 43 early," Seavey continued, once he had calmed down slightly. "It was pulled over to the side of the road. It didn't look good right away. We circled the area and then, then I found him."

He took another deep drink of water.

"Jesus," Bob muttered, shaking his head as he paced the length of the kitchen.

Last night wouldn't have been too soon after all, he thought bitterly. He smacked his fist into his open palm.

"You're sure you didn't see or hear anything?" Seavey said anxiously.

"I was out pretty late. I came home about an hour or so before dawn and went straight to bed. Didn't hear a thing."

He walked over to the kitchen window and looked out into the backyard. There was still a thin snow cover there, and what he saw made him gasp. He could plainly see the footprints that came from the trees, angled over to the side of the house just below the kitchen window, and then swung in a wide circle, disappearing again into the forest.

He had been out there last night spying on me, Bob thought.

"I went right to bed," he repeated as he turned and walked back over to Seavey. "Can I get you some more water?"

Seavey shook his head, apparently calmed down now. "What I can't understand is what he was doing out there, parked on the side of the road like that." Seavey scratched his head, perplexed. "Maybe he saw that dog and went after it."

Bob suddenly felt any sympathy he might have felt for Thurston disappear.

That bastard was snooping around here spying on me!

"Maybe that's what happened," Bob said softly. "Only it got him."

"Shit!" Seavey stamped his foot on the floor. "I just don't know what I'm gonna do. I guess I'm police chief now. I don't wanna be police chief. Hell, now it's gonna be up to me to organize the hunt. I ain't so sure I can hack it."

He looked at Bob with a sorrowful, pleading look. Bob did feel sympathy for him. "You'll do all right. Just keep doing what you've been doing all along. Rick had a plan, didn't he?"

Seavey nodded. "Yeah. We were setting out

traps and poison bait, 'n' checking 'em on a rotatin' basis."

"Well," Bob said, "just stick to that, for now."

"It ain't been the best thing goin', you know," Seavey said. "I mean, it's been over six months since that Stillman girl was killed. We've had a lot of sightings and a lot of evidence since. But, Christ! I don't know one man who's got off a clean shot at that bastard and lived."

"All you can do is keep trying," Bob said grimly. "Maybe his time has come."

"Let's just hope to God it has," Seavey said. He moved toward the door. "Sorry to bother you. I had to check, you know."

Bob nodded.

"I'll, I'll probably be by later for a statement," Seavey said at the doorway.

"Sure," Bob said. He swung the door shut behind the deputy and watched him drive away.

.II.

The sky was darkening as Bob and Lisa pulled into the church parking-lot. The snowman some children had built on the front lawn had melted and was now little more than a shapeless slush-ball.

Bob looked at the melting snowman and felt glad that at least not all life in the town had stopped. He noticed, though, that now that it was dark there were no children out playing. Bob looked up at the church, at the dim light of the candles filtering through the stained-glass windows.

"Please? Won't you come in with me?" Lisa asked, her voice edged with worry. "Reverend Alder will understand."

Bob lit a cigarette and exhaled noisily. "You know I can't, Lisa."

"Even after what happened to Thurston? No one's safe out there." She looked at him intently. "There must be someone who could go with you. Bob, you could get killed!" Tears glistened in her eyes. "Please, don't go."

"It's already too late. I have to go tonight!" He was surprised by the intensity in his voice. Reaching across in front of her, he snapped open her car door. "The time for talking is over."

With a wrenching sigh, Lisa swung her legs out of the car. Before she stood up, though, she leaned close to Bob and said, "I'll be praying for you." She kissed him lightly on the cheek.

"Stop worrying."

Bob started the car, put it into reverse, and slowly backed up. Lisa stood in the glare of the headlights, shoulders slumped, her head cocked to one side. She looked defeated. She raised one hand and waved.

Bob stuck his head out the window and shouted, "I'll stop by later tonight when I get back." Then he shifted the car into gear and slipped out onto the road. He hit his horn one quick beep and drove away.

As he drove down the road, something within him made him want to scream, to shout, to cry out. His emotions were twisted and confused. He reached into the back seat and picked up the rifle he had there. Laying it across his lap, he gripped the stock, and the ruggedness of the rifle helped steady him to his purpose. He drove up Railroad Avenue, heading toward the Simmons house.

"We've all suffered enough," he whispered, glancing at his pale reflection in the rearview mirror. His voice sounded like gravel to him.

.III.

When Lisa stepped out of the car in the church parking-lot and watched Bob drive away, she was surprised that her mind was functioning along clear and precise lines.

The man she loves is driving away from her.

In his backseat is a rifle.

In his pocket are three silver bullets.

He is going out to kill a werewolf.

She had to talk to Reverend Alder again. That was why she had Bob drop her off at the church.

Her feet crunched the ice on the sidewalk as she made her way to the front door of the church. At the top of the steps, she paused and looked out over the quiet street. Everything looked dead. The earth was covered with a layer of ice that the warming spring sun had not yet penetrated. She wondered if it ever would.

She swung the heavy door open and quickly stepped inside. The church was dark except for the glow of the candles on the altar. Lisa inhaled slowly, deeply, letting the quiet emptiness of the church calm her nerves. She could hear the blood rushing through her ears. She flicked the light switch and the church filled with light.

"Hello," she called softly. She stood with her hand resting on one of the pews. "Reverend Alder?"

Her call echoed dully from the front of the church. Cautiously, she walked up the aisle, aware of the floorboards creaking underfoot. Her attuned hearing magnified the sound, making her feel uneasy.

At the front of the church, she paused. Looking over at the door to the reverend's office, she could see that the room was dark. He had said he'd meet her but had probably forgotten, she figured.

She was about to turn and leave when the lights overhead suddenly blinked out, plunging the church into darkness. Slowly, Lisa's eyes adjusted to the faint candlelight. She stood beside the altar railing, both hands covering her mouth to hold back the scream that threatened.

Then, from the stairway leading to the basement, she heard heavy footsteps.

Could that beast have gotten in here? she wondered frantically. No! It could never enter a church. Could it?

Her throat closed with a gagging spasm.

This is a holy place! she thought. It should be safe!

The footsteps came to the head of the stairs

and paused. Lisa's lungs began to hurt as she held her breath, waiting.

It could never enter a church!

She wondered if she should cry out for help. Would anyone hear her? Her eyes widened with fear as a shapeless shadow moved across the far wall.

Run! Get out of here! her mind screamed, but her body remained tense, unable to move. Her throat made a clicking sound as she inhaled deeply. She looked longingly at the reverend's office door. She knew she could get out that way, if only her body would obey the commands of her mind.

Suddenly, there was a loud crash from the back of the church. Lisa let loose a shattering scream that filled the church. Overhead, the lights flashed on. Around the corner, Lisa saw the startled face of Reverend Alder peering at her.

"Lisa? Lisa," he said, striding rapidly toward her with his arms open wide.

"Oh my God!" she muttered weakly, feeling her knees buckle. She caught herself on the altar railing.

"I'm so sorry," the reverend said as he came up to her and gripped her by the shoulders. "I had no idea you were waiting for me up here. I saw the lights on and thought I had absent-mindedly left them on."

Lisa whimpered softly as she brushed her hair back from her face and tried to compose herself.

"I'm sorry I gave you such a start. Clumsy me,

I dropped my briefcase when I stumbled in the dark."

"I was— Bob dropped me off. I wanted to talk," she said, and then she began to cry.

.IV.

Bob stood in the darkness at the foot of the steps, looking up at the Simmons front door. He felt a sudden tightening in his stomach. The haunting, death-still face of Julie Sikes floated through his mind. He imagined her standing there, ghostly, in the open doorway, beckoning to him.

Right down there! he thought, glancing at the black cellar window set in the stone foundation. She's waiting. Right down there!

He shook his head and took several steps backward, but the feeling was strong; it was as if there was something pulling him toward the house.

Should I go down there and check? he wondered.

He wanted to convince himself that he had imagined seeing her corpse there. Perhaps his overwrought imagination had fabricated it that night from a discarded burlap bag or pile of trash or something. She wasn't really down there. She couldn't be! But he knew better.

She's right down there, waiting.

"She's dead. She's dead," he whispered softly, rubbing the length of his rifle with his gloved hand. But that thought gave him no comfort as he scanned the moon-washed side of the house.

Raising his gun to his shoulder, he walked gingerly over to the ground-level cellar-window. Bending down low, he squinted, trying to pierce the night-washed pane of glass. His heart almost choked him. At any second he expected to see Julie's white, desiccated face press against the glass, staring at him, beckoning him.

Right down there!

The grip on his rifle tightened until his hands began to hurt.

"There's nothing there," he said firmly. But he was bothered by the feeling that it was more wishful thinking than fact. Cautiously, his eyes riveted to the cellar window, he backpedaled away from the house. When he was about fifty feet away from the house, he turned and trotted across the field toward the distant woods.

As he entered the forest, he was surprised to find that he felt more secure in the closeness of the trees. The wind whistled in the pines. The full moon flooded the woods with a soft, blue light. Before he plunged too far into the woods, he took one last look at the Simmons house, standing alone and silent and waiting.

.V.

Tonight he had intended to climb the ridge behind the Simmons house, hike out to the falls, and from there cut north along the river up to

Martin's Lake. Now that he had the Simmons house between himself and the falls, Bob decided to follow the fire roads west, instead. He would walk out by the old Cushing place, loop-around until he hit Old Jepson's Road, and then call it a night.

Tomorrow night, he decided, would be time enough to go out by the falls.

Hefting his rifle to his shoulder, he bent low to avoid the low-hanging tree-branches and started walking west. He felt great relief to leave the Simmons house behind.

The deeper he got into the woods, the deeper the snow got. Quite a few times in the next hour he wished he had taken Lisa's advice and brought snowshoes. He kept sinking, up to his knees in spots, sometimes with every other step. It slowed him down considerably. He knew that if the beast came after him in the deep woods, he would have to count on the silver bullets to stop it; there would be no other escape.

Sweat formed on his forehead and ran down his face from the effort of hiking, but he had to laugh at the picture he must be presenting. He must look like he was drunk on his ass.

The silence of the night was broken only by the sounds of his labored breathing and walking. He paused now and then to catch his breath and listen intently. At any moment, he expected to hear a long, wavering howling in the distance. But if the animal was out hunting, it was keeping its presence a secret so far. Bob kept remembering a line from countless adventure movies: "It's too quiet out there. It makes me nervous."

Puffing for breath, he pushed on, making a wide arc that would eventually bring him out of the forest.

At last, he came to a wide clearing; there Bob decided to take a moment to rest. He checked, making sure there was at least twenty feet clear all the way around, before he hunkered down on his heels and lit a cigarette. He kept his rifle across his lap as he smoked, thinking that was just how a frontiersman would do it.

As the smoke from his cigarette wafted away on the night breeze, he kept turning his head, trying to watch the forest edge. He didn't want to be surprised and taken. He kept reminding himself that it wasn't just him hunting the werewolf. Like last night, it would be out hunting too!

With a sudden flick of his wrist, he sent the cigarette butt tailspinning off into the darkness. He rose, scanned the circumference of the forest clearing again, and headed off into the woods.

He plunged deep into the woods. The thick, crowded trees blocked out most of the moonlight, and the going got increasingly difficult. Thick, inky shadows shifted gently in the wind. Every sense was on edge, hair-triggered to spring at the slightest sign of anything. Bob felt confident that he would react in time if he was attacked.

After another hour of wandering through the woods, the trees began to thin out and, distantly, Bob could hear the hiss of traffic. He glanced at his watch and was surprised to see that he had been out for over two hours. He was exhausted and grateful that he had come to the road. He was also a bit irritated that he hadn't had even a sign of the werewolf.

As he came out onto the road, Bob realized that he had wandered quite far off track. He was up too far north on Route 43. He figured he was about three or four miles from Old Jepson's Road. He decided not to hitchhike, figuring he'd have trouble explaining what he was doing out at night with a gun when it wasn't hunting season. He struck off into the woods again, hoping that with any luck he would come out at his house. He had covered a lot of ground and was extremely tired.

After walking for another half hour, he saw the silver surface of Pemaquid Pond through a break in the trees. His house was still on the far shore of his approach, but he felt relieved that he was almost through for the night. Lisa said she would be home. He figured that once he got to his house he'd give her a call and ask her if she would drive him out to the Simmons place to pick up his car. After that, all he wanted was a hot shower and some sleep.

.VI.

Friday, April 16 (Good Friday)

"No one died last night?" Bob asked, amazed. It had been late afternoon before he got out of bed and came over to Lisa's apartment. They sat together on the couch drinking coffee.

Lisa looked over his shoulder at the darkening sky. "No, thank God," she whispered. Her apartment filled with silence as she and Bob stared at each other. Between them on the floor, was Bob's cleaned and oiled rifle. Lisa wondered if it was loaded now.

"I've been reading in this," she said, indicating the new, whole copy of *Witchcraft: Its Forms and Functions.* "The one I ordered for the library came in and I thought I'd glance through it."

"I half-read it," Bob said smiling. Lisa chuckled at his attempted joke.

"It's interesting, but cripes, it all sounds so, so wacky," Lisa said. "I mean, if you really believe in this—"

"Julie Sikes believed in it," Bob said sharply. "And look what it got her!"

Bob shivered as the mental image of Julie's corpse rose in his mind.

Lisa said nothing as she fixed her gaze on the open book on the coffee table. Still, deep inside, she rebelled at the idea that a werewolf was killing the people of the town. But she had also seen enough that night at Bob's house to convince herself that the cause of so many deaths in town was not entirely natural, either. Her talk last night with Reverend Alder had done nothing to settle her mind. Still, there was no denying that the cross, her silver cross, had glowed with blue light and had exploded when it touched the animal. She had wondered, briefly, if maybe the whole episode that night had been fabricated by Bob as a practical joke or something, but she dismissed it.

"You know," she said weakly, "it says in here that if someone is just bitten by the werewolf, that he too will become a werewolf."

"I didn't read that part, I guess," Bob said. He leaned over and picked up his rifle.

"Yeah. It's like with vampires. One can make another."

"Yeah, well, it's getting dark," Bob said, standing up and putting on his coat. "I've got to get going."

"Do you want the snowshoes tonight?" Lisa asked. She made a move toward the closet.

"No. Not tonight. This is the last chance I'll have this month. If I have to go out next month, the snow will be out of the woods. I was planning on staying pretty much on the roads. I figure the animal has to come pretty close to town now. It must realize that people are scared now and staying close.

"Take them, just in case," Lisa said.

"No, really," Bob said, hefting his rifle. "I'm just going to drive out to the falls, look around, and then swing around by Martin's Lake, where Julie's house used to be."

"Bob, please be careful."

"Don't worry, OK?" he said smiling. "I'll do everything I can to make sure it's him, not me, that gets it. Well, I guess I'm ready."

He turned and walked to the door. With one

last glance, he winked at Lisa, then shut the door firmly behind him. Lisa sat on the couch and listened until she heard his car start and drive away, then she let her held breath out slowly.

She picked up the witchcraft book from the coffee table and idly flipped through it. She paused to read the titles at the top of the chapters, then opened the book and began to read in the chapter titled, "Destroying the Werewolf."

After several minutes of silent reading, Lisa gave a startled gasp and sat bolt-upright on the couch. The book was clamped shut on her index finger, which still marked the paragraph she had just read.

"No," she said softly, intensely. She looked about herself strangely, as if unsure she had spoke aloud. Her face flushed, and she felt a terrible twisting in her stomach.

Her hands trembled as she slowly opened the book again and read the page out loud.

" 'There are, as would be expected, many ways of getting rid of a werewolf, both religious and quasi-magical. The most common way, of course, is to shoot the animal with a silver bullet; but this has not always been effective. A person can be cured of lycanthropy if he is addressed by his Christian name three times. In order to prevent the return of the werewolf, most folk customs require that the fur be burned entirely. Otherwise, there is the possibility that the werewolf will return as a vampire.' "

Her eyes were stinging as she closed the book and put it down on the coffee table.

Does Bob know this? she wondered, feeling her panic rising.

According to the book, the werewolf can't be killed—completely—unless the fur is burned!

The silver bullets won't end it! her mind screamed.

"Most folk customs," she whispered hoarsely, her eyes darting out at the darkening evening sky. It might not be important; it might not matter; but this was the book Julie used! And if Julie used the book to create the magic, wouldn't the remedies in the book be required to stop it?

She jumped up, raced into the kitchen, grabbed her coat, and raced down the steps to her car. She had to find Bob and tell him!

She stopped before getting into the car, a sudden thought slowing her down.

"If you need fire to kill it—gasoline!" She raced back into the apartment building to the workroom where the apartment-building manager kept his tools. Maybe there would be gasoline there.

"Damn!" she shouted, when she saw that the door was locked. She stood back with frustrated anger for a moment, staring at the padlock on the door. Looking to her left, she saw a fire extinguisher. She grabbed it, raised it over her head, and smashed the padlock. The door was old and rotten, and the padlock didn't hold. The door flung wide open, and Lisa ducked inside.

She reached blindly for the light switch, found it, and snapped it on. Frantically, she searched for a can of gasoline and, over in the corner beside the snowblower and the lawn mower, she found it. Two gallons. Full.

She raced out to her car and drove off.

.VII.

Bob left his car down by the deserted mine-office. The road to that point had been rough enough, and he didn't want to take a chance of bottoming out his car on the rutted road up to the falls. He walked over to the edge of the river and looked at the swiftly moving water. The river was swollen with the spring flood.

Looking up toward the falls, he saw the billowing plume of spray illuminated by the light of the full moon. The roar of the falling water was deafening, and Bob realized that he would have to be doubly on alert.

He turned and started up the road, past the mine offices, to the top of the falls. He knew that at the top was an old footbridge. He had decided to cross over there and follow the river downstream on the opposite shore until he could cross back on the Old Mill Bridge, about two miles downstream.

The road up to the top of the falls was steeper than it looked, and by the time he had made it to the top, Bob was just about out of breath. He stopped and rested, leaning against the rusted hulk of an old tractor that had been deposited about ten feet from the edge of the cliff. To his left, he could see the footbridge; down below, about thirty feet, he could dimly see his parked car and the abandoned mine-buildings.

Suddenly, faintly, he became aware of a sound rising from beneath the hissing of the falls. He frowned, listening with concentration, trying to distinguish the sound. It was faint and hollow, but then—he heard it clearly—the wavering, rising howl pierced the night.

It's nearby! Bob thought, squeezing his rifle. His thumb flicked off the safety catch, and he walked cautiously to the cliff edge and looked down.

Something is out tonight! Something is hunting!

A sudden panic rose in him, and Bob thought he might be safer if he made it to his car. It would offer him some protection, and would be better than standing out in plain sight at the edge of the cliff. It would also be a quick means of escape if he needed it.

He crossed his rifle over his chest and started down the steep incline. He had taken no more than a dozen steps when the howling rose again on the night wind. It swelled, eventually drowning out the sound of the falls.

Bob stopped short, almost falling down. His breath came in ragged gulps as his eyes darted about, trying to fix the direction of the howling. It would help to know from which direction the beast was coming, but with the roaring of the falls and the echoing ravine, it was impossible to tell.

The sound was closer; of that Bob was sure. The rifle with the three silver bullets didn't give him as much reassurance as he had hoped it

434

would. Suddenly, Bob felt very vulnerable. Some primitive alarm warned him that he was now the hunted!

Looking down at his car, he saw a rapid, shadowy motion. It was the beast! He watched as the animal ran over to where his car was parked, sniffed at the tires, and then threw its head back and howled. Bob crouched above, watching.

Judging from the direction the animal had come from, Bob figured that it had to have come from the mine. That was the only answer. He almost chuckled at the irony of a werewolf using an abandoned silver-mine as a lair.

The werewolf glared up at Bob, then howled again. This time the sound rose clearly on the night, wavering wildly, like a siren.

Bob snapped the rifle to his shoulder, drew a bead, and fired. The rifle exploded, slamming back into his shoulder painfully. Bob knew he would have a horrible bruise there, if he was alive in the morning.

The shot cut short the animal's howling, but Bob knew he had missed because the beast dodged easily to the side. It crouched down beside Bob's car, staying hidden in the shadow.

Suddenly, the werewolf rose to its feet and turned on the car. A steady growling sound rose as the beast savaged one of the tires. Bob saw the car suddenly shift to the side, dropping down on the flat tire.

Now that it had prevented his escape, the werewolf turned and started stalking up the rutted dirt road to where Bob waited, crouching with his rifle in his lap.

.VIII.

Lisa's mind was clicking fast and furiously. In an effort to calm herself, she switched on the radio. A song by the Eagles "Hotel California," was playing. Lisa had always liked the song, but she had never listened to the lyrics. This time, she heard some lines that made her freeze.

She turned the radio off and stepped down harder on the accelerator.

Suddenly, a winking blue light reflected in her rearview mirror, hurting her eyes. She pulled over to the side of the road.

"No! No! No!" she whined, banging her fists on the steering wheel. She squinted every time the revolving blue light hit her eyes. Then she heard a tapping on her window and looked up to see Ted Seavey leaning down. She rolled the window down and nodded a wordless greeting.

"Evenin', Mrs. Carter," Seavey said. "Just a bit late to be out drivin' like a bat outta hell, ain't it?" There was more than a trace of mockery in his voice. "Now what's the rush?"

Lisa looked up at him but was unable to speak.

" 'S there a fire somewhere we don't know about?" Seavey said.

"It's Bob, Bob Wentworth. I've got to find him." She knew she was disguising the agitation in her voice. "It's very important."

"Important enough to be drivin' through town at least twenty miles over the posted speed limit?"

"Yes," Lisa said. "It is."

" 'N just what would that something so all-fire important be?" Seavey asked with a grin. Lisa suspected that he thought the fire was in her pants.

"It's personal," she said. She glanced on the floor of the car and saw the two-gallon can of gasoline. She pushed it back with her foot, hoping Seavey hadn't noticed it.

You have to burn the werewolf! she wanted to yell.

"Personal, huh?" Seavey said. "Well, Mrs. Carter, now I know you're an honest, tax-paying citizen, but I'm afraid I'm gonna have to write you out a ticket. The law is the law," he said with a firm, scolding tone. "Now if you'll just hand me your license and registration."

Lisa opened her purse, took out her license, then snapped open the glove compartment and got her registration. She handed both to Seavey.

Fuming, she sat drumming her fingers on the steering wheel as Seavey went back to his cruiser and wrote her out the ticket. Her eyes kept glancing at the two gallon can of gasoline.

Only fire will stop the evil!

.IX.

Bob watched tensely, stood up, and took a few steps backward as he watched the werewolf stalk up the road toward him. He vowed to make the next shot count, to have it lined up perfectly before using his second silver bullet.

As the beast advanced slowly up the hill, Bob saw in the moonlight that its face was split with a wide grin. Long, shiny teeth caught and reflected the moonlight. Carefully, Bob snapped the lever back and let the second silver bullet enter the chamber. Above the roar of the falls, he could hear a low, steady growling. Bob kept backing up the hill, watching, waiting. The closer the beast got to him, the slower it moved. It was toying with him, he was sure.

"Come on, you bastard," Bob said with a sneer. "This is your last—" something sharp jabbed into his back, cutting him with a quick, tearing pain. He wheeled around and saw that he had backed up into the rusted fender of the derelict tractor.

He realized that if he hadn't hit the tractor, he might have backed up right over the cliff edge. He sighed softly. A trickle of blood ran down the small of his back.

"Come on, you bastard!" he shouted, waving the rifle at the animal. "Come on!" The echo of his voice bounced back from the distant cliff side and then faded beneath the hiss of the falls.

The werewolf raised its hackles but still approached at a slow, menacing pace. Bob scrambled around the tractor, using it as a shield. He crouched and took a careful steady aim. The werewolf was about twenty feet from him. He held his breath and squeezed the trigger.

With the crack of the rifle, the werewolf leaped wildly to the side. Bob saw the bullet hit the ground, kicking up a clod of dirt. With an ear-piercing howl the beast charged.

The jump carried the werewolf over the side of the tractor. It turned and jabbed at Bob, its jaws open wide. The beast jumped on him, pressing Bob to the ground. He was engulfed by a flurry of slashing claws and teeth.

They kicked and scrambled in the dirt, rolling back and forth, too close for either to seriously harm the other. The animal was twisting, trying to fasten its jaws on Bob's throat. Bob fought against the crushing weight of the animal, trying to get clear or at least to get enough room to fire the last silver bullet.

The beast's jaws shagged Bob's jacket, and then the needle sharp teeth raked his flesh, tearing his coat and his arm from the elbow to the wrist. Warm blood gushed over him as he kicked the animal in the belly.

Finally, he managed to get his foot firmly planted just under the beast's ribcage and, grunting loudly, he heaved up with everything he had. The snarling beast went flying through the air and hit the ground with a pained yelp, its legs crumbling beneath the impact.

Bob rolled over and got to his feet. He felt dizzy from blood loss as he dashed up the slope toward the wooden bridge. He gripped his rifle as though it was his last hold on life. It was.

His feet clattered on the loose boards, and the old structure swung wildly, threatening to fall apart with every step. Bob looked down at the dizzingly swift water. Before he gained the opposite shore, he expected to feel the weight of the werewolf bring him down, to feel the jaws clamped on his neck.

Miraculously, the werewolf didn't rush into the attack. It stood at the foot of the bridge, panting. Its teeth glinted with moonlight and saliva. Bob felt a measure of relief. At least there was the swift river between them. He looked down at his left arm, torn and hanging uselessly at his side. The pain was not yet too intense. Bob knew he would have to kill the beast before he passed out from loss of blood.

Bob thought of what to do next. Keeping his eyes fixed on the werewolf, he began to tear at the bridge's support boards. If the beast couldn't get at him, he figured, he could take his time for the third and final shot. If he missed that . . . .

The nails in the bridge were rusted and refused to give to his efforts. With his good arm, he swung the butt of the rifle at the boards, hammering them loose. One board loosened and dropped into the water. It was quickly swept away.

Bob looked up and saw the moonlit shape of the beast at the foot of the bridge, preparing to spring. Beyond the wolf, down by the abandoned office-buildings, Bob saw headlights coming up the road. The car jostled wildly, bouncing in the ruts, and then pulled to a stop beside his parked car. Someone got out and started running up the slope of the hill.

The werewolf turned, saw the new intruder, and snarled. The animal bared its teeth, then looked back at Bob. The steady rumbling of the beast rose up above the roar of the falls.

"Come on and get me, you bastard!" Bob taunted. Whoever this person was who had arrived, Bob wanted the werewolf to keep his attention on him.

"Ned! Ned Simmons! I know that it's you!" Bob shouted. He looked beyond the beast and felt a sudden sinking in his stomach. Lisa was running toward them, carrying something in one hand.

"I know it's you, Ned," Bob shouted, hoping to keep the werewolf distracted.

"Fire!" Lisa shouted as she ran up to them. "Bob! Fire!"

The werewolf started across the bridge. The growling rose steadily, breaking now and again into a sharp barking sound.

With his good arm, Bob raised the rifle to his shoulder. He had trouble aiming; the rifle kept sweeping in wide circles as he tried to draw a good bead on the beast.

Lisa was at the other end of the bridge now,

holding up whatever it was she was carrying. Bob couldn't see clearly enough. He was growing faint from loss of blood.

"Fire!" Lisa shouted again, waving the object in her hand Bob saw now, it looked like a gasoline can. Lisa bent down and screwed off the top of the can. The werewolf, caught between the two people, one at either end of the bridge, looked back and forth from one to the other, snarling.

"Well, you bastard," Bob said with a hiss. He pointed to the river. "It's either that or this." He shook his rifle.

Lisa stepped forward cautiously, splattering the bridge with gasoline. She got close enough to splash the werewolf.

Bob wondered why the beast didn't turn and attack Lisa. He had the gun. She was unarmed.

"All right!" Bob shouted, when he saw that Lisa was holding her silver cross in one hand. It was glowing with blue light.

"Ned," Bob shouted, feeling a wave of pity for whoever, whatever the beast confronting him was. "Ned! I don't want to do this!"

The werewolf snarled loudly and suddenly leapt into the air. The rifle shot split the night, and the silver bullet slammed into the beast, stopping it in mid-flight. It landed, crumpled, on the bridge, laying on its side.

"Stand back," Lisa shouted. She dodged forward, Bob saw, with a lit match in her hand. She touched it to the beast, and an orange ball of flame roared into the sky. The animal's pained howl filled the night. The wooden slats of the bridge caught fire too, lapping with flames.

The wounded beast scrambled across the bridge, trying to get at Bob. Bob stepped forward and with one strong swing of his rifle, knocked the werewolf over the side of the bridge.

The animal held on, its claws digging deeply into the burning, rotting wood. The snarling beast was consumed with flames, yet still it struggled to hold onto the bridge. Its flailing claws removed large chunks of wood as it tried to regain its footing.

Lisa had backed away. She was standing at the foot of the bridge, watching, horrified as Bob stepped closer to the burning animal. It looked up at him with death-clouded eyes and whined with pain. Its fierce rage was gone. Now it was just a suffering animal, about to die.

"Ned," Bob said, watching as the animal grasped, weaker now, at the burning bridge. "Ned."

Bob stepped back, shocked, when he heard a deep, gravely voice say, "Help, help me."

With sudden anger, Bob swung the rifle butt again. "Die! God damn you!" As he hammered at the gripping paws, Bob slowly became aware of the physical change that was gradually taking place.

The paws—thin, cruel, wolf's feet—were getting thicker, as if the fire that engulfed the animal was burning away the gray fur. Soon, they were no longer animal paws at all, but human hands trying desperately to hold onto the bridge. The flesh turned black and began to bubble. The flames billowed, roaring, consuming the wooden beams of the bridge.

"Help—me. help—me—please."

Bob looked down into the animal's eyes, glowing dimly with dying green fire. The face was shifting, changing, becoming more human.

With one wrenching scream, Bob swung the rifle butt and hit the beast squarely in the face. There was a loud crack as bone shattered. The rifle butt splintered and fell off. The hands released their grip and the now almost completely human shape of Ned Simmons dropped into the water trailing flames. Bob and Lisa watched as the twisting black shape rushed toward the edge of the falls and then disappeared.

They looked at each other. The blazing bridge was between them. Lisa held her arms out to Bob and shouted, "You did it, Bob! You did it!" Tears streamed down her face, which was glowing brightly as the flames consumed more of the bridge.

Bob's knees buckled and he almost fell. He sat down heavily at the end of the bridge and let it all hit him. He had done it! He had stopped the evil! He watched as the charred timbers and planks of the bridge collapsed and fell hissing into the raging river.

"We did it!" he said, softly but loud enough for Lisa on the other side to hear him. "We did it!"

Epilogue: Sunday, April 18 (Easter)

"One last thing to do, and then we can be sure," Bob said. He and Lisa were standing beside the abandoned mine-office, looking up at the open mine-shaft. Lisa's hand gripped Bob's elbow.

"You don't have to," she said softly. "It's over now. I know it is." She looked up at the clear spring sky and inhaled deeply.

"I have to be sure," Bob said. He patted the .45 revolver that was cradled in the sling that supported his wounded left arm. The cut was healing fast, but it still throbbed with a deep pain.

"You have the fire burning," he said. "If I find anything, we'll have to burn it to destroy it. If there's the slightest chance that Ned survived the fall from the bridge, he'll have his magic implements here in the mine. If we destroy them, he'll be powerless."

"Be careful." Lisa whispered hoarsely.

"I will." He started up the slope to the open cave-mouth and, with one backward glance, entered the thick darkness.

He was surprised at the numerous twists and turns of the mine. As he trained his flashlight beam along the mine floor, however, he could see a clear path in the dirt that Ned had made going into and out of the cave. Bob followed this path along the dark, echoing corridors.

Suddenly, he halted, staring. Up ahead, he saw a flickering light. It illuminated the walls and ceiling with a dull, cheery glow. He snapped off his flashlight, stuck it into his back pocket, and took the revolver from his sling. Cautiously, he stepped forward.

He entered a small room and knew immediately that this was Ned's campsite. In the warm glow of a low burning fire, he saw the mattress spread on the floor, the folded up sleeping bag, and the remnants of several meals. The room smelled of rotting food and garbage, and more.

He wondered how the fire could still be burning since Friday night, and concluded that, this far into the mine, there were no drafts that could have put it out or fanned it to burn fast.

Suddenly he froze, his eyes darting about when he heard a faint, shuffling sound.

There's someone hiding over there, he thought. Over there!

He pressed his back against the cold wall and waited tensely for the sound to be repeated. There was enough light from the campfire to see, so he didn't want to chance turning on his flashlight and revealing his presence. As he listened intently, the sound repeated. His heart-beat almost stopped as he saw a shadow on the far wall shift. Then, from the far end of the corridor, out walked Julie Sikes.

"God! No!" Bob whispered.

She was naked, and her body had somehow, miraculously regained its youth. Her full, firm breasts and smooth belly were lit from the glow of the fire. She smiled at Bob with a vacant stare as she walked slowly toward him.

Bob remembered the revolver, hanging uselessly in his hand, and he raised his arm, taking careful aim. He squeezed the trigger once, twice, three times. The roar filled the mine as the pistol spit orange flame. The bullets hit Julie, making her body twitch slightly, but she continued walking toward him. Walking through the burning fire, scattering embers on the ground, she stiffly raised her arms toward him. With a choking gag, Bob's hand opened, and the revolver dropped to the ground. A thin smile spread across Julie's face as she got closer to him. Her thick black hair framed her pale face, empty of emotion.

"Ahhh," she said, coming up to Bob and en-circling his waist with her arms. She pulled him closely to her body and held him tightly. The bone-deep cold of his wounded arm spread through his body at her touch. She tilted her head back and drew Bob's face closer. "I knew you'd come."

Bob tried to pull away, gasping for breath. "I, I. How can you be? How . . . ." The cold of her touch penetrated him, drawing his strength from him.

Julie looked up at him with deadened eyes. Her smile widened, displaying her pearly, pointed teeth. "You don't understand?" she asked softly.

Bob shook his head, trying to find air enough to scream.

"Don't you understand? Feel your arm, the one that was bitten by the beast. You should understand. More than anyone else in town, you should understand. But if you don't, if you don't." She moved her face closer until Bob felt her frozen breath on his face. "You will. Within a month, you will."

His scream was cut off as she pressed her cold, dead lips against his mouth.